Copyright

Published by Outpost Books

Produced by Christian Hurst Publishing

www.churstpublishing.com

Distributed by Ingram

Additional distribution by Draft2Digital and Amazon

Cover design by Max Young and Christian Hurst

Set in Ethnocentric by Ray Larabie (Typodermic Fonts)

and Allumi by Jean François Porchez (Typofonderie)

ISBN (Digital): 979-8993932750

ISBN (Paperback): 979-8218788032

ISBN (Hardcover): 979-8993932743

For retail, visit: LilyStarlingBook.com

Author blog: christianhurst.substack.com

Instagram & TikTok: @churstpublishing

This is a work of fiction. Names, characters, places, and incidents are either the product of the author's imagination or used fictitiously. Any resemblance to actual persons, living or dead, or actual events is purely coincidental.

Fourth Edition: June 2026

Lily Starling and the Voyage of the Salamander

By Christian Hurst
Book 1 in the Lily Starling Series
© 2025 Christian Hurst

••••

For John

A Note from the Author

This is the second edition of Lily Starling and the Voyage of the Salamander. It has been carefully revised and re-released under Outpost Books, with extensive editorial work to bring it fully in line with the standard of the series. This edition is tighter, with errors and continuity issues corrected, and the formatting refined for a smoother reading experience.

If you've read the original, you'll find the same story—now sharpened and polished. If this is your first time joining Lily and the crew, welcome aboard; you're experiencing the best version of the journey from the very beginning.

Thank you for exploring Lily's universe. I hope it carries you somewhere unexpected.

• • • •

Content Advisory:

This book explores themes of memory loss, homelessness, trauma, violence, and death. Identity and intimacy are explored through emotional and romantic relationships, with closed-door depictions only.

LILY STARLING

AND THE VOYAGE OF THE SALAMANDER

CHRISTIAN HURST

Introduction

Computer, this is Lily Starling... begin recording.

Well, here I am. On a spaceship. Probably. I mean, it looks like a spaceship. I've got stars whizzing past at what I can only describe as "completely bonkers speeds" and this whole thing smells like metal and ozone, so... yeah. I'm about 75% sure this is really happening. The other 25%? That's reserved for the possibility that I've completely lost my mind. Honestly, not ruling it out.

What really gets me, though, is the view. The cosmos—and yeah, I know how pretentious that sounds, but there's no other word for it—it's stunning. Like every science documentary you've ever seen but bigger. Realer. It makes you feel small in the kind of way that's supposed to be humbling but mostly just makes you wonder if the universe is secretly laughing at you. Or maybe that's just me.

But I'm getting ahead of myself. Let me back up.

The short version is, I don't remember much. No family, no childhood, no "happy place" to escape to when things get rough. The slate is wiped clean, except for a metal tag with the name "Lily Starling" engraved on it and a date that makes me think I just turned 17. So yeah, happy birthday to me. Or not. I'm still not entirely convinced that's even my real name.

Here's what I do know: I'm good at math. Stupid good. Like, "give me a second and I'll tell you how many nanoseconds it'll take to get to Alpha Centauri" good. I also know how to ride a bike, pick a lock, and spot a bad idea from about 50 paces. And yet, none of that has helped me figure out who I am or why I feel like I'm constantly juggling two different versions of myself. There's the worn-out old woman who's seen too much and the impulsive kid who'd rather eat expired peanut butter than ask for help. Balancing those two? It's exhausting.

But that's the thing about being 17—if that's even what I am. You're not a kid anymore, but you're not really an adult either. You're stuck in this weird in-between place where everyone expects you to have answers, and all you've got is a head full of questions. Questions like, "Why does everything feel like it's teetering on the edge of disaster?" and "Why am I the one who's supposed to fix it?"

Loneliness is a funny thing. Not "ha-ha" funny, more like "what even is this" funny. It sneaks up on you, settles in your chest, and makes itself at home like it's paying rent. You start out thinking, "Okay, I've got this," but then a few weeks, months, whatever go by, and suddenly you're in full-on survival mode. It's like a super weakness—the opposite of an origin story. There's no radioactive spider or alien ring. Just you, alone, and the constant hum of everything you're not.

But here's the twist. You don't stay alone forever. Connection happens. Sometimes it's fast, like lightning. Sometimes it's slow, like watching a tree grow. Either way, when it happens, it changes you. It's not magic—it's better. It's someone handing you a piece of their belief in you and saying, "Here. Take this. You'll need it." And just like that, the super weakness loses its grip. You start to see the edges of the cage, and if you're lucky, you figure out how to break it open.

But again, I'm getting ahead of myself. Let's rewind to before all that. Back to when loneliness was still winning. Back to when I couldn't see a way out, and the stars were just dots in the sky instead of the map to everything I'd ever wanted to believe in.

Because that's the real gift, isn't it? Not knowing all the answers. Not being invincible. Just being able to look up at the stars and finally understand: I'm not alone.

Chapter 1: Earth 2010

IT WAS AN UNSEASONABLY warm October in San Francisco, the kind of weather that clung to your skin and made the sidewalks feel sticky underfoot. In the Mission District, the changes were creeping in like a slow tide—inevitable and indifferent. Once the heart of the working-class backbone of the city, the Mission was now in flux, caught between what it had been and what it was becoming. The first signs of gentrification arrived years ago, but now they were impossible to ignore. A certain chain coffee shop—the kind that liked to decorate with reclaimed wood and mason jars—had popped up near the homeless shelter, which had promptly been rebranded as "artist housing." The irony wasn't lost on anyone who cared to look. But most people didn't.

Those who moved into the neighborhood came with their eyes half-shut. They walked fast, earbuds in, and clutched their oat milk lattes as if they were shields. To them, the street's worn faces and cracked sidewalks weren't stories; they were blurs, something to be ignored. But if you did choose to look—if you let your gaze linger—you'd see the people. Old men wrapped in blankets, young women clutching tattered backpacks, children too tired to cry. Their crime? Having less. Being without. Their existence had become a violation of the city's unwritten rules. The ones who needed the most help were the ones the city pretended not to see.

Lily shoved her hands deep into her hoodie pockets as she walked, even though the heat was almost stifling. The fabric was worn thin and had holes at the cuffs, but it was hers, and it kept her hands from shaking. She kept her head down, her pace brisk, ignoring the pangs in her stomach. Hunger wasn't new; it was just part of the rhythm of her days now. Still, it made her feel slow, like her body was dragging her spirit behind it.

She passed a row of half-demolished houses, their skeletal frames still clinging to bits of siding and broken windows. The city had sold the land to make room for luxury apartments, and apparently someone had thought it would be a good idea to dress up the ruins for Halloween. Fake cobwebs stretched across crumbling doorways, and plastic skeletons dangled from the beams. Lily's lips twisted into a bitter smile. Even she could see how tacky that was, and she was just a kid. Worse, it was counterproductive; they'd had to put up extra "KEEP OUT" and "NO TRESPASSING" signs because people kept sneaking in to explore. What did they expect? Make something look like a haunted house, and of course, people would want to go inside.

She brushed her fingers against the metal tag in her pocket, the familiar weight of it grounding her. It was cool against her palm, smooth except for the faint ridges of the engraving. *Lily Starling.* That's what it said. Her name. Her birthday. She didn't remember who had given it to her, but it was the only thing she had that felt real.

One time, she'd gone to the library and used one of the computers to look it up. She'd typed her name into the search bar, heart pounding as she waited for the results. But the closest thing she'd found was a brand of Japanese bubble tea. She'd laughed out loud in the quiet room, earning a sharp glare from the librarian. She really hoped her name meant more than that. It had to, didn't it?

She squeezed the tag once before letting it slip back into her pocket and kept walking. There wasn't time to think about things like that. Not when she had to figure out where she was going to sleep tonight.

A sharp voice cut through her thoughts. "What are you doing here, kid?"

Lily turned her head slightly, just enough to catch the scene unfolding by the corner. A little boy, probably no older than ten, stood rooted to the spot, his big brown eyes wide with fear. Looming over him was a cop, one hand resting on his belt as he rattled off questions. The boy clutched a backpack that was practically bigger than him, and his shoulders were drawn up like he was trying to make himself disappear.

Lily's gut twisted. She recognized the look on the boy's face—that mix of fear and hopelessness, like he already knew nothing he said would make a difference. She knew better than to get involved, but her feet were already moving.

A taco cart sat a few yards away, the vendor deep in conversation with a customer. Nearby, a lanky teen hovered, balancing on one foot like he had nowhere to be. Lily's sharp eyes pegged him instantly—another street kid, like her. And street kids knew how to handle themselves.

"Hey," she whispered, sidling up to him. "Do me a favor?"

He raised an eyebrow. "What kind of favor?"

"Make a commotion," she said, jerking her head toward the taco cart. "Knock something over, start yelling. Whatever you gotta do to get that cop's attention."

The kid eyed her warily. "Why?"

Lily pulled out her last five-dollar bill, crumpled but real. "Because I'm asking. And because I'll give you this."

The kid shrugged, took the bill, and pocketed it. "Sure. Why not?"

Lily didn't wait to see what he'd do. She straightened her hoodie, smoothed her face into an expression of exasperation, and marched straight up to the cop and the boy.

"There you are!" she said, her voice pitched just right to sound like an annoyed big sister. She grabbed the boy's arm gently but firmly. "What did I tell you about wandering off?"

The cop frowned. "This your brother?"

"Uh, yeah," Lily said, rolling her eyes. "He's always doing this. Drives me nuts. You know how kids are." She gave the boy's arm a small squeeze, willing him to play along.

The boy nodded quickly. "Sorry," he mumbled.

Before the cop could press further, a loud crash rang out. Lily turned just in time to see the teen by the taco cart knock over a bin of soda cans, sending them clattering across the pavement. The vendor started yelling, and the cop's head snapped toward the commotion.

"Keep a better eye on him," the cop said gruffly, already moving toward the chaos.

"Will do," Lily called after him, her heart pounding. She hustled the boy into a small corner shop, glancing over her shoulder to make sure they weren't being followed.

Inside, the air was cooler, the smell of fresh bread mixing with something faintly antiseptic. The shopkeeper, a tired-looking woman with gray streaks in her hair, raised an eyebrow but said nothing as Lily pushed the boy toward the counter.

"Can you call his mom?" Lily asked, keeping her voice low. "Or aunt, or... someone?" She glanced at the boy. "You do have someone, right?"

The boy nodded, clutching his backpack. "Yeah. My mom."

Lily relaxed a fraction. The shopkeeper sighed, motioning for the boy to follow her toward the back.

Lily's eyes flicked to the bins of apples near the counter. Her stomach growled. She hesitated for just a second before her hand darted out. An apple and a bag of chips disappeared into her hoodie pocket. Lily didn't wait for guilt to catch up with her. She was out the door before anyone noticed, running down the block like her life depended on it.

The world blurred as Lily tore through the streets, her sneakers pounding the cracked pavement in a rhythm that felt all too familiar. The sound of air rushing past her ears mingled with the thudding of her heartbeat, loud and insistent, like a drumline pushing her forward. She darted around corners and slipped between crowds, the city racing by in flashes of color and motion: neon signs buzzing faintly, puddles catching the glint of streetlights, shadows shifting with every step. Her mind raced just as fast, tumbling through a mix of relief, guilt, and the nagging fear of being caught.

For a moment, she wasn't sure if she was running from the shopkeeper, the cop, or something deeper she couldn't name. The streets twisted and folded around her like a labyrinth, but her feet seemed to know the way. She didn't stop until her legs burned and her chest ached, her breath coming in sharp, uneven gasps. She slowed to a stumble and leaned against a graffiti-splashed wall, blinking hard as her vision blurred. For a second, the streetlights and stars above seemed to merge, swirling into a dizzying constellation that made her head spin.

She closed her eyes and pressed her palms against the cool brick, waiting for the world to steady. When she opened them again, the stars were just stars, distant and indifferent, and the city had gone quiet around her.

The night was thick and cold, wrapping around the empty street like a threadbare blanket. The houses on either side were shells of their former selves: boarded windows, crumbling steps, doorframes that hung crooked as if yawning from exhaustion. Lily moved cautiously, clutching the bruised apple and now half-smashed bag of chips she'd pilfered. Her stomach growled loud enough to rival the distant rumble of traffic.

The block wasn't exactly quiet. Somewhere nearby, someone was arguing about a mattress, and an old transistor radio played tinny music in a doorway. Lily stepped lightly, scanning for a spot she could tuck into for the night—someplace safer than last time, when a couple of men had decided her stash was better off as theirs. She shivered at the memory and adjusted her hoodie.

Ahead, a woman sat on the stoop of a peeling Victorian house. She looked as worn as the wood beneath her: hunched shoulders, wiry hair tucked into a knit cap, and eyes that glinted like streetlights catching broken glass. She watched Lily approach with the kind of gaze that seemed to know too much.

"You new here?" the woman rasped, voice smoky and dry.

Lily hesitated. "Just passing through," she lied.

The woman snorted, as if to say, Sure, kid. She didn't press, just waved a bony hand toward the house behind her. "Number nine's empty. Don't leave no trace."

"Thanks," Lily murmured, already heading up the steps. She didn't look back, but she could feel the woman's gaze burning a hole between her shoulder blades.

Inside, the air was stale, thick with mildew and something metallic. The kind of smell that clung to places forgotten by everyone except time. Lily found a corner in what might have once been a dining room and sat cross-legged, pulling her hoodie tighter. She bit into the apple, its sourness making her eyes sting, and tried to tune out the creaks and groans of the house settling around her.

And then it came: a sound. Low and rumbling, like distant thunder, except it came from below, not above. The floor shuddered beneath her, just enough to make the empty cans on the counter clink together. Lily froze mid-bite.

"Earthquake?" she whispered to no one.

She peeked out a broken window. Across the street, the old woman was still on the stoop, looking calm as ever. She raised an eyebrow, tilting her head toward the horizon. Lily followed her gaze and squinted.

A bright light flared in the distance, blindingly bright for a moment, then vanished. Lily's breath caught. "You're right," she muttered. "Definitely not an earthquake."

Later that night, Lily woke to a sound unlike anything she'd heard before. A low beeping, faint at first but growing louder, rhythmic and insistent. She sat up sharply, heart hammering. The sound seemed to be moving, getting closer. Panic prickled under her skin. She'd heard stories about weird tech and weirder people. Cops. Squatters. Worse.

She slipped into the kitchen, finding a cabinet big enough to crawl into. It smelled like rot and rust, but it was tight and dark. She drew her knees to her chest, trying to make herself small. Through the slats of the broken door, she saw them.

Four pairs of legs, casually dressed but too clean, too crisp, like the mannequins in a department store. Their movements were deliberate but oddly stiff, their shoes spotless. Lily's pulse quickened.

"The signal's localized," said one voice, crisp and commanding. "Am I warm?"

"Your body temperature readings are normal," answered another voice, androgynous and unsettlingly calm.

"Very funny," the first voice snapped, with a sigh.

The second replied, deadpan, "I was not attempting humor, however I now see that I have inadvertently become the butt of the joke."

The beeping grew louder, sharper. Lily's hands clenched into fists. The panel in front of her shifted slightly as if someone had brushed against it. The commanding voice said, "Right about... here."

The panel swung open, and Lily reacted instantly, kicking out hard. Her foot connected with a shin, and there was a sharp yelp. She scrambled out of the cabinet, darting past the startled figure and toward the door. Her breath came in quick, panicked bursts.

Before she made it, something cold and strong locked around her wrist. She twisted to see a bald figure with unnervingly smooth, almost shiny skin. Their face was blank and unlined, like a mannequin brought to life. Their grip didn't hurt, but it was unyielding.

"Let go of me!" she shouted, yanking with all her strength.

The commanding voice spoke again, softer now. "Lily, please. Don't be afraid. My name is Caris. We're here to help you."

Lily froze just long enough to feel the grip on her wrist loosen slightly. It was all the opening she needed. She wrenched free, bolting out the door and into the night, her feet pounding against the pavement. She didn't look back.

Behind her, Caris sighed heavily. "That went well."

"If it is any consolation," the androgynous voice offered, "I calculate only a 23% probability of catastrophic failure in this mission."

"That's... not as comforting as you think it is," Caris muttered, gesturing for the others to follow. "Let's go. She won't get far."

· · · ·

Lily's chest heaved as she rounded the corner, her feet pounding the pavement hard enough to send little jolts up her legs. She darted down an alley, the air close and smelling of wet concrete and garbage. Her fingers gripped the wall as she turned sharply, pressing herself flat against the bricks.

She clenched her jaw, forcing her breathing to slow. Her heart thudded in her ears, so loud she was sure it would give her away. Slowly, she strained to listen, her muscles coiled tight. There was nothing but the faint hum of the city—a car in the distance, the drip of water somewhere nearby. She exhaled softly, her shoulders loosening just a little. Maybe they're gone.

And then, faint but distinct, the beep came again. It started soft, a low, rhythmic pulse, but it was growing louder with each passing second. Lily's blood ran cold. She blinked hard, willing it to stop, but there it was, echoing down the alley like some terrible homing signal. Her disbelief turned to panic.

"You've gotta be kidding me," she muttered under her breath. "They should really add a silent mode to that thing."

She launched herself forward again, her legs screaming in protest. Up ahead, the alley opened into a construction site, dimly lit by a single flickering bulb. Tall scaffolding rose against the night sky like a skeleton, and an old ladder leaned against a half-built wall. It wasn't much of a plan, but it was something. She bolted toward it, the beeping still haunting her steps.

Her hands gripped the ladder, splinters biting into her palms as she climbed. The rungs wobbled, but she didn't stop. She climbed higher, her breath coming in ragged bursts. The city stretched below her in a patchwork of light and shadow, but she couldn't afford to look down.

The beep grew louder still, joined now by the sound of footsteps. She was out of time. She reached the top of the scaffolding and swung herself onto the wooden platform, which creaked ominously beneath her weight. For a moment, she froze, realizing too late that there was nowhere else to go.

A figure stepped into view below, looking up at her with unflinching precision. The faint glow of the city lights reflected off their smooth, featureless skin. Lily's stomach twisted. They weren't winded. They weren't even sweating.

"Lily," the voice called, calm but unyielding. "There's no need for this. Please, come down."

"Yeah, sure," she muttered, backing away until her heels touched the edge of the platform. "I'll get right on that."

The platform groaned under her, and suddenly, the wood gave way. Her stomach lurched as she fell, the air rushing past her in a blur of sound and motion. She barely had time to scream before something caught her—a grip strong, unyielding, and cold.

She blinked, her heart hammering as she realized she wasn't on the ground. She was hanging, suspended in mid-air, cradled in the arms of the smooth-skinned figure from before.

"Got you," they said, their voice calm, almost detached.

Her vision blurred at the edges, stars dancing in the periphery. "Great," she muttered faintly before the world tilted sideways, and everything went dark.

• • • •

Glass exploded all around her, glittering shards spinning in slow motion, catching flashes of light like jagged stars. The world tilted violently, the crunch of metal twisting and collapsing around her ears. Her body jerked against the seatbelt, her breath punched out of her lungs, and then came the silence—thick and oppressive, like cotton stuffed in her ears.

Something warm and wet trickled down the side of her face. She reached up instinctively and her fingers came back slick with blood. The coppery tang filled her mouth, her head swimming in disjointed flashes of light and sound. There was yelling—someone screaming her name, but it was drowned out by the wail of sirens, distant but getting closer.

Her ears rang as the scene shifted suddenly, jarringly, like a film reel torn and spliced with something else entirely. She was no longer in the car. She was standing in the middle of the rundown neighborhood from earlier. The street was eerily still, frozen in time. Cracks in the pavement seemed to glow faintly, pulsing in a rhythm she couldn't quite place.

Ahead of her, the old woman sat on the stoop as before, her wiry hair tucked into her knit cap. Only now, the woman was bathed in light, impossibly bright, as if the sun had decided to take up residence in that exact spot. Lily shielded her eyes, squinting, but the light grew brighter, swallowing the street in its glow.

The old woman stood, her face unchanging yet vivid, as if carved from memory and something more ephemeral. Her lips moved, the voice distant and echoing. "Lily?"

Lily's chest tightened, her breath catching in her throat. Her eyes welled with tears she didn't understand, a sharp ache blooming in her chest—a raw, overwhelming sense of loss that threatened to knock her to her knees.

"Lily?" the woman repeated, stepping closer. The light framed her like a halo now, shimmering and alive.

"Lily?" The voice was softer this time, warmer. It broke through the dream, tugging her upward, away from the strange, glowing street. The old woman's face dissolved into white-hot brightness, and—

She opened her eyes.

The light was still there, but now it was different, morning light from high up. Above her was a face—disturbingly symmetrical, with eyes so crystalline and steady they didn't look real. A voice, soft yet precise, spoke again.

"Lily? Are you alright?"

She blinked, her mind struggling to piece together where she was. The face belonged to a young woman—or someone who looked like one. She was noticeably clean, dressed in crisp lines, her skin so flawless it almost shone under the light.

Lily's lips moved before her brain could catch up. "Where the hell am I?"

The tears from the dream were still there, hot and wet against her cheeks. She swiped at them angrily with the back of her hand, not wanting to show weakness to the stranger in front of her. Her legs wobbled as she pushed herself upright, her head spinning slightly, but she refused to stay down. "I'm fine," she lied, her voice sharper than she intended. "I just—where am I?"

The world came into focus slowly, a hazy blend of morning light and muted shadows. The air smelled faintly of dust and old wood, the kind of stale scent that lingered in abandoned places. Golden beams of sunlight filtered through the high, broken windows, cutting through the gloom in perfect slants that caught motes of dust mid-air. It was almost beautiful—if Lily weren't busy grappling with panic.

Her gaze darted around the room. Exposed beams stretched above her like the ribs of a giant, and stacks of forgotten crates loomed in the corners. But it wasn't the warehouse that made her heart race. It was them.

Four figures stood a few feet away, speaking in hushed voices. They looked strangely out of place, their casual clothes just a little too crisp, their postures just a little too rigid. Lily's eyes landed first on the one closest to her—the young woman with unnervingly symmetrical features. Her dark eyes seemed to catch the sunlight, giving her an almost radiant quality.

"Lily?" the woman said again, her tone kind but firm. "Do you remember what happened?"

Lily squinted, forcing her sluggish brain to catch up. She looked between the woman and the other figures: a tall, bald individual with a smooth, almost metallic sheen to their skin that shimmered faintly in the sunlight. Standing beside them was a man with strange purple markings snaking up the sides of his neck, so faint she thought they might be shadows at first. Tattoos? No, they were too organic, like beauty marks patterned by nature itself. He caught her staring and raised an eyebrow, a stern look on his face.

And then there was the last one—a stocky figure with a blunt, no-nonsense face and the kind of broad shoulders that said he probably bench-pressed cars for fun. He stood with his arms crossed, radiating disapproval like an overzealous bouncer.

Lily crossed her own arms, more out of defiance than comfort. "You're not cops? 'Cause I'm getting some serious cop vibes off this one." She nodded toward the stocky man.

The man raised an eyebrow but said nothing, his stony expression unchanging.

The young woman's lips twitched into a faint smile. "Correct," she said calmly, her voice carrying an authority that felt practiced but not overbearing. "My name is Ensign Leena Caris." She gestured to the smooth-skinned figure beside her. "This is Datch."

Datch gave a small, precise nod. "It is a pleasure to meet you," he said in a voice that was both neutral and strangely melodic. Lily couldn't decide if it was comforting or unnerving.

Caris continued, nodding toward the others. "That's Ensign Malik," she said, indicating the man with the markings, "and Mr. Garrow." Her tone shifted slightly as she said his name, making it clear that whatever authority he had was purely practical. Garrow offered nothing in return, his arms still crossed.

Lily's eyebrows shot up. "Great. So what are you, then? Special ops for runaway teens? Fight club?"

Caris took a slow step forward, her hands raised slightly in what Lily could only assume was supposed to look non-threatening. "We're here to help you, Lily. That's all. But we need to ask you some questions."

Lily took a step back, her shoulder blades pressing into the cold concrete wall. "Is that why you chased me through half the city like I stole something? Which, for the record, I didn't—at least, not from you."

There was a brief, uncomfortable silence. Caris opened her mouth to respond, but Datch spoke first. "We were not chasing you in the conventional sense," they said matter-of-factly. "Our efforts were to secure your safety while limiting external disruption. I estimate—"

Caris shot them a quick look. "Datch. not now."

Datch tilted his head slightly. "Yes, Ensign."

Caris adjusted her posture slightly, her hands at her sides, radiating calm. "Lily, do you remember anything? Anything at all about us?"

Lily crossed her arms tightly, her eyes narrowing. "Lady, I don't even know who I am. You think I'd remember you?"

Caris tilted her head, her expression neutral but patient. "Do we seem familiar at all? Even a little?"

Lily hesitated, the sharp retort dying on her lips. She hated how cornered she felt, like a rat with nowhere to run. "No," she admitted quietly. "Nothing. Believe me, I wish I remembered anything."

Datch stepped forward, his movement unnervingly smooth. "We tracked you using your com tag," they said in their usual flat tone.

Lily frowned. "Com tag?"

Datch gestured toward her pocket. "The object you carry."

Her hand instinctively went to the smooth metal tag in her pocket. She pulled it out, holding it up and glaring at it as if daring it to explain itself. It had always been plain—just her name and a date etched into the surface. But now, the letters glowed brightly, like they were lit from within.

"What the...?" she whispered, her stomach twisting. The tag felt alive in her palm, a sensation she didn't like. "It's never done that before."

"Your com tag," Datch continued, unfazed by her reaction, "is linked to your identification in our system. It confirms who you are."

Lily stared at the glowing tag, her throat tightening. "And who's that supposed to be?"

Caris's gaze softened slightly, and she took a cautious step closer. "You're Lieutenant Lily Starling. A member of the United Space Fleet."

"United..." Lily barked a laugh, shaking her head. "Is that supposed to mean something to me?"

"It should," Malik chimed in, his voice calm but firm. "You followed the Krythar to Earth and into the past."

Lily blinked, her brain tripping over the words. "Wait. Hold up. The past? Did you just say...?" Her words trailed off, her voice hitching.

Caris nodded slowly, her tone careful. "We're from the 26th century. We... followed your signal back through time."

Lily stared at them, her face blank for a beat before she laughed again, this time short and sharp. "Right. Okay. Sure. Time travelers. Makes sense."

Lily's head spun as she tried to process what they were saying. Her fingers tightened around the tag, the weight of it grounding her. "So you're not aliens?"

Caris shook her head. "Not all of us. I'm human, from Earth. Centuries ago, humans began exploring the galaxy and discovered... we weren't alone."

Datch added, "Countless species exist, spanning thousands of worlds."

Lily's mind reeled, the weight of their words settling heavily in her chest. She wanted to dismiss it all as ridiculous, but deep down, something about it clicked—like a piece of a puzzle she didn't know she'd been trying to solve.

Her voice softened slightly. "So... who am I? Really?"

Caris met her gaze, her voice steady and sure. "You're Lieutenant Lily Starling of the United Space Fleet. You were on a mission to stop the Krythar from deploying a weapon of unimaginable power."

Datch added, "They must have wiped your memory as a contingency."

Lily swallowed hard, her throat dry. The words hung in the air, heavy and unreal. A part of her wanted to call them crazy. But another part—the part that had always wondered who she really was—wanted to believe them.

She took a shaky breath. "So... what are you asking me to do?"

"To come with us," Caris said. "To our ship. It's in orbit."

Lily blinked. "In orbit?"

Datch stepped forward, holding up a small device. "Our shuttle is already here."

They pressed a button, and the air in the warehouse shimmered. A sleek, silver craft materialized in the middle of the room, its clean lines glowing faintly in the dim light.

Lily's jaw dropped despite herself. "Okay," she murmured. "That's... actually impressive."

Caris gestured toward the shuttle, her expression softening. "Will you trust us?"

Lily hesitated, the tag in her pocket suddenly feeling heavier. Every instinct told her to run, to find somewhere safe and familiar. But there was nothing familiar left. Only questions. And maybe, just maybe, these people had answers.

She snorted, a faint smirk tugging at her lips. "What's the worst that could happen? You turn me into a breeding sac for some alien experiment?"

Everyone froze, staring at her in wide-eyed horror.

"20th-century movies not part of your cultural studies?" she added dryly.

Caris blinked, then sighed, a hint of a smile tugging at her lips. "No. Definitely not."

Datch tilted his head slightly. "I assure you, no such threat exists."

Caris smiled faintly. "We'll keep you safe, Lily. I promise."

Caris gestured toward the shuttle, her tone calm but insistent. "Shall we?"

Lily stared at the craft, the glowing tag still tight in her hand. Against all odds, she took a step forward.

Lily glanced back at the warehouse full of morning light one last time, steeling herself. "Alright," she said, her voice steadier now. "Let's do this."

Species Profile: Cyranthians

Native to the lush world of Cyrantha Prime, the Cyranthians are a long-lived, deeply social people known for their grace and cultural refinement. Slightly taller than humans, they bear distinctive violet markings unique to each individual, with luminous grey eyes that seem to hold both curiosity and memory. They reach maturity at fifty, when some are granted the honorary title of Dryst—an acknowledgment of wisdom and communal trust that carries lifelong respect.

Cyranthian society prizes connection above conquest. Masters of diplomacy and artistic innovation, they have long favored alliances over aggression, blending beauty and function in their bio-organic technologies. Though not a warrior species, they helped found the Space Fleet alongside humanity and other allies, shaping a coalition devoted to exploration and peace. The devastation of the Krythar centuries ago tempered their idealism but strengthened their resolve: they would never again stand alone.

Chapter 2: The Salamander

THE SILENCE IS DEEP—NOT a vacuum of absence, but a fullness of being, a silence filled with the memory of creation. This is not loneliness, though it would be easy to mistake it for such. It is something richer, a stillness that cradles possibility, like a darkened theater before the lights rise, where every dream of what could be waits just out of reach.

The blackness is not lifeless. It holds multitudes. Invisible winds of solar particles whip through the void, a fiery breath from the sun scattering energy to the farthest corners. Gravity bends and pulls like an unseen sculptor, shaping orbits and destinies. The remnants of ancient collisions drift endlessly, a symphony of dust and ice which have witnessed the birth and death of stars. And somewhere out here, a speck of cosmic dust tumbles, infinitesimal against the backdrop of eternity, yet wholly a part of it.

To the dust, the universe is a kaleidoscope of extremes. It feels the sharp kiss of starlight, a fleeting warmth that fades as quickly as it arrives. It passes through the chill of endless shadow, the kind of cold that freezes not just life but time itself. It hurtles through this silence, surrounded by vast fields of nothingness so deep they feel like a whispered promise—this is the framework for all things. Every love, every loss, every war, every moment of joy and heartbreak—all of it begins and ends here.

And then—there. In the distance, a light. A pinprick of blue nestled among the black, so faint it seems unreal at first. But as the speck draws closer, the blue deepens, sharpening into focus.

At first, it is just a single point of light—a faint, flickering blue against the infinite black. It seems barely distinguishable from the distant stars. But as the dust draws nearer, that light sharpens and expands, revealing a thin, hazy ring encircling the blue. The atmosphere catches the sun's rays, scattering them into a halo of soft whites and golds that shimmer like silk spun in the dark.

Closer still, the reflections of oceans emerge, vast fields of liquid sapphire catching and refracting light in brilliant flashes that dance like signals to the cosmos. The haze resolves into ribbons of clouds, swirling in slow, mesmerizing patterns that trace the movement of winds over the planet's surface. The blue of the oceans deepens, crisscrossed by faint shadows of waves and currents, and just at their edges, hints of green and brown begin to appear—the contours of continents taking shape.

Then, the details multiply. The greens become forests and fields, the browns reveal rugged mountains and sprawling deserts, and here and there, tiny clusters of light begin to dot the surface. Civilization—bright pinpricks against the darker patches of land, glowing softly as if the Earth itself were breathing. The planet stretches out now, filling the view entirely, a living mosaic of motion and color, vibrant and alive.

Earth.

A sapphire suspended in a sea of ink, its light veiled by a thin blue haze. The dust drifts closer—past spiraled clouds, bright ice caps, and the greens and browns of living continents—drawn into the waiting atmosphere. Air gathers around it, friction sparking brief flares of light. Chaos and beauty in a single descent.

The curve of Earth opens wide beneath it, oceans tugging, forests breathing, lives humming in quiet rhythm. The dust is no longer alone; it becomes part of the whole. And beneath it all, the quiet remains—not emptiness, but the space where everything begins.

And the dust tumbles on, unnoticed. But in the distance, something else stirs—a faint ripple against the silence. A shuttle, its engines burning faint trails of blue, breaks free from the grip of Earth's orbit. And beyond it, invisible and waiting, lies a shadow. Something vast and hidden, watching from the void.

• • • •

Lily sat rigid in her seat, knuckles white against the armrests. The deck's constant vibration seemed to sync with the hammering of her heart. She wanted to take it all in, to absorb every detail, but the movement, the noise, the sheer strangeness of it all pressed in from every side.

She thought briefly about pinching herself, but the shaking deck and occasional flicker of lights on the console ahead left no doubt. This wasn't a dream—it was far too visceral, too alive.

Her eyes darted around the cabin, searching for reassurance in the others' faces. They were calm, focused—people who had done this a thousand times. Garrow stood beside the pilot's seat, hand resting lightly for balance, steady despite the turbulence. Caris, at the controls, moved her hands fluidly across a panel that seemed alive, forming and erasing symbols at her touch.

The shuttle's walls caught Lily's attention. They weren't pieced together like human vehicles, with bolts, seams, and rivets. They looked organic, almost grown—a smooth, unbroken surface curving like an eggshell. Only where walls met control panels and seats did a more utilitarian design appear—practical, worn, like the handle of a trusted hammer.

"Pressure stability holding at ninety-eight percent," Garrow said, steady and clipped.

"Primary systems green," Caris replied, not looking up.

"Engines steady, but keep an eye on the tertiary core," Garrow added, scanning a shifting data display.

The voices calmed Lily somewhat, though her chest stayed tight. She turned to the viewport—

—and her breath caught. Earth filled her view, a sphere of blue, green, and white swirls against the black. The sight hit her like a punch, stealing her breath. She hadn't even realized they'd left the atmosphere.

"How are we not... floating?" she asked, gesturing at Garrow, steady on his feet.

"Artificial gravity," Caris said with a smirk. "One of the better inventions for space travelers."

"Better?" Lily echoed.

"You'd be amazed what we've perfected out here," Caris said, eyes back on the console.

"We're taking a slow approach," Caris added. "So we won't attract attention. Dock in about five minutes."

"Dock with what?" Lily asked.

"The cloaking device is engaged," Caris said. "Bends light around the ship, makes it invisible—to the eye and most sensors."

Lily pressed a hand to the cold glass. "So I don't even get to see it?"

Caris chuckled. "Plenty of time later. And plenty to see once you're aboard."

The moment the tractor beam engaged, the shuttle shifted. The smooth, steady hum of their journey gave way to a gentle tug, then a subtle rocking, as though they were no longer flying through space but floating on water. The vibrations felt less like the controlled thrum of machinery and more like the uneven bob of a small boat coming into dock.

"Here we go," Caris murmured, her hands steady over the console. The shuttle jolted, a firm bump that made Lily's teeth click together.

Ahead, a shimmering barrier came into view, flickering faintly like heat waves on a desert road. The shuttle aligned with it, and Lily's stomach flipped as the craft seemed to pause mid-space. For a moment, it felt as though the universe itself had taken a deep breath. The barrier rippled, a delicate distortion like sunlight on water.

"We're transitioning through the mag-field," Caris said, her voice steady. "The bay's pressurized, but you'll feel the shift. Hold tight."

The shuttle passed through, and a soft hiss filled the cabin. Frost bloomed on the viewport, tiny crystalline webs that vanished as quickly as they formed. Lily's ears popped, and the hum of the engines shifted to a quieter, steadier tone.

The lights flickered—bright, then dim, then bright again—casting the interior in strange, shifting hues. Outside, Lily caught glimpses of dark, swirling colors, like oil slicks on water, before they faded into the more uniform glow of the shuttlebay beyond.

The craft jolted again, settling with a final, satisfying bump. A moment later, the rear hatch hissed and lowered with a mechanical whine, revealing the massive expanse of the shuttlebay.

Lily stepped out hesitantly, the soles of her sneakers squeaking on the smooth surface. The air carried an odd blend of scents: warm metal, the crisp edge of static, and the tang of machinery. It felt fitting for a space so vast and bustling.

The shuttlebay stretched around her, alive with motion. Dozens of crafts were docked in neat rows while crews in sleek uniforms moved purposefully between them. The sound of machinery clanked in rhythm beneath the murmur of voices.

"Decontamination first," Malik said, gesturing toward a nearby door.

"What's that mean?" Lily asked warily, but before she got an answer, they stepped into a small chamber lit with deep magenta light.

The moment the door sealed behind them, a burst of air hit her, strong enough to make her stagger. It roared around her like a wind tunnel, accompanied by flashes of light that danced over her skin in eerie, shifting patterns. She squinted against the brightness, feeling the warmth of the air, the prickling in her eyes, and the faint hum of energy beneath her feet.

When the door ahead opened, the shuttlebay was already a memory. They stepped into a surprisingly cozy hallway, the walls a soft brushed metal, sleek lighting casting a warm glow. A vase of delicate flowers sat on a small shelf, and a framed painting hung nearby—abstract swirls of deep blue and silver that reminded her of a stormy sea. It felt more like the lobby of a boutique hotel than the inside of a spaceship.

"This way," Caris said, her voice snapping Lily out of her daze. She fell into step, but her thoughts lingered on the shuttlebay. There had been so much to take in—an endless array of details, layered with a scale she hadn't imagined.

Caris stopped outside a pair of doors and turned back to the group. "Datch, escort Lily to her quarters. She could use a guide."

Datch inclined his head. "Of course. Follow me, Lily."

As they walked, the hallway curved gently, the brushed metal walls catching the light. The faint hum of the ship's systems provided a steady rhythm beneath their footsteps.

"You're... an android?" Lily asked after a moment.

"That is correct," Datch replied, his tone neutral but not unkind. "The term is far more accurate than 'robot.'"

"Right. Got it," Lily said quickly. Then, "Sorry if that was rude."

"There is no need to apologize," Datch assured her. "It is not easy to offend me."

"Not easy, but not impossible?" she asked.

Datch considered this. "My feelings are... different from yours. Less immediate. More deliberate."

"Were you built by humans?" she asked.

"While I was technically built, I prefer the term born. It more accurately reflects my experience."

"Born?"

"Yes." He offered a faint smile, both practiced and sincere. "My history is complicated. Perhaps I will share it with you sometime."

Before she could respond, he added, "For now, it is enough to say that you and I were good friends before your memory loss. I trust we will be again."

They reached her quarters, and the door slid open with a soft hiss. The room beyond was compact but inviting: brushed metal walls, soft lighting, a vase with a single white flower, and a small abstract painting. The bed looked plush, the kind she could sink into for hours.

Earth was visible through the window. Her chest tightened at the sight.

"The computer panel has been configured for you," Datch said, gesturing to a sleek display in the far wall. "It provides access to your personal file, as well as general information about the Space Fleet and the Union of Allied Systems. You may find it helpful as you acclimate."

"Thanks," Lily said.

"I recommend you rest. In about five hours, Dr. Thesari will meet with you, and the captain will want to see you as well." He paused. "Do not fear. He is a kind man."

With that, Datch inclined his head again and stepped back into the hallway. The door slid shut, leaving her alone.

The shower caught her eye, tucked into a corner behind frosted glass. She hesitated, half expecting it to spray her with fluorescent goo, but when she turned the handle, warm water poured out—clean and steady. It was simple, wonderfully ordinary, and exactly what she needed. She stayed in just long enough to feel clean for the first time in far too long.

When she emerged, she found a set of clothes laid out on the bed: a silver-white tracksuit with a faint sheen. She smirked as she slipped it on. "Why do people from the future always dress like this?" she muttered.

Clean and dressed, she approached the computer panel. The screen lit up at her touch, its surface smooth and responsive. She began scrolling through menus, but something about it felt different. As her thoughts drifted, so did the interface. Thumbnails bubbled up, each one reflecting a topic she'd just been considering. She flicked one upward, and it expanded into an array of subtopics.

"Man," she muttered, "you could go down quite a rabbit hole with this thing."

Her file caught her attention. She opened it—and froze. She was listed as the youngest human ever admitted to the Space Fleet, joining at sixteen and promoted to lieutenant by seventeen.

Her parents' names appeared next: Dr. Elaine Starling and Dr. Marcus Starling, Lead Researchers, Psionic Advancement Project. She swallowed hard. There would be time to cry later.

They had been famous scientists, controversial among humans but supported by many other worlds in the UAS. Their work had been instrumental in combating something called the Krythar.

"I guess there are politics in every time period," Lily muttered, leaning back.

She stared at the screen, questions swirling, but exhaustion tugged at her again. There would be time to learn more. At least, she hoped there would be.

• • • •

The door to the medical bay slid open with a soft hiss, and Lily hesitated on the threshold. The room was brightly lit, its walls curved and seamless like the rest of the ship. Sleek medical instruments lined the walls, their purpose unclear but intimidating. A faint, clean scent hung in the air, sharp and slightly sweet, like freshly peeled citrus.

"Come in, come in!" A melodic voice filled the room, warm and welcoming. Dr. Thesari turned toward Lily, her expression lighting with delight. The Cyranthian elder was tall and elegant, her pale lavender skin glowing faintly under the lights. Silver hair flowed in intricate braids down her back, and her wide, expressive eyes sparkled with genuine curiosity. "You must be Lily Starling! Oh, this is wonderful—please, sit, sit."

Lily stepped inside, glancing at Datch, who gave her an almost imperceptible nod of reassurance. She perched on the edge of the examination chair, trying to relax as Dr. Thesari bustled around her with the energy of a party host rather than a doctor.

"I must say, I've been looking forward to meeting you," Dr. Thesari said, placing a small device near Lily's wrist. It emitted a faint hum as it scanned her. "Human physiology is fascinating. Did you know your mitochondrial DNA shares similarities with a plant species we encountered on Verath-7? Remarkable. Oh, and your neural pathways—"

"Doctor..." Datch interjected, calm but firm. "Perhaps we should focus on the examination."

"Ah, yes, of course." Dr. Thesari smiled sheepishly, waving a hand. "Forgive me. I do get carried away." She placed a hand over her heart before continuing the scan. "Your vitals look excellent, Lily. No injuries, no significant anomalies—though your serotonin levels are a touch low. Understandable, given everything you've been through. We'll address that."

Lily blinked. "That's it? No needles or anything?"

Dr. Thesari laughed, warm and musical. "Needles? Goodness, no. We've moved well past those. I promise, this is painless. You might even find it relaxing."

As the scanner hummed, Dr. Thesari leaned closer, her eyes narrowing slightly in concentration, almost as if she could see right through Lily's skull—which, for all Lily knew, she could. "I've always wondered about the adaptability of human sensory systems in zero gravity. If you don't mind, I'd love to hear your thoughts once you've had more time aboard."

"She's barely been aboard for five hours," Datch pointed out, faintly exasperated. "Perhaps that conversation can wait."

Dr. Thesari chuckled. "Ah, Datch, always the voice of reason. You're right." She turned back to Lily, her expression softening. "You're in excellent health, my dear. And if you ever have questions—about your physiology, the ship, or anything at all—please don't hesitate to ask. We Cyranthians do love a good chat."

Lily smiled faintly, relaxing a little. Dr. Thesari's warmth was infectious, and though the examination was unlike anything she'd experienced, it was far less intimidating than she'd feared. "Thanks, Doctor."

"Call me Tess," Dr. Thesari said with a grin. "Everyone does."

"I'll try to remember that," Lily said, standing as Tess waved her off.

"Oh, and Lily?" Tess added, a mischievous glint in her eye. "When you meet the captain, don't mention his hat collection. Just... trust me."

· · · ·

The door to the Captain's Stateroom opened with the softest hiss of any she'd encountered on the ship. Lily was immediately struck by the contrast between the tranquil corridor behind her and the sheer presence of the room beyond. Dim lighting revealed a space cluttered like a cross between a cramped museum and a man cave, the kind of room belonging to someone who curated their life around stories. Artifacts and trinkets covered nearly every surface—ancient tools, faded photographs, holograms of distant worlds, and a sword mounted awkwardly on the wall beside a collection of old Earth medals.

What truly caught her eye, though, was the ceiling. Lining its edges was the sprawling collection of hats Dr. Thesari had mentioned—top hats, military caps, wide-brimmed sun hats, and headpieces so strange they barely resembled hats at all. Each seemed to carry its own history, the variety dizzying.

Her gaze swept the room but was abruptly pulled to the blaring opera. The deep, booming voice of a singer filled the air, dramatic and unrelenting.

At the far end, the captain stood with his back to her, silhouetted by the glow of a muted holographic display. Hands clasped behind him, posture radiating theatrical gravitas, he might have been carved from stone.

Lily's first thought: Is he for real?

"I have often thought," the captain began, his voice rising above the music, "that no creature is more noble than the salamander. Born of fire and dwelling in its embrace, it represents resilience, transformation, and an unyielding spirit. On ancient Earth, it was seen as a symbol of power and mystery. The choice to name our ship after such a creature was no accident—"

He paused for effect, lifting one hand as though delivering an oration to a crowd.

Lily glanced behind her, half expecting someone to interrupt. But the door had slid shut—she was alone in the room with this... performance.

The captain paced a step, voice warming to a sudden tangent. "You know, the salamander is remarkable. Amphibian. Lives both in water and on land, though some species are entirely aquatic. And their regenerative abilities? Extraordinary. They can regrow entire limbs—legs, tails, even parts of their heart or brain. Parts of their brain!" His movements were deliberate, measured.

"Think about that. A creature so unassuming, so often overlooked, yet carrying the potential for profound renewal. Nature's own little miracle workers—living proof that even the smallest beings can hold the key to survival."

He paused, seemed to reconsider, then waved a hand. "No, no, that's not quite it. Let me rephrase."

Straightening, his tone turned deliberate again. "The salamander is not just a symbol of adaptability or regeneration. It's a testament to resilience. To survival against odds. To thriving in places where others might falter. And it is that spirit that we carry forward—"

Lily blinked, unsure whether to interrupt.

"And so," the captain continued, voice dipping into a near whisper, "the Salamander represents not only our ship but our mission—our journey through the flames of adversity, emerging stronger, more united, and ever victorious."

He stepped to his desk, tapped a control, and the opera cut off abruptly, leaving a startling silence. Adjusting the lighting, he transformed the room: the dim, den-like ambiance gave way to stark brightness, the collector's sanctuary now a functional office.

Finally, he pressed the comm button. "Send her in," he said with finality.

A pause. The voice over the comm hesitated. "Sir..."

Lily cleared her throat, loud and deliberate.

The captain froze mid-turn, then wheeled around, his face a mask of surprise and embarrassment. His tall frame loomed over the desk as he quickly collected himself, straightening his jacket and smoothing back graying hair. Sharp blue eyes softened as they met hers, and he stepped forward with a hand extended.

"Well," he said, voice steady but touched with self-awareness. "You must be Lily Starling."

"That's what they tell me," Lily replied, stepping forward and clasping his hand.

His grip was strong but not crushing, a perfect balance of authority and approachability. Up close, she saw the details: broad shoulders, a chiseled face lined with years of experience, and the faintest hint of a smile at the edge of his lips. Silver streaked his hair, and his posture was impeccable—confidence and discipline embodied. He reminded her of a classic hero from an old painting: part charm, part determination, part unshakable certainty.

"Captain Griff Calan," he said, releasing her hand. "Welcome aboard."

Lily shifted in her seat, trying to stay composed, but the captain's piercing gaze made it impossible to relax. He leaned forward slightly, resting his hands on the desk. The brightness of the room no longer felt clinical—it felt like a spotlight, and she was center stage.

"So," she began, her voice faltering slightly, "it really is called the Salamander?"

The captain's face softened, just enough for a faint smirk to touch his lips. "The SFS Salamander," he said with measured pride. "Pride of the Space Fleet."

Lily blinked, brow furrowing. "But... Salamander?"

He raised an eyebrow, holding her gaze as if daring her to continue.

She straightened a little, her mouth twitching into a nervous smile. "Never mind."

His demeanor shifted. The faint glint of amusement in his eyes was replaced by something heavier, a shadow of the burden he carried. He leaned back, expression firm but not unkind.

"There are things you need to know," he said, voice steady but serious. "And I won't sugarcoat them. That's not how I operate."

Lily straightened, her stomach tightening.

"The doctor confirmed your identity," he continued, blue eyes searching hers. "But there's no treatment plan for your memory loss. Psionic trauma like yours is... complicated."

She nodded slowly, not trusting herself to speak.

The captain hesitated before continuing. "Your parents, Dr. Elaine and Dr. Marcus Starling, were murdered by the Krythar."

The words landed like a blow. Lily's breath hitched, and she stared at him, throat tightening as she fought the wave of emotion rising inside her.

"I won't lie to you," he added, voice softening. "Command didn't want me to tell you—not all of it, at least. But I believe in honesty. Transparency. So here it is." He leaned forward again, hands clasped on the desk.

"Your parents didn't serve in the Space Fleet," he said, each word deliberate. "They worked... separately."

Lily frowned, caught off guard. "What do you mean?"

"They answered only to themselves. Their work was..." He paused, searching for the word. "Independent. They pushed boundaries others wouldn't. And in their work, they created you."

Her breath hitched. "Created me?"

"They genetically engineered you," the captain said evenly. "Manipulated your DNA to enhance your psionic abilities. You were designed to be a weapon against the Krythar."

Her mind reeled. "A... weapon?" The word felt sharp, foreign, like it didn't belong to her—or anyone.

"Yes," he said, tone unflinching but not without sympathy. "And not everyone agreed with it. Many humans found it unethical—myself included. But other worlds in the Union of Allied Systems strongly supported your creation. The Krythar are a threat unlike any we've faced, and humanity's psionic potential was seen as a solution."

Lily shook her head, trying to make sense of it. "What makes the... Krythar such a threat?"

The captain leaned back, exhaling slowly, as if bracing for the question. "About two hundred fifty years ago, the Cyntharians—Dr. Thesari's people—made contact with Earth. Humanity's first introduction to an alien species. They're incredibly diplomatic, as you've probably noticed. But a century before they met humans, they encountered the Krythar."

His jaw tightened, his gaze flickering toward a hologram on the wall. "The Krythar nearly conquered them. They're a psionically powerful species—telepaths, empaths, manipulators on a scale most can't compete with. The Cyntharians barely survived and learned a harsh lesson: sometimes, friendliness isn't enough. Since then, they've relied on alliances like the Union for protection."

Lily leaned forward slightly, drawn in despite herself.

"For a long time, the Krythar Alliance kept to themselves," the captain went on, his voice heavy with history. "But something changed. They've grown hungry for conquest again, and they've focused their efforts on defeating the Union. For decades, we were evenly matched—until the Psion Core."

"The what?" Lily asked, her voice sharp with unease.

"A weapon," the captain said grimly. "A massive psionic amplifier. With it, they can focus their abilities on a scale that affects entire ships—or worse. It uses organic crystals as its core, crystals that take centuries to grow. The Krythar couldn't grow it fast enough to matter in the war, so they launched a desperate, terrifying plot. They sent it into the past, where it could grow and mature over hundreds of years."

Lily's eyes widened.

"In my time, it seemed to appear out of nowhere, fully operational," he continued. "It's turned the tide in their favor. The losses are devastating."

Her throat was dry. "So... how does that involve me?"

The captain's gaze locked on hers, steady and unflinching. "Before your memory loss, you tracked the Psion Core here. You found it and signaled us. And now that we know where it is—"

"You're going to go after it?" she interrupted.

"Yes," he said without hesitation. "We're planning an away mission to secure the Core before it can reach full development. And I was hoping you would consider going on the mission."

She stared in disbelief. "You're asking me to go after this thing?"

Calan nodded. "Back in my time, we're losing this war. You may be our best hope for turning the tide."

Her heart pounded, the enormity of it pressing down like a physical weight. "Holy crap," she muttered under her breath.

The captain allowed himself a faint smile.

Her head spun with everything she'd just learned, puzzle pieces falling into a terrifying, inevitable shape. Without thinking, she blurted, "It sounds like you're saying I was born for this."

• • • •

The mess hall wasn't quite what Lily expected. It had the cafeteria-like feel of a high school lunchroom, with rows of tables and chairs in neat, utilitarian order. The air hit her first—not unpleasant, but thick with the accumulated aromas of countless meals, like the ghosts of dinners past had settled into the very fibers of the furniture.

Along one side of the room stood a line of sleek machines, their surfaces blank until someone approached, at which point the panels flickered to life.

Lily's stomach growled as she took a hesitant step forward. Datch had walked her here but left without ceremony, explaining that eating was "unnecessary" for him. Now she stood alone, staring at what looked like a cross between an old ship's galley and a futuristic vending station. Sleek consoles hummed softly, ready to respond to a single touch, while further down, uniformed crew members moved through open chef's stations, plating dishes with the practiced ease of a high-end hotel kitchen. The contrast was striking—machines delivering meals with clinical precision while, just steps away, human hands added the personal touch of artistry.

Lily approached one of the consoles. "Okay," she muttered as the screen flared to life. "Food."

Nothing happened.

She leaned closer. "Uh... sandwich?"

A list of options appeared, overwhelming in her current state. "Sure, make it complicated," she grumbled, jabbing at the screen with mild frustration. After a few wrong selections and muttered curses, she cobbled together a tray: something resembling a sandwich, a steaming bowl of soup, and a glowing blue drink that looked questionable but smelled amazing.

Tray in hand, she slid into a seat by the window and dug in. The sandwich surprised her—warm, soft bread with a spiced vegetable filling that was oddly satisfying—and the soup tasted like actual cream and herbs. She barely came up for air between bites.

"You eat like a rescue dog," a voice said from behind her, dry but not unkind.

Lily jerked upright, nearly choking. Caris stood there, arms crossed, her expression neutral but with a flicker of amusement in her eyes.

"I didn't even see you come in," Lily said, swallowing quickly.

"I noticed." Caris slid into the seat across from her, movements casual but deliberate. "The captain didn't scare you off, then?"

Lily shrugged, still chewing. "He's... a lot. But I survived."

Caris smirked faintly, her gaze drifting to the window. For a moment, neither of them spoke, the hum of the ship filling the space. Then, without preamble, Caris said, "I lost my parents when I was your age."

The statement hung in the air, heavy and abrupt. Lily froze, her sandwich halfway to her mouth.

"I get it," Caris continued, her voice steady. "Not in the same way you do, but... enough to know it's going to mess with you. Maybe for a while. Just... don't let it stop you."

Lily swallowed hard, her throat tight. "Thanks," she said after a beat, her voice quieter than she intended.

Caris leaned back slightly, her expression softening. "The captain asked me to lead the away mission."

Relief hit Lily like a wave. Before she could stop herself, she leaned forward and hugged Caris, quick and tight.

Caris stiffened for a moment, unprepared, but said nothing. Lily pulled back almost immediately, face hot, and busied herself with her tray. Neither of them acknowledged the moment.

"You'll be ready," Caris said finally, standing and adjusting her jacket.

Lily glanced out the window, her gaze lingering on Earth as Australia rolled into view, its edges kissed by the soft glow of sunlight.

Caris followed her gaze. "Eight hours. Then we get to work." She turned toward the door, pausing just long enough to add, "And try not to get lost on your way to the briefing."

Lily smiled faintly, her appetite forgotten as her eyes stayed fixed on the planet below.

Species Profile:
The Krythar Ascendancy

The Krythar are a psionically formidable species whose very presence unsettles those who stand before them. Tall and statuesque, with opalescent skin that shimmers in shifting light and eyes of unbroken black, they seem less born of flesh than carved from some colder intention. Their tri-lobed minds allow them to perceive patterns others cannot, wielding telepathy, telekinesis, and emotional manipulation with terrifying precision—though such power demands focus, and even they are not invulnerable.

To the Krythar, order is sacred. They believe themselves chosen by a cosmic force known as the Vorran Imperative, destined to impose harmony upon a chaotic galaxy. Free will is not a right but a flaw to be corrected. Conquest, in their theology, is purification. They will negotiate when submission serves their design, but resistance is met without mercy. Their mastery of graviton manipulation and experimental temporal engineering reflects a singular goal: control of destiny itself. Yet beneath their certainty lies a weakness common to all empires—an unshakable belief in their own inevitability.

Chapter 3: The Fractured Path

THE AIR CRACKED WITH the sound of energy blasts, sharp and deafening, as the away team scrambled for cover. Lily pressed her back against the jagged remains of an old concrete pillar, her chest heaving, ears ringing. Dust and debris rained down with every impact, the oppressive heat of Krythar disruptor fire biting at her exposed skin. The smoky tang of the air burned her eyes, forcing them to water as she tried to see through the haze.

It wasn't like the movies. There was no dramatic soundtrack, no choreographed precision to the chaos. It was noise and pain, blood and panic. Her pulse pounded in her ears, louder than the explosions around her, and her hands shook so hard she could barely grip the weapon they'd handed her.

To her right, Malik crouched low, firing off bursts of plasma with calculated precision. He shouted something to Caris, but the words were swallowed by the roar of the fight. Datch stood further back, a model of eerie calm as he provided cover fire, his movements so measured they almost seemed out of place amid the carnage.

Lily dared to peek around the pillar, her breath catching in her throat. The Krythar were relentless. Their figures shimmered in the dim light, their opalescent skin glinting with every shift. They moved with an unsettling grace, their black eyes locking onto targets with predatory focus. She saw one lift a hand, and without a sound, a chunk of the ceiling tore free and hurtled toward them.

"Move!" Caris bellowed, yanking Lily back just in time. The concrete slammed into the ground where she'd been, sending up a cloud of dust and choking debris. Lily coughed, her vision swimming, but she had no time to recover.

Ahead of her, Garrow stood firm, his blaster pistol firing in rapid succession. He was the picture of courage, holding his ground as the Krythar advanced.

And then it happened.

A beam of green light sliced through the air, sharp and unforgiving. It hit Garrow square in the chest, and for a moment, everything seemed to freeze. His scream was short, a sound of pure agony, as the disrupter ray tore through his body. The smell hit Lily before her brain could process what she'd seen—burning flesh, sharp and acrid, turning her stomach.

"Garrow!" someone shouted, the voice filled with despair, but Lily couldn't tell who. He dropped to his knees, his weapon clattering to the ground. His face twisted in pain, and then he fell forward, motionless.

This wasn't supposed to happen. They had it all planned out—in and out, that's what they said. Quick, efficient, no surprises. This wasn't the plan. This wasn't supposed to happen.

Another blast struck the ground nearby, and the spell broke. Caris grabbed her arm, pulling her back into the shadows as Malik shouted orders. They were losing ground, and the Krythar weren't letting up.

The world blurred, her pulse thundering in her ears, the sounds of battle crashing over her like relentless waves. This was war—not the distant, romanticized version she'd seen in movies, but the real thing. Raw and terrifying, filled with blood, sweat, and the overwhelming certainty that she wouldn't leave this place alive.

• • • •

Four hours earlier.

Lily gripped the blast pistol tightly, its weight awkward in her hand. She stood in one of the ship's smaller training rooms, Garrow looming over her with an expression that suggested he'd rather be anywhere else.

"Point and shoot," he said flatly, folding his arms. "That's the gist of it. Keep it aimed downrange, don't touch the trigger unless you mean it, and for the love of everything, don't point it at anything you don't want dead."

Lily swallowed hard, glancing down at the weapon. Sleek, black, and cold, it caught the light in a way that made it seem more alive than it should have been. She raised it tentatively, her hand shaking, and Garrow immediately barked, "Steady grip. If you can't control it here, you've got no chance in the field."

"She won't need to fire," Datch said, standing nearby with his hands clasped behind his back. His voice carried the kind of certainty that left no room for argument. "This is a precaution only. Emergencies."

"Sure," Garrow muttered, skeptical.

Lily ignored them, her focus shifting to the target ahead—a simple circular marking on the far wall. She took a breath, tried to still the tremor in her arm, and fired. The blast was loud and bright, leaving a sharp tang in the air that stung her nose and burned like pepper on her tongue. She flinched as the shot veered wide, missing the target completely and leaving a dark scorch mark on the wall.

"Terrible," Garrow muttered under his breath.

"I heard that," Lily snapped, lowering the pistol.

"You were supposed to," he shot back, face set in disapproval.

Lily's grip tightened as her mind slipped back to the medical bay an hour earlier. Dr. Thesari had been kind, gentle even, as she tried every method she could think of to coax some spark of psionic ability out of her. The tests had been draining and fruitless. Lily had walked away no closer to the self everyone expected.

"We're relying on you," Thesari had said softly, her usually vibrant voice quiet. "But don't force it. Trust that it will come when it's needed."

Trust. The word felt hollow now, with a weapon in her hand and Garrow scowling at her every move.

"Let's try again," Datch said, his voice cutting through her thoughts. "You must focus, Lily."

She raised the pistol once more, her jaw set. This didn't feel like her—it couldn't be. The idea of firing at anything living made her stomach churn. But there was no time for doubt. The mission was clear: infiltrate the Krythar site undetected, rely on her psionic abilities to neutralize their security systems, and set charges to destroy the crystals.

"Just in stand out," Caris had said earlier. "Quick, clean, no surprises."

Lily didn't believe it for a second.

"Try again," Garrow said, motioning toward the target. His tone softened, almost imperceptibly. "If you're lucky, you'll never have to use it. But luck isn't something you count on in this line of work."

She took another breath, raised the pistol, and fired.

• • • •

The roar of the shuttle engines pressed against Lily's ears as she sat strapped into her seat, clutching the harness across her chest like it was the only thing keeping her tethered to reality. The hum of the machinery, steady and deep, vibrated through her bones, but it was nothing compared to the turmoil inside her.

Her stomach churned violently, and she swallowed hard, willing herself to keep it together. She stared at the floor, focusing on the pattern of the bolts in the metal as if grounding herself in the small details could stop the rising tide of nausea.

Caris, seated across from her, glanced up from her console. "You good?"

Lily nodded quickly, though she wasn't sure it was true. Her mouth felt dry, and her hands clenched into fists so tight that her knuckles ached.

Malik, sitting beside her, gave her a sidelong glance but said nothing. His quiet presence somehow made it worse. It was like he was waiting for her to crack, for the girl with no memory and shaky hands to confirm she didn't belong here.

She closed her eyes, the weight of the blast pistol strapped to her side a constant reminder of everything she didn't know how to do. The plan ran through her mind like a mantra: Get in. Stay undetected. Use the psionic abilities that might or might not exist. Get out.

Her stomach flipped again, and she thought for a moment she might actually be sick.

"Deep breaths," Datch said, his voice calm and measured. "Hyperventilation will not improve your odds."

"Thanks for the tip," she muttered, gripping the straps tighter.

The tunnels were worse.

After landing the shuttle in a rocky crevice far from any Krythar scans, the team had descended into the old subway tunnels on foot. Lily hadn't realized how steep the climb down would be or how heavy her limbs would feel after the cramped shuttle ride. Now, walking through the pitch-black tunnels, she could feel every muscle ache, every bead of sweat trickling down her back.

Datch and Garrow led the way, Datch scanning ahead with a device that glowed faintly blue in the dark. Lily found herself smirking despite the tension. *So that scanner does have a silent mode after all.*

Caris moved just behind Lily, her presence steady and reassuring. The group moved in a line, their footsteps muffled against the damp, uneven floor. The air was thick and stale, carrying the faint scent of mold and rust, and the darkness pressed in on them from all sides.

They'd been told not to speak unless absolutely necessary, and the silence gnawed at Lily's nerves. Every creak of the old tunnel, every distant drip of water, made her flinch. The glow from Datch's scanner cast long, eerie shadows, and she tried to focus on its light instead of the oppressive blackness around them.

Her thoughts wandered, grasping for anything to distract from the gnawing fear in her chest. *One mile,* she reminded herself. *Just one mile to the coordinates. Then we get in, we get out.*

The air was heavy and damp as they trudged through the abandoned subway tunnels, footsteps muffled on the uneven ground. Lily kept her head low, ears straining for any sound beyond the shuffle of boots and the occasional drip of water echoing through the dark. The smell of mold and stone hung thick, settling deep in her lungs.

Ahead, Datch's scanner glowed faintly, casting eerie light across cracked walls and exposed beams. Garrow walked beside him, blaster ready, eyes sharp. Caris brought up the rear, steady and unflinching.

Lily stumbled on debris, catching herself before she fell. Her heart spiked. She bit her lip, forcing focus.

They'd walked what felt like hours when Datch stopped and raised a hand. "We're here."

Lily squinted into the dark. A console glowed faintly in the wall ahead, its hum breaking the cavern's silence. Rusted metal and crumbling stone stretched out around it like the bones of some ancient beast.

Caris's voice was low but firm. "Lily, it's time."

Her stomach twisted. She nodded and stepped closer as Malik crouched beside the console, tools already working.

"Do you feel it?" Caris asked, eyes searching.

Lily hesitated. She felt nothing—only silence—but Caris's gaze carried so much hope that she nodded anyway. "Yeah," she lied.

"Good. Focus on it. Let it guide you."

Focus. The word echoed as she closed her eyes. The dream came back: the old woman's face, the blinding crash of the car, the strange brightness seeping into her soul. She clung to it, desperate. Maybe emotion was the key.

The console beeped. Malik's sharp intake of breath made her snap her eyes open.

"It's working! The psionic systems are opening. We're in!"

Caris leaned over his shoulder, relief flickering in her taut expression. "Keep going. Don't lose the window."

Lily stood frozen, the weight of their hope pressing down like gravity. Her hands trembled, but she pressed them to her sides.

At the edge of the group, Garrow looked back with a rare smile. "We might just pull this off."

Lily managed a faint smile in return. Maybe—just maybe—they would.

The moment shattered.

A shriek of energy ripped from the shadows, followed by the hum of Krythar disruptors. The ambush was instant, brutal. Blasts lit the dark like fireworks, scattering the team.

"Fall back!" Caris shouted.

Garrow fired, holding them off long enough for the others to retreat. He didn't make it far. A green beam hit him squarely in the chest. His scream cut through the air. Lily turned in time to see him drop, weapon clattering to the floor. The acrid smell of burning flesh hit her nose, turning her stomach.

"No!" she cried, but Caris yanked her back into the corridor.

"This way!" Datch's voice was calm but urgent. "The psionic chamber. It's impervious to disruptor fire. Move!"

They ducked inside. The heavy door sealed with an insect-like hiss. Crystalline walls glowed honey yellow, twisting Lily's stomach with some half-remembered familiarity.

"What now?" she asked, voice shaking.

"We've got thirty seconds before this chamber floods with nerve gas," Caris said, clipped and matter-of-fact. "Unless you can block the psionic alarm."

Lily's stomach dropped. Every eye turned to her as she stepped toward the pulsing node in the wall.

Focus, she told herself, but her mind was a mess. She reached out, clinging to the dream, the light, the old woman's voice—so close but still out of reach.

"It's not working," she whispered, panic rising.

A loud hiss filled the chamber. Lily froze, every muscle tensed, bracing for the end.

But the gas didn't fill the room. It poured outside instead, flooding the tunnels with a sickly green fog. Krythar screams echoed briefly, then fell silent.

When the hiss faded, Datch peered through the viewport. "The gas has dissipated. It's safe."

They stepped out cautiously. Krythar bodies lay scattered, their opalescent skin dull and lifeless.

Malik knelt beside Garrow's still form, draping his field jacket over him. Lily's chest tightened with guilt. She barely knew him, but it felt like her fault.

Datch turned to her, his neutral face softened. "You are not to blame. Garrow always intended to die in the line of duty. He died protecting us."

Lily nodded, swallowing the lump in her throat. She didn't believe him, not fully, but said nothing.

Caris radioed the ship, her voice steady as she requested a cleanup team. The mission wasn't over, but the loss hung heavy—a weight none of them could ignore.

• • • •

The mess hall was empty, the stillness punctuated by the faint hum of the ship's systems. Lily sat slumped at a table, staring at the melting ice cream sundae in front of her. The doctor's advice—"Something sweet can help"—was well-intentioned, but the cheerful swirl of chocolate and vanilla had dissolved into a sticky mess, ignored.

The mission was over. The crystals and all the Krythar equipment had been recovered. By every metric, the outcome was better than they'd hoped for. But all she could feel was the suffocating weight of everything that went wrong. Garrow's smile flashed in her mind, followed by the green light, the sound, the smell... Her throat tightened, and she swallowed hard, willing the memory away.

A voice cut through the quiet. "Datch said I could find you here."

Lily didn't look up right away, but when she did, the sight of Captain Calan surprised her. He stood just inside the doorway, his usually commanding presence diminished. His face, worn and shadowed, carried something heavier than fatigue. His usual confidence had bled out, leaving a man who, despite his stature, looked smaller.

He didn't sit. Instead, he paced a few steps toward her, then stopped, his gaze falling to the untouched sundae.

"I shouldn't have sent you," he said finally. His voice was quieter than she'd ever heard it, the words slow and deliberate.

Lily hesitated. "Captain—"

He cut her off, shaking his head. "I made a mistake. I thought I was doing what was best, but putting you out there so quickly... I was wrong."

She stared at him, unsure what to say. It was strange seeing him like this—vulnerable, uncertain. "I... I don't know," she said carefully. "Maybe it was important for me to be there. We got it done, and now I know firsthand how real the threat is."

The captain exhaled, his lips pressing into a thin line. "Perhaps," he admitted, though his tone was heavy with doubt. "Garrow would have agreed with you."

He took a step back, straightening slightly. "There's a memorial tomorrow. You're welcome to attend." He paused at the door, glancing back at her. "And tomorrow, we'll need to discuss... what happens next."

He left without another word, the soft hiss of the door closing behind him.

Lily sat in silence, his words lingering in the air. She knew what he was referring to. What happens next? The ship and crew were bound for the 26th century. Was her next step really to travel to the future?

She didn't have long to dwell; a loud metallic clatter from the kitchen jolted her from her thoughts.

She frowned, standing slowly and moving toward the noise. The sight stopped her in her tracks.

A slender, three-foot-tall biped stood by the counter, arms crossed, expression exasperated. He wore tailored clothes that accentuated his graceful frame, his knowing eyes glinting with bemused patience. His movements were fluid but almost theatrical, like a performer long used to an audience.

Next to him, a large quadruped—easily six feet tall at the shoulder—rummaged through drawers. His thick chestnut fur rippled with every motion, a cloth satchel slung loosely across his broad torso. With all that fur, it was hard to tell if he wore anything else at all.

"Must you make such a mess?" the smaller one asked, his voice surprisingly strong for his stature, yet melodious.

"Must you nag me while I'm working?" the larger one grumbled.

Lily blinked, unsure whether to laugh or leave. "Uh... hi?"

The smaller one turned, his face warming instantly. "Ah, good evening. Burning the midnight oil? I often come here to think—so does this lug, if you can call it thinking." He guided one of his companion's strong paws toward an object Lily didn't recognize. She couldn't tell if they were repairing the machinery or pulling it apart.

"We haven't met. I'm Ka-Lorrin, and my rather messy companion is Taran."

Taran grunted, turning his broad head toward her. His large snout sniffed her for so long it became uncomfortable. "Oh! You're the one Tess told us about. The one with the brain powers. I heard there was a casualty on your mission. Deepest regards. Sincerest sad."

Lily couldn't help but stare. "Sorry... it's just, all of this is new to me."

"Ah ha! And so it is, and so it is." Ka-Lorrin beamed, though Lily wasn't sure what exactly he was agreeing with.

"We're Raath-Ka," he explained gently. "Symbiotic partners. I provide vision, guidance, and decorum. Taran provides brute force, unrelenting curiosity, and the occasional disaster."

"Oh sure, oh sure, always the blame on Taran," Taran muttered, though without malice.

"I fix things too, you know. Not just break them."

"Yes, yes, your great triumphs with tools," Ka-Lorrin said with a weary sigh, rolling his eyes.

Despite herself, Lily laughed.

Taran sniffed her again, then rumbled in a tone unexpectedly tender. "You're on the fractured path."

Lily frowned.

Ka-Lorrin's expression turned solemn. "And so indeed, and so indeed..."

"What is—" Lily began, but Ka-Lorrin lifted a hand.

"An ancient legend from our homeworld, the beautiful but oppressive Korolith III. A young Raath-Ka pair, Sammat and Ka-Torrid, were separated during a terrible storm—the summer fire fell from the skies. Ka-Torrid, the thinker, found a river and followed it, believing it would lead him home. Sammat, the protector, did the same on another river.

"They faced trials along the way: hunger, predators, doubt. Ka-Torrid used his wits to evade danger but longed for the strength of his partner. Sammat fought valiantly but grew weary without guidance.

"Both rivers twisted and turned, but they never stopped flowing. Each kept faith the rivers would join again."

"And did they?" Lily asked softly.

Ka-Lorrin hesitated. "The story ends there... disappointing at first, I know. It's said the fractured path never truly ends—it simply leads us to where we're meant to be."

"It ends, it ends," Taran said, shaking his scruffy head. "You'll find your way. Just keep walking."

Ka-Lorrin's smile stretched wide with pride. "Different traditions say different things. Some more hopeful than others. Just stay by the river and let it guide you. You will be okay."

His large eyes seemed to pierce Lily's heart with kindness, enough for both of them. She felt something shift inside, their words settling over her like a warm blanket. She managed a smile. "Thanks. Both of you."

Back in her quarters, every muscle ached as she sank onto the bed. Exhaustion finally caught up to her. She lay back in the dark, the hum of the ship soothing her frayed thoughts. Outside the window, the stars stretched endlessly, and for the first time in what felt like forever, her mind stilled.

The night wrapped around her like a cocoon, and she drifted into a deep sleep.

Species Profile: The Raath-Ka

THE RAATH-KA ARE A symbiotic people born of partnership. On the storm-lashed world of Korolith III, two distinct beings evolved as one: the Raath—large, four-legged mammals of strength and instinct—and the Ka—small, luminous-eyed bipeds of perception and thought. Bound in lifelong pairs from early childhood, they move through life together, the Raath providing resilience and ingenuity, the Ka offering vision and reason. Alone, each is capable. Together, they are whole.

Their culture reveres interdependence above all things. Rivers, which carve through the forests and mountains of their dangerous homeworld, serve as their central metaphor: separate streams may wander, but they are always destined to converge. Through oral traditions and legends such as *The Fractured Path*, the Raath-Ka teach perseverance, trust, and faith in reunion. Though not known for grand technological innovation, their tools and ships reflect their dual nature—tactile, intuitive, and built for cooperation. Across the stars, they are valued not only for their skill but for the warmth and levity they bring, even in uncertain times.

Chapter 4: Into the Future

THE AIR SHIMMERED WITH heat. At first, Lily thought she was awake, standing under the sun of some alien world, but the colors weren't right. The sky above her was bruised and swirling, streaked with reds and purples that bled into one another. Beneath her feet, the ground pulsed faintly, like the glowing embers of a dying fire.

A low, guttural roar rumbled through the atmosphere. Her heartbeat quickened as she turned toward the sound.

It wasn't sunlight warming her skin—it was fire.

The realization struck her like a blow to the chest. She stood in the heart of a firestorm, yet it wasn't burning her. The flames moved with a sinister grace, rivers of molten fire weaving intricate patterns across the horizon. It was mesmerizing, even beautiful, but it left her cold.

Korolith III. The name surfaced unbidden in her mind, accompanied by the echo of Ka-Lorrin's voice describing the infamous firestorms. But this... this was something else—something surreal, twisted by the landscape of her imagination.

A sharp metallic groan tore through the roar of the flames, and the world shifted.

The firestorm collapsed into darkness, replaced by the suffocating confines of a subway tunnel. The walls glistened with dampness, the air heavy with the stench of decay. Her footsteps echoed eerily as she moved forward, drawn by the mournful groaning sound that seemed to come from everywhere and nowhere.

Ahead, a faint light flickered. The tunnel opened into a station, its cracked tiles smeared with graffiti and something darker—sticky, red streaks that her mind refused to name. A phantom train screamed past her in a blur, its wheels shrieking like tortured souls.

For a fleeting moment, as the train passed, a burst of green light seared her vision. It was vivid and violent, carving through the shadows like a blade. Her chest tightened as Garrow's death flickered through her mind, a ghostly afterimage that refused to fade.

The train vanished into the darkness, and she was no longer alone.

The Krythar face emerged from the shadows.

It wasn't the first time she'd seen it, but the terror hit her fresh and raw, as if her body remembered the fear even when her mind didn't. Its eyes were the worst part—two voids that seemed to devour everything, including her courage. She wanted to run, but her legs refused to obey.

"You don't belong here," it said, though its mouth didn't move. The words vibrated through her skull, a bone-deep resonance that left her trembling.

Before she could respond, the face changed.

The harsh, angular features softened, melting into the kind, lined face of the old woman she'd seen before. The oppressive weight of fear lifted, replaced by a calm so profound it brought tears to her eyes.

"Lily," the woman said, her voice gentle but insistent. "Follow the river."

The subway dissolved, and Lily found herself back in the overturned car. The details were sharper this time—the cracked windshield, the twisted seatbelt biting into her shoulder, the caustic scent of burning fuel. She struggled to turn toward the voice, desperate to see who was speaking.

"Lily... follow them home," the voice urged, closer now, achingly familiar.

She froze.

Her reflection stared back at her from the shattered glass. It was her face, but something was wrong—subtly, deeply wrong. The reflection's lips moved, though hers didn't.

"You must follow them home, Lily."

The voice was hers, but distorted, alien. She reached out, her fingers brushing the glass.

Her reflection smirked.

• • • •

The Salamander's lighting system simulated night almost too well. For Alpha shift, the ship was already waking up, the artificial dawn brightening the corridors to match the rhythms of a distant star.

Lily sat in the mess hall with a steaming coffee, studying the half-eaten muffin in her hand. She had bitten it into an odd shape she decided looked vaguely like a life form. Despite the strange dreams, she had managed some decent rest and was even starting to grow accustomed to life aboard the ship.

Across the table, Taran and Ka-Lorrin were in the middle of a heated debate.

"Waste of time, waste of time!" Taran said, gesturing emphatically with his fork.

"It's not a waste of time," Ka-Lorrin countered, his tone exasperated but laced with barely concealed teasing. "It's an artistic endeavor. You wouldn't understand."

"Oh, I understand. Pointless, pointless. What use is a sculpture made of engine parts?"

"It's not just engine parts," Ka-Lorrin said, dragging out the words with exaggerated patience. "It's a statement about—"

Caris's voice cut through the argument as she approached, her movements brisk and purposeful. "Lily, the captain wants you on the bridge. We're going through the time portal in ten minutes."

Lily set her coffee down, her pulse quickening. She glanced at Taran and Ka-Lorrin, who had both fallen silent.

"Don't worry," Ka-Lorrin said with a wink. "We'll still be arguing when you get back."

. . . .

Caris led Lily through the bustling corridors of the Salamander, her pace brisk but measured. Artificial sunlight glowed from the ceiling panels, warm against the sleek metallic walls. As they neared the bridge, the ambient hum of the ship grew louder, punctuated by bursts of intercom chatter.

The doors slid open with a soft whoosh, and Lily stepped onto the bridge for the first time.

It was larger than she'd imagined—two levels beneath a curved ceiling that shimmered faintly, ready to transform into a panoramic starfield at a moment's notice. At its center stood the captain's chair, raised on a platform and flanked by an array of consoles. Its high back tapered into elegant lines, subtle accents pulsing in rhythm with the ship's systems.

Beyond it stretched the main viewscreen, an enormous, semi-transparent display that filled the front wall. Holographic projections floated before it, layering real-time data over the vivid blues and greens of Earth below. To Lily, it felt like staring into an enchanted painting, alive with depth and motion.

Datch stood at his station to the captain's right, fingers gliding over a sleek console, his expression focused. He glanced up with a small nod before returning to work. To the left, Caris manned her compact but sophisticated console bristling with holographic readouts. Further ahead, the first officer—a Cyranthian male with calm, deliberate movements—worked quietly, the purple markings on his skin catching the faint glow from his display.

Around the bridge, officers and crew worked in steady rhythm, their voices blending into a low symphony of purpose. The layered hum of the ship's systems gave the space an almost organic energy.

Caris guided Lily to a seat beside her console, a compact chair with restraints that looked far too serious for comfort. "Strap in," she said, barely glancing her way.

Lily hesitated but obeyed, her stomach twisting as her gaze lingered on the towering viewscreen and glowing consoles around her.

"Captain on the bridge!" someone announced.

Startled, Lily turned. She hadn't even noticed him enter.

Captain Calan strode to his chair with practiced confidence, his presence commanding immediate attention. He lowered himself into the seat with ease, the glow of the consoles sharpening the lines of his face.

"All right, people," he said, his voice rich with authority and excitement. "Let's make history."

"Paradox Reactor is primed," Datch reported, his tone clipped and professional. "Stabilizing quantum variance fields now."

"Temporal coordinates locked," added the first officer, his hands moving quickly over his console. "The 26th century awaits."

Caris leaned into her console, her fingers dancing across the holographic controls. "Navigational alignment confirmed. Flux aperture holding steady."

The bridge buzzed with overlapping voices and the hum of coordinated activity. Lily couldn't follow most of the terminology, but the rhythm and precision made it clear they were on the cusp of something monumental.

Her thoughts drifted to the captain's words at Garrow's memorial service. *If there's one thing I learned from Garrow,* he'd said, *it's that sometimes you just have to make a choice and move forward. Even if it means diving in headfirst. The universe will either catch you, or it won't—but if you don't take that leap, you'll stay stuck in the past. Garrow showed us what it means to leap, and his courage will echo in the stars for generations to come.*

A faint vibration beneath her feet snapped her back to the present. Butterflies erupted in her stomach—they were about to time travel.

"Reactor power at 80%," Datch called out.

"Bring it up to 100%. Steady as she goes," the captain ordered, calm but brimming with anticipation.

"Adjusting matrix stabilizers," Caris added.

The captain turned slightly toward Lily and gave her a reassuring nod. The gesture caught her off guard, but she was grateful for it.

The bridge shook as the reactor reached full power, a deep hum filling the air. On the viewscreen, projections swirled into a vortex of light and color.

"Paradox Reactor is fully charged," Datch reported.

The captain leaned forward, his tone electric. "Engage."

The vortex exploded into brilliance. The bridge dissolved.

It wasn't gone, exactly, but everything warped as though viewed through rippling glass. Consoles, walls, even people shimmered and stretched, their edges refracting like beams through a prism.

Afterimages multiplied—ghostly silhouettes frozen mid-motion, smeared trails of light stretching behind every movement. They layered on one another until the air was thick with echoes, a kaleidoscope of shifting forms.

Bands of color spiraled through her vision, liquid rainbows poured through the cracks in reality. They had texture, as if she could run her hands through the shimmering threads.

Then came the sound. Not the hum of the ship, but something vast—like the groan of an ancient machine. Deep, resonant bellows overlapped with crystalline chimes, an eerie harmony that seemed to vibrate through her chest.

Her sense of movement unraveled, untethered. Afterimages broke apart and reformed into fleeting shapes—some of them her. Dozens of versions of herself scattered through the swirls, their faces blurring and warping before vanishing back into light.

The chaos collapsed inward. Colors folded, compressing into a single, blinding point. The ship, the bridge, the crew—everything smeared into light.

And then—

A piercing silence.

The bridge reassembled piece by piece, reality stumbling before regaining balance.

Lily opened her eyes—had they been closed?—and gasped. Earth was gone. The viewscreen now displayed a brilliant sprawl of unfamiliar stars scattered across the void.

She ran her palms over her arms, confirming she was solid. Everything felt normal—yet subtly wrong. Her pulse was calm, her breathing steady, her body lulled into an unnatural serenity. Around her, the others seemed to share the same eerie calm.

"Confirmed," Datch announced, his voice breaking the quiet. "We've arrived in the 26th century."

The words settled over the crew like a wave. Lily drew a long breath, grounding herself in the faint hum of the ship. Her gaze lingered on the stars, brighter and sharper than before, as if they belonged to an unfiltered reality.

"Well done, everyone," the captain said, rising from his chair. His voice carried pride and warmth, capturing a rare moment of calm authority. "Remember this moment—we've moved forward, not just in time but in—"

"Sir," an ensign cut in, her tone sharp with urgency. "I'm reading a ship under heavy fire. It's just crossed out of Krythar-controlled space and into the demarcated region. It's heading toward us at high speed."

The captain's expression tightened; all traces of celebration gone. "Hail them."

The viewscreen flickered, revealing a recorded message. A trembling voice, layered with static, filled the room:

"To any UAS vessel—we request asylum. We bring critical intelligence regarding Krythar operations. Please respond. I repeat, we request asylum and offer information vital to the war effort."

The captain didn't hesitate. "Extend our energy shields around that ship. Tractor them into the shuttle bay." He turned to Caris. "Coordinate with medical and security. Be ready for anything."

"Aye, sir," Caris replied, already moving.

Lily leaned closer. "Do you always have adventures back-to-back like this?"

Caris didn't look up from her console. "Only on Tuesdays," she said, so deadpan Lily almost wondered if she was serious.

The refugee ship had barely docked in the shuttle bay when the ensign's voice rang out again. "Sir, the Krythar are hailing us."

"On screen," the captain ordered, his tone steely.

The viewscreen flickered, revealing a Krythar commander seated in shadow. Its angular face gleamed faintly under green light, and its slitted eyes were sharp and predatory. Its voice, low and smooth, filtered through the ship's translation matrix.

"Union vessel," it said, "you are harboring fugitives of the Krythar Ascendency. Surrender them to us, and your ship will be spared."

The captain's jaw tightened, but his voice remained calm. "This is Union space. Anyone who requests asylum here is under our protection."

The Krythar tilted its head, its tone icy. "Your defiance will be remembered, captain."

"Good," the captain said evenly. "Now get out of our space."

The Krythar's image vanished, replaced once again by the open field of stars.

Lily exhaled slowly, her gaze lingering on the empty screen. For the first time, she'd seen the Krythar speaking not as shadowy monsters but as calculated, arrogant adversaries. She thought briefly about the translation matrix—how it turned countless alien languages into something comprehensible, erasing barriers of communication but not necessarily of understanding. The Krythar's calm menace lingered in her mind as she quietly excused herself from the bridge.

As Lily walked through the Salamander's winding corridors, the low hum of the ship and the bustle of activity buzzed around her. Her feet carried her toward the observation deck, drawn by an unshakable need to see the refugees herself.

Through the wide, curved windows, she spotted the refugee ship now nestled in the shuttle bay, battered but intact. **SS Manta** was painted in bold letters along its side. The transport vessel was much larger than she had expected, and she paused, momentarily overwhelmed by the sheer scale of everything around her.

A line of figures disembarked, guided by Salamander crew. Her gaze snagged on one of them—a tall, blue-skinned girl who looked about her age, maybe a little older. Silvery freckles glimmered faintly under the bay's lights. Her sharp, guarded expression and the defiant grace in her movements made Lily pause.

Butterflies stirred in her stomach, fleeting but impossible to ignore. Heat rose to her face, and she quickly turned away. *Get a grip, Lily,* she thought, heading back toward her quarters.

• • • •

The quiet of her quarters felt almost too still after the day's events. Lily stretched out on her bed, letting the silence settle like a heavy blanket.

A faint rustling broke the calm.

She sat up, squinting toward the kitchenette. The light flickered on, revealing a small figure rummaging through her cabinets.

"Excuse me?" Lily said, more curious than annoyed.

The figure yelped and spun around. A boy—small and wiry—clutched a ration bar like a shield. He looked about eleven or twelve, though undersized. Pale blue skin speckled with silvery freckles marked him as kin to the girl Lily had seen in the shuttle bay. His wide gray eyes darted nervously.

"The manifest said this room was empty!" he blurted.

Lily blinked, then smiled. "Well, I am new here. How'd you get past the lock?"

The boy grinned, mischief flashing. "That thing? Super easy to crack."

"Just so you know," Lily said, tilting her head, "you don't have to sneak around for food. The galley's open to everyone."

His grip on the ration bar loosened. "Really?"

"Really," she said warmly. "What's your name?"

"Alrek," he muttered.

"Well, Alrek," she said with a smile, "how about we find the mess hall? I'll show you where the good snacks are."

By the time they reached the galley, the room was quieter than she expected. Leaning against a table was the blue-skinned girl from earlier. Arms crossed, expression flat, she radiated irritation.

Lily steered Alrek toward her. "Hey. I stumbled across this little guy. Do you know him?"

The girl didn't even look up at first. When she did, her eyes were cold. "Do I look like someone who collects children?"

Lily blinked, caught off guard.

"Yiseffish oosaree," the girl hissed at the boy in a strange language. The translation matrix didn't catch it, but the disdain was unmistakable. She turned on her heel and walked away without another word.

"Wow," Alrek said softly.

"Yeah," Lily muttered, forcing a smile. "Don't worry. We've got better company waiting."

She led him to a table where Taran and Ka-Lorrin were locked in a lively debate.

"Hey, guys," Lily said as they looked up. "Meet Alrek."

Taran grinned, gesturing to an open seat. "Welcome, welcome. Hungry?"

Alrek nodded eagerly, sliding into the chair.

"Do you eat like a humanoid," Ka-Lorrin asked, completely serious, "or more like a photosynthesizer?"

"Like a humanoid, I guess," Alrek replied, wide-eyed.

"Good answer," Taran said with a laugh.

The tension of the day eased as the table filled with lighthearted chatter. Lily leaned back, watching Alrek dig into his food, his earlier nerves fading. Despite everything, a warm sense of camaraderie settled over her—a reminder that even in chaos, moments like this mattered.

• • • •

The recreation room buzzed softly with life, its walls glowing with shifting patterns that mimicked flowing water. Lily and Alrek stood side by side on a smooth platform projecting a holographic grid beneath their feet. The game was part ski-ball, part dance: players shifted their weight, jumped, and stomped to align with glowing targets pulsing to a rhythm. Hitting a target launched glowing spheres that arced into virtual hoops hovering above.

"Watch the red ones—they're crazy fast!" Lily called, her feet tapping rapidly to match the rhythm. A cluster of spheres shot from her position and swished cleanly through a hoop.

Alrek jumped a beat too late, sending his spheres clattering off the rim. "Ugh!" he groaned, stomping in frustration.

Lily laughed, sidestepping to catch another target. "You've got to time it better! Watch the rhythm lights—they cue you in."

"I'm trying!" Alrek said, grinning despite himself. He hopped onto a square, launching a sphere that clanged into the nearest hoop. He threw his arms up in victory.

"See? Told you," Lily teased, keeping her own streak going.

As the pace slowed, signaling the end of the round, Alrek leaned on his knees, catching his breath. "You're good at this."

"Thanks," Lily said, brushing back a loose strand of hair. "Some of the games don't make any sense to me, but this one's fun."

"I've never played anything like this," Alrek admitted, watching the grid reset. "We didn't have fancy holo-games back home."

"Where's home?" Lily asked, shifting her weight for the next round.

"Raskon III," he said softly. "It was a Saravethi colony in Krythar space. They took it over when I was little."

Lily stomped on a glowing square, sending another sphere sailing through a hoop. "What was it like?"

"At first, fine," Alrek said, his tone thoughtful as he jumped to another target. "Peaceful. I lived with my grandma after my parents died. She used to make sweet cakes—they tasted like warm clouds."

Lily smiled as she hit her mark. "Sounds like a good place to grow up."

"It was," he said more quietly. "Until the Krythar decided they didn't like 'rebel species' anymore. They rounded us up, separated families. They do that on purpose, you know. To make you feel like you don't belong anywhere."

Lily misstepped, her sphere veering off course. "They took you away from your grandma?"

"Yeah." His voice cracked, but he cleared his throat and stomped harder than necessary. "I got moved around a lot. The girl from earlier—you know, the rude one? She was in my group for a while. She was always yelling at the guards. I think she got separated from her family too."

Lily hesitated as the game reset. "I try not to judge people," she said softly. "We all deal with things differently."

Alrek nodded faintly, eyes down. "I guess."

The next round began, targets flashing faster. Alrek focused, stomping square after square, but his voice broke through. "Do you think they'll ever stop? The Krythar, I mean."

Lily missed a target but didn't care. "I don't know. But there are people fighting to stop them. And now you're here, Alrek. You made it out. That's something."

For the first time, Alrek smiled fully, his whole face lighting up. "Thanks, Lily."

"Anytime," she said with a grin. "Now don't think I'm going to let you win."

"Let me win? I'm just getting better!" Alrek shot back, nailing a streak of targets.

The game ended in a flurry of lights and cheers, leaving them both breathless but grinning.

. . . .

Later, as they wandered aimlessly down the corridor, the lighthearted energy of the game lingered between them. Alrek seemed unusually quiet, his steps slowing as though weighed down by a decision.

Finally, he looked up at Lily, his voice barely above a whisper. "I have a secret."

Lily glanced sideways at him, raising a skeptical brow as they walked through one of the quieter corridors of the Salamander. The steady hum of the ship's systems filled the space, her boots echoing softly against the polished floor. "Oh yeah? What kind of secret?"

"A good one," he replied, his glowing freckles brightening with excitement.

Lily smirked. "And you're just going to leave it at that?"

"Maybe." He darted a mischievous look her way. "What if I want you to guess?"

She sighed dramatically, running a hand through her hair. "Fine. It's a... secret candy stash you've been hiding in your jacket."

Alrek laughed, shaking his head. "Nope."

"Okay, then it's, uh... a tiny pet you smuggled on board. Some weird little slug creature?"

"Ew, no!" he said, wrinkling his nose. "That would probably smell awful."

Lily stopped walking and crossed her arms, her expression mock-serious. "All right, Alrek, spill it. What's this big secret of yours?"

He hesitated, his teasing grin fading into something more serious. "You have to promise not to freak out."

Lily's smirk softened, replaced by curiosity. "That's not exactly reassuring."

Alrek glanced up and down the corridor, then slowly reached into his jacket. He pulled out an old cloth, cradling it like something precious. "Okay, here."

He unfolded it carefully, revealing an object nestled inside.

Lily's breath caught. The item was an intricate mix of materials—polished wood gleaming under the corridor lights, interwoven with vein-like carvings that pulsed faintly with light. At its center, a glowing core radiated a subtle warmth, as though it were alive. A thin, looped strap suggested it could be worn as a necklace.

"What is it?" she asked, her voice quieter now.

"I don't know," Alrek admitted, holding it up for her to see. "But it's Krythar. I'm sure of that."

Lily's stomach twisted at the word. She stepped back, her arms dropping to her sides. "Alrek... are you serious? This is a Krythar artifact or something?"

He nodded, his earlier excitement replaced by unease. "I saw things like this back on Raskon III. I don't know what it does, but—"

"We need to tell the captain," Lily interrupted, her voice sharp, her heart racing.

Alrek clutched the object tighter to his chest. "Wait! I didn't steal it—I just found it on the transport. I'm not in trouble, am I?"

"You're not in trouble," she said quickly, her tone softening as she placed a reassuring hand on his shoulder. "But this could be dangerous. The Krythar use things like psionic amplifiers, trackers—stuff we don't fully understand. If this is one of their devices, it might be able to hurt people—or worse. We have to make sure it's safe."

Alrek hesitated, his fingers tracing the carvings on the object. "You really think it's dangerous?"

"I don't know," Lily admitted, her voice steady. "But we're not taking any chances. We'll tell the captain you found it and didn't know what to do with it. That's all. You won't get in trouble."

After a long moment, Alrek sighed and nodded. "Okay."

* * * *

The corridor outside the captain's stateroom was quiet, the hum of the ship's systems a steady backdrop. Lily sat on a small bench next to Alrek, the weight of the day settling over them.

Dryst Amaris, the ship's first officer, leaned casually against the wall, already mid-story.

"...and, of course, the eldest of my three wives, Zemira, handled all the logistics. She's brilliant at that sort of thing, thank the stars. You try keeping track of 27 children on a shuttle. Cyranthian children, no less! Turn around for one second, and three of them have climbed the bulkhead, one's stuck in the air vent, and another is trying to eat a fuel cell."

Lily pressed her lips together, trying not to laugh. Alrek let out a quiet snort before quickly covering his mouth.

Amaris didn't seem to notice. "The waterfalls of Shamtar are worth every bit of chaos, though. Oh, the sound! It resonates with your very soul, like a symphony conducted by the universe itself. The water is said to have restorative properties—not scientifically proven, mind you—but my youngest swore his eyesight improved after swimming there. He's always been a clumsy lad..."

Lily glanced at Alrek, whose wide eyes reflected polite alarm as Amaris launched into yet another anecdote, this one involving a child getting swept downriver and rescued by a particularly heroic tourist.

Her impatience bubbled. The captain was in a meeting, but every moment they waited made Alrek's discovery feel heavier. Should she interrupt? Find Ensign Caris? The thought tugged at her, but Amaris's lilting tone and endless detours made it nearly impossible to find an opening.

Just as she was about to gather the nerve to excuse herself, Amaris paused abruptly, his silver eyes narrowing as though he'd only just noticed them. "Wait a moment. Why are you two here again?"

Lily cleared her throat. "We need to see the captain about something Alrek found."

Alrek reached into his jacket, pulling out the cloth-wrapped object.

Amaris's easygoing demeanor vanished. His face sharpened, his tall frame leaning forward as he studied it. "You found this? Where?"

"On the transport," Alrek said quickly. "I didn't mean—"

"Why didn't you mention this in the first place?" Amaris interrupted, his voice urgent. "Follow me, please."

• • • •

The captain's stateroom was as eclectic as Lily remembered, its dim, golden lighting catching on the collection of artifacts lining the walls. Her gaze flicked up to the shelf of hats around the ceiling, and a small grimace crossed her lips as she recalled her first impression of the captain's peculiar collection.

The moment evaporated when her eyes landed on the Krythar seated across from the captain.

Panic struck like fire in her chest, heat rushing to her face as her pulse thundered in her ears.

"Lily," Amaris said gently, guiding her to a chair. "Sit. It's all right."

"That's a Krythar," she hissed, barely able to form the words.

The captain stood, calm but firm. "This is Shyra'thel," he said. "She defected from the Ascendency. She's here to help."

The Krythar turned its piercing gaze toward Lily.

"We find ourselves on the same side, Aberration," Shyra'thel said, the translation matrix lending her voice a cold, unsettling cadence. "Curious..."

Lily felt her skin crawl, static prickling over her arms as the Krythar's eyes bored into her.

The word "Aberration" hung in the air like a dagger. Its implications cut deeply, but no one dared acknowledge it. A single misplaced word could shatter the fragile diplomacy binding the moment together.

Amaris's jaw tightened, his usual smile faltering. Even Captain Calan's confident demeanor wavered before he masked it with a deliberate adjustment of his uniform. Alrek shifted stiffly in his seat, silent but tense.

Shyra'thel's sharp features betrayed no emotion, though her elongated fingers flexed faintly, as if testing the room's atmosphere. "I see," she said, her voice a metallic hum through the translation matrix. "Your silence speaks volumes."

She rose with fluid grace, her movements measured yet tense, like a predator stalking prey. "If you'll excuse me, Captain," she said, her tone cold and unyielding.

Amaris stepped forward, his steady voice cutting through the tension. "Shyra'thel, we invited you here in good faith. Please, stay for just a moment longer. You'll want to see this."

The Krythar paused, her gaze lingering on Amaris, weighing his words. Then, with a slight incline of her head, she stepped back. "As you wish," she said, icy but restrained.

Before the captain could interject, Alrek stepped forward, drawing every eye in the room. His movements were deliberate, but his shoulders were tight with apprehension. Slowly, he reached into his jacket and withdrew the strange object. Its glow pulsed faintly, casting eerie patterns across the walls.

The air seemed to change, thickening with an almost imperceptible hum.

Shyra'thel's reaction was immediate. Her cold composure cracked, and her angular eyes widened in unmistakable shock. "Where did you get this?!" she demanded, her voice sharp and accusatory.

Alrek flinched at the outburst, instinctively stepping back. Before he could speak, Amaris moved protectively to his side, his slender frame forming a shield between the boy and the Krythar. "You will not threaten him," he said evenly, calm but unyielding.

The tension in the room coiled tighter, as if it might snap at any moment. Lily, standing just behind Amaris, found herself stepping closer to Alrek, her pulse quickening. Her eyes darted between Shyra'thel and the glowing object. Whatever it was, it was significant—dangerous, even.

The Krythar raised a hand, her movements slow and deliberate. "Threaten? No. But you don't understand what he holds." Her gaze fixed on the object in Alrek's hands, her voice softening—not in kindness, but in something resembling reverence. "That is no mere artifact. It is the Memory Seed."

The name hung in the air like an unspoken curse. Even without understanding its purpose, Lily could feel its weight, as though the glow itself carried centuries of sorrow.

Shyra'thel stepped forward, her gaze never leaving the Seed. "This object is a key—one of several—designed for temporal warfare. It can unlock the past itself, rewriting history and bringing ruin to the unprepared."

Her voice grew quieter, more distant, as though pulled back into memories. "This Seed was used during the cleansing of the Ah'karyan Sect—my people. A test of Krythar weaponry during one of our civil wars. They erased entire bloodlines. Generations of history, gone."

Her words struck the room like a blow. Even the captain, usually quick to interject, stood silent, his expression grim.

Shyra'thel hesitated, her voice faltering for the briefest of moments. "My... my lover and I fled with this Seed, knowing its potential for destruction. We hoped to keep it from falling into the wrong hands. But she was killed smuggling it out of Krythar space. I believed it had been lost with her."

Her eyes hardened as they bore into Alrek. "And yet here it is."

Its shifting light played across the solemn faces in the room.

Amaris glanced at Alrek, his calm demeanor cracking just enough to reveal a flicker of unease, before turning back to Shyra'thel. "And now that it's here," he said quietly, "what are the risks?"

• • • •

The briefing room was a compact but efficient space tucked behind the bridge, its walls lined with holographic displays and tactical charts. A sleek table dominated the center, surrounded by high-backed chairs that hummed faintly with embedded technology. Above the table, the Memory Seed hovered on the primary screen, its faint glow pulsing with an unsettling rhythm. The air was heavy with silence, broken only by the soft whir of the ship's systems.

Malik stood at the head of the table, his hands clasped behind his back as he addressed the crew. "This isn't a weapon in the traditional sense," he said, his voice calm but weighted with urgency. "On its own, the Memory Seed is inert. But under specific conditions—location, temporal alignment—it becomes devastating, capable of rewriting history. That's why we must get it far from Krythar territory."

Captain Calan leaned back in his chair, his eyes fixed on the screen. "Agreed. As soon as the Manta's repairs are complete, it will transport the Seed, the refugees, and the defector to Starbase 12—deep in Union space. Safer, for now. We'll assign a security detail to ensure it arrives without incident."

Amaris nodded firmly. "I'll oversee the preparations personally, Captain."

Lily, seated near the far end of the table, glanced between the softly glowing Memory Seed and the Captain. Her curiosity finally got the better of her. "What about us—where's the Salamander going?"

Calan shifted his gaze to her, his tone softening slightly. "The Salamander has its own orders. We're heading to a Zephtari science station.

Their telepaths may help you recover your memories—and perhaps give us an edge against the Krythar."

Lily's stomach tightened at the reminder of her role in the war, but she nodded. The star map faded, replaced once more by the shimmering Memory Seed, its light casting faint, shifting patterns across the room.

"Captain," Ka-Lorrin said, leaning forward, "permission to take Lily aboard the Manta during the repairs. She can shadow me and Taran—routine maintenance, but it might be educational."

"Not to mention fun," Taran added with a grin, earning a sharp side-eye from his partner.

Calan raised an eyebrow. "Routine or not, I'm not sure we should be sending Lily out again so soon. The mission to Earth—"

Ka-Lorrin gently interrupted, tilting his head. "She'll only observe. It's low-risk, and it might give her valuable context for how things operate."

Calan sighed, rubbing his temple as though weighing the risks. "Fine. But keep her out of trouble. That's not a suggestion."

Lily's chest fluttered, though she kept her expression steady and formal. "Thank you, Captain."

As the crew rose and began to disperse, Lily caught Ka-Lorrin's eye. "Thanks for that," she said, her voice quiet but earnest. "I'm excited to see you two in action."

Ka-Lorrin smiled warmly, tilting his head. "Just try to keep up. And don't touch anything."

Lily watched him stride out with Taran, a smile tugging at her lips. She felt a flicker of excitement—not just about the adventure ahead, but about being part of the team.

•　•　•　•

The shuttle bay buzzed with subdued activity, its usual harsh lighting dimmed to simulate night. Refugees clustered in small groups, their voices low as they packed their belongings and prepared to reboard the Manta. The blue glow of the ship's night mode cast long shadows, and faint murmurs and clanging echoed through the cavernous space.

Lily stepped inside, scanning the vast space. She spotted Alrek near one of the staging areas, stuffing tools into a bag with the kind of focus that suggested he was avoiding his thoughts. Nearby, a flicker of movement caught her attention. The blue-skinned girl from earlier sat cross-legged near the far wall, her attention fixed on a glowing board. Small, luminous beads shifted under her quick, deliberate fingers.

Lily hesitated. Something about the girl's intense focus and her distance from the crowd drew her in. She squared her shoulders and walked over.

"That looks…" Lily searched for a casual tone. "Like a game. Solitaire?"

The girl didn't look up. "It's not a game," she said flatly, her hands moving with sharp precision. "It's a training tool. Reflexes, strategy, patience." The board chimed softly as she reset it. "Three things you clearly don't have."

The jab caught Lily off guard, and she blinked. "Fair enough," she said lightly, swallowing her irritation. "Look, I just wanted to apologize for earlier. I shouldn't have assumed you knew Alrek."

The girl's fingers paused for a moment before resuming. "It's fine."

"No, it's not." Lily leaned in, lowering her voice. "I know what it's like to lose family. I mean, I don't know your story, but—"

"You don't." The girl finally looked up, her cold gaze cutting through Lily's words. "You think losing someone means you understand? You don't know anything about me."

The words stung, but Lily held her ground. "Maybe not," she said softly. "But pushing everyone away doesn't help."

Xynn's expression flickered—puzzled, almost amused—before the walls snapped back into place. "It's about survival," she said evenly.

Lily couldn't tell if she meant pushing people away… or something else.

Xynn gestured impatiently at the board. "The tool. Reflexes, strategy. Not everyone survives."

Lily frowned, unsure how to respond. Before she could think of anything, Alrek's voice broke the moment.

"Hey, Lily—uh, everything okay?" he asked, approaching with his bag slung over one shoulder. His eyes darted nervously between the two girls.

The blue-skinned girl's smirk vanished. She glanced at Alrek. "You're going over to the Manta?" Her tone dripped with disdain.

"Yeah," Alrek said, nodding. "Ka-Lorrin said I could help."

The girl's lips curled, addressing Lily instead. "I hope you told them this zeeftash is useless at fixing things. That's why they work in the fields."

Lily's stomach twisted at the slur. Alrek flinched, his shoulders tightening. Before he could respond, Lily's voice snapped, "Hey! That's not okay."

The girl shrugged, unbothered. "Not my fault. That's just how things are." She reset her board, her attention shifting back to the glowing beads.

Alrek muttered something about checking his tools and retreated. Lily sighed, watching him go, then turned back. "For someone who acts so tough, you sure take a lot of cheap shots."

The girl didn't look up. She reset the board again, her fingers moving sharply. Just as Lily turned to walk away, her voice cut through the quiet.

"My name's Xynn," she said, her tone low with a touch of teasing. She gestured to the board. "And maybe you would... survive, I mean." Her lips curved faintly as she added, "Probably."

Lily froze, meeting Xynn's steady gaze. The comment hung in the air—part warning, part challenge. Before Lily could decide how to take it, Xynn was already focused on her training again.

Lily shook her head, a faint smile tugging at her lips. "Thanks, Xynn," she said softly, though she wasn't sure Xynn heard her. She walked away, leaving her alone in the faint blue glow of the ship's night.

* * * *

The Manta's interior buzzed with energy the next day. Bright overhead lights contrasted sharply with the dim ship-night of the evening before, illuminating riveted walls and exposed conduits that glowed faintly with soft blue energy. Scuffs and faded warning labels added to its rugged, utilitarian character, while the cheerful glow of the repair crew's portable lamps played off the metal surfaces, creating a lively, almost chaotic atmosphere.

Lily trailed behind Ka-Lorrin and Taran, watching as they deftly restored the transport's systems. Sparks jumped from their tools as they welded panels and tested circuits, their banter filling the space with easy laughter.

Alrek moved with quiet focus, sharp eyes scanning the equipment. He picked up a spanner—exactly the right size—and tightened a bolt without being asked.

Taran paused, raising a brow. "Well, well. Looks like we have a natural."

Ka-Lorrin nodded, attempting to mask his admiration. "Not bad for a first-timer."

Lily, crouched nearby and working under Ka-Lorrin's supervision, felt a genuine warmth as she watched Alrek find his place.

A sudden blur of blue caught her eye. Xynn stormed into the room, exasperation written all over her face. She ducked behind a console, then sprang forward, chasing something small and fast. A tiny creature zipped between her legs, squealing faintly—a round, furry thing with bright eyes and a stubby tail, somewhere between a hamster and a squirrel.

"Stop running!" Xynn hissed, diving for the creature and missing as it darted toward Lily.

Instinctively, Lily crouched, scooping it up before it could slip past. It wriggled in her hands, then settled, its nose twitching as it sniffed the air.

"Here," Lily said, holding it out. "Is this yours?"

Xynn caught the creature, cradling it carefully despite her irritated tone. "No. It's the refugees'. One of the kids let it loose. Again."

"Cute little thing," Lily said, smirking. "Looks like it's giving you a real workout."

Xynn shot her a sharp look, but her lips twitched into a smile before snapping back to neutrality. "You think this is funny? Try chasing it across the engine room."

Lily caught that brief crack in her armor, and the thought lingered as they returned to work.

Later, as Lily adjusted a panel under Ka-Lorrin's eye, her thoughts drifted. She remembered Caris from the day before—her calm but firm voice announcing her promotion to Lieutenant Junior Grade and command of the Manta mission. *See you over there,* she'd said with quiet pride. Bittersweet words, with Garrow's absence still pressing heavily on the crew.

A klaxon shattered her reflection. Red lights strobed, alarms blared. Ka-Lorrin's head snapped up, composure slipping to reveal a flicker of alarm. Taran bounded toward the nearest console, his bulk moving with surprising speed.

"What's happening?" Lily shouted.

Ka-Lorrin's voice was tight. "The Manta's engines have engaged."

Lily's stomach dropped. "Moving where?"

Ka-Lorrin didn't answer, already racing for the bridge. Lily and Alrek scrambled after him as the floor trembled beneath their feet.

On the bridge, the situation had gone from bad to worse. Shyra'thel stood near the console, her sharp features unreadable. The navigation display glowed ominously: their trajectory pointed straight into Krythar space. Light Factor 7 and climbing.

Ka-Lorrin was the first to break the silence. "What the hell is going on?"

Shyra'thel turned, her voice unnervingly steady. "I don't know. The controls aren't responding. I'm locked out."

Taran shoved a chair aside, his paws flying over the keys. "True words, true words. Override's in place—can't disengage!"

Alrek stared at the display, voice barely a whisper. "We're headed straight for Krythar space."

The bridge fell quiet, broken only by alarms and the whir of the engines. Lily's eyes darted from the frozen controls to Shyra'thel, whose calmness now felt chilling. Ka-Lorrin's jaw was clenched tight.

"This is bad," Alrek muttered, giving voice to what everyone was thinking.

Before anyone could respond, the Manta lurched violently, the engines roaring louder as the ship accelerated further—straight toward the dark expanse of Krythar space.

ONCE NATIVE TO THE world of Saraveth, the Saravethi are now a people scattered among the stars. Their blue- and ash-toned skin bears faint bioluminescent patterns—unique to each individual—that shimmer like embers in darkness, said to carry the memory of their ancestors. Traditionally marked by subtle facial tattoos denoting social roles, their society once followed a strict caste system of warriors, artisans, scholars, priests, and fieldworkers. Centuries of Krythar domination have fractured those divisions, binding the castes together in shared survival.

Though their homeworld was abandoned under oppression, the Saravethi endure. Large refugee settlements thrive where they can—most vibrantly on Adius II, where culture, language, and ritual persist despite surveillance and threat. Their traditions are rich with music, storytelling, and ceremony; festivals such as the Procession of Kar celebrate life even in exile. Across the galaxy, the Saravethi remain a resilient people—diminished in number but unbroken in spirit—carrying their history not as burden, but as light.

THE ALARMS ECHOED IN Lily's head, their shrill wail amplifying the tension gripping her chest. Each pulse hammered against her skull, a relentless reminder of the chaos around her. The Manta barreled through light space at breakneck speed, vibrations shuddering through the hull—a testament to its disturbing pace. The urgency was suffocating, leaving little room for thought.

She pressed a hand against the cool metal wall, grounding herself as she fought back rising panic. The bridge was in disarray. Shyra'thel had slipped away in the confusion, muttering something incoherent before vanishing down the corridor. Great, Lily thought. Guess we're on our own.

Ka-Lorrin's sharp voice cut through the noise, urgent but controlled. "The ship's systems are locked. We've got about an hour before we're deep in Krythar space, and the cloaking device has engaged. No chance of the Salamander tracking us like this."

Lily's stomach churned. She forced her voice steady. "What can I do?"

Ka-Lorrin glanced at her, jaw tight. "Locate anyone else on board, let them know what's happening, and keep them calm. Fortunately, most of the crew are still on the Salamander. Taran and I will head to engineering and try to stop the engines manually. The lifts are down—we'll use the crawlways."

Before Lily could respond, Ka-Lorrin was already striding toward the rear exit, Taran close on his heels. She turned to Alrek, lowering her voice. "Stick close. I don't want us getting separated in this mess."

He nodded, trying to mask his nerves with a brave face. Together, they started down the maintenance ladders toward the habitat level.

The shift was immediate. The habitat deck was eerily quiet. Common areas that should have buzzed with voices and movement felt hollow, unsettled. Only a handful of passengers lingered, their faces etched with confusion and fear.

Lily drew a deep breath, projecting more confidence than she felt. "It's going to be okay," she told them. "We're working on stopping the ship. Stay here, stay calm, and I'll keep you updated."

The tension in their postures eased, though unease still lingered. Before she could say more, a familiar figure approached from the shadows. Xynn. She moved cautiously, her usual sharpness dulled by hesitation.

"Alrek, right?" she began, her voice uneven.

Alrek stared at her, clearly shocked to be addressed by the tall young woman.

"I need to... apologize," Xynn continued, faltering as her gaze briefly flicked to Lily for support. "I've been cruel to you. I'm not great at this—at being around people. But I think..." She trailed off, the words catching in her throat.

Alrek blinked, still startled. "It's okay," he said after a moment, though his tone carried more confusion than forgiveness.

"Look, I... I can't change overnight," Xynn said firmly, squaring her shoulders. "But there's something you both need to know." Her expression darkened. "I saw that Krythar in the engine room earlier. Everyone here is too..." She searched for the right words. "Too tired or scared to act. But if we don't do something, I have a feeling she's going to get us all killed."

Lily exchanged a glance with Alrek, a spark of understanding passing between them.

"Well," Lily said, breaking through the awkward silence, "I think we can call a truce for now. Let's move. If Shyra'thel is responsible for sabotaging the ship, we need to figure it out—fast."

She cast a final look at the passengers. They seemed calm enough for now, and she mentally marked her orders from Ka-Lorrin as fulfilled.

Alrek's voice broke the moment. "If we can access the ship's internal sensors, I might be able to locate any Krythar life signs."

Xynn nodded sharply and turned toward a nearby access ladder. "This way. Either the bridge or the science lab—we can get to both on the same level."

Without hesitation, Lily and Alrek followed her toward the hatch, urgency driving them forward.

• • • •

The three of them moved quickly, the muted hum of the Manta's systems underscored by the engines straining at full capacity. With most passengers still aboard the Salamander, the ship felt like a ghost town.

Emergency lighting bathed the corridors in a flickering glow, shadows jittering across the walls. The crawlway lamps cast their faint green phosphorescence, making Xynn and Alrek's faces look ghoulish as they climbed. Sweat slicked Lily's palms as she gripped the rungs, her breath short and fast. The silence pressed in, broken only by the occasional groan of the ship's frame under its speed.

At last they reached Alpha Deck—and stopped short.

The passage Lily had come through minutes ago was now sealed by a blast door, its heavy surface gleaming in the dim light.

"What the hell?" Lily whispered.

Xynn tapped the door with two sharp fingers, eyes narrowing. "Looks like someone doesn't want to be disturbed."

Alrek leaned toward the panel, trying a sequence of commands. His brow furrowed. "Locked from the inside. We're not getting through."

Uneasy glances passed between them before they veered toward the science lab. The door hissed open, revealing a sterile white space lit too bright against the dim corridors. Equipment hummed faintly, a few monitors flickering awake.

Alrek hurried to the nearest console and pulled up a schematic. Clusters of dots flared into view, each marking a life sign. He zoomed on the bridge. "There's one person there." Another tap pulled up a biometric scan. His shoulders tensed. "It's Shyra'thel."

"Of course it is," Xynn muttered, shifting like a fighter preparing to strike.

Lily's stomach twisted. "If she's locked herself in there, we'll need another way."

"The service crawlways," Xynn said immediately, already moving toward the hatch.

"Wait." Lily's voice cut through the tension. "We should check in with Ka-Lorrin and Taran."

She keyed the comms to engineering. The feed blinked alive—both engineers slumped at their stations.

"That doesn't make sense..." she whispered.

Alrek's hands flew over the console. His face drained. "Engineering deck's flooded with gas. Everyone's out cold—probably for the next hour."

Lily's heart lurched, but Xynn sliced the moment apart with a sharp gesture at the exit. "Sorry about your friends. Can we go now?"

Worry clawed at Lily, but there was no time. If they didn't stop Shyra'thel, everyone aboard was doomed. She drew in a breath, steadied herself. "Let's go."

The crawlway hatch was narrow, more suited for drones than people. Xynn went first, vanishing into the cramped tunnel. Alrek followed, awkward but determined.

Lily took another deep breath and slid in after them. The crawlway was tighter than she had expected, the green glow of the lights reflecting off every surface in a way that was faintly disorienting. She moved on her hands and knees, the confined space pressing in on her from all sides. Every sound—the rustle of her clothing, the scrape of her boots—seemed amplified, echoing faintly down the tunnel.

Her mind drifted to half-remembered scenes from old movies, images of action heroes crawling through ventilation shafts to save the day. It might've been amusing, if the stakes weren't so devastatingly high.

"I think we're almost there," Xynn called back, her voice echoing faintly ahead.

Lily focused on the rhythm of her movements, trying to ignore the sweat dripping into her eyes and the ache in her legs. The crawlway seemed to stretch on forever, but finally, they reached a branching path.

Alrek paused to study a small marker panel. "The bridge should be this way," he said, pointing to the left, toward a tunnel that somehow looked even less inviting—its walls lined with tangled wires and blinking lights that pulsed angrily at uneven intervals.

Without hesitation, they pressed on, the weight of urgency pressing heavily on their shoulders as they neared their destination.

Then the floor vanished beneath them.

For a brief, weightless moment, Lily's mind scrambled to make sense of what was happening. The faint hiss of an automated mechanism, the rush of air, and the sudden plunge all seemed to unfold in slow motion. A trap, she realized, her heart lurching. They'd triggered some kind of defense mechanism.

Gravity took hold.

The impact was brutal. Lily hit the ground hard, the jolt rattling through her entire body. Nearby, Xynn landed with practiced precision, her knees absorbing the shock effortlessly. Alrek, less coordinated, sprawled awkwardly beside them, letting out a muffled groan as he rolled onto his side.

Lily blinked against the dim light, her breath coming in short gasps. The space they had fallen into was small and featureless, its corrugated metal walls giving no indication of a way out. A faintly glowing panel near the ceiling cast an eerie, sterile light over the room.

"This is a holding cell," Alrek muttered, rubbing his elbow as he sat up. His voice trembled slightly, though he tried to mask it with confidence. "I saw these on the schematics. Part of the ship's security system. If intruders are detected, they get dumped here."

"Perfect," Xynn growled, her fists clenching at her sides. She stalked toward the nearest wall and slammed her fist into it, leaving a faint dent in the paneling. "Now we're stuck."

"Hey," Lily said sharply, stepping between Xynn and the wall. "Take it easy. Punching things isn't going to get us out of here."

Xynn's glare softened slightly, and she stepped back, crossing her arms. "I don't like being trapped," she muttered.

Lily placed a steadying hand on the wall, trying to ground herself. "Let's focus. Alrek, can you do anything with this?"

Alrek nodded, already moving toward a small maintenance panel near the floor. With deft hands, he pried it open, revealing a mess of tangled wires. "I can bypass the system," he said confidently, his fingers dancing over the circuitry. "This shouldn't take long."

Xynn hovered nearby, her gaze flicking between Alrek's hands and the room's walls. "Careful," she warned. "If you trip—"

A harsh beep cut her off as the room's lights flared red, bathing them in an ominous glow.

"You tripped the system," Xynn snapped, her voice sharp with frustration.

"What does that mean?" Lily asked, her heart pounding.

The answer came in the form of a mechanical whirring. Panels along the walls slid open, and three sleek drones emerged, their matte-black surfaces gleaming in the crimson light. They hovered with unsettling precision, their insectoid forms bristling with weaponry that immediately locked onto the trio.

"Take cover!" Lily yelled, diving behind a metal support beam as the drones opened fire.

Plasma bolts sizzled through the air, the scent of burning metal filling the room. Xynn was already in motion, rolling smoothly to her feet and pulling a weapon from her belt. The baton-like device snapped open with a sharp crack, extending into an energy blade that pulsed faintly with a bluish glow.

Xynn moved like a blur. She darted forward, her blade carving through the first drone with lethal precision. Sparks and shards of metal flew as the drone crumpled to the floor, its weapon clattering beside it.

Lily watched, momentarily awed. "Nice work," she muttered under her breath.

But their reprieve was short-lived. More drones poured into the room, their numbers doubling in an instant.

"Stay behind me!" Xynn barked, slicing another drone cleanly in two.

Lily scrambled toward the downed drone's weapon, her hands shaking as she picked it up. The grip was unfamiliar, heavier than she expected, but she managed to aim and fire, the plasma bolt grazing one of the advancing drones.

"Good shot," Xynn muttered, her focus never wavering. "Now stay out of the way."

Alrek, emboldened by the chaos, tried to flank one of the drones. "I've got this!" he yelled, only to be struck by a glancing blow from a plasma bolt. He crumpled to the floor, unconscious.

"Alrek!" Lily screamed, her stomach twisting as she rushed to his side.

A sharp intake of breath drew her attention. Xynn stood frozen for half a second, her blade trembling in her grip. Then something shifted. Her movements became sharper, faster, fueled by a ferocity that seemed almost inhuman. With a guttural cry, she tore through the remaining drones, her blade leaving arcs of light and trails of smoke in its wake. The last drone barely managed to fire before she reduced it to a heap of smoldering scrap.

The room fell silent, the air thick with the scent of melted circuitry.

Lily knelt beside Alrek, gently brushing a strand of hair from his face. "He's breathing," she said softly, glancing up at Xynn. "I think he's going to be okay."

Xynn crouched beside her, pale and shaken. A tear slipped free before she wiped it away. "I lost my brother," she said hoarsely. "He was Alrek's age."

The weight of her words settled heavy in the silence. Lily felt it in her chest, an ache that wasn't just her own.

Xynn drew a breath, steadied herself, and continued. "You were right. I push people away. Because it hurts too much. But I'm not losing anyone else." She rose to her feet, blade still in hand, standing ready as if daring the room to throw more at them.

Lily placed a hand on her arm, squeezing gently. "Hey, you saved us. We'll get out of here together."

A faint groan broke the moment. Alrek stirred, blinking groggily as he tried to sit up.

"Don't scare me like that," Lily said, her voice trembling as she smiled down at him.

Alrek managed a weak grin. "Did... did we win?"

Xynn let out a shaky laugh, the tension in her shoulders easing slightly. "We won."

Alrek rubbed the back of his head, wincing. "Good... 'cause I know how to get us out of here."

Lily exchanged a glance with Xynn, who nodded.

"Then let's not waste any more time," Xynn said, helping Alrek to his feet.

Alrek's face glowed with renewed confidence as he turned to Lily and Xynn. "When I was knocked out, I saw the Memory Seed in my mind," he began, his voice steady but tinged with awe. "It was like I could see every room on the ship at once—like I already knew what was going to happen."

Lily frowned, skeptical, but she bit her tongue and let him continue.

"The readouts from when Mr. Malik scanned the Seed… they're burned into my head now, crystal clear. If I can tune the resonant frequency of the environmental controls to match the Seed's output, it should send out a pulse strong enough to disable every system in and around that room. Like an EMP."

Xynn raised an eyebrow, arms crossed. "There must be millions of combinations. How are you going to guess the exact one?"

Lily tilted her head, studying Alrek. "He had the Seed with him for a long time. Maybe it left some kind of imprint on him?"

"Or maybe you're both crazy," Xynn muttered, rolling her eyes.

Alrek didn't flinch. He was already kneeling by the exposed panel, his fingers flying over the tangled wires. The faint glow of the emergency lights caught his determined face. He glanced up, meeting Lily's eyes. "Trust me," he said softly, with a conviction that made her chest tighten.

Lily held his gaze, then nodded once.

Xynn sighed, muttering under her breath, but didn't stop him.

Alrek twisted a final connection. A shower of sparks cracked against the metal, and a wave of energy rippled outward, cascading through the walls like a tidal surge. For a breathless moment, every system went dark—the ship plunged into black silence.

Then came the faint clicks of systems rebooting. Lights flared dimly back to life. The holding cell door hissed open.

Alrek stared, wide-eyed. "It worked," he whispered.

They didn't waste a second. Sprinting down the corridor, their shadows flickered wildly under the stuttering lights. They climbed hard for Alpha Deck, lungs burning, until the bridge doors parted and spilled them inside.

Shyra'thel lay sprawled on the floor, groaning as she pushed herself up. Around her neck, the Memory Seed glowed faintly on its leather strap. The shockwave had knocked her flat, her grip on both the Seed and the moment slipping.

Lily's pulse thundered as she took a cautious step forward.

"Shyra'thel," she said carefully. "Let's talk about this."

The Krythar turned, her movements deliberate, her expression eerily calm. But her eyes burned with a mix of desperation and conviction. "There's nothing to discuss," she replied, her voice steady yet unyielding.

"The course is set. The star will guide us, and the memory seed will restore what was lost."

Xynn's hand twitched toward her weapon. "Not if I stop you first."

Shyra'thel didn't flinch. "Do what you will," she said softly. "If my death fulfills the prophecy, so be it."

Lily tensed, her gaze darting between them. "Xynn, wait!"

It was Alrek who moved first, stepping between Xynn and Shyra'thel. "We might need her," he said, his voice firm but edged with urgency. "She knows more about the seed than we do."

Xynn scowled but didn't lower her hand. "She's about to kill all of us. We don't have time for this!"

Her fingers danced across a nearby control panel, and the display flickered to life. The screen showed their trajectory—a rapidly shrinking distance to the core of a red dwarf star. A timer blinked ominously at the top of the screen: 02:47.

"We're heading straight into it," Xynn hissed. "In less than three minutes, we'll be past the point of no return. It will incinerate us all!"

Shyra'thel tilted her head, almost serene. "You don't understand. This is Ah'karya's greatest truth. The star is divine. Its fire is not an ending—it is a restoration. The memory seed is the key to unlocking its power, to bringing back all that we've lost."

Lily glanced at Alrek, her chest tightening as the timer ticked down. "Can we override the controls?"

"I'm trying!" Alrek said, furiously tapping at another console. Sparks flickered, and an error message flashed on the screen. "She's locked us out. If the Raath-Ka couldn't crack it, there's no way I can."

"The prophecy is clear," Shyra'thel continued, her tone taking on a reverent quality. "The star's core must embrace the memory seed. Its divine pulse will ripple across the void, bringing the Ah'karyan people back to their rightful place. It will restore our glory, our unity... our lives."

Xynn's laugh was sharp and bitter. "I'm so glad you've thought this through. But I, for one, don't feel like dying for your guilt-driven fantasies."

Lily's mind raced. "Alrek, what about—"

"Don't you see?" Shyra'thel interrupted, her voice rising with fervor. "This is the cycle of renewal! My life, this ship, the seed—all of it is but a small price for the salvation of my people!"

Her words hung in the air, heavy and poetic, but Lily wasn't listening anymore. Her breath faltered as something stirred in her memory—almost like an itch she couldn't reach. She closed her eyes and let the image take shape.

The heat of smoke surrounded her. The searing pain of the seatbelt digging into her shoulder. The reflection in the shattered glass. A voice, faint but insistent, calling her name.

Her eyes snapped open. The world seemed sharper, as if every detail had been etched into her vision. Somehow, she now knew what to say.

"Shyra'thel," Lily said, her voice steady yet filled with emotion. She took another step closer, her hands open in a gesture of peace. "I understand your loss. I understand the pain of feeling like you've been shattered into pieces and left behind. But we can't undo what's happened. Loss changes us—it becomes a part of who we are."

Shyra'thel blinked, her resolve flickering for the first time.

"A necessary part! We're all on a path," Lily continued, her voice soft yet unwavering. "At different points along... along a river. The river of our lives, we're shaped by the currents. We can't go back upstream, but we carry the strength given to us by those we've lost. Their hope, their trust—it gives us the power to move forward."

Shyra'thel's grip tightened on the memory seed's strap.

"This new version of us," Lily said, "this version shaped by loss—it's capable of forming new connections, of giving others the strength to endure and move on. That's how the cycle of connection continues. Breaking it would dishonor everyone you've lost, everyone who believed in you." She took one more step. "We need you, Shyra'thel. And there are others out there—countless others—who may need you too. Don't throw that away."

The room was silent except for the soft hum of the ship's systems.

Lily stared right through Shyra'thel as she spoke. "Her name? What was your lover's name?"

Shyra'thel's hand trembled as it hovered over the console. Her eyes brimmed with tears, and for a long moment, she stood frozen.

"Loryn'na," she said in a defeated tone.

Slowly, she lowered her hand. Her fingers moved across the controls, and with a soft whir, the ship's trajectory shifted. The timer stopped, and the engines wound down as the ship decelerated.

They had survived for now, and the soft glow of the memory seed served as a reminder of what had been saved.

• • • •

Ka-Lorrin and Taran were already stirring by the time the team reached engineering. The gas had begun to dissipate, and their groggy voices filled Lily with relief. Alrek had taken the lead in stabilizing the systems, his confidence growing with every flicker of control restored. Within minutes, the team coordinated a safe rendezvous with the Salamander, guiding the battered transport ship into a secure docking position.

Back aboard the Salamander, Lily stood at a window on the observation deck, watching as the Manta underwent repairs. What had initially seemed rugged and sturdy now looked fragile, a testament to how close they'd come to disaster.

Her thoughts lingered on Shyra'thel, who now sat under guard in one of the Salamander's holding cells. The memory seed had been safely retrieved, its faint glow locked away behind layers of security.

Lily sighed, her breath fogging the window in front of her. She wanted to hate Shyra'thel for what she'd done, but she couldn't. The Krythar's pain, her desperate belief in the prophecy—it all felt too familiar. Lily had seen that same kind of grief in herself, in the way it could twist hope into something dangerous. She only hoped Shyra'thel would have a second chance to find healing, to use her conviction for something good.

The ship's intercom buzzed, and Captain Calan's voice came through, calm but commanding. "This is your captain. We'll be arriving at Star Base 12 within the hour. My thanks to everyone for getting the crew of the Manta here safely. We'll remain at the station for two days. I encourage you all to take some well-earned leave."

Lily smiled faintly. She was grateful the captain had chosen to transport the Manta and the memory seed to Star Base 12 aboard the Salamander. After everything that had happened, the thought of rest felt like a luxury.

As they arrived at Star Base 12, the Salamander's corridors were quieter than usual, the crew and passengers settling after the ordeal. Lily stood near the main airlock, her arms crossed as she gazed at the gangplank. Beyond the viewing portal, Star Base 12 caught the light of the nearby star, its spires gleaming against the void.

Measured footsteps sounded behind her. She turned to see Xynn approaching, her tall, guarded posture less rigid than before.

"Heading out?" Lily asked softly.

Xynn nodded, pausing a step away. "I've got a transport to the Saravethi relocation effort on Adius II. I'm going to try to do some good for my people." She hesitated, then added, "But... I wanted to say something before I go."

Lily locked eyes with her, waiting.

"I've spent so long trying to bury my past, to pretend it didn't matter," Xynn said, her voice quieter than Lily had ever heard it. "But what you said to Shyra'thel—it made me realize... maybe acknowledging that pain doesn't make me weaker. Maybe it makes me stronger."

Before Lily could answer, Xynn leaned down and surprised her with a kiss. It was brief, but it said more than words could. When she pulled back, a faint, daring smile curved her lips. "Don't get yourself killed, okay?"

Lily blinked, caught off guard, but managed a small laugh. "I'll try."

Xynn turned and strode away with a confidence that Lily couldn't help but admit to herself was attractive.

As Lily watched her go, Alrek appeared at her side, a small bag slung over his shoulder. "I talked to Captain Calan," he said.

Lily raised an eyebrow. "And?"

"I'm staying," Alrek said simply, a grin spreading across his face. "The Raath-Ka have offered to take me under their wing and train me in engineering."

Lily smiled and gave him a playful punch on the arm. "Best news ever. You're going to do great."

He blushed, adjusting his bag awkwardly. "Yeah, well... somebody's gotta keep the ship running."

The intercom crackled to life once more. "Welcome to Star Base 12," Captain Calan announced. "Thank you all for your hard work and service."

Lily exhaled, the tension in her shoulders easing as the Salamander's engines powered down. She turned to look at Alrek, who gave her a nod of encouragement.

As the crew and passengers filtered across the gangplank, Lily felt a flicker of something unexpected: anticipation.

Whatever lay ahead, she was ready.

Galaxy Today: Special Report

Tensions Mount as Peace Talks Continue on Star Base 12

By Kyn Thaliss, Senior Correspondent

STAR BASE 12 — Under the glow of the Union's most opulent orbital hub, the galaxy's fragile hope for peace rests in the hands of an unlikely coalition of leaders, skeptics, and survivors. The talks, spearheaded by Prince Zayir Ishraan of Ishreth Prime, are being described as the Union's most critical diplomatic effort in decades.

The station itself hums with unease. Markets brim with exotic goods, luxury resorts gleam against the void, yet security patrols march every corridor. "Given the Krythar Ascendancy's history of subterfuge, we cannot afford to take any chances," said Captain Eryk Dalren, the Union officer tasked with coordinating the defense of the talks.

The Players at the Table

Prince Zayir Ishraan arrives cloaked in both wealth and controversy. Admired for his humanitarian projects and defiance of Ishrethi tradition, the young prince's optimism collides with his mother's shadow. Queen Ishraan, herself a fixture of political intrigue, has been blunt in questioning her son's resolve. Their dynamic has become as much a sideshow as the negotiations themselves.

Representing the Krythar — though critics argue they are little more than mouthpieces — are the Varrothi, led by Ambassador Thal-Zrenn. Observers describe him as brilliant, glacial, and painfully aware of the precarious line his species walks between autonomy and servitude.

The Union has sent both its diplomats and its muscle. General Oryk Bessan, once a soldier, now a hawkish voice for "peace through strength," shares the table with Ambassador Karex L'Varis of the Zephtari Commonwealth, a telepath whose calm presence and famed knack for detecting deceit have already drawn notice.

A Station Under Guard

Orbiting a crime-scarred world, Star Base 12 was once better known for smugglers than statesmen. Now it has been transformed into a diplomatic stage: parks, markets, glittering towers, and — for the moment — military checkpoints at every junction. The Union has enacted a partial lockdown, restricting movement and keeping the entire complex under Dalren's watchful eye.

Rumors swirl in its corridors: whispers of backroom deals, nervous talk of covert sabotage. Some factions within the Union whisper that compromise is inevitable, while others mutter that only a decisive military victory can secure the galaxy's future.

What's at Stake

Beyond the intrigue, the stakes could not be higher. The Krythar war has scarred entire worlds and displaced millions. To the refugees crowding Union space, these talks represent not just politics but survival.

Can Prince Zayir's idealism survive the weight of galactic reality? Will the delegates find common ground, or fracture under the pressure of their own agendas?

For now, all eyes remain on Star Base 12, where the future of the galaxy hangs in the balance.

Chapter 6: The Prince and the Rogue

STAR BASE 12 WAS NOT so much a station as it was a city adrift in the stars. From the outside, its lattice of silver spires and glowing domes shimmered like a jewel in the dark. It hovered in stark contrast to the barren world below, a planet reduced to little more than dust and desperation, where smugglers and pirates ruled the ruins of a long-forgotten civilization. Down there, life was hard and short; up here, life was anything but.

The station was a marvel of ambition, a place where the Union's brightest minds and deepest pockets had come together to build something extraordinary. It wasn't just a hub for interstellar travel or a diplomatic outpost; it was a world unto itself. Vast parks stretched out beneath towering skylights that let in filtered sunlight, so real you could almost believe you were planetside. Entire forests hummed with birdsong, their trees rooted in hydroponic soil. Resorts lined the edges of habitat rings, where waterfalls spilled into crystalline pools, and honored guests could sip on cocktails while watching the planet rotate below.

Then there were the markets—endless, vibrant, and alive. The air buzzed with the voices of traders and buyers, a medley of languages that overlapped and spilled into one another. Every scent was an invitation: alien spices that prickled the nose, luxurious textiles that glistened as though infused with liquid light, sweet fruits with skins so delicate they bruised at a touch.

Lily walked among the stalls, her eyes wide, her thoughts racing to keep up with her senses. Here, a vendor was selling something that looked like an emerald but smelled like citrus. There, a gleaming mechanical bird whirred to life, singing a melody from a world Lily didn't recognize.

Everywhere she turned, there was something new—jewelry made from crystals that seemed to pulse with their own light, stacks of books printed in a dozen different alphabets, even a device shaped like a metal flower that radiated heat like a small sun. It was impossible not to imagine the stories behind every object, every person. Who had carved that intricate wooden box? Where had the strange blue vines growing in a glass terrarium been harvested?

"This place is amazing," Alrek said, his voice bright with awe as he leaned over to inspect a cluster of hand-painted spheres that hung like fruit from a vendor's stall. "I could spend days here."

Lily smiled and thought, Days? I could spend a year here and never learn it all. Her mind danced with curiosity, touching on each strange and wonderful thing as if it might unravel its secrets at a glance. This was the kind of place where you could lose yourself in the best way, where every turn held a story waiting to be uncovered.

But Alrek was already moving on, darting between the stalls with an eagerness that made Lily laugh. "You better go," she said, nudging him gently. "You don't want to be late for Ka-Lorrin."

He hesitated, his gaze flicking back to the markets. "You'll be okay?"

"Of course," she said, waving him off. "Go. I'll be fine."

And as he disappeared into the crowd, Lily turned back to the world around her, letting herself sink into the wonder of it all.

Lily drifted through the labyrinth of stalls, her senses overwhelmed by the market's kaleidoscope of sights and sounds. The warm glow of alien lanterns reflected off polished metals and gemstones, casting shimmering patterns across the narrow pathways. Spices perfumed the air—sharp, sweet, and strange—mingling with the scent of ozone from small machines churning faintly behind vendor tables.

"Starling..."

The voice came from nowhere and everywhere, slipping through the noise of the bustling market like a cold draft. Lily paused, her head turning toward the stalls around her.

"Lily Starling..."

This time, the voice was clearer, wheedling and sharp, like an old hinge groaning open. Her gaze darted from one vendor to the next, her pulse quickening as she scanned the crowd. Finally, her eyes landed on a small, shadowed booth tucked between two towering displays of shimmering textiles.

The proprietor of the booth—a diminutive alien woman—grinned at her with unsettling familiarity. Her skin was a sickly green, folded and sagging like wrinkled leather, with deep-set eyes that gleamed a sickly yellow. Moles and age spots dotted her face, and her chin jutted forward slightly, wobbling as she cackled. A colorful scarf tied haphazardly over her head barely tamed the tufts of wiry white hair poking out in all directions. Around her neck, a cascade of gaudy necklaces jingled with every movement, each adorned with beads, baubles, and bits of metal that looked more scavenged than crafted. Rings crowded her spindly fingers, their mismatched stones glinting like stolen treasures.

"Come closer, child," the woman rasped, her voice as rough as sandpaper. "I've been waiting for you."

Lily hesitated, but curiosity outweighed caution as she stepped closer to the cluttered table. The trinkets piled across it were a chaotic assortment—carved amulets, metallic scraps strung into pendants, and odd mechanical objects that clicked faintly.

"How do you know my name?" Lily asked, her brows drawing together.

The woman tilted her head, her grin stretching disturbingly wide. "Sneeheehee... I know many things, child. Your name is but a fragment of the truth I see."

"Like what?" Lily challenged, folding her arms.

The alien's grin widened, and Lily suddenly became more aware of her surroundings. Heavy, patchwork cloth draped down on all sides, embroidered with swirling, hypnotic patterns in purples and greens. Lanterns flickered overhead, their light casting restless shadows across shelves of trinkets, making the space feel larger than it was. The scent here was stronger than in the open market—spices layered with something metallic and cloying that made Lily's stomach twist.

She glanced over her shoulder and realized the opening she'd walked through wasn't as obvious as it had been. The hanging fabric, combined with the dim light, made it feel like she was already caught in the web of this strange little lair.

"Oh, the stars have told me much," the alien crooned, leaning forward. The folds of her face cast eerie shadows under the lantern light. "Your parents... murdered by the Krythar. You, pulled through the threads of time and space. You carry the weight of secrets, child. Secrets that would crush the strongest of souls."

Lily's heart skipped a beat. How could she know about the Krythar, about her parents? After everything she'd witnessed—the Psion Core, the impossible leap through time, the Memory Seed—she couldn't dismiss the woman's words outright.

"What secrets?" she asked, her voice softening.

"Secrets... and a curse." The alien's grin deepened, her voice dropping to a whisper. "A shadow follows you, child, clinging like smoke. But fear not! The stars whisper of protection—of salvation!"

From beneath the table, she produced a small object, holding it reverently as though it were sacred. "Behold."

Lily leaned closer as the alien revealed a tarnished metal talisman, its surface etched with faint, swirling patterns. At its center, a cracked gemstone gleamed faintly.

"This," the woman said, her voice heavy with theatrical awe, "is imbued with ancient cosmic magic. It will shield you from harm, repel darkness, and guard your very soul."

Lily turned the talisman over in her hands. The weight was uneven, the etchings suspiciously uniform—then she spotted a faint manufacturer's stamp on the back. The illusion shattered.

She stepped back, skepticism hardening into resolve.

The woman snatched the trinket away. "It is a treasure of immeasurable value. And it's yours... for only fifty credits."

"I should have guessed," Lily said flatly. "Thanks, but I'll pass."

She turned to leave—but two hulking figures stepped into her path, faces hidden beneath scarves, patched armor marking them as enforcers. They loomed silently, their bulk making the message clear.

"Now, child," the woman pressed, producing an even gaudier talisman, "perhaps this one—seventy credits, and you'll never fear the dark again!"

Lily scowled, the sting of betrayal sharp. "Right, I'm needed back on my ship." She tried to back away, but the alien's bony hand shot out, clamping around her wrist with startling strength.

"You cannot leave unprotected!" the alien hissed, her grip tightening.

Before Lily could react, a smooth, amused voice cut through the tension.

"Camilla, what are you doing to this nice girl?"

Lily turned to see a young man leaning casually against the edge of the stall. He was human, tall but not too tall, with dark, slightly unruly hair that curled just enough to frame his sharp features. His gray eyes gleamed with a mix of mischief and intelligence, and his grin carried the kind of charm that could win over a crowd—or get him into trouble.

His clothes had a rugged flair: a fitted jacket with asymmetrical closures and faint scuff marks, dark pants tucked into sturdy boots, and a utility belt that hinted at more than just casual wear. He looked like he belonged on an adventure to either save the galaxy or line his own pockets—maybe both, Lily couldn't decide, but there was an edge to him that suggested he knew how to handle himself.

"Rhyder," Camilla spat, her jovial mask slipping into a sneer. "This is none of your concern."

"Hmm," he said, his tone light but laced with impatience. "You know how I hate to see an honest market sullied by shady dealings."

The alien bristled, her many necklaces jangling as her yellow eyes narrowed. "Oh, is that right? That's rich, coming from a common smuggler."

"You wound me. I am an exceptional smuggler. And I prefer freelancer," he corrected, his grin widening. "Also, you owe me one for that mess on Haskari Prime."

Camilla's eyes narrowed. "Wrong again, boy. You're the one who owes me. My nephew died on that little... errand. My favorite nephew, too!"

Rhyder raised an eyebrow and took a small step back, as if just now recalling the event. "Hey now, I thought we decided that wasn't my fault."

Lily had been inching toward the edge of the booth this entire time, but one of the large guards shifted his massive frame, blocking her escape with a sharp glance.

Camilla leaned forward, her grin stretching unnervingly wide to reveal rows of cracked and broken teeth. Her voice dropped to a hiss. "You may have decided, but I intend to collect my debts—either in money or in blood."

Rhyder's grin didn't falter, but his tone cooled. "Well, how much do I owe you, then?"

Camilla somehow smiled even wider, her sharp teeth glinting in the flickering light. "Oh, I think I'll be collecting this one in blood!"

The guards closed in, their steps heavy and deliberate, one of them reaching under his coat.

Rhyder bounced on his heels awkwardly as though weighing his options. "Oh, well, that won't do," he said, straightening abruptly. Then, with a quick glance at Lily, he mouthed, Run.

Before Lily could fully process his words, Rhyder lunged forward and flipped the table, sending trinkets and talismans flying in every direction. Camilla screeched, scrambling backward as the guards stumbled.

"RUN!" he shouted, grabbing Lily's hand and pulling her into the chaos.

They darted through the maze of booths and stalls, weaving between startled vendors and shoppers. Lily's breath came in short bursts, her heart pounding as they dodged carts and pushed past startled patrons. Behind them, Camilla's enraged shrieks and the heavy footfalls of her guards echoed faintly.

Finally, Rhyder pulled her into a narrow alcove, pressing a finger to his lips as he glanced back toward the market. They were packed close together, his body blocking her view of the alley. His breathing was steady, in stark contrast to her frantic gasps, and he radiated an almost infuriating calm.

"What in the—what?" Lily stammered.

"Rhyder Dayne," he said smoothly, as if they weren't hiding from potential danger. "And you're Lily Starling, though you already knew that."

"How did she know my name?" Lily demanded, ignoring the faint warmth rising to her cheeks.

"That's Camilla," Rhyder said with a roll of his eyes. "She's a telepath. Uses her gift to scam people, hook them in with all that 'prophecy' nonsense, then sell them overpriced junk. Pretty sure she pegged you as an easy mark the moment you stepped into her stall."

"Hey!" Lily protested.

Rhyder's grin widened. "I didn't say she was right." He reached for her hand, lifting it with exaggerated elegance. "Still, it was my pleasure to assist a lovely image of starlight such as yourself."

Before she could pull away, he kissed her knuckles lightly, his stormy eyes gleaming with mischief.

Lily snatched her hand back, glaring. "Well, thanks, I guess."

He only laughed, leaning against a nearby stack of crates. "We should be fine now. Those things she calls her nephews don't like to run."

"She should really be more careful," he added, shaking his head. "Using telepathy on customers is illegal."

Everything about him seemed calculated—his grin, his nonchalance, even the way he moved, like he was daring someone to call his bluff. Lily admitted to herself that he was attractive but found herself doubting every word he said. Did his saccharine charm really work on most people?

Movement caught Lily's eye—first a ripple in the crowd, then a hushed murmur spreading like wildfire. The clinking of ornamental chains and the rhythmic thud of armored boots broke through the market's lively noise, echoing like distant thunder.

A procession emerged from the far end of the bazaar, their presence commanding instant attention.

At the front marched guards clad in sleek, angular armor that shimmered like obsidian under the market's lanterns. Their helmets were sculpted into elegant curves, adorned with intricate gold filigree that caught the light with every step. Their movements were precise, almost mechanical, each step landing with exact synchrony. The ground beneath their boots seemed to vibrate with their heavy, unified rhythm, a sound both mesmerizing and oppressive.

Behind them came robed figures, their garments flowing like liquid silk, embroidered with constellations in glinting metallic threads. They carried banners of deep sapphire blue, emblazoned with a sunburst crest surrounded by angular, alien script. Above them, enormous holo banners no smaller than thirty feet tall hovered, each displaying the image of a young man wearing a crown. His face, regal and serene, was illuminated in shimmering light, giving him an almost divine presence. The banners drifted in perfect sync with the procession, their celestial glow adding to the spectacle.

A faint hum filled the air, and Lily realized it came from small hovering drones trailing the procession, projecting ethereal beams of light that flickered like celestial patterns. The entire display was a breathtaking combination of tradition and technological precision, an overwhelming reminder of the grandeur and power on display.

As the group advanced through the common area and toward the main exhibition hall, their deliberate, synchronized march amplified, drowning out the murmurs of the crowd. The noise echoed off the market's high ceilings, a resonant pulse that seemed to declare their authority. The crowd instinctively parted, their awe-struck silence giving way to whispers of speculation as the procession disappeared into the grand hall.

"That's Prince Zayir Ishraan Kaseer," Rhyder said in almost a whisper, but with a lilt to his voice, "and the Ishrethi royal delegation. Pretty big deal for this humble station."

"Prince?" she echoed.

"Don't you watch the news?" he asked, raising an eyebrow.

"Well, I'm... new... to... everything," she admitted sheepishly.

Rhyder studied her for a moment, his gaze sweeping over her just long enough to make her shift uncomfortably. She cleared her throat, deliberately breaking the silence.

"Ahrrrmm."

His attention snapped past her. His grin faltered. "Speaking of... everything. That's station security. I should probably take this opportunity to... scram."

He backed away, his movements fluid, and melted seamlessly into the crowd. His patchy, earth-toned clothes, Lily realized, were a deliberate choice, blending into the market's muted chaos with uncanny ease.

"Enjoy your afternoon, Lily Starling," he called with one last sparkle of a smile before disappearing completely.

Lily stood there, catching her breath as the market's bustle resumed around her, the surreal encounter leaving her both curious and unsettled.

Lily shoved her hands deep into her pockets and began trodding toward the transit system. Working her way through the crowd proved difficult; apparently, everyone was trying to catch a glimpse of the prince. Her patience was wearing thin when she spotted a familiar and very welcome bald head in the throng.

Datch's glistening skin was instantly recognizable among the flow of people. Relief washed over her as she waved him down.

"Datch! Am I glad to see you," she said, falling into step beside him.

Datch turned his head, his face neutral but softened by a small, appreciated smile. "Hello, Lieutenant. Any trouble?"

"Not exactly," she hedged, brushing off the question. "And I'm not sure about the whole 'Lieutenant' thing yet. Command is waiting to reinstate me until we figure out if my memory is coming back. Which, for the record, I agree with."

Datch nodded, steady as ever.

"Where are you headed?" Lily asked, hoping for an escort.

"To the Salamander," he replied. "But I have a stop to make first. Care to walk with me?"

"I would be very grateful for the company," Lily said with a small nod.

As they weaved through the throngs of travelers and market-goers, Datch shared some background on the prince's presence and the upcoming peace talks.

"When the Salamander diverted here with the Krython defector, this entire region of space was thrown into upheaval. Prince Zayir has taken advantage of the political momentum and hopes to host a successful exchange for not only a ceasefire but a continued treaty."

Lily scrunched her face, thinking about the politics of it all. "Do you think it will work?"

Datch paused for a moment. "The odds are not in the prince's favor. However, there are many who would prefer to see peace triumph."

"And I imagine an equal number who want it to fail," Lily offered.

"Indeed," Datch confirmed. "Many also feel this is as much a show of power by the prince as anything else. The Ishrethi are known for their grand displays of wealth and influence. It's woven into their culture."

They stopped outside an elegant structure flanked by statuesque guards in immaculate uniforms that looked freshly pressed that morning. The arched doorway glowed with faintly lit carvings, framed by curved holographic panels scrolling names and titles in flowing Ishrethi script.

"This is the Luxury Residence," Datch said, his voice even but edged with quiet respect. "They're famous for their hospitality—hosting some of the galaxy's most powerful figures. Entire wings can be reshaped into palatial replicas of a guest's home culture."

He led her inside. The foyer shimmered with understated luxury: a polished floor gleaming like glass, light pouring down from a geometric skylight that scattered shifting patterns across the stone. Exotic plants in sleek planters lined the walls, some glowing faintly, their leaves stirring as if touched by an invisible breeze.

"I won't be long," Datch said, nodding toward the grand lobby beyond. "I've been invited to confirm some security arrangements in person. The Salamander is offering support. Ahh, there is Captain Dalren now."

A figure approached, his steps sharp and deliberate against the gleaming floor.

"Mr. Datch," the man said in a gravelly voice, extending a hand.

Captain Dalren's white hair was cropped into a precise military cut, framing his weathered but commanding face. His uniform was immaculate, its dark fabric contrasted by colorful medals and a silver insignia over his heart. His brown eyes, sharp and assessing, flicked briefly to Lily before settling back on Datch.

"Captain Dalren," Datch replied evenly, shaking his hand.

"I appreciate you coming down to assist," Dalren said, gesturing toward a hallway lined with ornate doors. "Shall we?"

"Of course," Datch replied.

As the two men walked off in lockstep, Lily lingered, her gaze drifting toward the grand lobby. She stepped inside and felt instantly dwarfed by its sheer scale.

Enormous pillars reached toward a domed ceiling alive with a projection of the galaxy, stars shifting slowly overhead. The polished stone floor gave way to a mosaic of glowing tiles arranged into a vast celestial map.

At the center, a fountain cascaded in glittering arcs, its water flecked with light that shimmered as if defying gravity. The sound was soft and steady, blending with the murmur of voices and the chime of graceful automaton attendants moving among guests.

The air carried a rich, herbal fragrance—a mingling of spices and flowers Lily couldn't name. Conversations rose and fell around her, their rhythm almost as carefully orchestrated as the room itself.

As Lily paid more attention, she noticed a blend of holographic and flesh-and-blood attendants circulating the space. Her boots, scuffed from the dusty markets, felt wildly out of place against the pristine tiles. Worse still, she realized with a pang of self-consciousness that her black jacket and boots closely resembled the uniforms worn by the attendants.

She folded her arms, leaning against a nearby pillar and trying to disappear into the background. It was one of those moments she wished she could simply vanish.

Lily's eyes caught on a group near the far side of the lobby. At first glance, they could have been ordinary travelers, but their look was too polished—crisp neutrals cut to perfection, every detail deliberate. The dark sunglasses indoors only made them stand out more, as if trying to blend in and failing spectacularly.

Her curiosity piqued, Lily edged closer, threading her way through the bustling lobby. The tallest figure in the group—a young man with sharp features and impeccable posture—stood out the most. His presence was magnetic, as though the air around him held a faint charge, and there was something familiar about his face.

Actually, he looks quite like the image of the prince, she thought, her eyes narrowing slightly. Could he be a member of the Ishrethi royal family?

Before she could draw any firm conclusions, an eccentric-looking alien bustled into view. The maitre d'—an elephantine creature with a long, sinuous trunk and silken hair cascading to his shoulders—moved with dramatic flair, his booming voice cutting through the hum of the lobby.

"Your Majesty!" he cried, his trunk bobbing as he gestured wildly. "I cannot express my deepest apologies enough! The very idea that you, of all people, have had to wait for even two seconds—unforgivable! When I discover how this mix-up occurred, there will be... consequences!"

The young man was striking in a way that commanded attention. Tall and lean, he carried an effortless elegance, his posture so regal it seemed carved into his bones. His copper skin glinted under the lobby's light, like molten metal in motion. Vivid orange birthmarks curved gracefully over his ears and down the sides of his neck, an earthy contrast to his luminous complexion.

His long black hair was pulled into a precise bun, accentuating the sharp lines of his reflective brown eyes. Flowing white garments draped over him in soft folds, embroidered at the collar and cuffs with subtle geometric patterns—a quiet display of wealth and tradition without ostentation. He radiated refinement, authority, and an unshakable confidence.

"Please, that's not necessary," the young man replied, his tone polite but laced with quiet exasperation.

"Not necessary?" The maitre d' gasped as though physically wounded. "It is essential!"

Without waiting for further instructions, the maitre d' shoved two bags into Lily's hands with such enthusiasm that she staggered backward. A luggage cart, laden with more cases, was rolled into place and seemed to magnetically lock onto her.

Lily blinked, trying to process what just happened. "Oh, I—"

But the maitre d' had already moved on to further ingratiating himself. Now addressing an older, very beautiful woman who seemed to be in charge, his tone shifted to a mix of reverence and alarm.

"What of the grand atrium? I want to see it with my own eyes before we go a step further," the woman said, her voice calm yet commanding.

The maitre d' looked as if he were going to turn inside out with mortification, his trunk quivering with the effort to respond. "Your Grace, of course, we are ready for your personal inspection. Allow me to rectify my egregious failure by escorting you in person this instant!"

The woman nodded imperiously and swept past, her attendants falling into step behind her. The maitre d' trailed after them, still issuing apologies.

The young man remained behind. "I'll head to the suite, mother," he said, addressing the retreating figure. He turned to Lily with a faint, amused smile. "Shall we?"

The luggage cart hummed as it followed Lily across the lobby and toward the long ramp leading to the residences. They walked in silence at first, the sound of their footsteps amplified in the pristine corridor.

After what felt like an eternity of walking, Lily stopped abruptly and turned to him. "Excuse me, but do you know what number residence we're going to? Or... how to get there?"

The young man blinked, a suspicious smirk crawling across his face. "I assumed you would know."

Lily forced an awkward smile. "Here's the thing..."

"Yes?" he questioned, his grin widening.

Lily winced, running a hand through her hair. "Okay, I don't actually work here. The maitre d' just handed me the bags, and I didn't have the heart to tell him because... well, did you see him? He was one bad moment away from a meltdown."

The young man's eyes lit up as he bellowed with sincere, childlike laughter, a genuine, hearty sound. "That is... fantastic. Absolutely brilliant."

She gave him a skeptical look. "I'm glad you find it funny. I didn't expect—well, I mean, you're taking this rather well for a... Prince? You are the prince, aren't you?"

His grin turned sheepish. "Guilty as charged."

Lily squinted. "So, what about that fanfare and madness outside?"

"Ahh, yes," the prince began, a touch of conspiratorial amusement flickering in his eyes. "We're never actually in those. We have doubles who fill in for us. Both for security reasons—and also, sitting on that ridiculous floating platform for hours is mind-numbingly dull."

Lily snorted. "Makes sense to me. I'm Lily, by the way. Lily Starling. I serve on the Salamander."

The prince's eyes widened with recognition. "You're Lily Starling!?"

Lily grimaced awkwardly. "This time, I'm guilty as charged."

The prince took a step closer, his intensity catching her off guard. "This is fate!" He gestured animatedly, almost as if conducting an orchestra. "I've wanted to meet you ever since I read your captain's report. This can't be a coincidence. I am here to usher in a new era of peace in the galaxy. You, Lily Starling, you are meant to be by my side. I'm sure of it. A beauty among the beasts of diplomacy!"

Lily stared at him, unsure how to respond. "Look," she said finally, "I'm just a 17-year-old who can't even remember who she is. Dating isn't exactly high on my priority list right now."

The prince tilted his head, his enthusiasm dimming only slightly. "Of course, of course," he said quickly, adjusting his tone to something gentler but no less determined. "But what a team we could make. Would you at least visit me here? We could just talk—get to know one another. Learn about what I'm trying to accomplish."

Lily hesitated. "I don't know..."

The prince pressed on, his voice earnest. "This galaxy in which we live—everyone's fighting over something, but really, we all want mostly the same things. People just need someone to show them..."

"And you're that someone?" Lily asked skeptically.

Prince Zayir nodded solemnly. "It's my calling. Ever since my father died, I've known that I'm meant to make a difference. What use is having all this wealth and influence if you don't use it to do a little good?"

"That's... noble," Lily said after a beat. "If maybe a little oversimplified."

He tilted his head, studying her thoughtfully. "You sound like my mother."

Before Lily could respond, the older woman from before reappeared with her entourage and a proper attendant. The maitre d' hovered nearby, looking visibly relieved. The attendant took charge of the luggage, and the group moved toward the correct residence.

"Who have we here?" the woman asked, her gaze sweeping over Lily with sharp precision.

"Mother, this is Lily," Prince Zayir said, gesturing toward her as though she were a work of art hanging in a gallery. "She is my destiny, Mother. Isn't she the most beautiful creature you've seen in the galaxy?"

Lily's face flushed with embarrassment as she stared wide-eyed.

The woman arched a perfectly sculpted brow, her lips curling into a wry smile. "I am Queen Karyah Ishraan," she said, her voice rich and smooth. "But you may call me Karyah. I must apologize for my son. He can be a bit of a dreamer."

"Nice to meet you," Lily managed, summoning every ounce of composure she had. "As I was telling your son, I'm not really in a place to be anyone's destiny right now."

The queen laughed, a deep, genuine sound that filled the space. "Of course not, my dear." She turned to her son, her tone softening. "You're right, though, Z. She's a special girl, this one."

Lily wondered if they always talked about people as if they weren't standing right there.

"I like you," the queen continued, her gaze locking with Lily's. "An honest girl. And brave eyes too. Oh, you must dine with us tomorrow. I won't take no for an answer."

At that moment, Datch reentered the lobby, his sharp gaze narrowing slightly when he saw Lily speaking to the prince and queen.

Lily opened her mouth but hesitated. There was something about Karyah's commanding presence, the way her words left no room for argument, that made resistance feel vain. "Okay," she said finally. "Dinner. And thank you for the invitation."

She dipped into a small, awkward curtsy, catching herself halfway through and straightening with a sheepish smile. Karyah let out a deep, irreverent laugh. "This one," she said, shaking her head. "Oh, my dear, you are too much."

The royal group began to move toward their suite, the queen leading the way. The prince lingered for a moment, turning back to Lily with a dazzling smile. "Until tomorrow, Lily Starling! The thought of it will help me survive these dreadful meetings."

Lily watched him go, her thoughts a mix of disbelief and bemusement. The whole encounter felt like something out of a sappy movie—one she wasn't entirely sure she wanted to be a part of.

Datch raised an eyebrow as Lily turned toward him.

"Stop," she said with mock sternness, brushing past him toward the exit.

As they walked toward the transit station, Datch broke the silence. "You might want to request a briefing from the captain about the peace talks. The prince is... central to Union affairs."

Lily sighed, her shoulders slumping under the weight of the day. So much for rest and relaxation.

• • • •

As Lily and Datch approached the Captain's Stateroom, raised voices carried into the corridor.

"This is an insult to the Varrothi delegation! We will not forget such slights!" a raspy voice hissed, sharp with indignation.

The doors hissed open and two Varrothi swept past, their crimson robes glinting with metallic threads. Pale, elongated faces framed by jagged bone crests turned briefly toward Lily and Datch, eyes gleaming with disdain, before they vanished down the corridor.

Inside, Captain Calan stood with his broad shoulders squared, his expression calm but watchful as he tracked their departure. He caught sight of Lily and Datch and straightened further.

"Lily. Datch," he greeted them with a nod, his tone softening as they stepped into the space.

"Captain," Lily said, offering a slight smile.

Datch gestured toward the departing Varrothi. "Trouble?"

Calan exhaled through his nose, shaking his head. "A last-minute change in the speaking order. Typical Varrothi—turning every minor adjustment into a galactic insult. Unfortunately, their theatrics don't make them any less dangerous."

He gestured toward a small table in the corner of the waiting area. "Have a seat. What's on your mind?"

Lily briefly explained her invitation to dine with the Ishrethi prince and her desire to better understand the peace talks and his role in them. Calan listened with a look of quiet focus, nodding occasionally.

"Prince Zayir Ishraan Kaseer," Calan began, leaning back slightly in his chair. "He's young, ambitious, eager to prove himself. After his father's death during the Solar Passage—a ritual signaling the transfer of power to the next generation—he assumed leadership of the Ishrethi monarchy. The Solar Passage stirred debate on Ishraan Prime. The younger generation seeks change, a new vision for their government. Zayir has a great deal to prove—not just to the old guard, but to the younger generations of his people. And now, to the galaxy as well."

"And his mother?" Datch asked.

"Queen Karyah Ishraan," Calan said, his voice carrying a hint of gravity. "She represents the old guard—traditionalist, cautious. She doesn't always agree with her son's bold approach to diplomacy but has publicly supported him thus far. How long that support will last is anyone's guess. The Ishrethi monarchy is walking a fine line, balancing its long-standing culture with Zayir's vision of progress."

Lily tilted her head, processing the information. "Do you think the peace talks have a chance?"

Calan's expression darkened slightly. "It's a long shot. The Krythar don't negotiate in good faith. But if Zayir can rally the other delegations, he might just tip the balance. It's an uphill battle, but not impossible."

Lily nodded. "Thank you, Captain."

Calan stood, signaling the end of their meeting. "Stay sharp. This situation is a powder keg just waiting for a spark."

As they stepped back into the corridor, Datch turned to Lily. "The public opening statements for the peace talks will be streamed to the ship's theaters tonight. It might give you a better sense of the bigger picture."

Lily offered a small, tired smile. "I'll see you there."

Datch gave a slight nod, the faintest hint of approval on his face, before heading off toward another part of the ship. Lily continued toward her quarters, the weight of the day settling over her like a thin, persistent fog.

. . . .

Lily leaned back in the plush velvet seat, her eyes adjusting to the gentle glow of the holoprojector as the room around her seemed to fade into shadow. The Salamander's theater was a marvel of contradictions—a 14th-century Venetian playhouse reborn in the vacuum of space. Overhead, cherubs cavorted in baroque murals, their painted faces frozen in eternal mischief. Ornate balconies lined with crimson drapes curved around the walls, their gilded railings shimmering faintly in the dim light.

Despite the grandeur, the space was quiet, with only a few murmured conversations. Tonight, the stage was not for Shakespearean drama; instead, the holoprojectors filled the room with the opening ceremony of the peace talks.

From her balcony seat, Lily could see the proceedings as though they were happening just beyond the gilded rail. A miniature version of the scene hovered in front of her, shimmering with a faint, otherworldly blue light. With a subtle flick of her fingers against the projected controls, she zoomed in on the Ishrethi delegation. The prince's copper-gold skin caught the chamber's light, every nuance of his posture projected with startling clarity.

She shifted the view once more, pulling up the Varrothi in their crimson robes. The precision of the hologram astonished her—it felt like the theater was an extension of her own senses.

Though the setting pulsed with quiet luxury, Lily's attention was riveted on the scene unfolding. Diplomacy was its own kind of theater, and tonight, the stakes felt impossibly high.

She glanced at Datch beside her. His serene presence was a quiet anchor in the swirl of politics. They'd been nearly inseparable since arriving at the starbase, and she was grateful for his steady companionship.

On the stage, Prince Zayir stepped forward to deliver his opening address. His presence was magnetic, commanding without effort.

"Esteemed delegates, honored guests," he began, his voice resonant, carrying an emotional weight that drew in his audience. "We gather here not as representatives of fractured alliances, but as beings who share a common desire: peace... The Krythar may not sit among us today, but they too crave survival, as we do. I ask you—can we not forge a path that spares the next generation the pain we have endured?"

Lily's fingers tightened on the armrest. His words were compelling, but her thoughts snagged on Earth—the Krythar's brutal attack, Garrow falling in the chaos. She struggled to reconcile their ferocity with Zayir's optimistic vision.

"Lily."

Datch's soft murmur pulled her back. He inclined his head toward the Urrathi delegation, whose armored spokesperson was taking the floor.

"The Urrathi," Datch said quietly, "oppose any ceasefire."

The delegate's voice boomed: "We have not come here to entertain fantasies of peace. Our soldiers have bled, our families have grieved. To seek reconciliation while the Krythar thrive is an insult to their sacrifice. We demand justice, not compromise."

The elegant surroundings seemed at odds with the raw anger in his voice.

Time slipped past as speeches continued. Lily managed to stay focused—except during the Raath-Ka ambassador's twenty-minute tangent on fruit imports for colony children. Her imagination wandered, conjuring cheerful robots unloading crates of alien fruit onto docks, the scent of it filling the air, until she realized she'd lost the thread entirely.

Captain Calan's voice finally brought the chamber back to order. "And now, as we near the conclusion of this historic opening ceremony, it is my honor to introduce our final speaker: Elder Yzatra Vel, Senior Ambassador of the Zephtari."

The Zephtari ambassador's tall, graceful figure shimmered into view, her patterned skin reflecting the light like water. "Distinguished delegates," she began, her voice smooth and melodic, "I speak not merely as a representative of the Union, but as a witness to what is possible when cooperation triumphs over conflict."

A gleaming station filled the holographic display. "The Zephtari Science Center," Vel said with pride. "Here, diseases are studied and cured. New food sources are perfected, ensuring sustenance for countless worlds. Clean energy solutions are developed to power generations yet to come. This station is not merely a facility—it is proof that exploration and discovery can bind us together."

She paused, then gestured again. The display shifted to show Zephtari and Varrothi scientists working side by side. "Yes, Varrothi—members of the Krythar Ascendancy—engaged in joint research with us. Even the greatest divides can be bridged through science."

Lily turned to Datch, whispering, "Is this true?"

"It's classified," he said softly. "But yes. I didn't think they'd reveal it here."

Vel's speech ended in polite applause, holographic banners filling the chamber.

As the ceremony closed, Lily stood and stretched. Datch lingered, his gaze fixed on the fluttering banners.

"Don't forget," he said, "movie night tomorrow. They're showing a 20th-century classic, *Death on the Nile.*"

Lily raised an eyebrow. "Sounds dramatic."

"It is," Datch replied evenly. "Humans loved stories where everything was neatly solved. It's... comforting."

She smiled faintly. "I could use a little certainty right now. Assuming I survive dinner with the prince and his mother."

Datch tilted his head, his tone almost wry. "Ahh yes, complicated dynamics."

"You can say that again. They're royalty. I'm... me. I don't even know which fork to use."

"Cultural differences are often messy," he said. After a pause, he added quietly, "On my homeworld—Gherion Prime—there are no kings or queens. Just us. Androids."

"Really?" Lily asked softly.

"Generations of us," Datch said. "We don't know who built us, but we've lived there for thousands of years. We procreate by building new generations. We wear out and die, just like you. I was born twenty-six years ago. We're a people, just like any other."

His eyes glowed faintly. "But the Union doesn't see it that way. Some think we're just machines. Others think we're a threat. That's why I'm here as a volunteer, not an officer. My personhood is still... debated."

Lily swallowed. "That's... awful."

"It's reality," he said. "Diplomacy is complicated. Sometimes it's about showing people who you are, even when they've already decided who they think you are."

She tried a small smile. "Then I'll just have to show them who I am tonight."

"You will," he said, his lips curving faintly. "And if all else fails, use the fork closest to your plate."

Lily laughed, some of her nerves easing. "Thanks, Datch."

"Always happy to help a friend."

At the door, she turned back. "Actually—would you come shopping with me tomorrow? I need something to wear, and I'd rather not go alone."

He considered, then nodded. "Of course. The promenade at 09:00."

"Thanks," Lily said, her smile widening.

"I'll add it to the list," Datch replied, his tone noticeably lighter as she walked away with her head held a little higher than before.

· · · ·

The artificial morning light streamed through the arched windows of Star Base 12's central promenade, casting a soft glow on the bustling crowds. Lily stood in front of a shop displaying shimmering fabrics and sleek, alien mannequins posed in overwhelmingly stylish outfits. Alrek had made it abundantly clear that he hated shopping, and Caris had been conveniently busy, leaving Lily no choice but to drag Datch along. To his credit, Datch stood beside her with the serene patience of a good friend, though his mind was clearly elsewhere.

"Okay," Lily sighed, stepping through the doors. "Remember, dinner with an actual prince and a queen to boot. So far, my best option is my hoodie from Earth."

Datch raised an eyebrow, his eyes briefly scanning the racks of clothes as though analyzing a complex data set. "I can assist by providing contextual analysis. What message are you hoping to convey with your attire?"

Lily sighed and grabbed a flowing dress in a deep emerald shade. "I don't know! I just need to look... confident? Polished? But not like I'm trying too hard. Definitely not like I'm interested in the prince's... advances."

Datch tilted his head, his reflective gaze shifting to the garment. "Emerald green conveys prosperity and stability, traits valued in diplomatic settings. However, the high neckline might suggest formality over approachability. A less structured silhouette might balance the impression."

Lily blinked at him. "Right. Noted. Thanks, Datch." She grabbed the dress and a few other options before disappearing into the changing room.

One by one, Lily tried on various outfits, stepping out to show Datch her favorites. His critiques were consistent, if frustratingly neutral.

"Okay, what about this one?" she asked, now wearing a sleek black dress with silver embroidery.

Datch considered it. "The black communicates authority, though the silver detailing adds an element of intrigue. However, the overall tone may lean too somber for a social dinner."

Lily groaned. "This is impossible."

Datch's comm tag buzzed, and he tapped it. A voice crackled through, requesting his presence for a security planning meeting. He glanced at Lily. "I'm needed elsewhere. Will you be fine on your own?"

"Yes, go," she said, shooing him away. "No offense, but you're better at security than fashion."

Datch gave a polite nod and exited, leaving Lily surrounded by racks of alien couture. She picked up a bold red jumpsuit, holding it against herself in the mirror with a sigh.

"I'd skip the red," came a familiar voice from behind her. Lily turned to see Rhyder leaning casually against the doorframe, his ever-present smirk firmly in place.

"What are you doing here?" she asked, narrowing her eyes.

"Browsing," he said with a shrug. "You looked like you could use a second opinion. Your friend doesn't exactly scream 'style icon.'"

"And you're an expert, I assume?" Lily shot back, though she couldn't help a small smile. "So what's wrong with the red?"

Rhyder stepped closer, his eyes assessing the jumpsuit with surprising seriousness. "Red's too aggressive. Unless you're planning to either seduce him or start a fight, I'd say no."

Lily rolled her eyes but quickly set the garment aside. "I just want to look confident. Like I belong at the table—but not in his lap."

Rhyder tilted his head thoughtfully. "Confidence without romantic interest? What about something from Tavari."

Lily frowned. "Tavari?"

"They're a gender non-binary species known for their smart style. You really are new; everyone knows about the Tavari," Rhyder explained, gesturing toward a section of the shop where mannequins displayed sharp, tailored outfits with unique accents. "Powerful, elegant, but not overly formal. It'll set you apart, but in a good way."

Curious, Lily picked out a sleek pantsuit in deep navy with subtle iridescent patterns that shimmered under the light. She slipped it on and stepped out of the dressing room, glancing at Rhyder for his verdict.

He gave a low whistle. "Now that's confidence. You'll knock them dead."

Lily turned to the mirror, studying herself. The suit fit like a dream, the structured jacket and wide pants struck just the right balance of authority and approachability. She smiled, finally feeling like she'd found the right choice.

"Thanks," she said, glancing at Rhyder. "You're surprisingly good at this."

"What can I say?" he replied with a wink. "I have an eye."

Lily narrowed her eyes.

Rhyder feigned innocence. "What?"

Lily didn't break her stern gaze. "Why are you helping me? You want something, don't you?"

"Who, me?" Rhyder asked with phony innocence. "I mean, if you're offering, I could use a hand with something. You do owe me after I saved you the other day."

Lily smiled but was indignant. "Saved me? That might be a bit of an exaggeration."

She looked at Rhyder's intoxicating smile.

"Fine," Lily muttered. "What can I help you with?"

"Oh, nothing dangerous," he said breezily, already turning toward the exit. "Come on, I'll explain on the way."

Lily glanced at the suit in the mirror one last time, then sighed. "You better not get me killed."

With that, she followed him out of the shop, her new outfit already en route to the Salamander. She might regret her choice later, but for now, she was grateful for the distraction—it kept her mind off the evening ahead and the nerves that came with it.

· · · ·

The shuttle ride to the planet's surface was quiet, almost too quiet, leaving Lily alone with her thoughts as they descended. She watched the landscape below shift into view, a chaotic sprawl that couldn't have been more different from the vibrant, organized environments of Star Base 12. The city buzzed with activity even from this height, its narrow streets crammed with stalls and dingy offices, shadowy corners hinting at secrets waiting to be uncovered. The stark contrast left her uneasy, a nagging tension twisting in her chest as they drew closer to the ground.

"This is charming," Lily shouted over the roar of the engines, her voice thick with sarcasm. "You really know how to show a girl a good time."

"Ah, New Cordova," Rhyder said, his voice dripping with mock grandeur as he swept his arm wide. "One of the first Earth colonies in deep space, and now a haven for... let's call it creative enterprise. You're going to love it. Of the humans left here, half feel abandoned by the Union, and the other half would rather it stay that way. Being left alone is kind of their thing—helps keep their business dealings nice and... flexible, if you catch my drift." He shot her a sly grin. "You should fit right in."

Lily glared at him. "Nice. Thanks for that."

The shuttle landed with a jarring thud on a dusty platform, and Rhyder led Lily along a winding path through a dense ghetto. Each step deepened her regret for agreeing to this.

"You'll like Ash. He's got a certain... charm," Rhyder said as they ducked past a vendor hawking suspiciously glowing fruit.

"You mean like you?" Lily shot back, earning herself a trademark smirk.

They rounded a corner into a quieter side street, where a modest, nondescript cinder block building squatted between towering warehouses. For a brief moment, Lily felt a pang of familiarity—it reminded her of the run-down corners of the Mission District, where she used to search for vacant spots to crash. The memory was an odd mixture of comfort and gravity.

Rhyder pushed open the building's battered metal door and gestured for her to step inside.

The dimly lit interior was stark, nearly devoid of furniture except for a few outdated machines that looked like they'd been salvaged from a junkyard. The air buzzed with a loud, grating hum—somewhere between a broken alarm clock and a relentless door buzzer. Near the back, a tall man with broad shoulders and flaming red hair stood beside a cart-mounted console, his hands deftly moving across flickering holographic controls.His hometown grin was more folksy than charming, the kind of smile you'd expect from someone who grew up wrestling brothers in the dirt. But the cool, appraising glint in his blue eyes hinted at something sharper beneath the surface.

"Ash Prynn," Rhyder announced, his tone carrying a note of camaraderie as he stepped forward. "This is Lily Starling. She's new," he added, casting a glance her way. "New to, well, everything, I'm told. But don't let that fool you—she's got the talent you're looking for."

"Talent? For what?" Lily asked, her suspicion sharpening her tone. Neither of them answered.

Ash's grin vanished, replaced by a flat stare as he jabbed a finger into Rhyder's chest. "I'd just about given up on you. I'm over here sweating bullets, and yet here he is—the galaxy's very own Rhyder Dayne—finally showing up with a girl in tow."

He started pacing, throwing his hands up for emphasis. "Do you know how close you cut this? Ten minutes. Ten minutes!"

Rhyder shrugged, completely unfazed. "I'm sure what he meant to say," he said smoothly, turning to Lily, "was: Lovely to meet you, Lily. I'm Ash. We appreciate your help." He said the last part through gritted teeth as he turned back to his friend.

"Yes, nice to meet you, now can we please get going?" Ash was already heading toward a parking garage attached to the building.

The speeder truck rattled along the uneven streets of New Cordova, its open sides letting in gusts of warm, dusty air. Lily sat in the back, wedged between a stack of worn crates and a metal bar that dug into her side every time they hit a bump. Across from her, Rhyder lounged with practiced ease, one boot propped on a crate, while Ash leaned forward from the driver's seat, his red hair gleaming under the pale sunlight.

"So," Lily began, crossing her arms. "Are either of you going to explain why I'm here? Or do I just keep blindly following you into increasingly sketchy situations?"

Ash glanced over his shoulder, his grin as easy as ever. "Patience, Kiddo. We're getting to it."

Lily bristled. "Don't call me kiddo." She turned to Rhyder. "Who is this guy?"

Ash shrugged slightly, unbothered, but Rhyder didn't waste the moment. "Here's the deal. We had someone lined up for this—Katya. She's a regular on these kinds of things, knows the drill. But she had to back out last minute."

"Emergency manicure?" Lily quipped, eyebrow raised.

"Something like that," Rhyder replied with a smirk. "Point is, the people we're meeting are expecting her. Specifically, a Russian woman."

Lily raised an eyebrow. "And?"

"And," Ash interjected, "that's where you come in. You go in, give them the name, and pick up the package."

"Wait a second," Lily said, sitting up straighter. "You want me to pretend to be this Katya person?"

"Exactly," Rhyder said, leaning back as if it were the simplest thing in the world.

"Using a Russian accent," Ash added, deadpan.

Lily blinked. "You can't be serious."

"Using a Russian accent... wait, why are there Russian accents millions of miles from Earth?" Lily asked, genuinely confused.

"Well, probably because there are Russians millions of miles from Earth," Rhyder replied, shrugging.

"Keep up, Starling," Ash said, his tone flat but amused.

Lily shook her head, half-smiling. "I had to ask."

Rhyder snapped his fingers twice in quick succession, his voice nearly drowned out by the roar of the speeder truck's engine. "Look, all you have to do is walk in, say her name—Katya Ivanovich—and ask for the case. They'll hand it over, and we'll be on our merry way. Easy peasy."

"Easy peasy," Lily repeated flatly, almost shouting to be heard over the noise. "Because nothing about this screams 'potential disaster.'"

"It's foolproof," Ash said. "And you're the perfect fool for the job."

Lily glared at him, but Ash quickly tried to save himself. "Look, they're expecting a Russian woman. Neither of us can pass for that, obviously. You're our best shot."

Lily sighed, leaning back against the crate. "Fine. But if this goes sideways, I'm not bailing you two out."

"Noted," Rhyder said, his grin unwavering. "Now, let's hear your accent. Give us your best Katya."

Lily rolled her eyes but straightened up, putting on a mock-serious expression. "Da. I am Katya Ivanovich. Vare is da package?"

Rhyder clapped his hands, clearly delighted. "You're a natural."

Ash gave a measured nod. "Just keep it simple. As long as you mostly keep your mouth shut, you should be fine."

"Great," Lily muttered under her breath as the truck's engine finally slowed to a stop in front of an unmarked building. The air was thick with dust and tension as they climbed out.

"Alright, Starlight," Rhyder said, giving her a playful nudge. "Time to shine."

Lily squared her shoulders and took a deep breath. "I hate you both."

Ash chuckled, his voice light. "That's the spirit."

The speeder rolled to a stop, and the three of them climbed out. The sun was sinking low, casting a dull amber glow across the grimy streets as Lily tugged at the fur-lined trapper hat perched awkwardly on her head. She pulled the collar of her borrowed leather coat higher around her neck and frowned up at the faded sign above the doorway: **Tetra Freight and Logistics**, the letters peeling and half-burned out. It looked every bit as sketchy as she had imagined.

"I look ridiculous," she muttered, fidgeting with the hat again.

"Whatever gets the job done," Rhyder said from his crouched position against the wall, posture relaxed, trouble radiating off him like a second skin. Beside him, Ash leaned casually, his kind blue eyes giving her an encouraging nod.

Lily shot them both a glare before pushing open the door, her boots clicking against the scuffed floor as she entered. The interior was dimly lit, the air thick with dust and a faint metallic tang. Shelves stacked haphazardly with crates and cartons loomed around her like makeshift walls. Behind a cluttered desk, two hulking figures stopped their murmured conversation to size her up.

"I am Katya Ivanovich," Lily said, her voice a strained approximation of a Russian accent. She pursed her lips, trying to channel the haughty confidence she imagined a Russian operative might have. "I am here for the package."

The larger of the two men squinted at her, then turned his attention to a console on the desk. He tapped a few buttons before muttering something to his companion. After an uncomfortably long pause, he shoved a black metal box across the desk toward her.

"Sign," he grunted, sliding the datapad her way.

Lily picked up the datapad, her hand trembling slightly as she did her best to scrawl the name in a way that looked effortless. As she signed, she could feel the men's eyes on her, sizing her up. There was a look in their gazes—a silent question of *aren't you a little young to be playing courier?* But she came to the conclusion that they didn't really care who picked up what.

She picked up the box, heavier than it looked, offering a terse nod as she turned toward the exit.

Just as Lily reached for the door, it swung open with a heavy thud, nearly hitting her in the face.

A woman entered, her presence like a thunderclap. Tall, commanding, and radiating authority, she wore a sleek leather jacket, and her platinum blonde hair was pulled back into a severe ponytail. Her sharp gaze locked onto Lily, and her lips twisted into a thin, dangerous line.

"I am Katya Ivanovich," the woman said, her thick Russian accent cutting through the air like a blade. Her eyes flicked down to the metal box in Lily's arms. "Who the hell are you?"

Lily's stomach dropped. "Uh... hi," she managed, her voice squeaking a little. "I can explain."

Before she could say more, Katya's hand shot to her belt, pulling out a sleek blaster and aiming it directly at Lily. "You have five seconds."

Lily's heart hammered in her chest, her mind scrambling. "Okay, so... I'm guessing you're not working with Rhyder, are you?"

The mention of Rhyder made Katya freeze, her eyes narrowing with fury. "Rhyder?" she snarled, her voice dripping with venom. "That bastard." Her glare shifted to the two men behind the desk. "Check the back! He knew I'd be here—he's probably robbing you blind right now!"

As if on cue, alarms blared through the building, confirming Katya's suspicion. One of the men shouted something unintelligible, and a volley of blaster fire erupted from the back of the building. Katya stormed toward the security console, her eyes glued to the footage. She saw Rhyder unloading something from her speeder pod parked outside, while Ash was inside the warehouse, removing a large case.

The realization hit like a freight train. "Damn, Rhyder, damn that kid!" Katya growled, fury flashing across her face as she watched the scene unfold. "Come on, get the doors open!"

The two men were still fumbling with the console, desperately trying to bypass the lockdown. They yelled at each other, their hands frantically moving over the buttons, but the system wouldn't release. The building was sealed tight.

Katya's eyes flicked back to Lily, her hand still gripping the blaster. "Where are they going with my static field generator?" she demanded, advancing on her with cold fury.

"I don't know!" Lily stammered. "They left me out here! I swear, I didn't know they were going to... whatever this is!"

The two men continued to struggle with the system. Katya's gaze darted between the security feed and the men, and for a brief moment, Lily thought she might pull the trigger. Instead, Katya growled in frustration and hit a button on the console, her blaster still trained on Lily. "Get out of here. Before I change my mind."

Lily didn't need to be told twice. She bolted for the exit, her heart pounding as she dashed down the hall. She heard the click of the doors opening as the lockdown was overridden and pushed herself to run faster, knowing Katya and the men were hot on her heels.

Outside, the chaos gave way to a tense stillness, broken only by the distant hum of the speeder truck's engine. Lily's heart sank at the sight of it revving to life. Rhyder was perched in the passenger seat, grinning with that infuriating smugness of his, while Ash manned the controls, giving her a casual wave.

"Rhyder!" Lily called, breathless. "What the hell?!"

He cupped his hands around his mouth and shouted back, "Sorry, Starling! Nothing personal!"

The speeder began to lift off, dust swirling in the air as its repulsors kicked into gear. Rhyder leaned out of the side, his grin widening. "And hey, now we're even!"

"Even?!" Lily snapped, storming forward, though the speeder was already picking up speed. "You—ugh!"

With a whoop, Rhyder smacked the side of the truck, and they roared off into the distance, leaving Lily choking on the dust storm they'd kicked up.

She stood there for a long moment, fists clenched, adrenaline still coursing through her veins. "Well, Lily, what did you expect?" she muttered bitterly, brushing dirt off her jacket.

Her frustration simmered as she turned and started walking back toward the starport. She could only hope dinner with the prince that evening would go better than this little disaster of a mission.

• • • •

Lily adjusted the hem of her tunic, wishing once again that Datch—or anyone, really—could have come with her. But the prince's invitation had been specific, leaving her no option but to face the evening alone. The decision had felt noble at the time, but now, standing in front of the towering doors of the Ishrethi Luxury Residence, she was starting to regret it.

Getting ready for this dinner had been a journey in itself. After her "adventure" with Rhyder—a polite way of describing the three miles of dusty terrain she'd slogged through just to reach the starport—she'd practically sprinted through Star Base 12 back to the Salamander. The grime from that ordeal had clung to her like a second skin, and she'd spent an embarrassing amount of time in the shower trying to scrub away the dirt and, more importantly, the frustration.

Her nerves hadn't calmed during the ride over. The shuttle had been a luxury model, its interior plush and quiet, but even the thick carpet and soothing ambient music hadn't done much to settle her stomach. She'd spent the entire transit staring at her reflection in the tinted window, fidgeting with her hair and wondering if she'd made the right choice by coming at all. Now, as the ornately dressed Ishrethi servant gestured for her to follow, Lily was painfully aware of the ache in her feet and the tension in her shoulders.

The dining room was nothing short of breathtaking. It wasn't just a room—it was a statement, every detail whispering of wealth, tradition, and meticulous design. The ceiling arched high above, painted in rich blues and silvers that shimmered like starlight. Delicate crystal fixtures dangled down, casting soft, diffused light over the scene below. The centerpiece of the room was a massive table, low to the ground and surrounded by plush cushions that seemed to promise a level of comfort Lily didn't quite trust.

The table itself was a masterpiece, carved from a single piece of dark, polished wood that gleamed under the chandelier's light. Intricate carvings of Ishrethi symbols and floral patterns adorned the edges, their silver inlays catching the light and drawing the eye. The table was set with an array of dishes that looked almost too beautiful to eat—delicate bowls filled with vibrant, steaming broths, platters of jewel-toned fruits arranged like works of art, and golden plates stacked with breads that glistened faintly with what Lily guessed was some kind of edible shimmer.

She hesitated at the threshold, feeling every inch the outsider. The servant motioned for her to sit, their movements graceful but impersonal. Lily nodded awkwardly, stepping forward and lowering herself onto one of the cushions. She couldn't help but shift a little as she tried to find a comfortable position. The cushion was softer than she expected, its embroidered fabric cool against her legs.

The room smelled incredible—spices she couldn't name mingling with the warm, earthy scent of freshly baked bread. Her stomach grumbled softly in response, a traitorous reminder of how little she'd eaten all day. She pressed a hand to her abdomen, silently willing it to behave.

Lily shifted uncomfortably on her cushion, her gaze drifting over the ornate table as the dining room began to fill with voices. A cluster of new arrivals swept in, their polished presence making her suddenly acutely aware of how much she didn't belong here.

She recognized them immediately: the Zephtari and Urrathi delegations. They had been front and center at the opening ceremony broadcast the previous night. The memory made her stomach twist. These weren't just people; they were the kind of individuals whose decisions altered the course of history. She suddenly wished the cushion beneath her could swallow her whole.

Minister Velnak approached her first, his smile genuine and disarming as he offered a slight bow. "Ah, you must be Lily Starling," he said, his voice smooth and practiced. "The guest of honor, I see. Let me introduce you to some of the others."

Lily blinked, startled by the unexpected attention. "Oh, uh, thank you," she managed, rising slightly as Velnak gestured toward the group.

"This is Elder Vel of the Zephtari Council," Velnak began, his tone deferential as he motioned toward the elder, who inclined her head just enough to be polite. Her elegant figure was framed by a long, flowing garment that shimmered like liquid silver. Her expression was sharp, her luminous gray eyes scanning the room with a calm but discerning gaze.

"And Envoy Taro Lethra," he continued, nodding toward the Zephtari delegate. The envoy's acknowledgment was minimal, his focus already elsewhere. His tall, willowy frame was draped in layered robes of deep green and gold. His movements were smooth and deliberate, as though every step made a statement.

"Premier Athrex Varn," Velnak added. The premier gave a curt nod, his eyes barely glancing her way. Varn was stern, broad-shouldered, with a square jaw set in a perpetually neutral—almost callous—position.

"And myself, of course, Minister Shyra Velnak." He chuckled lightly, as if to diffuse the tension in the air. Lighter in demeanor, his warm smile contrasted with the tense energy of the others.

"Nice to meet you all," Lily said, her voice careful. Her attempt at friendliness was met with varying degrees of indifference, though Velnak seemed pleased by her effort.

Nearby, Elder Vel turned to the minister with a wistful sigh. "A shame Captain Dalren couldn't join us tonight," she remarked, her tone pointed. "His insights would've been valuable."

Premier Varn's smile twisted into something sharper, his eyes gleaming with unspoken malice. "The captain," he said, letting the words linger, his tone almost too polished, "he's likely... occupied elsewhere. Wouldn't be the first time he's been... preoccupied with matters of a personal nature, would it?"

Elder Vel's face remained composed, though her brow arched ever so slightly—a subtle but unmistakable rebuke. Varn ignored her entirely, turning his critical gaze toward the room with a theatrical sigh. "As for this…" He waved a dismissive hand at the table and the lavish decorations. "Gaudy, overwrought, and absolutely suffocating with the smell of over-spiced mediocrity. Honestly, it's as if they're trying to disguise a lack of sophistication with excess."

The jab hung in the air like a shard of glass, sharp and deliberate. Lily's stomach tightened, her fingers curling into the edge of her cushion as she resisted the urge to retort. A glance at Elder Vel showed the slightest twitch of her lips, as if she were holding back the urge to reprimand him outright.

Varn leaned back, entirely pleased with himself. "But then, I suppose that's to be expected. One doesn't come to a place like this hoping for refinement."

Before the conversation could continue, a soft chime rang out, and the side doors of the dining room slid open. A procession of Ishrethi servants filed in, their movements precise and synchronized. The guests around the table rose in unison, and Lily quickly followed suit, trying not to feel too conspicuous as she copied their actions.

The lead servant, a figure dressed in elaborate robes of midnight blue trimmed with silver, stepped forward. Their voice rang out clear and formal, carrying an air of ceremony. "Presenting His Highness, Prince Zayir Ishraan, Crown Heir to the Ishrethi Dominion, Protector of the Ten Systems, and Regent of the Luminous Path. Accompanying him, Her Majesty, Queen Ishraan Talyssa, Keeper of the Solar Flame and Matriarch of the Ishrethi Lineage."

Lily's eyes flicked toward the entrance, where the prince and queen appeared, flanked by attendants. They moved with regal precision, though their expressions hinted at a different story. Prince Zayir's face was set in a polite mask, but his jaw was tight, and his posture betrayed tension. The queen's gaze was sharp and calculating, her lips pressed into a thin line. Even from across the room, Lily could feel the lingering energy of whatever argument they'd just been having.

As the two took their places at the table, the prince gestured for the guests to be seated. "Please," he said, his voice warm but slightly clipped. "Be seated, and thank you for joining us tonight."

Lily obeyed, lowering herself back onto her cushion. Her heart skipped when she realized where she was seated: directly to the prince's right, the first position on his side of the table. Across from her, to the prince's left, was the queen. The proximity to both of them made Lily's pulse quicken. *What am I doing here?* she thought, her nerves threatening to overwhelm her.

The prince offered a faint smile, leaning slightly toward her. "I hope the evening finds you well, Miss Starling."

"Uh... yeah," Lily replied, trying not to sound as awkward as she felt. "Thank you for inviting me."

The prince nodded, the look on his face one of self-satisfaction, the kind that practically invited you to notice it. Across the table, the queen's gaze lingered on Lily for just a moment—cool and unflinching, like she was peeling back the layers of her soul. The contrast sent a shiver down Lily's spine, and she quickly averted her eyes.

The queen turned her attention to Lily, her sharp gaze softened by a practiced air of courtesy. "Miss Starling," she began, her voice melodic but laced with subtle authority, "I understand you've had quite a difficult time with your memory loss. It must be disorienting, not knowing your past."

Lily blinked, caught off guard by the sudden shift in focus. "It's... definitely been an adjustment," she began, her words careful.

The queen nodded, her expression almost sympathetic. "Yes, I imagine it's like losing a part of yourself," she mused, her tone thoughtful. "But I'm sure you've found ways to adapt. Tell me, what are you studying aboard the Salamander?"

"Well, I haven't really started any formal studies yet," Lily replied. "I'm still—"

"Oh, of course," the queen interrupted, waving a hand as though she already understood. "Still finding your footing, naturally. But I assume you'll gravitate toward something practical, like navigation or communications. Those seem like the sort of skills that would suit someone your age."

Lily's lips parted, but before she could respond, the queen leaned forward slightly. "Speaking of life aboard the Salamander, do you find it enjoyable?"

Lily hesitated, searching for the right words. "It's... interesting," she offered. "I've been learning a lot—"

"Ah, of course it must be fascinating," the queen said, nodding as if Lily's answer had confirmed her own thoughts. "All those new experiences. Have you made many friends yet?"

Lily managed a faint smile. "A few. Everyone's been pretty welcoming—"

"Oh, but it must still be hard," the queen said, cutting her off once again. "I imagine people are so busy with their duties, and with your memory loss, it's no doubt difficult to connect. Do the doctors think they'll be able to restore your memories?"

"They're not sure yet," Lily admitted, her voice quieter. "It's something—"

"Yes, so unpredictable," the queen interjected, her tone laced with authority. "Memories are such delicate things. But you're young. How old are you, dear?"

"Seventeen," Lily replied, doing her best to keep her tone even.

The queen's brows lifted slightly, and a faint smile touched her lips. "Seventeen? By that age, I was already married. My husband and I began our family soon after. Five daughters, all grown now and thriving—one a renowned scientist, another a diplomat, two in politics, and my youngest is a surgeon. We'd about given up on having a son when Zayir finally arrived." She smiled fondly at the prince, who shifted uncomfortably in his seat.

Lily tried to form a polite response, but the queen pressed on, her tone tinged with something almost wistful. "It's difficult, you know, to have only one son after so many daughters. And then, when it was my husband's time to take up the Solar Passage—"

"Mother," Zayir interjected, his voice firm but laced with irritation, "Lily doesn't want to hear about that."

The queen tilted her head, her sharp eyes narrowing slightly. "Oh, she doesn't know?" Her gaze turned back to Lily, her smile reappearing as though she were offering a gift. "Zayir, explain it to her. She should understand our ways."

Zayir's jaw tightened, but he obliged, his voice quieter now. "The Solar Passage is a ritual, a tradition of the Ishrethi. Every male ruler of our people must undergo it when they reach seventy. It's... a ceremonial death, so their heir can take their place."

Lily's stomach twisted. "Ritual suicide?" she asked, her voice barely above a whisper.

"It is more than that," the queen said smoothly, her face laced with the faintest hint of impatience. "It is the ultimate act of devotion to one's people. To step aside so the next generation can lead—it is a sacrifice that ensures the prosperity of our society."

Zayir's lips thinned, and he looked away. "The younger generation doesn't see it that way anymore," he muttered. "They think it's barbaric. And they're not wrong."

The queen's eyes flashed. "That is because they lack the wisdom to understand its importance. Fifty years ago, we extended the age from sixty to seventy to reflect longer lifespans, but that was a concession, not an abandonment of our values."

Zayir's hands clenched on the table. "And yet, no one asked if those values still make sense in this modern age. Maybe it's time we reconsider what's important."

The queen's gaze hardened. "Your father never would have wasted his time chasing dreams of change. He understood the weight of tradition."

The table fell silent, the tension palpable. Lily glanced around, catching the uneasy expressions of the other guests. Even Minister Velnak seemed uncharacteristically subdued, his usual smirk replaced by a wary glance between mother and son.

The silence lingered, heavy and awkward, after the queen's pointed remark about Zayir's father. Lily shifted slightly on her cushion, wishing she were anywhere else. Across the table, Minister Velnak cleared his throat.

"Well," he began, his voice light and almost cheerful, "I hear the storms on the planet's surface are quite something this time of year. It's said they can last for days, the winds strong enough to topple even the sturdiest of structures."

A faint murmur of acknowledgment rippled around the table, but it was more out of politeness than interest. Elder Vel raised a single eyebrow, while Premier Varn merely took a slow sip from his goblet. The silence that followed was deafening.

Velnak's smile faltered briefly, and he shifted gears. Lifting his glass, he stood and offered a broad smile. "A toast," he said, his voice ringing with forced enthusiasm. "To Prince Zayir. Though we may occasionally differ in our methods and philosophies, let us remember that, in the end, we all seek the same goal: peace and prosperity for our worlds."

The guests raised their glasses, the movement coordinated yet subdued. "To peace," they murmured in unison before sipping their drinks.

The tension eased slightly as the conversation turned to less contentious topics. Time passed in a blur of polite but restrained chatter, and Lily found herself caught in the ebb and flow of the evening. Discussions ranged from diplomatic gossip to cultural anecdotes, each topic carefully chosen to avoid further conflict.

Gradually, the guests began to leave, one by one, until the dining room grew quieter. The grand table, once full of voices, was now nearly empty. Lily glanced up and realized she was alone with the queen and the prince.

The queen studied her for a moment, her sharp eyes softened by something that almost resembled approval. "Miss Starling," she said, her tone even but firm, "a word of advice, if I may."

Lily blinked, startled but intrigued. "Of course."

The queen leaned forward slightly, her gaze unwavering. "No one will ever give you anything in this galaxy. If you want something done right, you must do it yourself. As an Ishrethi woman, I have learned that everyone expects me to wait for the man to make the decision. But I have a mind of my own, as I suspect you do as well."

Lily nodded slowly, the weight of the queen's words settling over her. "Thank you," she said, her voice steady.

The queen inclined her head gracefully. "You're welcome, my dear. Now, if you'll excuse me." She rose smoothly, her movements as deliberate and regal as ever, and left the room with a soft rustle of fabric.

Lily exhaled, feeling some of the tension dissipate, but she wasn't entirely sure she'd escaped unscathed.

Zayir turned to her, his look shifting from neutral to something closer to admiration. "You handled yourself well tonight," he said. "Not many people could stand up to a room full of delegates and my mother and still hold their own."

"Thanks," Lily said, managing a faint smile.

The prince hesitated, his gaze lingering. "I mean it. You're... impressive."

Before Lily could respond, he leaned in slightly, his intent clear.

Her heart jumped into her throat, and she shifted quickly, dodging the kiss with a well-timed turn of her head. "Uh... yeah, no," she said, trying to sound light but firm.

Zayir sat back, his expression flickering between surprise and something more subdued. "You're not going to stay, are you?" he asked, his tone quieter now, almost defeated.

Lily shook her head. "No," she replied. "But... we're having movie night on the Salamander. If you really want to get to know me, why don't you come along? My friend Datch will be there, and we can watch something together."

The prince's brow furrowed slightly, and for a moment, Lily thought he might decline. But then he nodded, though his expression remained grumpy, like a boy whose grand plans had been derailed. "Alright," he said. "I'll come."

Lily suppressed a sigh of relief as they made their way to the prince's shuttle. The ride was as luxurious as she'd expected, all plush seats and velvet silence, the engines a low whisper beneath their feet. Zayir sat across from her, his gaze lingering a little too long for her liking, and she found herself hoping he wouldn't get any fresh ideas. At least Datch would be there when the evening wound down.

She turned to the viewport as the shuttle glided into the void. The Salamander loomed larger with each passing second, its familiar profile a steady anchor against the chaos of the day. For all the complications, she felt a flicker of pride. She'd made it through the gauntlet—and she was ending the night on her terms.

The next thing she knew, she was stretching in the quiet of her quarters, morning light spilling from the ship's panels. Her arms arched high over her head as the faint vibration of the Salamander's systems reminded her she was still home. Her muscles ached from the past few days, but it was the good kind of soreness—the kind that meant she'd survived, and even earned her rest.

She smiled faintly as the memories returned. Against all odds, the evening had ended on a surprisingly warm note. The prince had laughed along with her and Datch during *Death on the Nile*, tossing out wry comments about Earth's melodramas. For a little while, there had been no war, no diplomacy, no royalty—just three people sharing a story. True to his word, Zayir had left as soon as the film ended, his regal airs softened by the easy laughter. For the first time in weeks, Lily had slipped into sleep without replaying her worries a hundred times over.

Now she pulled on her Fleet-issued tracksuit, grateful for the simplicity. No gowns, no forks to choose from, no royalty to impress. Just breakfast and the chance to catch up with Datch, Alrek—or maybe even Caris and the ever-entertaining Raath-Ka.

But when she stepped into the mess hall corridor, something felt wrong. The usual din of voices and clatter of utensils was muted, the air heavy as though the entire crew were holding its breath.

Her steps quickened.

Alrek skidded to a stop in front of her, his wide eyes and flushed cheeks spelling trouble before he even spoke.

"Lily," he blurted, his voice low and urgent. "Have you heard?"

Her stomach dropped. "Heard what?"

"There was a murder last night!" He thrust a datapad into her hands before she could answer.

The headline jumped out in stark black letters:

Delegate L'than Veirr Found Murdered in Quarters – Lead Varrothi Negotiator Dead Amid Peace Talks

Her breath faltered. No suspects. No motive. Only a single, chilling clue: a Krythar static field generator used as the weapon.

Lily's grip tightened around the datapad. L'than Veirr's death wasn't just a tragedy—it was a spark in a powder keg. The peace talks, the fragile alliances, the precarious balance of trust...

This changes everything, she thought, her pulse hammering in her ears. And she had the sinking feeling she was about to be caught in the middle of it.

The Raath-Ka
and the Lost Memories

THE DIM GLOW OF KA-Lorrin's console cast shifting patterns on the walls of the small engineering lab aboard the *Salamander*. His thin fingers danced over the holographic interface, the soft clicks and chirps of the system punctuating the otherwise quiet space. Ka-Lorrin's brow furrowed in concentration as he sorted through a seemingly endless stream of files. To an outsider, it might have looked like tedious busywork, but to Ka-Lorrin, this was bliss—a carefully constructed puzzle just waiting to be solved.

Across the room, Taran was far less preoccupied. The towering, shaggy Raath lounged against a stack of equipment crates, his large paws expertly shaping a ball from a leftover chunk of rubber-like material. It was meant to clean anti-grav plating, but to Taran it took on a new purpose. With an almost childlike glee, he tossed the ball into a makeshift hoop cobbled together from an impulse manifold and the post of a blast coupling.

"Kal," Taran drawled, catching the ball on its rebound, "ya don't have to organize the whole darn database tonight, ya don't, ya don't. Captain Calan said to take a break while we're at Star Base 12. Best not to disappoint the cap'n."

"Yes, yes, we'll rest," Ka-Lorrin replied, not looking up. "But first, we must finish our work. I've been meaning to clean out these miscellaneous files for months."

Taran threw the ball again, watching it bounce around the lab before he caught it with a satisfied grin. "And they've waited months, months, they have. A few more won't hurt."

Ka-Lorrin ignored him, his attention narrowing to a single file that had just appeared on his display, flagged by the location filter. His sharp eyes skimmed the details, his breath catching when he saw the names attached to it.

"Come here," he said, his voice suddenly serious.

Taran dropped the ball, his ears perking up. He lumbered over, peering down at the console. "What's got ya all worked up?"

Ka-Lorrin pointed at the screen. "This file was created here—at Star Base 12. Look at the names."

Taran squinted, his expression softening as he read. "Kiran and Lenore Starling. Lily's folks."

Ka-Lorrin nodded, his fingers flying over the interface. "It seems they archived a data pod at a secure facility on the station. It's listed under the Vault Center of Terrestrial Artifacts and Assets." He paused, his eyes narrowing as he examined the timestamp. "The date coincides with their work on psionic enhancements. This could be important, vital even."

"Could be," Taran said, rubbing his chin. "Could be a grocery list."

Ka-Lorrin's glare was sharp enough to cut steel. "A grocery list? At the zenith of their groundbreaking research? Preposterous!"

Taran's ears twitched. "Alright, ya got me, ya got me. So, what do we do?"

"We must speak to the captain," Ka-Lorrin declared, rising from his seat. "Immediately."

Taran's wide eyes blinked slowly. "Now? Captain'll be asleep, for sure."

"This is important!" Ka-Lorrin said, already marching toward the door. "Time is of the essence."

Taran sighed and followed. "Just what ya didn't need—a new obsession. So much for time off, here we go, here we go."

• • • •

The door to Captain Calan's quarters slid open with a soft hiss, revealing the captain in Fleet-issue pajamas. The silky fabric shimmered under the corridor lights, faintly patterned with the insignia of his rank. Ka-Lorrin had often wondered if anyone actually wore those—but now that he knew, it was a revelation he wished he could unsee.

"Gentlemen," Calan said, his voice rough from sleep. "Do you know what time it is?"

"Yes, I'm terribly sorry to disturb you," Ka-Lorrin said without a hint of remorse. "But this cannot wait."

Calan ran a hand through his hair, sighing. "Give me a moment." He disappeared back into his quarters, returning a minute later with his uniform jacket hastily thrown over his pajama top and his hair somewhat tamed. From inside, the faint sound of a bubbling kettle drifted out. "Come in."

The two Raath-Ka stepped inside, Taran ducking slightly to avoid hitting his head on the low doorway. Ka-Lorrin wasted no time, projecting the file onto the wall-mounted display.

"Captain, we've discovered an archived data pod linked to Lily's parents," Ka-Lorrin began. "It's located in the Vault Center of Terrestrial Artifacts and Assets on Star Base 12. The date aligns with their work on psionic enhancements... their work on Lily."

Calan's grogginess faded away as his attention locked onto the display, his expression turning thoughtful. A steaming mug of tea, seemingly conjured out of nowhere, rested in his hand. He took a slow, deliberate sip. "That's... interesting. Have you accessed the contents?"

"No," Ka-Lorrin admitted. "The file only provides the location. But if we retrieve the pod, we may uncover something valuable."

Calan nodded slowly. "Alright. I'll authorize the retrieval in the morning."

"Thank you, Captain," Ka-Lorrin said, though his tone suggested that waiting until morning was an unnecessary delay.

Taran smiled, giving Ka-Lorrin a rough nudge with his scruffy head. "See? Easy. No need to get all worked up."

Ka-Lorrin sniffed. "We'll see how easy it is when we're dealing with Star Base bureaucracy."

Calan ushered the two out and leaned against the door as it slid shut, rubbing his temple, already wondering what kind of adventure he'd just unleashed.

* * * *

The public transport system of Star Base 12 was a marvel of efficiency—or at least, that's what Ka-Lorrin kept telling himself as he clung to the overhead handle with one hand, the other clutching the requisition orders as if they were sacred scrolls. The small transport pod rocked back and forth as it sped along its suspended track, its interior crammed to capacity with an eclectic mix of species, all packed like sardines in a tin can.

Ka-Lorrin stood tall, his posture ramrod straight despite the crowded conditions. The glowing emblem of the Space Fleet's Office of the Commander and Chief stamped on the requisition orders was prominently displayed on the data pad clutched to his chest, and he exuded an air of self-importance that might have seemed comical to those who didn't know him. Those close to Ka-Lorrin, however, would recognize sheer conviction.

Taran, on the other hand, was having a much harder time. His massive, fur-covered frame loomed over the sea of passengers, and every time the transport jolted, he unintentionally bumped into someone. "Sorry, sorry," he repeated with increasing frequency as his tail swished, brushing against an annoyed insectoid alien, whose antennae twitched furiously.

"Ya mighta picked the busiest time to travel, Kal," Taran said, gripping a pole with one paw and trying to keep himself from toppling over a diminutive reptilian passenger. "Feels like a barrel of eels in here, it does, it does."

"It is not my fault that the Vault Center is located at the furthest possible stop," Ka-Lorrin replied primly, refusing to acknowledge the chaos around him. He gestured with the requisition orders. "Do you see this? Stamped by the Office of the Commander and Chief of the Space Fleet. This is an official matter, and the urgency must be respected!"

The transport jolted again, and Taran accidentally stepped on the tail of a feline-like passenger, who hissed in irritation. "The passengers' toes must be respected, they must," Taran muttered, followed by another, "sorry, sorry!"

By the time they reached their stop, Taran had apologized no fewer than twenty times, and the relieved passengers practically pushed them out of the transport pod as the doors slid open. Ka-Lorrin led the way, the requisition orders held aloft like a torch.

The signs pointing to the Vault Center of Terrestrial Artifacts and Assets, or VCTAA, were sparse but clear. The journey took them through a series of long, featureless corridors. The walls were bare metal, and the lighting pads overhead cast an even, sterile glow. The further they walked, the quieter it became, the hum of the station fading into an unsettling stillness.

After the fourth identical turn, Taran's ears twitched. "Feels like we're headin' into a ghost ship, it does."

Ka-Lorrin didn't break stride. "There's no need to be melodramatic. The signage is clear, and there's only one way forward."

"Clear as mud, clear as mud," Taran muttered, glancing over his shoulder at the empty corridor behind them. "I don't like it. Ain't no doors, no people, no nothin'. Just walkin' and walkin'."

They continued on, and soon, the pristine lighting gave way to dim, flickering panels. The hum of the station was replaced by the faint sound of dripping water. One of the light pads overhead sparked and went dark as they passed under it.

Finally, they came to a ladder mounted into the wall, leading downward into a shadowy shaft. A handwritten sign, taped haphazardly to the wall, read: VCTAA with an arrow pointing down. The crude lettering seemed wildly out of place on a station known for its precision.

"You have to be kidding me," Ka-Lorrin muttered, staring at the sign in disbelief.

Taran peered down the shaft, his nose wrinkling. "Looks like somethin' outta one o' them horror movies from Earth, it does."

Ka-Lorrin sighed, tucking the requisition orders into his coat. "There's no point in complaining. Let's go."

The climb down was long and arduous. The ladder rungs were cold and slightly damp, and the faint sound of water dripping echoed through the shaft. Taran descended carefully, his large feet making each rung groan slightly under his weight.

At the bottom, they emerged into a dimly lit antechamber. A rusted metal door stood before them, its surface scratched and dented from years of wear. A faded sign above it read Vault Center of Terrestrial Artifacts and Assets in blocky lettering. Beside the door was a small comm panel, its screen covered by a piece of paper with the word "Broken" scrawled in thick marker.

Ka-Lorrin frowned and pressed the call button. A high-pitched, gravelly voice crackled through the speaker. "YES?"

Ka-Lorrin straightened his jacket and cleared his throat. "This is Ka-Lorrin of the Starship Salamander. I am here on official business to access one of your storage pods. I have the requisite orders from Space Fleet Command." There was silence for a few moments, so he added, "directly from the office of the C&C."

There was a moment of silence, followed by the grating sound of a loud buzzer. The door clicked open with a metallic groan.

"Not the most professional," Ka-Lorrin muttered as he pushed the door wide.

The lobby of the VCTAA was enormous but dimly lit, its large circular space entirely surrounded by heavy metal doors about 12 feet tall each, leading to separate corridors of vaults and storage pods. At the center of the chamber sat a solitary desk, framed by an imposing arch of cabinets behind it. The desk's surface was cluttered with scattered papers and devices. The room was eerily silent, and a faint smell of mildew lingered in the air.

Taran craned his neck, his wide eyes taking in the scene. "Well, this is somethin', somethin'."

Ka-Lorrin stepped forward, his sharp gaze scanning the room. "Let's hope the service is better than the decor."

They approached the desk, at first mistakenly thinking no one was there, but soon noticed the source of the voice from earlier: a small alien who looked almost like a piece of yellow dried fruit with limbs. Barely two feet tall, he was dressed in a scratchy-looking suit—a miniature version of something you'd expect to find in a thrift store on Earth, untouched since the 1970s.

The little alien behind the desk barely glanced up as Ka-Lorrin and Taran approached. Without preamble, he launched into what was clearly a well-rehearsed monologue.

"Welcome to the Vault Center of Terrestrial Artifacts and Assets, or VCTAA—pronounced Victa," he began, his gravelly voice rapid and clipped, devoid of any trace of emotion. "We are the longest continuously operating secure storage facility of our kind in this quadrant, with over five hundred cycles of uninterrupted service. Trusted by royalty, governments, interstellar corporations, and private collectors alike, VCTAA offers unparalleled protection for your most valuable possessions. Utilizing state-of-the-art molecular shielding, gravitational displacement locks, and a proprietary encryption system rated top-tier by the Interstellar Security Bureau, our services are unmatched in security, discretion, and peace of mind. Whether you are storing historical artifacts, sensitive documents, or priceless heirlooms, we guarantee—"

Ka-Lorrin cleared his throat, lifting a hand to interrupt, but the alien steamrolled on without missing a beat.

"—that your items will remain in pristine condition, safeguarded against environmental fluctuations, theft, or unauthorized access. Our vaults are monitored twenty-four-seven by an elite team of security drones equipped with advanced neural AI algorithms, ensuring maximum oversight with minimal intrusion into your privacy. We offer a range of packages tailored to meet the needs of our diverse clientele, including short-term, long-term, and indefinite storage options. Additionally, all storage pods are insured up to—"

"Excuse me," Ka-Lorrin interjected more forcefully, but the alien's speech did not so much as falter.

"—five million credits as a standard feature, with higher coverage limits available upon request. Our clientele includes luminaries such as the Imperial Zathorian Dynasty, the Galactic Federation of Mercantile States, and—"

"Hey, uh, Kal, does he ever breathe?" Taran muttered out of the corner of his mouth, glancing at the alien with a mix of curiosity and concern.

"Apparently not," Ka-Lorrin hissed back, his grip tightening on the requisition orders.

"—the Tri-Council of Hevaron Prime. For inquiries regarding new accounts or upgrades to existing packages, please consult our onboarding department during regular business hours. Now, how may I assist you today?"

The abrupt end of the speech left an almost tangible void in the air. Ka-Lorrin blinked, momentarily stunned by the torrent of information.

"We're not here to open an account," he said sharply, stepping forward and extending the requisition orders. "We are here on official Space Fleet business to retrieve a data pod belonging to Kiran and Lenore Starling.

I have the proper authorization from the Office of the Commander and Chief."

The alien's beady eyes darted to the document Ka-Lorrin held, then back up to his face. Without a word, he reached out with one spindly hand, took the data pad, and examined it briefly.

"Please hold," he said flatly, as if addressing a disembodied voice on a call. Then, with complete indifference, he picked up a glossy magazine from his desk. The cover displayed a sleek, angular speeder in shimmering black, with alien text Ka-Lorrin and Taran couldn't read. The little alien flipped the pages leisurely, pausing occasionally to examine an image of yet another luxury vehicle.

Ka-Lorrin bristled, his fingers twitching as though itching to snatch the requisition orders back. "Excuse me," he said after a few moments, his tone edged with irritation. "This is an urgent matter."

The alien didn't look up. "Thank you for your patience. Please continue to hold. We will be with you as soon as one of our representatives becomes available."

Taran tilted his head, his ears twitching in confusion. "Uh, we're right here, ya know, we're right here," he said, gesturing between himself and Ka-Lorrin.

The alien ignored him, flipping another page.

Ka-Lorrin's eye twitched, and for the first time in a long while, Taran thought his friend might actually snap. "Kal, deep breaths," he said quietly. "Ya don't wanna scare the little fella. He's just... uh... doin' his job?"

Ka-Lorrin muttered something under his breath—unclear but distinctly unkind—and folded his arms across his chest. "This," he hissed, "is intolerable."

Taran leaned on the desk, lowering himself to the alien's eye level. "So... you like speeders, huh?" he asked, nodding toward the magazine.

The alien glanced up briefly, blinked once, and then looked back down without replying.

Ka-Lorrin threw his hands in the air. "Unbelievable."

• • • •

In the ancient forests of Korolith III, where the undergrowth was thick and impenetrable, and the canopy stretched so high it seemed to touch the skies, the Ka developed a unique ability to locate their Raath companions. Separated by miles of dense thicket and obscured by the omnipresent mist that clung to the jungle floor, they evolved what they called the Raath Summon. To call it a "very loud sound" would be akin to describing a volcanic eruption as "a bit of a rumble."

The Raath Summon was a ground-shaking bellow, a thunderous mix of a roar and a screech that could strip leaves from branches and send entire flocks of avian creatures—ranging from tiny birds to the great winged pteranodons of Korolith—scattering in every direction. It reverberated through the dense vegetation, shaking the trees and echoing for miles. No creature of Korolith III, no matter how fearsome or indifferent, dared to ignore it.

Taran saw the telltale look in Ka-Lorrin's eyes. It was a combination of utter determination and a touch of dramatic flair, and it sent a bolt of alarm straight through him. His ears twitched, his tail stiffened, and his large paws instinctively rose to cover his ears, his palms forming a tight seal over the fur-lined canals. "Oh no, no ya don't, Kal, no ya don't," Taran muttered, bracing himself.

Ka-Lorrin's diminutive form seemed to contract momentarily, his shoulders hunching inward as if pulling energy from some deep reserve. Then, with a suddenness that defied expectation, he sprang to his full height, his body straight as a spear, and opened his mouth.

The sound that erupted from him could not truly be described by language. It was a force of nature, a wave of pure auditory destruction that defied all attempts at categorization. The Vault Center lobby seemed to tremble under the onslaught. Papers lifted from the desk in a chaotic flurry, and the walls themselves seemed to vibrate in protest. Somewhere in the back of the facility, a door creaked open and slammed shut as if in startled response.

The small, pruney alien behind the desk froze. His eyes went impossibly wide, bulging as though trying to escape his head. His long, spindly fingers gripped the edge of the desk for dear life, his scratchy suit rustling in the wake of the reverberations.

And then, silence.

Taran cautiously lowered his hands, his ears twitching as he dared to peek at the aftermath. The lobby seemed eerily still, the air heavy with the residue of the bellow.

The alien blinked slowly, his wide eyes shrinking back to their usual size. His face, previously a tableau of shock, reset itself to its usual blank expression. He straightened his tie and cleared his throat.

"Thank you for holding," he said in the same fast, emotionless monotone as before. "My name is Morty. How can I help you?"

Taran stared, his jaw slack. Ka-Lorrin, by contrast, smoothed his jacket and replied with a level voice, as though nothing unusual had occurred, "We're here to retrieve a storage pod."

Morty stared at the requisition order displayed on the data pad, his face now utterly blank. "This will take two to three business days to process," he said in a flat, almost robotic tone, as if reciting from a script. Without looking up, he handed the data pad back.

Ka-Lorrin's jaw tightened. "Two to three days? That's absurd. We need the item today."

Morty blinked slowly, his voice unchanged. "If you'd like to expedite the process, there's a rush form you can fill out. Exceptions can be made under specific circumstances."

"Fine," Ka-Lorrin said, exasperation creeping into his voice. "Give me the form."

Morty stared blankly at Ka-Lorrin for a moment, as if buffering, before swiveling his chair to face the towering stack of mismatched cabinets behind him. Without a word, he opened the top drawer of the nearest cabinet, rummaging through a chaotic mess of loose papers, outdated brochures, and what looked like a half-eaten sandwich wrapped in foil. Taran's ears twitched at the faint crinkle of the foil, his nose wrinkling slightly.

"Is he... looking for the form?" Taran whispered, leaning down toward Ka-Lorrin.

"Obviously," Ka-Lorrin muttered, clutching the requisition orders tighter. "Just give him a moment."

Morty slammed the first drawer shut and moved to the next cabinet, opening three drawers in quick succession. Each produced an increasingly chaotic flurry of debris—bundles of mismatched files, a stray sock, and even what appeared to be an ancient potted plant, its leaves browned and curling. With the same robotic calm, he set the plant aside and continued his search.

Ka-Lorrin's fingers drummed against the data pad, his patience thinning with each drawer Morty explored. Taran, on the other hand, seemed mesmerized by the unfolding spectacle, tilting his head as Morty opened a slim folder, examined it briefly, and then filed it away in a completely different drawer.

At last, Morty reached the smallest cabinet, located on the floor beneath his desk. He sank down, his wiry limbs folding awkwardly as he fumbled with the latch. The drawer creaked open, and he withdrew a single sheet of paper, holding it aloft like it was a sacred artifact.

"Here," Morty said, placing the form on the desk with great ceremony. The paper was pristine, its edges sharp, its surface gleaming with a faint watermark that read *Official Documentation – VCTAA* in elegant script.

Ka-Lorrin straightened, his eyes narrowing. "Finally." He examined the tiny boxes and fields on the form, its print head-acheingly small.

Morty blinked at him. "Efficiency is the cornerstone of our service," he said without a hint of irony. He slid a pen across the desk. "Please print clearly."

Ka-Lorrin glanced at Taran, who had managed to contain his chuckle to a low rumble. "Right," Ka-Lorrin muttered, sitting down to begin the arduous task.

He filled out the form with meticulous precision, his handwriting small and perfect, every word placed just so. Taran peeked over his shoulder until Ka-Lorrin shot him a sharp glare.

Once completed, he handed the form back to Morty, who examined it with the same methodical slowness. After a long pause, he nodded. "This exception form requires the signature of a senior station official. You'll need to have it signed and return it to me."

Ka-Lorrin's face twitched. "We don't have time for that!"

Morty nodded again, his tone unchanging. "There is an alternative. I can provide you with a waiver that overrides the signature requirement."

Ka-Lorrin breathed a sigh of relief. "Yes, do that."

Morty retrieved yet another form, this time from a towering stack of yellow half-sheets. With deliberate precision, he hefted a rubber stamp that seemed comically oversized for his small frame, yet he wielded it with surprising ease. The loud *thwack* of the stamp echoed through the room, a sound imbued with the gravity Morty clearly believed the moment deserved. He followed up with an impressively ornate signature, executed using a glowing fountain pen that shimmered with an otherworldly elegance, before stapling the new form to the original exception request. Nodding solemnly, he surveyed his handiwork with an air of bureaucratic finality.

"There," Morty said. "The waiver has been processed."

Ka-Lorrin reached for the stapled forms, but Morty snatched them away and deposited them into a large bin behind the desk. Ka-Lorrin frowned. "What are you doing?"

"Submitting the exception form," Morty replied as if it were the most obvious thing in the world.

"How long will *that* take to process?" Ka-Lorrin asked warily.

Morty tapped the side of the bin. "Oh no worries, it only takes between six and eight weeks once the courier picks it up."

Ka-Lorrin blinked. "Six weeks?"

Morty tilted his head. "Yes. Is that a problem?"

Ka-Lorrin's voice rose. "The exception takes *longer* than the standard request?"

Morty's expression remained neutral. "Huh. I never considered that."

Taran, who had been remarkably patient up until this point, ran a paw down his face. "Even I'm gettin' frustrated, I am, I am."

Morty's blank gaze shifted to Taran. "You think *you're* frustrated? I have to work here every day."

Ka-Lorrin slammed his hands on the desk, his patience finally evaporating. "I want to speak to your supervisor!"

Morty froze, blinking up at him with wide, unblinking eyes. Without a word, the small alien turned and began rifling through one of the many drawers behind the counter. Papers rustled, filing cabinets squeaked, and a metal box slammed shut with a hollow clang.

Ka-Lorrin exchanged a glance with Taran. "Are you... looking for something?"

Morty didn't respond, his small hands now shuffling through a stack of forms on a shelf. He moved with unnerving precision, methodically inspecting each document before casting it aside in his search.

"Morty?" Ka-Lorrin pressed, his voice sharp with irritation.

Still no answer. The little alien muttered something inaudible under his breath as he opened yet another cabinet, peered inside, and shut it with a decisive bang.

Finally, with a triumphant noise that sounded vaguely like "Aha!", Morty turned around and placed a pristine, pink sheet of paper onto the counter. It was printed on high-quality stock and adorned with an ornate, almost holographic watermark of the VCTAA's logo.

Taran raised an eyebrow. "Let me guess..."

"This," Morty interrupted, his tone businesslike, "is the form you requested." He slid it toward Ka-Lorrin with a flourish.

Ka-Lorrin's jaw clenched as he picked up the sheet and read the bold text across the top: Form 4722 - VCTAA Official Request to Speak to a Manager.

Taran's ears twitched as he leaned over to get a better look. "Fancy paper, I'll give ya that. Musta cost a fortune to print."

Ka-Lorrin's hands trembled with suppressed rage. For a moment, he stared at the form, his mouth a tight, thin line. Then, with deliberate precision, he began to crumple the paper into a ball.

What happened next defied description. It was as though each crease and fold in the paper sent shockwaves directly into Morty's very being. His small, wrinkled frame seemed to convulse with every audible crunch of the fibers, and he began to wail, "No, no, no, no!" The sound rose in pitch, gaining urgency as the paper compacted into a tighter and tighter sphere.

Taran's eyes widened, his concern mounting as he watched his companion wind back his pitching arm. "Kal, maybe—" But it was too late.

With a decisive swing, Ka-Lorrin launched the paper ball with precision. It struck Morty squarely in the chest with what seemed to be an unnaturally loud thwack, as if the very laws of physics had momentarily exaggerated the impact. Morty staggered backward, clutching at his chest as though mortally wounded, his wide eyes filled with indignation.

"BANNED!" Morty screeched, his voice hitting an otherworldly register. "You are BANNED! Never to return! GET OUT!"

He scrambled to retrieve the crumpled form, smoothing it out with trembling hands as though trying to restore its dignity. His entire body shook with righteous fury, the crumpled paper held aloft like a flag of war.

Ka-Lorrin blinked, his mouth opening and closing like a fish out of water. "What?"

"BANNED!" Morty repeated with even more fervor, waving the mangled form for emphasis. "From this facility! Never to return! Now GET OUT before I call security!"

Ka-Lorrin started to retort, his finger rising in defiance, but Taran gently but firmly placed a paw on his shoulder, steering him toward the exit. "C'mon, Kal. Ain't worth it, it ain't, it ain't."

"But—" Ka-Lorrin began, only to be interrupted by Morty's escalating tirade.

"BANNED!" Morty shouted again, now hopping up and down, the motion jostling his too-large suit. "OUT! OUT!"

Ka-Lorrin's lips pressed into a tight line as Taran tugged him closer to the door. "Kal, we're just makin' it worse, we are. Let's go, let's go," Taran urged, his voice low but firm.

The door slammed behind them with a metallic clang, Morty's muffled voice still echoing faintly from the other side, something about regulations and banned individuals.

The ride back to the docking bays was eerily quiet. The transport pod, now nearly empty, swayed gently as it moved along the track. Ka-Lorrin sat stiffly, arms crossed, staring straight ahead. The data pad with the requisition orders, once his prized possession, now rested unceremoniously in his lap.

Taran sat beside him, sneaking glances at his friend with growing unease. He opened his mouth several times as if to say something, but each time he closed it again, the silence stretching on. The only sounds were the soft chime of station announcements and the clunk of the transport doors at each stop.

Finally, as the docking bays came into view, Taran cleared his throat. "What're we gonna do now, Kal?"

Ka-Lorrin turned to him, his eyes sharp, his resolve fully restored. "Don't fret, my friend," he said, his tone steady and confident. "I have a plan."

• • • •

Ka-Lorrin crouched in the narrow maintenance shaft, his lithe frame just barely fitting between the tangle of conduits and glowing energy lines. Sweat beaded on his forehead as he adjusted his comm link. The air was thick with the metallic tang of recycled oxygen, and every sound—the hum of the station, the soft creak of the panels—seemed amplified in the confined space.

"This is going precisely as planned," Ka-Lorrin whispered, though the quaver in his voice betrayed him.

"Planned?" Taran's voice crackled in his ear, heavy with disbelief. "This ain't a plan, Kal. It's a disaster waitin' to happen, it is."

Ka-Lorrin ignored the jab, focusing on the glowing map displayed on his data pad. His mind briefly flickered back to the planning stage—hours hunched over schematics he'd procured using his Fleet clearances, meticulously marking weak points, crafting contingencies. He had outlined everything down to the second, dubbing it "The Victa Heist" with a flourish that Taran had immediately dismissed as unnecessary.

"Kal, it's a bad idea, a bad idea," Taran had said then, leaning against the table, his large arms crossed. "This place literally advertises that it can't be broken into. What part o' that don't ya get?"

Ka-Lorrin had waved him off, his voice laced with the overconfidence of someone who had solved one too many puzzles in his life. "If they think it's impossible, they won't expect anyone to try. That's where we have the advantage."

Taran had considered going straight to Captain Calan. The thought had lingered as Ka-Lorrin went on about bypass codes, restricted zones, and security protocols. But then he'd noticed the gleam in his friend's eyes, the sheer determination that bordered on obsession. This wasn't just about the data pod anymore; it was personal. The VCTAA, and specifically Morty, had challenged Ka-Lorrin's competence, his pride—and that was something no Raath-Ka could let slide.

With a resigned sigh, Taran had finally muttered, "Just don't get us both thrown in the brig, Kal. I mean it, I mean it."

Ka-Lorrin eased through the narrow maintenance shaft, his sharp eyes scanning for the next obstacle. His data pad displayed a live map of the facility's schematics, and a bright red marker blinked on the screen, indicating his first hurdle.

"Taran," he whispered into the comm link, "I'm approaching the magnetic lock. Prepare to be amazed."

Taran's skeptical voice crackled in his ear. "You just make sure ya don't get zapped, Kal. I got no idea what to tell the captain if ya end up fried like a crispy critter."

Ignoring the warning, Ka-Lorrin crouched in front of the lock, a sleek, circular device embedded into the corridor wall. Pulsing with a faint blue glow, it radiated an energy field strong enough to dissuade any ordinary intruder.

But Ka-Lorrin was no ordinary intruder.

He pulled a small tool from his belt—a modified resonator he'd crafted during one of his many late-night engineering experiments. With a flick of a switch, the device emitted a soft hum, and Ka-Lorrin placed it carefully against the lock's surface.

"This," he murmured with a hint of pride, "is where preparation meets genius."

The resonator vibrated gently, syncing with the magnetic pulses of the lock. Ka-Lorrin's hands moved deftly, adjusting the settings with practiced precision. The blue glow began to flicker, and after a tense moment, the lock released with a soft click.

"There," he said, allowing himself a small smile. "One obstacle down."

"Nice work," Taran said grudgingly. "Still think this is a bad idea, but that was pretty slick, it was."

Ka-Lorrin pressed forward, his confidence bolstered by the success. The map on his data pad updated as he approached the next challenge: a lightning field that crackled menacingly across the corridor ahead. Arcs of electricity danced between emitters mounted on either side, filling the air with the sharp tang of static.

"Taran," Ka-Lorrin said, his tone a mix of excitement and trepidation. "I've reached the lightning field."

"I don't like the sound o' that, Kal. Lightning and you ain't a good mix."

Ka-Lorrin smirked. "Don't worry, I'm ready." From his bag, he pulled out a set of insulated gloves and a small device resembling a tuning fork. "This is what I always try to tell you, Taran—planning is everything." You could almost hear Taran rolling his eyes over the comm link.

Crouching low, Ka-Lorrin slid the fork-like device into the base of the emitter, carefully aligning its prongs with the electrical pulses. Sparks crackled as the field intensified, but he held steady, his gloved hands unflinching.

"I wish you could see this," he said, his grin widening as the device emitted a low hum. The lightning field flickered, its arcs sputtering before finally vanishing with a faint crackle.

Ka-Lorrin straightened and dusted off his hands, his expression smug. "And that," he declared, "is how you neutralize a lightning field."

"Don't get cocky," Taran replied over the comm, his tone dry. "Every time ya start braggin', trouble ain't far behind."

Ka-Lorrin chuckled, moving further down the corridor. His map now indicated a third obstacle: a pressure-sensitive floor grid. Rows of faintly glowing tiles stretched out before him, each one rigged to trigger an alarm if even the slightest weight was detected.

He stopped short, his eyes narrowing as he studied the grid. "Taran, this one's tricky. But I've accounted for it."

"I hope you're right," Taran was closing his eyes trying not to panic.

Ka-Lorrin pulled a lightweight grappling device from his bag, attaching its hook to a beam above the grid. With a graceful leap, he swung across, his feet never touching the ground. He landed lightly on the other side, turning to admire his handiwork.

Ka-Lorrin brushed off his coat with exaggerated nonchalance. "Still doubting me?" he asked, casting a smug glance at nothing in particular.

"Every second," Taran replied, though there was a grudging note of admiration in his tone. "But ya made it, Kal. I'll give ya that."

Ka-Lorrin's smirk widened, but it faltered as a faint, unfamiliar hum reached his ears. It wasn't the steady thrumming of the station's systems—this sound was sharper, mechanical, and growing louder. He cocked his head. "Taran, do you hear that?"

"Uhh, Kal," Taran muttered over the comm. "I got a blip."

"A blip?" Ka-Lorrin repeated, his voice rising. "What do you mean, a blip?"

"A blip! A blip!" Taran shot back. "I'm pulling up the audio for the security system."

Before Ka-Lorrin could protest, a sharp, mechanical tone filled his earpiece, followed by an automated voice: "Unauthorized access detected. Security drones deployed."

Ka-Lorrin froze, the weight of those words hitting him like a bulkhead door slamming shut. "Taran," he whispered, his earlier bravado vanishing. "Deployed? Where?"

"Ohh dear," Taran groaned. "Didn't I tell ya not to celebrate?"

The sound of motors spinning to life drowned out Ka-Lorrin's reply. The hum intensified, becoming an ominous cacophony of mechanical whirrs and clicks echoing down the corridor.

Ka-Lorrin's instincts kicked in, his legs propelling him into a frantic sprint. The neatly mapped-out corridors on his schematics blurred into a confusing maze as he ran. Overhead alarms blared, their shrill cries mocking his earlier confidence.

"Turn left!" Taran yelled through the comm.

Ka-Lorrin veered into another hatchway, only to skid to a halt as he came face-to-face with a cluster of blinking red lights. Drones! He ducked back into the corridor, barely avoiding the sharp hiss of energy weapons slicing through the air.

"Not left! NOT LEFT!" Ka-Lorrin shouted into the comm. He barreled around a few corners, tripping more alarms as he went, his heart pounding. "I'm lost!" he cried.

"Calm down, calm down," Taran urged, his voice steady. "You need to head East."

"What part of 'I'm lost' don't you understand?" Ka-Lorrin snapped.

"Ya can't get lost, Kal! It's a straight shot!" Taran protested, though his voice carried a note of helplessness.

Ka-Lorrin glanced wildly around at the crisscrossing hatchways and identical corridors. "Straight shot? Oh, really? Tell that to the endless labyrinth of doom I'm currently trapped in!"

"Three turns, Kal. Ya took three turns."

"Well, maybe those three turns were my undoing!" Ka-Lorrin shot back, his voice cracking. He bolted into another corridor, his foot catching on an uneven panel, sending him sprawling into a heap. "This station is actively trying to kill me!" he muttered, scrambling back to his feet.

He darted through a narrow service duct, the cold metal scraping his coat as he slid to the other side. Behind him, the hum of the drones grew louder, their glowing eyes casting an eerie red light as they fanned out like a swarm of mechanical wasps.

"I'm doomed," Ka-Lorrin hissed into the comm, his breaths coming fast and shallow. "I am absolutely doomed."

"Not if I can help it," Taran replied, the sound of his heavy breathing evident over the link. "Just... hold tight. I'm heading to the main office. I'll shut 'em down."

Ka-Lorrin froze for a moment, his ears twitching at the sound of the drones drawing closer. "Hold tight? Hold tight where? There are no tight places to hold!"

"Kal, ya gotta find a place to hole up!" Taran urged. "Somethin' small and metal—preferably with a door that locks."

Ka-Lorrin grumbled something unintelligible, his sharp eyes scanning the area before he spotted a maintenance compartment. Without hesitation, he threw himself into it, slamming the panel shut just as the whir of a drone passed by outside.

His chest heaved as he tried to steady his breathing. "Taran, if I survive this, we're taking a vacation. Somewhere quiet. With no drones. Or hatchways."

From the comm came Taran's calm, steady reply. "That's the spirit, Kal."

• • • •

Taran barreled down the corridor toward the VCTAA's main office, his earlier misgivings replaced by a singular focus: fixing the mess they were in. His broad shoulders brushed against the narrow walls as he pushed forward, the sound of his hurried footsteps echoing in the dimly lit hall.

The familiar metal door loomed ahead, its battered surface appearing even more worn under the flickering light. Without hesitation, Taran reached for a tool from his belt, his large paws working with surprising finesse as he forced the lock open. The door groaned in protest before swinging inward.

The office looked exactly as they'd left it—disheveled and dimly lit, the faint glow of a single overhead light casting jagged shadows across the room. At the center of it all sat Morty, slumped in his chair. The little alien's shriveled figure was hunched over, his tiny head cradled in his hands. His usual rigid demeanor had collapsed into something unrecognizable—defeated and small.

Taran hesitated in the doorway, his ears twitching uncertainly. He hadn't expected Morty to still be there, much less looking so utterly miserable. "Morty?" Taran ventured, his deep voice softening.

The little alien groaned but didn't lift his head. "What do you want now?" he mumbled, his sharp tone dulled to a weary murmur.

Taran took a cautious step forward, his large shape casting a long shadow across the cluttered desk. "Umm... are ya okay?" he asked, his tone supremely gentle. "I'm, uh... a real good listener, if ya wanna talk."

For a moment, there was silence, broken only by the faint hum of the station. Then, unexpectedly, Morty began to sob.

· · · ·

Ka-Lorrin huddled in the cramped maintenance compartment, his ears twitching at the unmistakable sound of security drones closing in. Their metallic whirrs echoed around him, growing louder with each passing second. The faint sizzle of cutting tools scraping against the compartment's exterior was his first real sign of how truly out of options he was.

"They're cutting through," he muttered to himself, his voice trembling. "These guys are going to kill me. I am going to be obliterated by a swarm of glorified vacuum cleaners."

Frantically, he tapped at his comm unit. "Taran? Taran, come in!" Static crackled back at him. "Taran?" Nothing. Silence.

His heart sank. He couldn't just sit there waiting for the inevitable. Spotting the hatch below his feet, Ka-Lorrin gritted his teeth. "Well, it's this or become Swiss cheese."

With a grunt, he wrenched the hatch open and dropped into the dark void below. The fall wasn't far, but he landed hard on his rear, the jolt sending a sharp pang up his spine. "Ah! Great. Perfect. Just what I needed," he hissed, clutching at his back.

For a moment, everything was silent. The pitch-black space around him felt calm, the only sound his own labored breathing. He allowed himself a single, shaky sigh of relief.

Then, faintly at first, came the telltale hum of drones. His ears perked up as he saw the faint glow of their red lights appearing in the shaft to his left. Then to his right. Then ahead of him. Then behind.

"Oh dear," he whispered, spinning in place as the lights converged from all sides.

He closed his eyes, bracing for the inevitable, his mind racing through all the unflattering ways his demise would be described. *Ka-Lorrin, killed over an argument with a raisin.*' He winced.

But the expected onslaught never came.

Instead, a deafening silence descended over the corridor. Ka-Lorrin opened one eye, then the other, his head darting around as the red lights on the drones flickered and dimmed. The mechanical hums died out one by one, leaving nothing but stillness.

He blinked. "Am I dead?" He patted his chest, as if confirming his own existence. "No holes. Not vaporized. How?"

Before he could puzzle it out, an arrow illuminated on the wall beside him, pulsing softly. Then another appeared further down the corridor, pointing the way. Ka-Lorrin squinted, unsure if his brain was playing tricks on him, when Taran's voice crackled to life in his comm.

"Follow the arrows, Kal," Taran said, his tone calm but firm. "I've got ya."

Ka-Lorrin didn't need to be told twice. His legs felt like jelly, but he forced himself forward, moving from one glowing arrow to the next. The corridor stretched on endlessly, the path winding and disorienting. His nerves remained taut, his ears twitching at every faint creak of the station.

Finally, a door loomed ahead. It was larger than the others, its surface gleaming faintly under the flickering lights. As Ka-Lorrin approached, it swung open with a sharp crack, the sound making him jump.

Blinking against the sudden brightness, he stepped inside and froze.

There, standing in the center of the lobby, were Taran and Morty. Taran had his paws folded in front of him, his expression a mix of exhaustion and quiet triumph. Morty, for his part, looked as unperturbed as ever, tapping away at his console with his usual mechanical precision.

Ka-Lorrin stared at them, his mouth agape. He couldn't speak.

Taran grinned. "Told ya I had ya, Kal."

Morty looked up from his console as Ka-Lorrin stepped cautiously into the lobby, his face still marked by the wide-eyed disbelief of someone who had just narrowly avoided being vaporized. Taran gave Ka-Lorrin a warm, reassuring smile, but before he could speak, Morty broke the silence.

"I owe you an apology," Morty said, his gravelly voice uncharacteristically soft.

Ka-Lorrin blinked, momentarily dumbstruck. An apology? From Morty? His jaw worked silently as his mind tried to process the words.

Morty continued, his tone calm and sincere, as if the events of the past hour hadn't happened. "Earlier, I wasn't at my best. You see, your companion here—" he gestured to Taran, whose ears perked at the mention, "—is a remarkably kind soul. A good listener. A rare thing in this galaxy."

Ka-Lorrin glanced at Taran, who gave a small, self-conscious shrug, his fur rippling slightly. Morty's expression shifted, and for the first time, his perpetually indifferent demeanor cracked, revealing a faint trace of sadness.

"My pet bush-beetle, Suki, passed away two days ago. She'd been with me for eighty years, since I was just a youngling of one hundred and ten. She was my companion, my confidant." Morty's small hands clasped tightly on the desk as he took a steadying breath. "Losing her... well, it's been difficult."

Ka-Lorrin didn't know what to say. He'd been prepared for a lecture or perhaps a flogging, but not this.

"Taran reminded me," Morty continued, his voice steady but quiet, "to focus on the good memories. To savor life, even when it feels heavy. He said there's meaning in all things." Morty's small eyes turned to Taran with genuine warmth. "He's right, you know."

Ka-Lorrin's gaze shifted to Taran, who beamed, his tail giving a small wag of pride. Despite the chaos and absurdity of the day, Ka-Lorrin couldn't help but smile back at his companion, though he remained speechless.

Morty stood, retrieving a small metallic object from behind the desk. He held it out to Ka-Lorrin. "Oh, this is for you."

It was the data pod.

"I hope you two find what you're looking for," Morty said.

Ka-Lorrin stared at the pod for a moment before reaching out with trembling hands to accept it. He gave a slight nod of thanks but still couldn't form any words.

Taran stepped forward with a bright smile. "Now don't forget to call me, Morty," he said. "We'll set up a time to visit the Star Base Zoo. I hear they've got a fantastic exhibit of wild bush-beetles." He turned to Ka-Lorrin, adding, "They're cat-like furry insects from Morty's home planet, Zelch."

"I won't forget," Morty said, his lips twitching into a small smile. "I'll look forward to telling you all about them."

Ka-Lorrin didn't speak another word as they ascended the ladder and made their way through the winding corridors back toward the transit platform. The entire journey passed in a blur, his mind still trying to reconcile the events that had unfolded.

When they reached the platform and boarded the transport pod, Taran finally broke the silence. "I knew it would all work out," he said with a grin, giving Ka-Lorrin a hearty pat on the back.

"Hehhh," was all Ka-Lorrin could manage.

. . . .

The next day, the Salamander's briefing room hummed softly with the ambient sounds of the ship. Captain Calan leaned back in his chair, his hands loosely clasped as he regarded the Raath-Ka seated before him. Ka-Lorrin's posture was stiff, his expression guarded, while Taran leaned on the edge of the table, his casual demeanor a stark contrast to his companion's.

"So," Calan began, a hint of puzzlement tugging at the corner of his mouth, "tell me again how the Zelchian plays into this? Morty, was it?"

Ka-Lorrin's composure faltered ever so slightly. "We don't need to talk about Morty."

"Yeah, Morty ain't important. Best leave that one alone," Taran added quickly, scratching the back of his head with one paw.

Calan raised a brow but didn't press the issue. "Alright. What did you find out from the data pod?"

Ka-Lorrin cleared his throat, sitting a little straighter. "Two things, Captain. The first was... scientific information we definitely didn't expect to find."

Taran leaned forward, his ears twitching with excitement. "Top secret stuff, Cap'n. Turns out it's from a project worked on by the Zephtari and the Varrothi. That's a real head-scratcher, it is, it is."

Calan rubbed his chin thoughtfully. "I heard about the Zephtari and the Varrothi working together on a project, but the details are classified. What did you learn?"

Ka-Lorrin took a deep breath. "They were researching an experimental type of energy they called Rencor Waves. Highly volatile, and more disturbingly... they can be weaponized."

"Weaponized how?" Calan asked, his tone sharpening.

"They can mimic the energy signature of virtually any known weapon," Ka-Lorrin replied, his voice grave. "If weaponized, Rencor Waves could leave no traceable signature. Any attack could be pinned on another party. It's a technology that could destabilize the entire quadrant if it fell into the wrong hands."

Calan's brow furrowed. "That's... disturbing, to say the least. And what was the second piece of data?"

The Raath-Ka exchanged a glance. For a moment, Ka-Lorrin's confident demeanor softened, and Taran's usual joviality gave way to a quiet solemnity.

"It was... a personal letter," Ka-Lorrin said.

* * * *

The lights in Lily's quarters dimmed as she sat cross-legged on her bed, her console glowing faintly before her. With a trembling hand, she activated the file the Raath-Ka had delivered. A holographic image flickered to life—a man and a woman, their faces worn but kind.

She recognized them only from their files. No matter how hard she tried, her mind held no memories of her parents.

The woman, her hair and eyes identical to Lily's, spoke first, her voice steady but tinged with sorrow. "Lily, if you're watching this... it means we didn't make it. We're sorry."

The man took over, his tone firmer but equally laden with emotion. "The Krythar are hunting us. That's why we disappeared. If you've found this, it means they must have succeeded."

The woman's expression softened. "You'll hear things about us. That we created you to be a weapon against the Krythar. And while we gave you gifts—special abilities—we want you to know you're so much more than that."

The man nodded, his shoulders heavy with regret. "Your destiny is your own, Lily. Whatever choice you make—whether to fight or not—it's your choice. But if you do, don't do it alone."

The woman leaned closer in the projection, as if trying to bridge the vast distance of time and space. "You have a loving heart, Lily. Rely on those who see you for who you truly are. Let them give you strength, especially when the road ahead feels impossible."

Tears streamed silently down Lily's face as the man's voice softened. "We love you, Lily. We're so proud of you."

The woman smiled faintly. "Goodbye, my sweet girl."

The holograms faded, leaving only the soft hum of the console.

Lily wiped her cheeks, her heart aching. "I wish... I could remember you," she whispered. But even as the sadness lingered, a faint spark of hope flickered within her.

She lay back on her bed, staring at the ceiling. Her thoughts turned to Ka-Lorrin and Taran. Their loyalty, their bond, their determination to help her even when it wasn't their fight. They'd shown her something she hadn't dared believe in—a connection that was real.

As the ship's gentle hum filled the silence, she let herself smile, a quiet gratitude washing over her.

Thanks to them, Lily didn't feel quite so alone anymore.

Chapter 7: The Shadow of Betrayal

A HOLOGRAPHIC BANNER scrolled across the top of the news feed in bold red letters: BREAKING: VARROTHI DELEGATE MURDERED DURING PEACE TALKS.

The broadcast transitioned to a dimly lit studio where a somber figure sat behind a sleek, metallic desk. The anchor, a being of strikingly alien appearance, projected a quiet gravitas that matched the weight of the moment. His green, seaweed-sheened skin shimmered faintly under the studio lights, pulsing veins just visible beneath the surface. A lattice of tentacles framed his face, twitching slightly as he spoke, their movements almost hypnotic.

"Good morning, viewers," the anchor began, his voice steady and rich, carrying the air of practiced authority. "I am Mren Volthrask, and you're watching Galactic Current, your trusted source for interstellar news."

His multiple limbs moved with fluid efficiency—papers in one hand, a glowing data pad in another, a control wand in a third. Dark, intricately wrapped robes and an elaborately tied cravat lent him an air of somber authority.

"We begin today's coverage with shocking news from Star Base 12." His small, polished-stone eyes fixed on the camera. "Delegate L'than Veirr, the lead Varrothi negotiator for the fragile peace talks, was found dead in his quarters late last night." He paused before adding, "The murder weapon—a Krythar static field generator—delivers lethal precision even through multiple walls."

A graphic of the device materialized, spinning slowly. "This weapon is more than a tool—it is a statement. Its use is forbidden under interstellar accords, yet whispers of its existence have haunted the edges of Krythar technology for years. That it has appeared here, now, raises profound concerns."

The hologram shifted to a map of Star Base 12 and nearby New Cordova, red markers blinking ominously. "In the wake of this tragedy, station security, Union enforcement, and planetary officials have launched a joint operation. The suspect is believed to have fled to New Cordova, now under lockdown. Authorities insist capture is imminent, though the suspect's identity remains undisclosed."

The map dissolved into a live feed of New Cordova's empty streets, checkpoints glowing at intersections, Union patrol ships hovering overhead. "As New Cordova tightens its grip, the galaxy watches with bated breath," Mren intoned. "Will this bring answers—or only deepen the questions?"

The screen split, revealing the anchor now joined by a silver-haired commentator with razor-sharp features and a glint of mischief in his eyes. A glowing caption read: Tyrell Grover, Host of Galactic Truth Hour.

"Joining us now is Tyrell Grover," Mren said. "Tyrell, your take on this shocking development?"

Grover clasped his hands, his voice dripping with practiced concern. "Mren, this raises a lot of questions, and none of them look good for the Krythar. But here's where it gets interesting."

Lily sat cross-legged on her bed, face lit by the feed. She reached for her tea but kept her eyes on the screen.

"First, Prince Zayir," Grover continued. "Polished, charming, all the right lines rehearsed—but barely out of his teens. Leaders that green make rash choices. Is it so hard to believe this was a Krythar power play he couldn't handle—or didn't want to?"

Lily scowled, grabbing a stress ball and lobbing it at the control panel to pause the feed. "Ridiculous," she muttered—yet after a beat, she sighed and hit play again.

Grover leaned closer, lowering his voice as though unveiling a scandal. "Then there's Captain Dalren. Decorated, respected, sure. But what about the whispers of his early career? Rogue missions, coverups polished so clean they gleamed. Could this murder be one of those shadows returning to haunt him?"

Lily tilted her head. *What rumors?*

"And finally," Grover said, his voice dropping into a near-whisper, "Premier Athrex Varn. His disdain for the Krythar is legendary. He's dismissed the peace talks from the start. Is it so unthinkable he staged this as a message—to force the galaxy's hand?"

The anchor's tentacles shifted subtly. "Those are certainly... thought-provoking ideas. Of course, we draw no conclusions here—"

Grover cut in smoothly. "No conclusions, Mren. Just pointing out the truth may not be what the Union spoon-feeds us."

Lily shut the feed off with a sharp jab. The screen went black, the whine of silence pressing in around her. Grover's theories were garbage—carefully crafted, sensationalized nonsense.

But as she sat there, one thought refused to let go: Prince Zayir would need an alibi.

And she had one.

• • • •

The energy aboard the *Salamander* had shifted overnight. The easygoing camaraderie Lily had grown accustomed to had given way to something far more disciplined, a kind of military precision she hadn't yet seen from the crew. Officers moved briskly through the corridors, their voices clipped as they relayed orders or consulted their data pads. Even the usually genial engineering team now wore expressions of grim focus. There was no laughter or idle chatter—only the white noise of the ship's systems and the determined footsteps of a crew that had fully shifted into crisis mode.

Lily stepped aside as a pair of security officers marched past, their postures straight and their gazes unyielding. She wasn't used to this version of the crew, but she couldn't deny the effectiveness of it. It was as if the murder had flipped a switch, and every member of the *Salamander*'s crew now moved with a singular purpose.

Her thoughts turned to the task at hand as she made her way to the captain's stateroom. She had tried to contact Prince Zayir directly to confirm his alibi but had only been met with a messaging system—a clear indication that the Ishrethi comms network was currently overwhelmed or intentionally throttled. Given the chaos of the situation, it wasn't surprising, but it left her feeling uneasy. The prince needed someone to vouch for him, and she was the only one who could do it.

When she reached the stateroom, she was greeted by Dryst Amaris, who stood just outside the door, his usual easygoing smile lighting up his face. "Lily!" he said warmly, his tone as bright as his expression. "The captain mentioned you might stop by. He said you can go straight in." His warmth was almost tangible, a small comfort in the tension that gripped the ship.

"Thanks," Lily said, taking a steadying breath before entering.

The door slid open with a soft hiss, revealing Captain Calan seated at his desk, flanked by Datch. The captain's expression was as serious as she'd ever seen it. He was leaning forward slightly, his hands folded on the desk, his tone calm but firm.

"Datch, this is on you to get right," Calan said, his voice low and weighted with importance. "This whole situation has turned into a galactic embarrassment for the Union. This man was killed on our watch. Command believes there's a strong chance this was an internal Krythar matter—that they killed their own Varrothi delegate—but it's up to us to reach our own conclusion. We're to avoid speculation and focus on the evidence. Any misstep could escalate into an intergalactic incident."

Datch nodded solemnly. "Understood, Captain."

Calan leaned back slightly, catching sight of Lily standing just inside the door. His sharp eyes softened briefly. "Lily. Come in. Perfect timing."

Datch turned to glance at her, his usual serene look, though his eyes seemed slightly more focused. Lily stepped forward, clasping her hands in front of her.

"I have some information," she said.

Calan's gaze sharpened. "Yes?"

Lily paused, gathering her thoughts. "Prince Zayir was with me last night."

"The captain's expression faltered, and he cleared his throat. 'Umm... all night?'"

Lily's face flushed as she realized the misunderstanding. "NO, Captain. The prince was at movie night with me and Datch," she explained quickly. "He left around 11."

Datch nodded in confirmation. "I've already informed the authorities of the prince's alibi. The murder took place at 22:30, so he was with us well before and shortly after the incident."

Calan exhaled, a flicker of relief crossing his features. "Good. Of course, someone like a prince wouldn't likely carry out such an act in person. Still, having a clear alibi should help keep his name out of the headlines."

Lily nodded, feeling a small weight lift from her shoulders. Datch's eyes stayed on her for a moment before turning to the captain.

"Anything else before I begin?" Datch asked.

"Just keep me updated," Calan replied. "Dismissed."

Lily fell into step beside Datch as they left the stateroom. He walked in calm silence for a few paces, thoughtful in that way of his, before finally speaking.

"I appreciate your willingness to offer your insights," he said, his tone measured but tinged with camaraderie. "Though, sticking your neck out for others is something I've come to expect from you."

Lily paused mid-step, glancing at him. "I—well, thanks. I didn't think it was much, to be honest."

"On the contrary," Datch replied, tilting his head slightly, his steps unbroken. "Your willingness to contribute, even without knowing how it might be received, is notable. It reflects an instinct to act when others might hesitate."

Lily's brow furrowed faintly. "Hopefully that's a good thing," she said, a soft laugh escaping her to ease the moment.

"It is," Datch said without hesitation. "This investigation will require more than logic and procedure. There are elements of human interaction—emotions, intuitions—that are not my strengths. That is why I would like to ask for your assistance."

She blinked, her pace faltering for a moment. "Me? Really?"

Datch gave a small nod. "You have a perspective I do not. It may prove invaluable."

Lily felt a tug of empathy at his words. Datch wasn't just a tactical mind in a humanoid body; he was her friend, and his sincerity was unmistakable. "I'd be happy to help," she said. "Actually, I welcome the opportunity. I've been feeling a little helpless since finding out about the murder—plus learning about what my parents were working on..." She hesitated, the weight of her thoughts catching up to her. "It's a lot. Helping you feels like a step toward making a difference."

Datch inclined his head in acknowledgment, his version of a smile. "Then we'll work well together. But I need to ask for your discretion."

"Discretion?" Lily echoed, her brow furrowing.

"The captain hasn't explicitly approved your involvement. In fact, the crew has been instructed to ensure you're not placed in unnecessary danger after... recent events. If you're assisting me, it may be best to keep it between us."

Lily mulled over this, then nodded. "I can do that. Besides, I'm technically on leave—what I choose to do with my rest time is up to me. And I'm choosing to help you."

"Thank you," Datch said, his tone warm and genuine. "Your insight will be invaluable."

Lily felt a small sense of pride at his words. "So, what's our first move?"

"First," Datch said, "we need to interview the prince and the other delegates. Even though the prince has an alibi, we can't overlook the possibility that he might have noticed something or have information that could help us. And we'll need to get the Zephtari and Urrathi delegates' statements as well."

Lily nodded thoughtfully. "I met both groups when I had dinner with the prince. Their cultures seemed... vastly different."

"An astute observation," Datch replied, his tone taking on the measured cadence of someone delivering a lecture. "The Zephtari and Urrathi represent two extremes in interstellar society. The Zephtari are a species known for their logical minds and telepathic abilities. Many of the Union's top scientists hail from their worlds. Their contributions to exploration and technological advancement are unparalleled, and their science station on the edge of Krythar space stands as a symbol of perseverance and intellectual achievement—even during this period of conflict."

Lily raised an eyebrow. "Telepathic scientists and symbols of achievement. They sound like the ideal Union members."

"They are, as a culture, methodical and introspective," Datch continued. "However, their telepathy doesn't exclude them from suspicion. While it might make deception among themselves difficult, it could also mean they are capable of executing plans with a precision others can't match."

Lily nodded slowly, letting that sink in. "And the Urrathi?"

"The Urrathi," Datch said, his tone shifting slightly, "are warriors, forged by centuries of conflict. They have been at war with the Krythar for longer than any species in the Union, aside from the Cyranthians. Their history is one of resistance and loss. Many of their border worlds were annexed by the Krythar for decades, and efforts to reclaim those territories have led to catastrophic losses."

"I see, did they ever get their territory back?" Lily asked, her voice tinged with concern.

"Some border worlds remain occupied to this day," Datch confirmed. "The Urrathi value strength and directness. A murder committed with subtlety and subterfuge is outside their cultural norm—but that doesn't necessarily exclude them as suspects, or as potentially being set up as a misdirection."

Lily considered his words, glancing out the window of the transit as the bustling streets of New Cordova came into view. "So, two cultures—one valuing logic, the other strength. Both have reasons to want peace... and reasons to sabotage it."

"Correct," Datch said. "Our task will be to discern which path—if any—leads us to the truth."

Lily frowned, considering his words. "So, we're looking for answers—but also for patterns, connections, anything that doesn't add up."

Datch nodded. "Exactly. We will head to the base and start with the prince."

As they made their way toward the docking bay, Lily couldn't help but feel a certain excitement, despite the seriousness of their situation. This wasn't just about solving a murder; it was about uncovering truths that could shape the course of peace—or war. And she wasn't about to sit on the sidelines.

• • • •

The transit vehicle glided smoothly through the tubes connecting the Salamander's docking bay to the Luxury Residence. Lily stared out at the sleek, curving architecture of the station's interior, her thoughts tangled.

She wasn't sure how to bring it up—wasn't even sure she should—but the more she considered it, the more her gut told her she had to.

"I need to tell you something," she said finally, breaking the silence.

Datch turned toward her, his expression calm as always, but there was a distinct curiosity in his eyes.

"It's about the static field generator," Lily said, her voice measured. "Some friends of mine, well not exactly friends..."

Datch's brow lifted slightly, a rare display of surprise. "Go on."

She exhaled deeply. "Two people—Rhyder Dayne and Ash Prynn. Rhyder's that guy I mentioned—the one I met in the market. He's a troublemaker, possibly a smuggler. Definitely a thief. At least sometimes," she admitted, picturing his infuriatingly cocky grin. "And Ash? They team up occasionally. I don't know much about him, but he has a knack for trouble too."

"What does this have to do with a static field generator?" Datch asked, his tone calm but focused.

Lily looked down, fingers fidgeting in her lap. "I helped them steal one... Well, I was there when they did it."

Datch's gaze didn't waver, but the weight of his attention pressed on her. "You stole a static field generator?"

"Not quite," she said quickly, shaking her head. "I mean, they dragged me into one of their schemes. They didn't tell me what they were really doing until it was too late. I saw them steal the generator, then they left me behind as a distraction. I assumed it was just a job. I had no idea... I didn't think it would be connected to something like this."

Datch nodded, concern on his face. "Why haven't you mentioned this until now?"

Lily hesitated. "What they did was against the law, but they stole from another smuggler. And what they did to me—leaving me behind like that—was a jerk move. But I don't believe they're killers. Rhyder is reckless, sure, but he's not someone who would take a life. And Ash... he's a little harder to pin down, but I just can't picture him doing something like that either. I know it's crazy, but it's just... a gut feeling."

Datch considered her words carefully before replying. "It's possible they weren't directly involved in the murder but were used to obtain the weapon. This could be an important lead."

"I don't want to tell the captain," Lily admitted, her voice quieter now. "Not yet. I don't want to drag their names into this if there's no reason to. But if they were working for someone else…"

"It's a possibility we have to explore," Datch agreed. "The authorities are pursuing a person of interest connected to the generator's theft. They haven't released a name yet."

Lily's stomach twisted uneasily. "Do you think it's one of them?"

"I don't know," Datch said evenly, his gaze steady. "But your information adds another thread to follow. It could make all the difference."

Lily leaned back in her seat, her gaze drifting to the transit's softly glowing ceiling. "I knew Rhyder was trouble, but I didn't think he'd get caught up in something like this."

"We all get into trouble now and then," Datch said, his tone firm but laced with understanding. "What matters is how we react. Speaking up now was the right choice. Let's see how the dots connect."

The transit vehicle slowed as it neared their destination, the city lights casting shifting patterns through the windows. Lily straightened in her seat, determination settling over her. As far as unraveling the mystery went, this was just the beginning.

The Luxury Residence, once a hub of hospitality, now felt like a fortress. The polished obsidian floors gleamed under dim chandeliers, but warmth had been replaced by tension. Guards stood at every doorway, their gazes sharp, while attendants whispered as though the galaxy's anxiety had seeped into the walls.

Lily and Datch were greeted by an Ishrethi attendant who moved with clipped precision, his navy and gold uniform impeccably tailored, every fold and seam sharp enough to cut. His dark eyes darted between them as if sizing them up, though his expression remained carefully blank. The tension in his jaw and the hurried cadence of his steps betrayed a man on edge, acutely aware of the weight of the moment. Without preamble, he gestured for them to follow and led them through a series of elaborately carved archways, their intricate designs lit by the soft amber glow of recessed lighting. The silence of the corridors was unnerving, broken only by the muted click of boots against polished obsidian floors.

The grand reception room they were led to was a testament to Ishrethi opulence. Towering stained-glass windows cast kaleidoscopic patterns across the floor, their hues muted by the somber atmosphere. The usual warmth of the space, with its flowing silk drapes and low tables arranged for diplomatic mingling, was conspicuously absent. Instead, the air carried a chill that wasn't physical but emotional—a palpable sense that the weight of the galaxy's gaze had transformed this once-hospitable haven into a gilded fortress.

"The prince isn't available," the attendant announced curtly, his words brisk and clipped. His slight bow was perfunctory, almost impatient, as though the act itself was too much of a delay in his duties. Before either Lily or Datch could respond, the sound of a door opening behind them froze him in place. The color seemed to drain slightly from his face, and he took a step back, retreating down the hall without another word, his movements now hurried, as if eager to be elsewhere.

Lily's heart quickened at the figure who stepped into the room. Queen Isharia entered with effortless grace, her gold-and-orange lehenga shimmering like a living flame. A delicate crown rested in her dark, coiled hair, catching the light like a constellation. She carried herself like someone who had never once hurried, every movement calculated, regal.

Despite her somber expression, a faint curve lingered at the corner of her lips—an echo of the smile she often wielded like a weapon, subtle and knowing, as though she could see every secret you tried to hide. Her dark eyes, lined with a hint of kohl, held Lily's gaze, warm on the surface yet unfathomably deep, like the black holes Lily had once seen on a science broadcast.

"Lily Starling," the queen said, her tone soft, velvety, but underpinned by a maternal authority that brooked no argument. Her voice filled the room effortlessly, commanding yet calm, as if she were the only person in the universe who could bring order to chaos. "What brings you here at such a delicate time?"

Lily's palms were slightly damp, and she clasped them behind her back, trying to maintain her composure. Her heart pounded as she stood in the queen's presence, feeling as though she were being examined under a microscope. The room felt heavier, not just because of the queen's commanding presence but because of the unshakable sense that, in this moment, Lily was a mere piece on a grand chessboard, and Isharia was already thinking three moves ahead.

"We came to speak with Prince Zayir," Lily replied, her voice steady. "We have questions we need to ask him as part of the investigation."

The queen's expression shifted, a flicker of something—disapproval?—crossing her face. "I'm afraid Zayir isn't in the best state to answer questions. This tragedy has affected him deeply. He... fears this failure will now define his legacy."

Her words were calm, almost kind, but there was a deliberate weight to them. "You must understand, Miss Starling. He has the memory of his father to uphold. A legacy of strength and leadership. This disaster... he believes he's let his people down."

Lily's jaw tightened, but she said nothing. The queen's gold-and-orange robes whispered faintly against the polished floor as she stepped closer, her delicate crown catching the light like a constellation frozen in time.

"The galaxy," the queen began, her tone slow and measured, as though weighing each word for significance, "is a tapestry of wars fought and empires risen. For every victory, a hundred defeats are buried beneath it, forgotten in the dust of history. Yet, those who endure—those who survive—become the keepers of the keys. They write the stories. They decide what is remembered and what is lost."

Lily blinked, the queen's words landing heavily in her thoughts. She couldn't tell if it was a philosophical musing or something far more deliberate, but it felt weighty, important. She logged it away in her mind, a puzzle piece she might need later.

The queen's gaze softened as she turned to Lily, her voice dropping into a more intimate, almost conspiratorial tone. "He is so fond of you," she said, the faintest smile playing at the corners of her lips. "Perhaps he would speak to you, if not to others. Would you mind trying? You might persuade him to reason."

Lily opened her mouth to reply, but the queen continued, her tone growing just a touch heavier, her words laced with a subtle undercurrent of exasperation. "If only Zayir would call off the peace talks himself. It would spare everyone the agony of watching them collapse on their own."

Datch's face remained steady, but Lily felt his presence beside her like an anchor, steady and unyielding. She fought to keep her own expression neutral, though the queen's sentiment churned in her stomach. Call off the peace talks? It was the opposite of everything they were working toward.

Before Lily could formulate a response, a quiet but resolute voice cut through the tension. "That won't be necessary."

Lily turned, and there was Zayir, standing just beyond the threshold of an adjacent corridor. His posture was upright, his expression guarded, but there was a flicker of defiance in his eyes.

"I will spare a moment for you, Lily," he said, his voice steady but carrying the weight of weariness.

The queen's smile faltered for just a fraction of a second, but she stepped aside gracefully, gesturing toward Zayir with a sweep of her hand, as though the entire moment had unfolded precisely as she had orchestrated it.

Lily followed Zayir into a private sitting room, where he sank into a chair with an audible sigh. He gestured for her to sit across from him, but he avoided meeting her eyes.

"Zayir," Lily began gently, "I know this feels... overwhelming. But you can't let this break you."

He shook his head, his gaze fixed on the intricate patterns of the rug beneath his feet. "This isn't just a setback, Lily. It's proof. Proof that I was never ready for this. I wanted so badly to believe that peace was possible. But now?" He let out a bitter laugh. "This will be my legacy. A failure."

Lily leaned forward, her voice firm but kind. "Don't give up on peace. You may be seen as an idealist, and maybe this won't work out. But you tried, Zayir. That's more than anyone else can say. Please don't let this setback turn you into what your mother and everyone else wants you to be. You're not like them."

Zayir looked at her then, his eyes heavy with exhaustion but searching, as if trying to uncover some fragment of the conviction she spoke of within himself. For a moment, the silence between them stretched, filled only by the faint hum of the chandeliers overhead. His hand moved hesitantly before brushing against hers, the lightest of touches, like the ghost of a connection he was too weary to grasp fully.

"If only," he murmured, his voice barely above a whisper, the words carrying a weight that felt far older than his years.

Lily opened her mouth to respond, but the words caught in her throat. There was something raw in his expression—a vulnerability she hadn't seen before, as though he were standing at the edge of an abyss and could see no way back. Her heart twisted, wanting to say something, anything, that might bring him back from the brink of despair. But before she could find the right words, he stood abruptly, his movements fluid but deliberate, and turned away.

He didn't look back as he exited the room, the quiet sound of the door closing behind him like a final punctuation mark on their conversation. Lily remained where she was, her chest tight with frustration and sadness. Had her words reached him at all? Or had they only added to the weight he already carried? She exhaled slowly, pressing her palms against the table to ground herself as she pushed herself to her feet.

When she rejoined Datch and the others in the grand hall, the atmosphere had shifted again. The tension was palpable, a current of unease humming beneath the surface. Datch stood at the edge of the room, his usually composed demeanor replaced with an uncharacteristic tension. His hands were clasped tightly behind his back, and his gaze flicked toward her the moment she stepped into view.

"We have to leave," he said, his voice clipped and low, though it carried an urgency that sent a ripple of unease through her.

Lily frowned, her steps quickening as she approached him. "What's wrong?" she asked, her tone sharper than she intended.

Datch turned fully to face her, his eyes steady but his jaw set. "Captain Dalren has confessed to the murder."

• • • •

The office complex shared by the Union of Allied Systems and the Station Authority towered above the central hub of Star Base 12 like a shimmering beacon of authority. Lily had never ventured to this part of the base before, and the sheer scale of it took her breath away. The building's exterior gleamed with reflective alloys and duraglass panels that caught starlight in shifting hues. Tiered terraces overflowed with silver-tipped trees and flowering vines, cascading fountains winding between them. It was futuristic and imposing, yet oddly tranquil—like a bridge between nature and order.

Inside, the atrium soared to dizzying heights, crisscrossed with elevated walkways. A monumental fountain rose at the center, its streams spiraling upward before falling back in synchronized arcs. Holographic projections pulsed across the walls, shifting between abstract art and official data feeds. The Union's dominance was unmistakable: its crest inlaid in silver and blue metals dominated the lobby floor, while the Station Authority's presence was acknowledged only in smaller banners.

Despite the grandeur, Lily felt uneasy. The air was charged, decisions made here carrying the weight to tilt entire alliances.

At the security checkpoint, gleaming sensors swept over them, beams glowing faintly as they scanned. A human officer observed with sharp eyes, making notations on a pad. "Please stand still," he instructed briskly. At his side, a holographic hospitality guide materialized, beaming an insincere smile. "Welcome to the Union Office Complex. Thank you for your patience."

The juxtaposition was almost comical, and Lily had to bite back a laugh.

Once cleared, Datch led her up a spiraling ramp. The third level was subdued, the soaring architecture giving way to plain, functional corridors. Datch stopped at a door labeled *Security Liaison Office* and placed his hand on the glowing panel. The faint hum of the scan ended in a soft chime, and the door slid open.

The room inside was stark and suffocating—metallic walls, no windows, only a single monitor showing the adjacent interrogation chamber. Through it, Captain Dalren sat alone at a table. His shoulders hunched at first, but then he adjusted his uniform collar with a deliberate precision, as though clinging to dignity even here. His gaze never lifted from the surface before him.

A figure rose from the corner of the room. Tall, broad, his dark skin catching the muted light, he moved with the ease of someone used to commanding attention. Datch stepped forward to clasp his hand.

"Good to see you, Commander Bassey," Datch said, composed as ever.

"Likewise, Datch," Bassey replied, his deep voice carrying easy confidence. His sharp gaze flicked briefly to Lily, appraising, before returning to Datch. There was a looseness to him, a casualness in his stance, that suggested someone who cared more for results than appearances.

Datch gestured subtly toward Lily. "Pretend my observer isn't here. She's training with me."

Caught off guard, Lily straightened quickly, trying to look composed.

Bassey's eyes lingered on her for a moment, then he gave a small nod. "Understood. Shall we begin?"

Lily nodded stiffly, trying to seem professional, though her inner thoughts were anything but. *I cannot believe this is happening.*

Moments later, Lily leaned against the console, watching the monitor. The room on the other side of the glass was stark, with its unadorned walls and a single table at its center. Captain Dalren sat stiffly in one of the chairs, his expression inscrutable, a man carved from stone. Lily wasn't sure if it was discomfort or a deliberate choice, but she was glad Datch had agreed to let her stay in the observation room.

Datch and Commander Bassey entered the interrogation room, the older man's firm, deliberate movements a stark contrast to Datch's calm precision. Bassey's voice was warm and coaxing as he broke the silence.

"I spoke to your wife, Eryk," Bassey said, settling into a chair opposite Dalren. "She's worried sick. We all are. Just help us understand what's going on here. You tell me the truth, and we can clear this up. You might even be home for dinner."

Dalren didn't respond, his gaze fixed on the table.

Datch's voice, sharper and more clinical, cut through the room. "Unlikely, Commander. Captain Dalren has been implicated in a capital offense."

Bassey shot Datch a sidelong glance, his tone shifting as he leaned forward. "Ignore him, Eryk. My friend here is all by-the-book, but me? I'm here for you. Just tell me what's going on, and we'll figure this out together."

Still, Dalren said nothing. The silence stretched uncomfortably, and Lily's heart thudded in her chest as she watched from the monitor.

Datch cleared his throat and spoke with measured precision. "I too would like to understand some things. First, there is no plausible motive for you to commit this crime. Second, you waived your right to counsel, which, as a starship captain, you are fully aware is inadvisable. Third, there is only circumstantial evidence linking you to the murder."

Bassey picked up where Datch left off, his voice rising slightly in frustration. "Yes, you were seen on security cameras at the Luxury Residence around the time of the murder, and your codes were used at customs on New Cordova to approve transport of a large object that matches the description of the static field generator. You know how this works, goddammit, Eryk! It feels like you're deliberately implicating yourself here. But I know you, and there's no way you killed that Varrothi."

Dalren remained unmoving, his hands resting on the table. After a long moment, he spoke, his voice low and even. "I stand by my statement."

Datch's expression didn't change as he responded, his tone unwavering. "Which leads me to item four: You do not actually confess to the murder in your statement, and yet it has been logged as an official confession. If you are connected to the theft of the static field generator, then—"

Dalren's head snapped up, his eyes locking on Datch. "Wait. What did you say?"

Datch tilted his head slightly. "I said, if you are connected to the theft of the static field generator—"

"No one said anything about a theft," Dalren interrupted, his voice tinged with confusion for the first time.

Bassey frowned, his eyes darting between Datch and Dalren. "What is he talking about?"

Datch straightened, his calm exterior unchanged. "If you'll excuse us momentarily." He rose, motioning for Bassey to stay as he exited the room, making his way back to Lily in the observation area.

Bassey folded his arms, his expression guarded but expectant as Datch returned to the observation area. "Alright, catch me up," he said, his tone calm but edged with curiosity.

Datch's gaze was steady. "I cannot go into detail," he began, "but on the day of the murder, a Krythar static field generator was stolen from a known smuggler on New Cordova. I mentioned it during our questioning in the hopes of gauging the captain's reaction. Its absence from both his statement and the official report is... significant."

Bassey raised an eyebrow, his interest visibly piqued. "You think he knew about the robbery?"

Judging from his emotional response," Datch replied, "I would say the theft is central to the reason he's withholding information. It's possible his life is under threat if he were to expose his co-conspirators. Alternatively, he could be protecting the actual killer."

Lily, who had been listening intently, finally spoke up. "Or... the thief."

Both men turned toward her, Datch's head tilting slightly in curiosity. "Explain," he prompted.

Lily hesitated for only a moment. "Well, if we're starting with the assumption that the thief and the killer are the same person, maybe he did too. What if he helped someone steal the generator, and now he thinks they used it in the murder? He could be trying to protect them."

Datch nodded, his tone thoughtful. "An interesting observation. It would fit with the captain's psychological profile. He places the needs of others ahead of his own, often to a fault."

Bassey's expression grew grim. "I'm not sure we're going to get much more out of him. The man's as tight-lipped as they come."

Datch's gaze flicked briefly back toward the monitor showing Dalren, who was still seated, staring at the table. "Perhaps one more question," he said quietly.

Bassey let out a slow sigh, gesturing toward the door. "Your show," he said.

The two men reentered the room, Lily watching from the monitor as they resumed their seats. Datch leaned forward slightly, his voice even but deliberate. "Captain Dalren, I have one more question for you."

Dalren's weary gaze shifted to him, his shoulders slumping.

"Your wife will grieve your separation if you are sent to a penal facility," Datch continued. His tone was neutral, but the words seemed to land like a blow.

Dalren's jaw tightened, his hands curling into fists. "That's not a question."

"Do you love your wife?" Datch asked, his calm persistence unwavering.

"Of course I love my wife!" Dalren snapped, his voice sharp and immediate.

Datch's face didn't change as he pressed on. "Then who could be so important to you that you would risk your life with her to protect them?"

Dalren immediately looked down again, his body language closing off like a door slamming shut. He said nothing.

. . . .

Lily and Datch walked side by side through the expansive lobby of the office complex, their steps echoing faintly against the polished floors. The atmosphere was quieter now, the earlier bustling activity tapering to a subdued hum. The centerpiece fountain commanded attention, its cascading streams catching the light in a way that scattered faint rainbows across the room. The air here was cooler, tinged with the faint scent of mineral water and a hint of the greenery from the terraces outside.

Lily glanced at it, momentarily mesmerized by the rhythmic flow of water. The gentle rush seemed to contrast sharply with the tension winding through her thoughts. She glanced at Datch, whose expression remained as composed as ever, though his pace was brisk and purposeful. It was as if the weight of their discoveries was propelling him forward.

As they grew closer, Lily's gaze lingered on the holographic Union crest projected above, shimmering faintly in the mist. The sight stirred something in her—a mixture of awe and unease. This place, with all its grandeur, was meant to symbolize order and unity, but the cracks beneath the surface felt impossible to ignore.

Datch's posture straightened as he broke the silence. "Do you think Dalren was telling the truth when he said he loves his wife?"

Lily tilted her head, considering the question. "Yes. Well, ninety percent sure," she said with a small shrug. "He doesn't seem like that good of a liar. And he's definitely not, like, a sociopath or anything."

"Agreed," Datch replied, his tone thoughtful. "Then why would he risk his life with her to protect Rhyder and Ash? Or whoever the killer is."

Lily frowned, her steps slowing as she pondered the question. Finally, she looked up at him, determination flickering in her eyes. "I don't know. But I think it's time to ask them."

Datch gave a slight nod, moving with his even gait as they headed toward the exit.

• • • •

The market felt quieter than usual, its vibrant chaos dulled by the lockdown. Colorful stalls sat half-empty, their usual clamor muted under the weight of a galaxy on pause.

Lily walked a familiar stretch, her boots crunching softly against the uneven pavement as she scanned the rows of stalls and shadowy alleys where she'd run into Rhyder before. She knew it was a long shot; Rhyder Dayne wasn't the kind of guy to stay in one place. But doing something, anything, felt better than standing still. Her earlier attempts to reach him via comms had gone unanswered, which didn't surprise her. Typical Rhyder, she thought, kicking a loose stone and watching it skitter away. He didn't seem like the type to check messages in the middle of a crisis.

As she rounded a corner near a cluster of fruit vendors, a sharp, familiar voice broke through her thoughts. "Well, if it isn't my favorite accidental troublemaker."

Lily turned and saw Camilla, her sharp edge softened today. She was adjusting the glowing flowers on her cart, their faint light haloing her against the dim street.

"Camilla," Lily said, her eyebrows lifting in genuine surprise. "Last time I saw you, you threatened to kill me."

Camilla smirked, wiping her hands on her apron. "Technically, I threatened to kill Rhyder. But don't take it so personally, child. That's just how we operate out here." Her dark eyes softened slightly, and she gestured to the sparse crowd around them. "Life in places like this teaches you to adapt. You learn when to fight and when to... cooperate. Mutual benefit, you know?"

Lily tilted her head, intrigued. "Believe me, I know," she replied, a rueful smile tugging at her lips. The faintest memory flickered—dodging unfriendly faces and empty glances on the streets of San Francisco. The ache of a hoodie full of holes in the damp chill. She pushed it aside. "I'm looking for Rhyder. Any chance you know how to get ahold of him?"

Camilla snorted. "That boy's a ghost when he wants to be." She leaned in slightly, lowering her voice. "But... there's always a way to leave a message. Follow me."

Camilla led her to the back of her stall, where a weathered terminal blinked faintly, embedded into the wall like a relic. With deft fingers, Camilla tapped at the controls, bringing up a flickering menu. "This is The Wall. Us market rats leave messages here, subtle-like. Gotta know what you're looking for."

After a moment, Camilla's lips curved into a grin. "There he is. Filter by his handle—Otter-Van."

Lily raised an eyebrow but didn't ask. The list loaded, and Camilla gestured toward a recent entry. "This one's for you."

The message read: **Hey, Starlight. Sorry about leaving you in the dust. I have to lay low a bit. Drop me a note here if you need me.**

Lily hesitated before typing: **Your sooty friend is in deep. Meet me...** She glanced at Camilla. "Where should I suggest?"

Camilla didn't hesitate. "Level 47. There's a spot in the hangar bay where they park stolen vehicles. Rhyder calls it the playground."

Lily nodded and finished her message: **...Meet me where the children go. 19:00.**

She turned to Camilla with a grateful smile. "Thanks. I owe you one."

Camilla gave a knowing smirk. "Don't mention it. Welcome to the rat pack."

Lily caught the unspoken hint and quickly slipped a 50-credit chit into Camilla's hand. Camilla accepted it with a sly wink but didn't linger. "Good luck, child."

Lily nodded, gratitude tugging at her chest as she turned and made a brisk exit.

She found Datch near the docking bay, his composed presence steady as ever amidst the subdued bustle. He turned slightly as she approached, his expression calm but questioning.

"Any luck?" he asked.

"Sort of," Lily replied. "I left him a message. I'm going to try to meet him tonight."

Datch gave a faint nod. "Progress. Now we must continue."

"What's next?" Lily asked, falling into step beside him.

"It's past time the delegates gave us their version of the story," Datch said, already striding toward the transit terminal.

· · · ·

The Zephtari chambers at the Luxury Residence embodied their culture's ideals: a meticulous blend of formality and refinement. The walls curved elegantly, adorned with intricate patterns inspired by nature, rendered in muted earth tones and metallics. Warm, ambient lighting emanated from concealed sources, casting a serene glow that complemented the restrained beauty of the space. The furniture was a study in contrasts—sleek and modern, yet clearly designed for comfort. A sweeping sectional framed the room, its modular design appearing seamless, as though grown rather than constructed. The atmosphere was calm and measured, a physical manifestation of Zephtari logic and precision.

Elder Yzatra Vel and Envoy Taro Lethra awaited their visitors with carefully composed expressions. Elder Vel, her elegant figure adorned by a flowing garment that shimmered like liquid silver, inclined her head slightly in acknowledgment as Lily and Datch entered. Her luminous gray eyes, sharp and discerning, studied them with the calm detachment of a scientist observing an experiment.

Beside her, Envoy Lethra exuded a quieter intensity. His tall, willowy frame was draped in layered robes of deep green and gold, the subtle interplay of colors hinting at status and tradition. His movements were deliberate, each step and gesture carrying a sense of unspoken purpose. Despite his outward poise, his long fingers toyed with the edge of his sleeve—a tell that betrayed a trace of unease.

"Mr. Datch, Ms. Starling," Vel greeted them, her tone smooth and measured. "Welcome to the Zephtari chambers. Please, sit."

Lethra offered a nod of acknowledgment, though his eyes flickered briefly with what might have been impatience. "We understand you have questions," he said, his voice low and even.

Lily followed Datch to the sectional. The cushions were firmer than she expected but surprisingly comfortable. She couldn't help but feel that the space, while not overly opulent, was meticulously curated to leave nothing to chance—every angle, every texture, a calculated statement of the Zephtari's values.

Datch inclined his head politely as he took his seat. "Thank you for meeting with us. We will try to make the interviews as efficient as possible."

Lethra shifted slightly, a flicker of discomfort crossing his features. "I was under the impression we would be giving a joint statement."

Datch's response was measured, his tone steady. "Besides being standard procedure, it is also ideal in its efficacy to conduct interviews separately, avoiding unintentional influence."

Vel's professionalism did not falter, though her eyes held a glint of impatience. "We will follow your protocol, of course."

As Lethra opened his mouth, his face tight with protest, Vel silenced him with a sharp glance. The unspoken command was clear.

"Leave us," she said, her tone brooking no argument.

Lethra rose and bowed deeply, an exaggerated show of deference to his superior, before turning and leaving the room without another word.

The room settled into an almost palpable stillness after Vel's cool welcome. Datch's calm demeanor as he began was a sharp contrast to the simmering tension that hung between them. "Thank you for providing your written statement to the authorities," he said evenly. "It was quite informative."

Elder Vel inclined her head, her elegant posture as rigid as a sculpture. "I pride myself on precision, Mr. Datch."

Datch's hands rested lightly on the table, his every movement precise and deliberate. "Indeed," he replied. "However, I noticed certain omissions."

The room seemed to contract with Vel's sharp inhale, her calm veneer showing its first crack. Her silvery eyes narrowed. "Omissions?" she repeated, her tone cutting. "I assure you, nothing of relevance was omitted."

Datch's unflappable exterior betrayed not even the faintest shift. "In your speech at the opening of the peace talks, you referenced the Zephtari collaboration with the Varrothi on a classified project. Yet this was not mentioned in your written statement."

Vel bristled, her voice cool but edged with steel. "I don't see the connection."

Datch tilted his head slightly, his tone still neutral. "I'm referring to the question during your deposition explicitly asking you to reveal any and all connections to the Varrothi."

Vel's already-perfect posture somehow straightened further, her expression hardening. "I understood the question to pertain to personal connections," she said crisply.

"Were you not personally involved in the project?" Datch's question cut through the air, direct and pointed.

Vel's lips pressed into a thin line, her hands tightening together in her lap. "As you said, that information is classified."

Datch didn't miss a beat. "Classified or not, I should inform you that the Salamander recently came across information regarding this joint effort and the development of Rencor Waves—a project that, according to the records we obtained, you oversaw personally."

A subtle tremor passed through Vel's carefully composed mask. Her fingers twitched slightly against the folds of her garment, and she chewed her lip, a momentary lapse in her otherwise unflappable demeanor. "I oversee many projects," she said after a long pause, her words slow and deliberate. "What of it?"

Datch leaned forward slightly, the calmness in his voice edged with an undeniable firmness. "And one of those projects was, in fact, the development of Rencor Waves in cooperation with the Varrothi. Was it not?"

Vel's irritation flared, eyes narrowing. "Where did you get this information?"

Lily, seated nearby, found herself marveling at Datch's poise. He was unshakable, his tone remaining even as he pressed on. "There were also other names connected to the experiments—names relevant to the peace talks. What I found particularly intriguing was the source of the funding for this project: a regime with substantial influence and a vested interest in maintaining secrecy..."

Vel cut him off, her voice rising. "I fail to see how this is relevant to your investigation, Mr. Datch."

Datch's tone sharpened, though his posture remained steady and composed. "It is relevant because any connection with the Varrothi—personal or otherwise—must be disclosed. Failure to do so constitutes perjury, Elder Vel."

The thin thread of Vel's composure finally snapped, and her voice rose with rancor, echoing slightly in the room's stillness. "Are you accusing me of committing a crime? Let me remind you, Mr. Datch, that despite whatever information you may have... obtained, this project is classified. I strongly suggest you refrain from prying into matters you do not fully understand, or I will have no choice but to contact the Office of the UAP President to have you removed from this investigation."

Datch didn't flinch. Instead, he shifted gears, his tone cooler now. "I see. Very well."

For a moment, Lily thought he might be wrapping up, but he continued after a deliberate pause. "One final question, then."

Vel's shoulders remained rigid, but her expression sharpened, suspicion flickering behind them.

"Why did you lie about being in the Zephtari chambers during the hours surrounding the murder?" Datch asked, his words precise and cutting.

Vel's reaction was immediate. Her expression cracked, her gaze darting to Datch and then quickly toward the door, as if seeking an escape. "I... I don't know what you're referring to," she stammered, her poise faltering as hints of panic flickered across her face.

Datch's voice remained steady. "Security footage and badge access logs show that you left the Zephtari chambers to meet with Captain Dalren during the hours surrounding Delegate Veirr's murder."

Lily, seated nearby, leaned forward slightly, her pulse quickening. This was the first she'd heard of this development, and the weight of its implication pulled her full attention to the exchange.

Vel's hands clenched tightly in her lap, her knuckles pale against the flowing silver fabric of her garment. When she finally spoke, her voice was strained, barely above a whisper. "He asked me to come over and help him with... He made a request of me... A personal request."

Datch inclined his head slightly, as though filing her words away for future analysis. "I see." He paused longer this time, his stillness amplifying the tension in the room. If he had been human, Lily might have thought he was enjoying watching Vel squirm in her seat. "Very well, Elder Vel. That will be all for now. Please ask Envoy Lethra to join us." He lowered his gaze to his datapad with intentional dismissal.

Vel rose abruptly, the movement so sudden it seemed to vibrate through the space. For a moment, she hesitated, lingering by the door. Her gaze flickered with what seemed to be an internal battle—whether to say more or retreat with her dignity intact. Finally, she chose the latter. With a faint sneer of disdain, she swept from the room without another word.

The door hissed shut behind her, leaving the room blanketed in a brief, heavy silence. Datch turned to Lily, who was perched on the edge of her seat, her brow furrowed in thought.

"I do not believe Elder Vel is the murderer," Datch said, his tone as calm and clinical as ever. "The security logs verify her location throughout the crime."

"But she's hiding something," Lily said, her voice quieter, her mind working quickly to piece together the growing puzzle. Datch gave a slight nod. "Indeed. And I suspect it will connect at least in part to the larger conspiracy." Before Lily could respond, the door opened again and Envoy Lethra entered in a storm of impatience. He dropped into the seat across from them, his layered robes swirling around him like an extension of his irritation. His sharp eyes glared at Datch, his voice a growl. "Let's get this over with."

Datch, as ever, appeared unperturbed. "Thank you for joining us, Envoy Lethra. I'll aim to make this brief." His calm, measured tone only seemed to irritate Lethra further.

"If you need someone to verify my whereabouts..." Lethra began, but Datch raised a single finger, silencing him with a small, disarming gesture.

"Envoy," Datch said, his voice even. "I'd like to ask you some questions about your career."

Lethra blinked, clearly caught off guard. "My career?" he repeated, suspicion lacing his words.

"Yes," Datch said, leaning forward slightly. "You've had an impressive tenure in Ambassador Vel's office—top of your class in the diplomatic corps—but there's an unusual gap in your records. Specifically, the period between your graduation and your assignment under Elder Vel."

Lethra shifted uncomfortably, his gaze darting briefly toward the door before he masked his unease with irritation. "I don't see how this is relevant to the investigation."

From her seat, Lily observed the exchange with growing intrigue. I really need to start asking Datch to brief me before these interviews, she thought. He does his homework.

Datch continued as though Lethra hadn't spoken. "During that time, you resided on New Cordova. Records show you were engaged in a humanitarian mission," he said, pausing for effect, his head tilting slightly. "An effort to aid those affected by the uprising of 2523—a notable endeavor."

Lethra stiffened, his posture becoming rigid. "As you said, it's on the record."

"Indeed," Datch said smoothly. "I imagine you must have formed some strong connections during that time—connections that persisted for over a decade." He tapped a note on his datapad. "For example, the individual you contacted just last week. Public comm records indicate a series of calls between you and someone you worked closely with during your time on New Cordova."

Lethra's composure cracked. "What are you implying?" he snapped, his voice rising.

Datch's face remained unchanged. "Simply this: The people you communicated with are known members of the resistance movement. A group classified as a terrorist organization by the Union."

Lethra's face darkened, his mouth opening to retort, but he stopped himself short. His jaw tightened as he processed the accusation, his expression a storm of barely contained anger and unease.

"The static field generator was stolen in the same sector of New Cordova where your communications were directed," Datch continued, his voice calm but unyielding.

Lethra's fingers tightened around the edges of his chair as though it were the only thing keeping him anchored. His silence stretched for a moment before he exhaled sharply. "All right," he said finally, his voice strained. "All right. I'll tell you, but... please, it's my career. If Ambassador Vel were to find out..." He trailed off, the weight of his implication filling the air.

Lily leaned forward slightly, her attention riveted as Lethra's composure unraveled. When he spoke again, the words spilled out in a rush, tinged with equal parts defiance and regret. "I was a member of the resistance. A young activist. A true believer. And yes, we used violence—occasionally," he admitted, his voice thick with emotion. "But it was the only way to make them listen. Even now, I still help them—sometimes with information, sometimes financially." He paused, his hands rising as if in self-defense. "But I didn't kill anyone. And if the field generator was stolen—and I'm not saying I know anything about that—but if it was, then I'd venture a guess it wasn't stolen to be used as a weapon. It was taken to be destroyed. It's weapons like that that keep marginalized communities subjugated on forgotten planets like New Cordova!"

His impassioned words lingered in the room, thick with the weight of his confession.

No one spoke for a moment. The air felt charged, as though the declaration itself had altered the dynamic in the room. Datch's steady gaze remained fixed on Lethra, unblinking. Finally, he inclined his head ever so slightly. "Thank you for your time."

• • • •

Lily and Datch walked side by side, their footsteps echoing faintly as they passed through the grand lobby.

"Where did you dig up all that?" Lily asked, her voice a mix of admiration and incredulity.

Datch glanced at her, his calm demeanor carrying the faintest hint of satisfaction. "It is a capital mistake to theorize before one has data," Datch recited evenly. "Insensibly, one begins to twist facts to suit theories, instead of theories to suit facts."

Lily tilted her head. "Sherlock Holmes?"

"Indeed," Datch replied with a nod.

Lily's lips curved into a small smile. "Makes sense." Then she pressed on, her tone more serious. "Do you think they actually destroyed the field generator?"

"It's an interesting twist," Datch admitted. "I have yet to establish any motive for Envoy Lethra to be involved in the murder, but some of these pieces will surely fit together."

Lily nodded, though her thoughts churned with the growing web of connections and secrets. As they approached the Urrathi chambers, she squared her shoulders, bracing herself for what promised to be a volatile encounter ahead.

• • • •

The Urrathi chambers were a stark contrast to the meticulous formality of the Zephtari quarters. Where the Zephtari emphasized artful precision, the Urrathi prioritized function over form. The space was unapologetically practical, with oversized, durable furniture arranged for comfort rather than display. Against one wall, arcade-style consoles blinked and flashed, their colorful lights scattering patterns across the room. A faint hum of mechanical noise blended with the occasional clang of metal—a constant reminder of the Urrathi's unpretentious culture.

Premier Athrex Varn leaned back in an enormous chair, his broad shoulders dwarfing the already imposing furniture. He exuded authority, his gruff demeanor as sharp-edged as a blade.

"Let's get on with it, then," he growled, his deep voice rumbling through the room.

In another chamber nearby, Minister Shyra Velnak offered a disarming warmth that belied his people's reputation for bluntness. Seated comfortably in a deeply cushioned chair, he smiled at Lily as though they were old acquaintances. "It is delightful to see you again, Ms. Starling. I hope things have been going well for you."

The contrast couldn't have been sharper—Varn's voice rising in tirades while Velnak spoke with measured calm.

"Those spineless bureaucrats wouldn't know strategy if it hit them in the face!" Varn barked, his hand slashing through the air. "The only thing worse than a Varrothi is a Krythar itself!"

"The Varrothi?" Velnak echoed, his tone smoother, but his words no less cutting. "They're weak—too obsessed with optics and alliances to act decisively. If *we* acted, there wouldn't be any questions about who was responsible."

Lily's thoughts flickered between the two men. Different approaches, same contempt.

"If I wanted to kill the Krythar delegate," Varn continued, leaning forward now, "I wouldn't bother with subtlety. A good blade, clean and honorable. Not some fancy microwave contraption."

"Let me tell you something, Mr. Datch," Velnak added with a dry chuckle. "If the Urrathi wanted the Krythar gone, they'd be gone. No tricks, no games. Just good, old-fashioned precision."

The interviews blurred together in Lily's mind, the edges of one bleeding into the other until their voices became an echo. Varn's fury, Velnak's composure—different instruments playing the same refrain. Both men expressed an unshakable faith in Urrathi efficiency and a disdain for the art of subterfuge.

By the time both interviews wrapped, Lily and Datch exchanged the same subtle glance. The message was clear: blunt, unpleasant, even bloodthirsty as they might be, the Urrathi were not responsible for the murder.

The transit platform was quieter than usual, the hum of activity dulled by the weight of the investigation. As they waited, Lily checked her comm—and her heart skipped when she saw Rhyder's response. Characteristically cryptic: a simple checkmark.

Datch leaned closer, brow furrowed. "What does that mean?"

Lily slipped the comm into her pocket with a sly smile. "It means," she said, her voice carrying a mischievous edge, "I have a date."

· · · ·

The docking bay known as "the playground" was a labyrinth of mismatched ships, broken parts, and questionable repairs. The air was thick with engine oil and ozone, dim lighting casting long shadows across the cluttered space. Lily approached cautiously, her boots clinking against the grated floor.

Rhyder leaned against a battered freighter, hands tucked into his jacket. His easy posture didn't fool her; tension flickered in the way his eyes darted to meet hers.

"Hey," he said simply, his voice softer than she expected.

Lily stopped a few steps away, crossing her arms. "You made it. I wasn't sure you'd show."

"I had to," Rhyder replied, his tone carrying a rare sincerity. He hesitated, then added, "I'm sorry, Starlight. For leaving you like that. For putting you in danger. It wasn't fair."

Her expression softened slightly, but she kept her stance firm. "No, it wasn't."

Rhyder nodded, shadowed with regret. "We were hired by the resistance to steal the field generator. It wasn't supposed to be a big deal—get in, grab it, get out. They wanted to destroy it, take another weapon off the board. But Ash..." His jaw tightened. "Ash is a true believer. Always has been. He's more... intense about the cause. And now he's in over his head. The mercenary force backing the provisional government is after him. On top of that, he's the person of interest the authorities are hunting." He looked up. "He's in serious trouble."

Lily's lips pressed into a thin line. "So, you're asking me to help clean up your mess?"

Rhyder gave her a lopsided grin that didn't reach his eyes. "Something like that."

She sighed, rubbing the back of her neck. "Fine. But we're not going alone."

At that moment, Datch stepped out from behind a parked ship, his calm, deliberate steps echoing in the bay. "I regret coming along as the 'third wheel,' so to speak," he said, his tone as dry as ever.

Lily rolled her eyes, suppressing a grin.

Rhyder shrugged, smirk tugging at his lips as he shot Lily a wink. "The more the merrier," he said.

The shuttle ride to New Cordova was anything but merry. The small craft rattled as it tore through the atmosphere, its aging systems groaning with each maneuver. Lily gripped the armrests, knuckles white. Across from her, Rhyder seemed entirely at ease, one leg bouncing casually. Datch, seated beside her, remained composed, remarking at one point, "Statistically, these older models are less prone to catastrophic failure than their appearance would suggest."

"Comforting," Lily muttered through clenched teeth.

When they finally touched down, the transition was jarring. The shuttle's chaos gave way to the stark quiet of New Cordova's surface. The landing site was a stretch of dusty ground surrounded by craggy outcroppings and sparse vegetation, bathed in the dim light of a distant sun.

Rhyder led the way, a handheld scanner blinking with Ash's location. "This way," he said, his tone serious now.

The shadows of New Cordova's underbelly stretched long and jagged as they turned into a dimly lit industrial lot. The air reeked of fuel and rust, the ground littered with scraps and glowing embers from the incinerators.

They spotted Ash instantly—bound and struggling as mercenaries shoved him into the back of a hovering transport van.

"Damn it!" Rhyder hissed, reaching for his weapon.

The van's thrusters roared, casting a harsh blue glow over the cracked pavement. Datch raised his sidearm, firing with calm precision, but the blast ricocheted off reinforced plating.

"They're moving!" Lily shouted.

Rhyder's eyes darted to a nearby speeder. "Cover me," he barked, sprinting toward it. With a deft hand he overrode the lock.

"Get on!" he yelled as the van surged forward.

They piled onto the speeder as it leapt into motion, tearing after the transport.

The chase was on.

The streets of New Cordova turned into a blur of neon lights and jagged architecture as the speeder wove through narrow alleys and open industrial corridors. Mercenary bikers on sleek, single-rider speeders swarmed from side alleys, their weapons trained on the pursuing trio.

"Lily, take the gun!" Rhyder shouted, tossing her a blaster as he struggled to keep the speeder steady.

"What—now?!" she stammered, clutching the weapon.

"Now!" Datch affirmed, his tone calm but commanding.

A mercenary pulled alongside them, his blaster rifle charging with a high-pitched whine. Lily squeezed the trigger, her hands trembling. The first shot went wide, singeing the edge of a building. The second hit home, striking the mercenary square in the chest and sending him spiraling into a pile of scrap metal.

"Good shot!" Rhyder called over his shoulder, his grin wild despite the chaos.

The van swerved sharply, cutting through a crowded thoroughfare and sending bystanders diving for cover. The speeder barely managed to follow, its hover field sparking as Rhyder pushed it to its limits. Behind them, a Union patrol ship descended into the fray, its sirens blaring.

"Now the authorities?" Lily shouted, firing wildly at another mercenary. Her shot clipped the rider's bike, sending it careening into the side of a building in a spectacular explosion.

"We're popular today," Rhyder quipped, swerving to avoid a barrage of plasma bolts.

Ahead, the van veered toward an abandoned shipping yard, its heavy chassis smashing through a barricade. Rhyder followed, the speeder barely clearing the wreckage. Lily and Datch exchanged fire with the remaining mercenaries, the air thick with the acrid smell of plasma discharges.

As they neared the van, Datch pulled a handheld EMP device from his belt. "Get closer," he instructed.

Rhyder gritted his teeth, maneuvering the speeder dangerously close to the van's rear. Datch hurled the device onto the van's roof, its magnetic clamps engaging with a satisfying thunk. A moment later, the EMP detonated, sending a pulse of blue light rippling through the area. The van shuddered, its thrusters sputtering.

"They're slowing down!" Lily shouted, her heart pounding.

But their victory was short-lived. Overhead, a squad of mercenary fighters roared into view, their sleek, black ships cutting through the smog like blades. Their weapons lit up the shipping yard, forcing Rhyder to swerve wildly to avoid the incoming fire.

"We need to end this now!" Datch declared.

The speeder skidded to a halt as they leapt off, using the brief cover of wreckage to exchange more fire with the mercenaries. Rhyder sprinted toward the van, his blaster barking as he took down the remaining guards. Lily covered him, her shots growing steadier with each pull of the trigger.

Finally, they reached Ash. Rhyder ripped the van's doors open, hauling his friend out with a grunt. "You're alive, you idiot," he muttered, his tone equal parts relief and exasperation.

"Not for long if we don't move!" Lily shouted, pointing to the descending patrol ships.

They scrambled back onto the speeder, Ash slumped against Rhyder as they tore off again. Lily fought to keep her eyes open against the blur of lights and wind, her stomach lurching as Datch pushed the vehicle harder than she thought possible. She had never felt speed like this in an open craft.

The shuttle loomed ahead, and for a heartbeat she thought they would smash straight into the hatch. At the last moment Datch swung them in, the speeder skidding across the deck as they piled out.

Plasma bolts rained down the instant they cleared the ramp. Datch sprinted to the controls, ship's defenses roaring to life as his fire met theirs with methodical precision. Lily and Rhyder hauled Ash into the cargo hold, strapping him down as explosions lit up the night sky.

With a final, wrenching maneuver, Datch slammed the shuttle into ascent. The craft punched through atmosphere, leaving New Cordova and its chaos behind.

Ash winced as Datch steadied him onto a stretcher. His shirt was torn, a jagged bruise spreading across his ribs, cuts and burns scattered across his arms and face. Lily hovered close, her hands fidgeting as she watched, worry etched deep into her features.

Datch retrieved a sleek med kit from beneath the seat, opening it with his usual precision. Tools and instruments gleamed in neat compartments. He selected a handheld scanner, adjusted the settings, and a faint blue light swept across Ash's battered frame.

"The ribs are fractured but stable," Datch reported evenly. "Shallow lacerations. Minor burns on the forearms."

Ash hissed through clenched teeth. "Can you stop listing everything like I'm a lab experiment?"

Lily offered a weak smile. "I mean, you kind of look like one."

Ash gave her a half glare, half grin before slumping back, letting Datch continue.

• • • •

The med bay was quiet save for the hum of equipment and the steady beep of monitors. Sterile surfaces reflected the blue glow of the scanner as it swept across Ash's ribs.

Dr. Thesari leaned over him, movements practiced and precise, though the tension in her jaw betrayed her focus. Lily stood nearby, arms crossed, the same glow flickering over her face.

"This won't take long," Tess said, her tone professional but gentle.

The scanner chimed softly. The doctor froze, brow furrowing as a holographic readout flickered above the device. Her sharp gray eyes cut to Datch. "You need to see this," she said, voice low but urgent.

Ash glanced up, suspicion breaking through his fatigue. "What now?"

"Do I have your permission to share these findings?" she asked, still professional, though her voice carried something heavier.

Ash blinked, too worn to care. "Sure. What do I care?"

Tess straightened, her hand falling from the scanner. She exchanged a loaded look with Datch, who gave a single nod.

• • • •

The briefing room was stark and utilitarian, its long metal table reflecting the overhead lights. Captain Calan sat at its head, his sharp gaze sweeping the group. Lily sat stiffly beside Datch, hands clasped in her lap. Rhyder leaned back with his usual air of nonchalance, though curiosity glinted in his eyes. Ash, pale and bandaged, slouched low, staring at the chair's armrest instead of the tension around him.

Calan leaned back, tone heavy. "All right. Fill me in."

Dr. Thesari rose, scanner in hand. "Captain," she began, voice calm but carrying weight, "the DNA results from Ash's medical scan revealed something unexpected."

Her gaze softened as she turned to Ash. "You are the biological son of Captain Eryk Dalren."

The words seemed to hang in the air. For a long moment, no one moved.

Rhyder let out a low whistle, leaning forward. "Well. Didn't see that coming."

Lily's eyes darted to Datch, who inclined his head slightly.

Ash looked more bewildered than anything. "You're kidding," he said flatly, though a flicker of shock crossed his face.

Tess shook her head. "The genetic match is irrefutable."

Calan steepled his fingers, expression darkening. "Well," he said slowly, "that certainly complicates things."

The room seemed to shrink under the weight of the revelation, implications branching in every direction.

• • • •

The lab had been dimmed for ship night, the glow of consoles the only light. Lily sat at a workstation, her face washed in blue-white, one hand propping her chin as the other tapped restlessly against the console. The screen's shifting patterns reflected the churn of her thoughts — fragments of the case refusing to settle into order.

"Burning the midnight oil?" a familiar voice asked.

Lily turned to see Alrek lingering in the doorway. His usually buoyant energy was muted, a trace of weariness clouding his eyes, though his smile still held.

"I heard you've been busy," he said, folding his arms in a casual stance that looked just a shade too tired to be effortless.

"Not as busy as you," Lily countered with a faint smirk. "Go rest. More knowledge awaits you tomorrow."

He chuckled softly, shaking his head. "Fair enough. Don't let the mysteries of the galaxy keep you up too late." With a wave, he slipped away down the corridor.

Moments later, Caris appeared, leaning against the doorframe. "I hear you've been busy."

Lily shot her a mock glare. "Is that everyone's new greeting?"

Caris grinned, stepping inside. "Word travels fast. Even on a ship this size."

Lily leaned back in her chair with a sigh. "All these pieces... I feel like I'm missing something obvious."

Caris rested a hand on the console, her expression gentler than usual. "You and Datch will figure it out. You're a good team. I even hear the captain isn't planning to reprimand him for dragging you into this."

A small smile tugged at Lily's lips. "I'll be fine here. Go. Get some rest."

Caris gave her a knowing look, but didn't press. "Good luck."

When she was gone, Lily returned to the monitor — only to hear another voice.

"Still working, eh?"

She startled at the sound of Rhyder's voice. He lounged against a nearby console, his tone light, his smile crooked.

"I'm really trying to think," Lily said, a little sharper than she intended.

He held up his hands in mock surrender. "Talk it out with me. Remember, I helped you solve your fashion problem. I can be useful."

Lily huffed, but her resolve slipped. "Fine. Let's lay it all out."

She lifted her hand, ticking points off with her fingers as she spoke.

Point One: Dalren's Connection to Ash

"Dalren is Ash's father. The result of a love affair early in his career with a diplomat."

Rhyder's eyebrows shot up. "Sordid," he said with relish.

"Dalren covered up a bar fight when Ash was eighteen. Someone died, and Dalren's been shielding him ever since. Ash used Dalren's codes to smuggle the field generator, not realizing whose they were. Dalren panicked when he saw his son tied to the theft and implicated himself to throw suspicion off."

Rhyder leaned in to study the screen. Lily glanced at him for a beat, then quickly looked away, pretending not to notice her body's unhelpful reaction.

Rhyder gave a thoughtful nod. "Messy. But it tracks."

Point Two: Lethra and the Field Generator

"Envoy Lethra — past ties to the True Believers. She helped arrange the theft of the static field generator. The resistance wanted it destroyed. And they succeeded, with some unwitting help from you."

Rhyder gave a sheepish grin. "Guilty as charged."

"We confirmed the generator was dumped and detonated an hour before the murder. That thread is closed."

"Lucky for me," he muttered.

Point Three: Cleared Suspects

"The Urrathi, the human delegation, the Raath-Ka — none of them connect cleanly to the crime. Which leaves us with..."

Point Four: Elder Vel

"Ambassador Vel. She's kept a lid on Varrothi experiments, but the motive doesn't hold. The Zephtari want peace. Their history and respect for the Varrothi is all on record."

"It just doesn't fit," Rhyder said, frustration edging his tone to match hers.

His gaze drifted to the monitor. "And this question mark? Just says money."

Lily's eyes followed his. "That's the benefactor for the Rencor Wave experiments. I don't have access to the files, but Datch mentioned it."

Rhyder leaned back, arms crossed. "Sounds like a big question mark to leave hanging."

"It is," Lily admitted, the weight of it pressing in her chest. She closed the file with a decisive tap. "Speaking of Datch, he called a meeting to tie up loose ends. I should get going."

Rhyder straightened, brushing off the console. "Oh, I also received the invite." His grin softened. "Hey, you've got this, Starlight."

Lily rolled her eyes, ignoring the unwelcome lump in her throat. With a steadying breath, she powered down the console and followed him out into the corridor.

The ship was quiet under night cycle, their footsteps the only sound against the polished deck. The hush carried with it a strange gravity, as though the walls themselves knew the weight of what was about to be said.

They entered the multi-use room together. The faint scent of incense lingered from a morning service, mingling with the sterile tang of recycled air. Cushioned chairs were arranged in neat rows facing a modest podium where Datch stood, posture as composed as ever. The chapel-like arrangement gave the space an unintentional solemnity, amplifying the tension gathering there.

Captain Calan sat front and center, arms crossed, his sharp gaze moving between the participants. Lily sat beside Rhyder, her posture stiff, her fingers idly smoothing the fabric of her pants. Ash slouched further back, bandaged and pale, though his gaze no longer avoided the others. Rhyder leaned casually in his seat, though the glint in his eye betrayed his curiosity. Elder Vel and Envoy Lethra occupied seats to the side, their composed expressions carefully neutral. In the back row, Dalren sat next to a uniformed Union officer, his face a mask of quiet resolve. On a monitor mounted at the side of the room, the stony faces of Veylon and Daalis of the Varrothi delegation loomed, framed by the stark gray backdrop of their ship.

Datch's calm, measured voice filled the room as he methodically laid out the investigation's findings, pulling disparate threads into a coherent narrative. The weight of his words was almost tangible as he reached his conclusion. "Analysis of the destructive field detected a communication signature. A Krythar communications signature."

Lily's eyes rested on the holographic image Datch had displayed—a distinct 3D rendering resembling an upturned pink horseshoe encircled by a green spiral. Her brow furrowed as she studied it, the design as foreign as the implications it carried.

The silence that followed was heavy, pressing down on the room like a stormcloud. Captain Calan finally broke it, his voice sharp and authoritative. "Fleet Command has reviewed the evidence and is fully convinced this was a Krythar operation. They assassinated their own delegate to derail the peace talks."

The Varrothi delegation erupted. Veylon's voice crackled through the speakers, his tone scathing. "This is an internal Krythar matter. We do not require Union interference!" With that, the monitor went dark, their transmission abruptly severed.

Datch turned his attention to Dalren and Ash, his gaze steady and unflinching. "The charges against you have been dropped concerning the events of the last few days. However, your past actions remain unresolved. That is your burden to bear."

Ash pushed himself to his feet, his movements careful but deliberate. He turned to Dalren, his expression more open than Lily had ever seen. "Then I'd like to face them together," he said quietly.

Dalren's face softened, his usual stoicism giving way to something deeper. "Together," he agreed. The two men embraced—raw, unguarded despite the gathered witnesses. When they parted, they turned to follow the waiting Union officer at the back of the room.

As the others began to filter out, their voices low and subdued, Lily turned to Datch. "I have an appointment to see the prince," she said, her voice soft but purposeful.

Datch inclined his head slightly, his posture as composed as ever. "An important farewell," he remarked. "I imagine he will appreciate your presence."

Lily hesitated as she moved toward the door. Glancing back at Datch, she asked, "By the way, who was the benefactor you mentioned for the Rencor Wave project?"

Datch's response was measured, almost dismissive. "I don't know for sure. Captain Calan requested the record be unsealed, but now that the investigation is over, it's unlikely to be a priority."

Lily frowned slightly but chose to let the matter drop. As she turned back toward the exit, Rhyder appeared at her side, his smirk softening into something more genuine. "Guess this is where we part ways—for now," he said.

Lily raised an eyebrow. "For now?"

"Let's just say you'll probably see me sooner than you think," Rhyder replied with a wink.

As he moved in for a hug, Lily extended her hand for a handshake, throwing off their timing. Rhyder adjusted, offering his hand just as she leaned in for the hug. They both laughed, the tension breaking as easily as their awkwardness.

Then, quick as a heartbeat, he leaned in and kissed her. It was brief, surprising—leaving her uncertain what to think about it. But against her better judgment, she liked it.

When he pulled back, his grin returned. "Take care of yourself, Starlight."

Lily watched him go, the sound of his boots fading into the quiet corridor. She lingered for a moment before exhaling deeply, squaring her shoulders as she turned to the door. The next destination awaited her—the prince.

• • • •

The opulent Luxury Residence felt eerily hollow as Lily stepped inside. The usual bustle had been replaced by the muted shuffling of attendants packing away priceless artifacts and furnishings. Sunlight streamed through towering crystal windows, fracturing into rainbows that danced across the marble floors. The scent of exotic blooms still lingered faintly in the air, a fading whisper of the Ishrethi presence.

Lily wandered through the grand hall, her footsteps a soft echo in the vast, empty space. The melancholy of the moment hung heavy; the peace talks lay in ruins, and she imagined Prince Zayir must be crushed. As she waited, her eyes traced the intricate patterns woven into the tapestries that adorned the walls—each depicting scenes of Ishrethi triumphs and legends, a silent testament to their storied past.

"Ah, Miss Starling," a regal voice broke the quiet.

Lily turned to see Queen Ishraan entering the room. Though her attire was far more casual than expected—a form-fitting ensemble resembling high-fashion athletic wear—it did nothing to diminish her commanding presence. Her silver hair was pulled back into an elegant style, and her makeup was impeccable, subtly emphasizing her sharp cheekbones and piercing blue eyes. Even in practicality, she wore her majestic jewelry—necklaces and bracelets gleaming softly with her every movement.

"I trust you're finding everything satisfactory?" the queen inquired, her voice smooth, her smile poised.

"Queen Karyah," Lily replied, nodding respectfully. "Yes, thank you. I'm just waiting to see your son."

"Just Karyah, dear, remember?" the queen said, her tone warm but edged with the authority that never quite left her words. "He'll be along shortly. These departures are always so... hectic." Her gaze drifted to the half-packed crates lining the corridor, and she sighed lightly, her expression momentarily weary.

An attendant approached the queen, whispering something urgently. Karyah's composed expression tightened, her poise marred by a flicker of irritation. "Did you tell them to adjust the Rencor levels?" she murmured, her whisper sharp enough to cut, and just loud enough for Lily to strain to hear. Without waiting for a reply, she waved the attendant off. "Never mind... I'll handle it myself."

Turning back to Lily, she offered a faint smile, the mask of regal politeness slipping back into place. "Excuse me for a moment, my dear."

As the queen glided from the room, her movements as seamless as ever, Lily's mind churned. Rencor. The word echoed in her thoughts, pulling at fragmented memories until the connections snapped into place. Rencor Waves—the experimental technology developed with Varrothi collaboration, capable of imitating any energy signature. Funded by a mysterious benefactor...

Her pulse quickened as the realization hit. If the benefactor was the Ishrethi royal family, if it had been the king himself...

Her feet moved almost without her realizing, carrying her to the nearest console. Its sleek, luminescent interface awaited input. Her fingers skimmed the surface, navigating quickly through the menus. One folder caught her eye—marked "secure" but already open, its contents displayed like a warning sign left in haste.

There it was: a shimmering 3D image of a pink horseshoe encircled by a green spiral. The Krythar communications signature.

Except it wasn't. Lily's breath caught as the pieces solidified. It wasn't a Krythar signature at all. It was fabricated—engineered with Rencor Waves. She heard Ka-Lorrin's voice in her memory, explaining how the technology could mimic any energy signature, any transmission. It could pretend to be anything.

"Now, my dear, where were we?"

Lily spun to find the queen returning, her sharp eyes narrowing as they landed on Lily standing by the console. The shift in her expression was subtle but unmistakable—a flicker of suspicion under the polished veneer.

"It was you," Lily whispered, the words barely escaping her lips.

The queen tilted her head gracefully. "What do you mean, child?"

"You killed L'than Veirr," Lily said, her voice growing stronger with each word. "You had access to Rencor technology because your husband's administration funded the experiments. You used it to fake a Krythar communications signature and sabotage the peace talks."

The queen's lips curled into a slow, chilling smile, her eyes gleaming with something that made Lily's stomach turn. "My son was right about you. You are a very special girl indeed."

Lily's voice sharpened with accusation. "I can't believe you would undermine your own son like that," she said, her fists tightening at her sides. "Is this what you meant when you said the keepers of the keys are the ones who write history? Is this the history you want for your children?"

The queen's expression hardened, her regal composure giving way to something colder, sharper—a steel edge beneath the velvet exterior. "The galaxy is forged by the strong, not the weak," she declared, her voice ringing with conviction. "This is an opportunity for true leadership. To unite the systems against a common enemy. To bring the Krythar to their knees. That will be my son's legacy—not a naive and fleeting peace, but lasting order under Ishrethi dominion once again."

Lily stepped back instinctively, her mind racing, every nerve screaming for escape. She slipped her hand into her pocket, pressing her comm tag to signal Datch. "You're risking everything," she argued, her voice wavering but determined. "If anyone finds out—"

"Enough." The queen's voice cracked like a whip. In a fluid motion, she raised a sleek blaster.

Lily froze, her heart slamming against her ribs. "Are you going to murder me?" she asked, almost as if it was a challenge.

The queen tilted her head, as if considering. "I wasn't planning on it," she said with an unsettling calm. "But perhaps it's cleaner this way. Loose ends have a way of unraveling even the best-laid plans."

Lily thought fast. Her eyes flicked past the queen's shoulder. "Are you sure you want to shoot me in front of your own son?"

The queen's gaze flickered ever so slightly toward the doorway—a split-second diversion. Seizing the moment, Lily lunged, slamming her hand against the queen's wrist. The blaster clattered to the floor, skidding across the polished surface.

But the queen moved with startling speed, delivering a sharp, well-aimed kick to Lily's temple. Stars burst behind Lily's eyes as she crashed to the floor, pain radiating through her skull. Adrenaline forced her onward. Gritting her teeth, she scrambled to her knees just as the queen reclaimed the blaster.

"And now my dear, this is goodbye." The queen hissed, her voice cold and final as she leveled the weapon at Lily's head.

"Mother?"

Prince Zayir's voice rang out from the doorway, confusion and alarm woven into the single word. "What on Ishreth is going on here?"

The queen froze, her regal composure cracking as she turned toward her son. "Zayir, Z—this isn't what it looks like," she began, her tone shifting, practiced and placating.

"Zayir," Lily interjected, her voice sharp and urgent. "She killed the Varrothi delegate. She's been orchestrating this entire plot to sabotage the peace talks."

Zayir's gaze snapped between Lily and his mother, disbelief giving way to something colder. "Is this true?" he demanded.

"Everything I've done, I did for you," the queen said, desperation cracking through her polished facade. "You are to be the most powerful ruler in the galaxy, To secure your father's... our... your legacy."

Zayir's expression darkened, heartbreak etched in the furrow of his brow. "Mother," he said quietly, "why don't you ever listen? I've tried so many times to make you understand, but—you don't know me at all."

"I'm your mother!" she countered, taking a step toward him. Her voice softened, imploring. "Everything I've done has been for our family, for you, for Ishreth."

"And yet, you've never cared to see me," Zayir replied, his voice steady, every word deliberate. "I am Prince Zayir Ishraan Kaseer, heir to my father's name, to the throne of Ishreth. I will use that title to bring peace to this galaxy—not plunge it into war."

The queen faltered, her face twisting in a storm of sorrow and defiance. "I'm sorry, my child," she whispered, her voice barely audible. "I didn't want it to end this way."

Her fingers tightened on the blaster, the barrel beginning to rise toward her son.

"Look out!" Lily shouted.

A sudden flash of light burst from the doorway—a stun beam striking the queen squarely in the chest. She crumpled to the floor, the blaster slipping from her grasp. Standing behind her, Datch lowered his weapon with practiced precision.

"Are you unharmed?" he asked Lily, stepping forward as security officers rushed into the room, their movements efficient and purposeful.

Lily nodded shakily, relief flooding through her. "Thank you," she said, her voice barely above a whisper.

Prince Zayir remained rooted in place, his gaze fixed on his mother's unconscious form. The weight of betrayal carved deep lines into his face, his usual composure replaced with something raw and fragile.

"I'm so sorry," Lily said softly, taking a hesitant step toward him.

He turned to her slowly, a flicker of resolve sparking in his eyes amidst the turmoil. "You have nothing to apologize for," he replied, his voice quiet but steady. "Thank you for helping me see the truth."

"What will you do now?" Lily asked gently, her tone careful, almost reverent.

Zayir straightened, and though his shoulders still bore the weight of the moment, a quiet determination began to take shape. " I will not let this define my path. The peace talks may be over for now, but I won't stop fighting for what I believe in."

Lily offered a small, encouraging smile. "If anyone can make a difference, it's you."

He inclined his head slightly in acknowledgment. "I hope our paths cross again, Miss Starling."

She returned the nod with a warmer one of her own. "Call me Lily."

"Lily," he said, as though testing the word, before adding, "Thank you."

As the prince turned to address the security team, Lily felt Datch step closer.

"Well done," he said simply, his voice calm but carrying the faintest trace of approval.

She took a deep breath, the tension of the day finally catching up to her. "I couldn't have done it without you," she admitted.

"Indeed," he replied, a hint of something almost like warmth in his tone.

Lily couldn't help but feel a mix of relief and sorrow. The peace talks were in ruins, but she wanted to believe there was hope on the horizon.

• • • •

The Salamander sang with the quiet efficiency of a ship easing back into its rhythm. In the mess hall, Lily sat with Caris and Datch at a small table by the viewport. The sprawling expanse of Star Base 12 slowly shrank in the distance, its gleaming structure fading into the backdrop of the stars. A steaming mug of tea warmed Lily's hands as she stared out at the void of deep space, a mixture of exhaustion and quiet reflection settling over her.

Caris leaned back in her chair, her usual sharp edges softened by a rare moment of relaxation. "Feels strange leaving all that behind," she mused, nodding toward the disappearing station. "Not that I'm going to miss the diplomatic drama."

Lily smiled faintly. "Feels like we packed a whole year's worth of chaos into a few days," she said, her tone wry. "I can't help but wonder what's waiting for us out there."

"Statistically speaking," Datch interjected, his even tone carrying the faintest hint of humor, "the odds favor more chaos."

Caris snorted, shaking her head. "Thanks for the reassurance, Datch."

Lily chuckled and took a sip of her tea. She was about to reply when Datch spoke again, his voice shifting to something more measured. "Speaking of developments," he began, "I received a communication earlier today. The Space Fleet has bestowed upon me an honorary rank of Lieutenant Commander."

Caris straightened, a grin spreading across her face. "Datch! That's amazing!" she exclaimed. "Congrats!"

Lily grinned, raising her mug in an impromptu toast. "To Lieutenant Commander Datch!"

Datch inclined his head slightly. "Thank you. However, I must clarify that the title is purely honorary. The Fleet still does not officially recognize my personhood."

The atmosphere around the table shifted slightly, the weight of his words settling over them. Lily's smile faltered for a moment, replaced by a look of quiet determination. "It's still a step," she said firmly. "And one they wouldn't have taken without you."

Datch considered her words, his face set with his usual poker face, but he gave the smallest of nods. "Perhaps."

The moment hung in the air, a quiet camaraderie between the three as they shared in this small victory. The ship's hum seemed almost peaceful, a rare reprieve from the chaos of recent days.

Then, a murmur began to ripple through the mess hall. Heads turned toward the monitors lining the walls as the sound of hurried footsteps grew louder.

Lily frowned, setting her mug down. "Oh no, what now?" she muttered, already bracing herself.

"Not again," Caris grumbled, rising from her seat.

The three joined the growing crowd gathering around the central holodisplay. A newsfeed flickered to life, the headline emblazoned across the screen in bold, chilling letters:

Frontier Station Destroyed: Zephtari Science Station on the Edge of Krythar Space Obliterated by Krythar Interceptor Ships. 300 Dead.

Gasps and whispers filled the room, but Lily barely heard them. Her stomach dropped, her chest tightening as the weight of the words settled in. She glanced at Caris, whose jaw was clenched, and then at Datch, whose expression remained even but whose gaze lingered on the screen, as though analyzing every detail.

Lily's voice was barely a whisper. "What kind of storm are we headed into next?"

Neither Datch nor Caris answered. The three stood in stunned silence, the newsfeed playing on, the gravity of what lay ahead pulling them all back into the unknown.

Chapter 8: Hearts of Glass

THE SMALL CARGO BAY thrummed with the steady rhythm of the Salamander's systems, a heartbeat of engineered precision. The artificial gravity was off, leaving everything untethered and drifting—small tools and bits of equipment hovered in lazy arcs, casting long, soft-edged shadows against the smooth walls. The faint blue glow of emergency lights mixed with the golden shimmer of safety beacons, creating a subdued, almost dreamlike atmosphere.

Lily squinted at her target—a narrow rail by the control panel—and kicked off from a support beam. The magnetic soles of her EV suit hummed faintly with potential energy, ready to anchor her as soon as she landed. But her trajectory wavered, and her momentum carried her just wide of the rail. She missed, her hands grabbing at empty air.

Her stomach tightened, a rush of self-reproach bubbling up. "Relax your movements," Caris's voice crackled through her helmet's comm system. Calm and steady, like the voice of someone narrating a scenic tour.

Lily turned her head to see Caris floating effortlessly near the opposite wall, her arms crossed in a way that made her look almost bored. The sleek curves of her EV suit caught the ambient light, the segmented plates of silver and black making her look as polished and seamless as the ship itself. Her boots hovered inches from a floating toolkit that she didn't even glance at.

"You're overcompensating," Caris continued, her tone both amused and encouraging. "Smaller kicks, less panic. The suit will do the work if you let it."

Lily nodded, taking a moment to re-center herself. Her own EV suit felt bulky, like wearing a too-heavy jacket underwater. The panels flexed and adjusted as she moved, but every joint creaked just a little, the sound sharp in her ears. She tried to remember the instructions from their earlier briefing: *minimal movement, controlled momentum, trust the tech.*

She kicked off again, her eyes on the rail, but her focus faltered for a fraction of a second.

The comm tag in her locker chirped.

Her trajectory wobbled, and she stopped herself mid-drift with a hand on a nearby wall, turning her head toward the sound. It wasn't even loud—just a soft *beep-beep*—but it cut through the white noise in her mind like a blade.

"Third time," Caris said, her smirk audible. "You wanna go check that?"

"No," Lily said quickly. "It's probably nothing."

Caris floated closer, her movements effortless, like a fish slicing through water. "You're distracted. And you're not helping yourself by pretending you're not."

Lily hesitated, heat rising to her cheeks. "Fine," she muttered, pushing off toward the locker. Her movements were stiff, graceless compared to Caris's fluidity. She fumbled with the latch before retrieving the comm tag.

The holo display flared to life, casting faint blue light onto her face. Lily scanned the message, her heart giving an unsteady flutter.

It was from Xynn.

She could hear Xynn's voice in her head, playful but sharp, like a blade wrapped in silk. It wasn't the words themselves—simple, casual, asking how Lily was doing. It was the subtext, the rhythm of their connection that still felt so new and so... fragile.

For a moment, she was back in the observation lounge from a few weeks ago, watching Xynn tilt her head, her piercing gaze fixed on Lily. They'd been arguing, in that charged way that wasn't really arguing. Something about Alrek, something about protocol. Lily couldn't even remember the topic now—only the way Xynn had smiled afterward, the way her sharp edges softened for just a moment. It had been disarming, dizzying.

"You're blushing," Caris's voice pulled her back to the present.

Lily flinched, almost dropping the comm tag.

Caris laughed, the sound light. "Is that from your girlfriend?"

"She's not my girlfriend," Lily said quickly, but the protest sounded weak even to her own ears.

"Uh-huh." Caris floated closer, her tone teasing. "It looks like a girlfriend message."

"It's complicated," Lily said, tucking the comm tag away.

"Complicated how?" Caris asked, now clearly intrigued.

Lily sighed, the sound heavy in the quiet of the cargo bay. She shifted her grip on the comm tag, running her thumb over its smooth surface as if the motion might help her untangle the knot in her chest. "Xynn... she's amazing," she started, the words careful, like she was laying them out in a line to inspect them. "But her culture has a caste system. There's a lot of prejudice baked into how she sees the world. It's not her fault—it's just how things are for her. She's trying, though. She made an effort with Alrek, and I could see it—it's just... there's still a lot of hate there. I don't know if I can look past that."

Caris didn't answer right away. Instead, she tilted her head slightly, her eyes sharp behind the visor of her EV suit, the way a teacher might when weighing whether to push a struggling student. "Do you like her?" she asked, her tone soft but direct.

The question hit Lily like a bump in the road, jolting her thoughts loose. She hesitated, her grip tightening on the comm tag as she turned the words over in her mind. Did she like Xynn?

"Yeah," she admitted finally, the word barely a whisper. "A little. But it's hard."

Caris nodded slowly, her expression pensive but kind, like she was seeing Lily in a new light. "I get that," she said, her voice quiet but firm. "But when it comes to prejudice, you've got to give people the chance to change. I was..." She paused, a faint, rueful smile tugging at the corner of her mouth. "Let's just say I was no saint about this stuff. I used to be pretty bigoted against the Cyranthians."

Lily blinked, her grip on the comm tag loosening slightly as the confession caught her completely off guard. "You?" she asked, her voice rising with disbelief. "Against the Cyranthians? How? Why?"

"It's a long story," Caris began, her voice softening. Her gaze drifted, as if she could see the memory playing out in the soft glow of the cargo bay. "When humans and Cyranthians first made contact, they treated us like children. Sabotaged our scientific efforts so we'd stay dependent on them, like they thought we weren't ready to stand on our own." She shook her head slightly, the movement barely perceptible in the weightless air.

"When my parents died, I ended up in a Cyranthian foster home. For a while, it became trendy for them to take in human kids—a way to show

how charitable they were, 'giving the poor humans a better life.'" Her lips tightened, her tone edged with an old bitterness. "But the way they looked at me, with the subtle prejudice of low expectations... like I was some fragile thing they needed to fix. It left a mark. For years, I was uncomfortable around Cyranthians. Sometimes, I still have to remind myself not to judge them too quickly."

Lily floated silently beside her, the words sinking in like stones dropped into still water. "What changed your perspective?" she asked after a moment, her voice quieter now.

Caris's smile softened, the weight of the memory easing slightly. "Malik," she said simply. "He's not your typical Cyranthian. Grumpy as anything." The faintest laugh slipped into her voice, a thread of warmth weaving through the words. "On Cyranthia, that's kind of like being autistic among humans. Most of their population has this natural positivity and charm. If you're not constantly outgoing, it's hard to fit in.

"Getting to know Malik—and seeing how the Dryst on board still accept him, even though he's different—helped me realize their friendliness isn't always fake. Sometimes, it's just... complicated."

Lily turned the comm tag over in her hand, her gaze falling back to Xynn's message. Her thumb brushed the edge of the holo display, and she let herself reread it, just once more. For once, she let herself enjoy the butterflies.

The captain's voice crackled over the ship's comm system, cutting through the stillness. "Lily, Lieutenant Commander Caris, report to the bridge."

Caris smiled, breaking the quiet moment. "Duty calls!"

With a practiced motion, she tapped a control on her EV suit. The segmented panels shifted and folded with a faint hiss, collapsing into compact pieces that clung seamlessly to her shoulders and hips. Lily followed her lead, activating her own suit just as the artificial gravity reactivated with a soft hum.

They floated gently downward, landing with a light thud on the polished floor.

Caris glanced over, her smirk faint but teasing. "Let's hope you're a little less clumsy on the bridge."

Lily shot her a mock glare, though the smile tugging at her lips gave her away as they headed for the door together.

· · · ·

The Salamander's bridge was alive with its usual quiet efficiency. Console light rippled across the curved walls, and the low murmur of the crew blended with the steady chime of readouts. Beyond the wide viewport, stars drifted past in a glittering stream.

At the back of the bridge, the sliding glass doors of the conference room whispered open. Lily followed Caris and Malik inside, her boots landing with soft thuds as gravity reclaimed her. The holo-projector in the center of the table was already powered on, casting a faint blue glow across the high-backed chairs. Wall panels gave off their steady light, serene as ever—but the tension that filled the room was anything but.

Captain Calan stood at the head of the table, his expression as steady as the stars beyond the viewports. "We have new orders from Command," he began, his voice measured and calm. He nodded toward Lily, and for a moment, she thought she saw a flicker of something almost fatherly in his gaze. "After the tragedy at Frontier Station, we haven't had a solid plan for assisting with Lily's recovery. This mission may finally offer some answers. At the same time, it aligns perfectly with our goals of exploration and humanitarian assistance."

His words pressed down on the room—not oppressive, but heavy enough that Lily felt them settle on her shoulders. A reminder of all the eyes on her, both here and across the Union.

"Dryst Amaris is our resident expert on the Xyridren people," Calan continued, stepping back. "I'll let him explain."

Amaris rose with his usual confidence, movements smooth and deliberate. Lily noticed Malik shift in his chair, his jaw tightening as Amaris began to speak.

"The Xyridren," Amaris said, his voice carrying a low, steady authority, "are rare—and fascinating. They are distantly related to the Krythar, but centuries of interbreeding with the Varrothi have changed them greatly. They resemble the other humanoid species now—though they retain formidable telekinetic abilities, powerful enough to disrupt Krythar psionics during their long years of subjugation."

The holo-projector flared to life, casting a faint glow over the table as an image of a Xyridren rotated above it. Reflective, scaly skin shimmered faintly in the light. Their large, glowing eyes gave them a striking, almost beautiful look—alien, yes, but not threatening. Lily found herself leaning forward, studying them, as though trying to memorize every sharp and elegant line.

The holo shifted again, this time to their homeworld: a swampy, fog-laden expanse. Dark trees jutted from murky water, tangled roots vanishing into the depths.

"They resisted Krythar domination for generations," Amaris went on. "Eventually, the Krythar deemed them too much trouble to control and allowed them to leave their territory. They resettled on the planet Xyrrhos, where they have lived in isolation ever since, fiercely protective of their independence."

Calan stepped in again, his voice cutting through the quiet. "Until now. They've reached out to the Union for assistance."

Amaris inclined his head smoothly, picking up the thread. "Their planet is experiencing severe magnetic storms, triggering seismic activity and mudslides. The Sacred Marshes—a site of profound cultural and spiritual importance—are under immediate threat of destruction."

"Sacred marshes?" Malik cut in, his voice sharp, almost sneering. "More like *sacred mud*."

Amaris didn't miss a beat. "The Xyridren come from a swamp world, Mr. Malik. To them, the marshes are not mud. They are history. Identity. A way of life." His tone was even, but there was an edge beneath it—a quiet reprimand sharp enough to land.

"Gentlemen," Calan interjected, his voice clean and firm. "The Union has agreed to provide assistance in the form of a gravimetric flux engine. This technology will stabilize the magnetic field and restore the region. In return, the Xyridren have offered to help Lily with her psionic training. This is an extraordinary opportunity. They rarely speak with outsiders, let alone invite them to their world."

Amaris clasped his hands behind his back, his gaze sweeping the room. "I will lead the away team. Caris, Lily, and Malik will accompany me, along with a support science detail. This mission will require cooperation and discretion."

"Any questions?" Calan asked, his eyes scanning the room.

Silence followed, thick with unspoken thoughts.

"Good," Calan said finally. "Dismissed."

As Lily rose, she caught Malik's expression. His mouth was set in a hard line, his shoulders taut, his dark eyes simmering with a quiet anger he wasn't bothering to hide. It wasn't just the Xyridren. It was deeper, sharper—like a wound twisting beneath the surface.

Lily lingered, watching him leave. Whatever was boiling in him, she had a feeling it wouldn't stay buried for long.

. . . .

The shuttle cut through the expanse of stars, its sleek form slipping through the void on approach to Xyrrhos. Inside, the atmosphere was subdued but tense. Lily sat near the front of the cabin, her eyes flicking to Malik, who was slouched in his seat with arms crossed tight. His gaze was locked on the floor, his expression drawn and distant.

Dryst Amaris stood at the controls, his movements smooth as he adjusted the course. "We'll make planetfall in approximately thirty minutes," he announced, his voice as measured as always.

Caris, seated beside Lily, gave a small sigh. "Looks like we're in for some turbulence," she muttered, nodding toward a faint flicker of energy on the console.

Lily nodded absently, her attention still on Malik. Something in his posture unsettled her. It wasn't just his usual gruffness—it ran deeper, coiled tight in his shoulders, as if it lived in his bones. After a moment, she rose and motioned for Caris to follow her into the small breakout room off the cabin.

"What's up?" Caris asked, leaning casually against the wall as the door slid shut.

"It's Malik," Lily said quietly. "He looks... physically uncomfortable being on this mission. Like he'd rather be anywhere else."

Caris's expression softened with recognition. "Yeah. Fitting we were talking about prejudice earlier. Malik's colony had some ugly run-ins with the Xyridren."

Lily tilted her head. "Ugly how?"

"They're territorial," Caris said simply. "Malik's colony settled too close to theirs. The Xyridren didn't ask. They demanded relocation—and it turned into a full-blown conflict. Families uprooted, homes lost. For Malik, that's not a story in a briefing file. It's his."

Lily frowned. "Do you think it'll interfere with the mission?"

Caris shook her head. "He's a professional. He'll get the job done. But that doesn't mean he has to like it."

Lily opened her mouth to press further, but the shuttle jolted violently, throwing them both sideways. A low rumble tore through the hull, and the lights flickered.

"Environmental interference!" Amaris's voice barked through the comm.

Lily and Caris scrambled back to the cabin, gripping the walls as the shuttle bucked again. Warning lights strobed red and orange across the displays, alarms layering into a chaotic din.

Amaris's hands flew over the controls. "Magnetic fields intensifying—readings off the charts. We're losing altitude."

"Can you stabilize us?" Caris asked, bracing herself against the wall.

"Not with this interference," Amaris shot back, his composure cracking. "Prepare for emergency landing."

The shuttle shook violently, metal groaning under the strain. The ground rushed up in the viewport.

"Brace for impact!" Amaris shouted.

The shuttle slammed down with a deafening crash. Dirt and debris blasted across the view as Lily jolted hard against her restraints. When the shaking stilled, silence fell—broken only by heavy breathing.

"Everyone all right?" Amaris called, already moving to the panels.

Lily unbuckled and glanced around. "Caris?"

"I'm here," Caris said through clenched teeth, cradling her arm. Her face was pale.

Malik was already at her side, steady and deliberate. "It's not broken," he said, his voice unexpectedly gentle. "But it'll hurt like hell for a while." He fashioned a sling from the med kit, his movements careful as he wrapped her arm and gave her a quick injection for the pain.

Lily hovered nearby, watching them. She thought she might have noticed more than duty in Malik's movements—there was a tenderness there, a softer side she had never seen in him before.

At the controls, Amaris tried the comm panel. "Salamander, this is Shuttle Omega. Do you copy?" Only static answered. His jaw tightened. "Interference is blocking the signal. We're on our own for now."

Malik secured the emergency packs with clipped efficiency. "Then let's move."

The hatch hissed open, and the swamp air of Xyrrhos rushed in—thick, damp, heavy with the scent of mud and decay. Lily adjusted her pack and glanced at Caris, her usual confidence muted by pain.

Together, they stepped out into the murky horizon, the alien world stretching endlessly ahead.

· · · ·

The canopy above was an unbroken sheet of green, so dense and interwoven it was as if the sky itself had been sealed away. Only faint ribbons of light filtered through, their muted glow barely reaching the ground below. What little sky could be glimpsed shimmered a deep green—the color of oxidized copper—casting the world in a dreamlike haze.

The trees were towering sentinels, their trunks slick with moisture and draped in vines that seemed to writhe in the damp air. Between their branches flitted a kaleidoscope of life. Insects with shimmering carapaces darted in zigzag patterns, their wings beating so fast they merged into the forest's constant song. One hovered too close to a cluster of leaves—and in an instant, a lizard-like creature pounced, swallowing it whole. Its body was lean and scaled, its limbs long and sinewy like a primate's. With clawed fingers and an opposable tail, it swung effortlessly through the canopy before vanishing into the depths of green.

Above, swarms of winged creatures glinted like shards of crystal, their calls blending into a chaotic symphony that filled the upper air.

On the lower branches, a snake-like creature coiled lazily, its body slick with a wet sheen. It had no eyes—only a line of heat-sensitive ridges that pulsed faintly as it scanned for prey.

Closer to the ground, mist curled around gnarled roots and stagnant pools. Tiny bipeds scavenged in the muck, their quick movements darting between patches of fog.

The bog seemed alive, every inch of it shifting, breathing, teeming with hidden energy. The dense humidity pressed against Lily's skin, slicking her hair to her forehead and making every breath feel like pulling water into her lungs. She wiped her brow, her hand coming away damp.

"It's like breathing soup," she muttered.

Caris, walking just ahead, shot her a glance over her shoulder. "Once we get to the path, it should prove a little easier—but we've got a ways to go."

Lily glanced down at the ground, where her boots sank slightly into the mud with every step. Each footfall released a sour scent of fermenting vegetation, the mist wrapping her in a cool, mineral tang. She adjusted her pack, forcing herself forward through the thick humidity.

The trek was grueling. The forest pressed close, vines tangling like fingers while unseen creatures called from the shadows. Even the sunlight dissolved into a muted green haze beneath the canopy.

Ahead, Malik studied the scanner, its screen glowing faintly in the gloom. "The path is just up ahead," he muttered.

But when they reached the crest of the ridge, the forest fell away to reveal a sheer drop. The gorge yawned before them, its depths lost in swirling mist.

Caris groaned, clutching her injured arm. "You've got to be kidding me. Did you even check the readings?"

Malik bristled. "The scanner's not exactly precise in this mess. The forest is throwing everything off."

Caris closed her eyes, shaking her head. "Sorry. The heat's getting to me. Let's just figure out how to get across."

Lily edged forward, the drop dizzying. "We could try to go around," she offered, though the thought of hours more slogging weighed heavily.

Before anyone could respond, the mist shifted. Dark shapes emerged at the edges of the clearing—Xyridren.

They were nothing like the polished holo-images Lily had seen. Their mottled scales blended seamlessly with the forest, their forms draped in vines and moss. Glowing eyes fixed on the group, weapons in hand.

The largest stepped forward, locking his gaze on Amaris.

Amaris raised a hand. "We are en route to Mirefall City to meet with the Collective. We mean no harm."

The leader studied him for a long moment, then gestured for them to follow.

Caris gave a faint shrug. "Better than wandering aimlessly."

The Xyridren moved with eerie grace, leading them down a narrow path that twisted through the mist. Doubt gnawed at Lily, but Amaris followed without hesitation.

At last, the path opened at the base of a massive tree. From its roots stretched a bridge of woven wood and vine, arching across the gorge as though grown from the forest itself.

They crossed cautiously, their footsteps muted. On the other side stretched the main road, cutting cleanly through the dense swamp.

"Well," Caris said, her voice a mix of relief and awe. "That's convenient."

Amaris turned to thank their escorts, but the clearing was empty. The Xyridren had vanished like smoke.

"They're gone," Lily murmured.

"I suppose that's one way to avoid small talk," Amaris replied.

The road wound onward until the mist began to thin. Shafts of green-tinted light filtered through, and the ground grew firmer under their boots. Soon, the silhouette of an archway emerged from the fog.

It was no mere gate but a monument. The base seemed to rise directly from the earth, entwined with ancient roots. From there, it climbed breathtakingly high, trunks braided together in an intricate, hypnotic lattice.

Flanking the arch stood two statues—Xyridren warriors over 300 feet tall. Their scaled armor gleamed beneath moss and streaks of slime, their glowing eyes forever fixed on the swamp. Weather had scarred the city walls, but the statues endured, untouched.

Beyond the arch stretched Mirefall City, sprawling in chaotic beauty. The wall encircled it like a scar, but inside, life pulsed. The closer they came, the more sound filled the air: chatter of voices, clatter of wheels on stone, the hum of tired hovercars. The air reeked of wet earth, spice, and faint metal.

Some residents passed without a glance. Others stared openly, their glowing eyes wide with curiosity. Children tugged at parents' sleeves, pointing at the strangers.

"It's like we've grown two heads," Caris muttered.

"They've probably never seen aliens before," Lily said, watching a group of teenagers whisper from a vendor's cart.

The streets swelled with traffic: pedicabs rattling, vendors shouting in melodic tones, livestock bleating against the din. Even amid the chaos, Amaris walked unhurried, his stride purposeful.

"We need to find the capital center," he said.

"I kind of expected a welcome committee," Caris quipped.

"The Xyridren aren't known for ceremony," Amaris replied with a faint smile.

They pushed through the bustle until Malik found a public transit station. Vines tangled with sleek metal supports, commuters flowing briskly through. An attendant gestured to a map, and Malik's scanner flickered with translation.

"There," he pointed. "Center of the city."

Moments later they boarded a transit pod, a transparent dome humming to life as it sped through tunnels. Caris leaned back with a wry grin. "Just your everyday commute."

The pod eased into a grand station built at the capital's base. Vaulted ceilings soared overhead, carved with patterns that echoed the archway outside. Light filtered through crystalline windows, scattering color across the polished floor.

Guards closed in, armor gleaming faintly as a delegate in flowing robes approached. His voice rang warm and practiced: "Welcome, welcome."

Malik's mouth twitched. "They're really rolling out the red carpet."

Inside the capital, the air hit Lily like a damp cloth—humid, but controlled. The corridors gleamed under shifting lights, their polished walls and braided arches too bright, too artificial. The inhabitants were as polished as the halls: glossy skin, immaculate clothes, postures unnervingly straight.

It was a jarring contrast to the outer city, where weathered hands and mud-stained clothes spoke of labor and survival.

A painting drew Lily's eye—an image of the Sacred Marshes, but glorified, almost celestial. The swamp waters shimmered unnaturally, the mist glowing as if divine. Not a painting of the marshes, but of an idea.

"This feels... different," Lily murmured.

"Civilization, snobbery—take your pick," Caris replied.

The endless corridors blurred together, sterile and dazzling, until Lily's eyes ached.

And then, abruptly, it ended.

Ahead of them, a brilliant light poured through an opening at the end of the corridor, dazzling after so much shadow. For a fleeting moment Lily's heart skipped — the glow reminded her of the stories of people walking into the afterlife.

When they stepped through, it might as well have been heaven.

The atrium soared a hundred feet high, its walls all glass, the rainforest canopy looming beyond. Light filtered through the green sky, bathing everything in a verdant glow. At its center was Mirefall itself — a perfect circular break in the canopy where sunlight poured down in a single column, a natural spotlight for the city's heart.

Lily turned slowly, awe pressing the breath from her chest. Spiraling ramps climbed the walls toward gilded doors, like golden threads woven through the vast chamber.

"Wow," she whispered, the word barely audible.

They crossed the atrium, their footsteps echoing. Every detail seemed designed to overwhelm: gilded railings, towering glass walls, the single shaft of sunlight illuminating everything.

At the far end, sleek doors opened without a sound, leading into another chamber. Light still poured through tall arched windows, softened by glossy stone floors and precise arrangements of lush plants.

Their escort halted abruptly. Amaris stepped forward, polite but firm. "Excuse me—"

The attendant turned sharply on his heel and walked away without a word.

"Charming," Amaris muttered.

Before Lily could react, a voice rolled out from a corner deliberately cast in shadow: smooth, mocking, and resonant.

"I assume you're accustomed to a heroes' welcome when you visit other worlds."

A figure stepped forward, framed by the dramatic contrast. His scales were pale and opalescent, reflecting the light like pearls. Regal posture, cool disdain.

"The pride of the mighty Union," he went on. "Gilded knights, riding in to rescue the poor savage planets. Bringing order to chaos. Turning the wild into yet another sterile jewel in your crown."

Lily's jaw tightened. Amaris stood rigid. Malik muttered something dark under his breath.

"Do you ever consider the cost of your benevolence?" the Xyridren pressed, pacing now. "The cultures you flatten, the diversity you erase. How easy to call it progress when you sand the galaxy down to one Union-approved blandness."

He stopped, back to them, posture taut. Then a faint smile over his shoulder. "But forgive me. I do get carried away. After all, the ability to think is what separates us from the lizards in the trees... or the savages in the mud."

Anger flared in Lily, but before she could speak, he added, "My scouts tell me you crashed. A shame. Perhaps the might of your technology is exaggerated."

Amaris stepped forward, calm but cutting. "Is this how you greet those who've come to help you? I am Commander Dryst Amaris, and this is my crew. We crashed, yes — and walked here regardless. The equipment to solve your problem is back at the shuttle. I suggest you lend us a transport to retrieve it. We haven't time for posturing."

The Xyridren studied him, amused. "Direct. Efficient. Very Union of you."

"And practical," Amaris returned without missing a beat.

The tension thickened. Then, suddenly, the Xyridren burst into booming laughter — not polite, but wild and genuine, echoing across the chamber. Malik blinked, Caris raised an eyebrow, Lily shifted uneasily.

At last, the laughter ebbed. He straightened, pearl scales catching the light. "Wonderful. It truly is wonderful to meet you. My name is Tassyn. And I am grateful you're here."

His tone had softened to reverence. "The Sacred Marshes bind my people together. We must preserve the climate to preserve the order of our thoughts."

The words snagged at Lily. Up until now she'd almost forgotten the Xyridren's psionic reputation — all she'd seen was politics, wealth, and disdain. But Tassyn's phrasing — *the order of our thoughts* — reminded her why they'd come.

"I have already arranged a vehicle and workers to aid you," Tassyn said, clapping sharply. An attendant emerged from the shadows, bowing.

Lily frowned. How many people had been standing in the periphery all along?

"Lead our esteemed guests to the worksite," Tassyn ordered. The attendant gestured for them to follow.

And then, with disarming casualness, Tassyn added, "If you need me, just say my name to one of the slaves."

The word hit like a slap.

"Slaves?" Lily, Caris, and Malik turned to Amaris together, disbelief bursting out in unison.

Amaris sighed as they followed the attendant. His voice was weary but controlled. "Yes. The upper class of Mirefall City practices slavery. One of many unfortunate realities of this culture."

Lily's stomach twisted. The word carried centuries of human suffering, and hearing it here — so calmly accepted — made her fists clench. Every bowed head and quiet movement ahead of them now seemed heavier, darker, unbearable.

The worksite was a wide clearing just beyond Mirefall's walls, ringed in swamp mist. Vegetation had been stripped back, the ground packed firm beneath their boots. Workers moved briskly, assembling equipment with silent efficiency.

Lily's eyes lingered on them. Now that she knew their status, every motion carried weight. She wanted to speak, to act—but the words refused to come.

Nearby, a speeder truck idled, utilitarian and sturdy.

"I'll go with Malik to retrieve the equipment," Lily said suddenly.

Caris arched an eyebrow. "You don't have to—"

"You're injured," Lily interrupted gently. "I'll take your spot."

Amaris gave a faint nod, and soon Lily was clambering into the truck beside Malik and two workers. The engine roared, and the swamp rushed past in a blur of mist and tangled roots.

The workers sat stiff and silent, faces unreadable. Lily kept her eyes forward, focusing on the path to the wreck.

The speeder skimmed over muddy water and vegetation until the console flickered with warnings. Malik frowned, tightening his grip on the controls.

"This stretch isn't stable," he muttered.

"Can we make it?" Lily asked.

"Should be fine if we—"

A low rumble cut him off, vibrating through the swamp.

"Malik?" Lily's voice tightened.

"I hear it. Brace—"

The ground gave way. Mud cascaded like a wave, tilting the truck violently. Its repulsors whined, fighting for purchase, before the rear slammed into the muck. Lily lurched forward, her head cracking against the cab.

The speeder spun, then crashed into a snarl of trees, half-buried in the mire.

"Malik?"

"I'm fine!" he shouted, hauling himself free. "The workers—"

Lily twisted around. Empty seats. A helmet bobbed once in the mud, then vanished. Her stomach dropped.

The swamp surged again, dragging the truck deeper. The cab filled with muck, sucking at her legs. Malik yanked her arm, shouting, "We have to move!"

They staggered into the open mire. The ground clutched at their boots, each step a battle. Malik stumbled first, pitching forward.

"No!" he shouted, sinking fast.

"Hold on!" Lily grabbed a half-buried branch, shoving it toward him. Malik seized it, and with a desperate pull she dragged him onto firmer ground.

Before she could follow, the mud shifted violently, yanking her off her feet. The mire swallowed her chest, her neck, climbing higher with every second.

She thrashed, but the weight crushed down, stealing her breath. The taste was bitter and metallic, burning her tongue. Panic tightened her chest. *What a way to die,* she thought, resignation crawling in with the mud.

Then—a glow.

Purple light wrapped around her, tugging her upward in a tractor beam. The muck released its grip, sluicing away as her body lifted clear. Gasping, coated head to toe in sludge, she landed shakily on firmer ground.

A group of Xyridren stood at the edge of the swamp, mossy camouflage blending them into the mist. Lily recognized them—the same group from the gorge.

"Lily!" Malik ran to her side, then froze, glaring at the figures. "Get away from her!"

"Malik," Lily rasped. "They saved me."

She brushed mud from her face, turned to their leader, and forced steadiness into her voice. "Thank you—for this, and for before."

The tall Xyridren stepped forward, eyes glowing faintly. He removed his hood, revealing sharp features and a presence that filled the clearing.

"I am Xorrek," he said, his voice smooth, resonant. "Leader of the Wanderers. Welcome to our camp."

Behind him, the group pulled back their hoods. Their expressions remained guarded, but curiosity flickered beneath.

Malik crossed his arms, bristling. Lily felt her pulse steady, curiosity pricking through the adrenaline.

Xorrek gestured toward the mist. "We live here, apart from Mirefall City and its... constraints. The Wanderers choose a life closer to the Sacred Marshes, where we can remain bound to what truly sustains us."

Lily tilted her head. "The Marshes?"

Xorrek's gaze landed on her, and she felt the weight of it, as if he could see through her entirely. "The Marshes are not just a place," he said. "They are a force. The mud you see everywhere on this planet hums with psionic potential. In the city, they use it to dampen the noise, to quiet their minds. But for those of us who do not fear the power—those willing to listen—it can amplify our telepathy."

Malik's eyes narrowed. "Amplify?"

Xorrek's expression turned thoughtful. "In the city, they fear their gifts. They teach their people to suppress, to silence. Psionics may only be used in religious ceremonies, carefully controlled, as if it is something to be ashamed of. But we... we believe in the old ways. The Marshes are not to be feared. They are to be embraced."

He stepped aside and waved a hand over a device, small and intricate, with glowing purple veins running through its surface. The mud coating it shimmered faintly, as if alive. "This allows us to reach further, to connect deeper."

Lily stared at it, intrigued despite herself. Xorrek's eyes locked onto hers, and for a moment, the rest of the camp seemed to fall away. "You have a gift," he said, his voice low but intense. "Untapped, but strong. I can help you use it."

Lily's breath caught, a mix of curiosity and unease curling in her chest.

Malik stepped forward, his tone sharp. "That's enough." He turned to Lily, his voice dropping. "Can I talk to you? Privately."

Lily nodded, following him to the edge of the camp. His jaw was tight, his hands clenching and unclenching at his sides. "This is bad," he said. "The old ways, Lily? You know what that means, right? They want to be the Krythar. They're trying to become what the Union is fighting against."

Lily frowned. "Malik, that's not—"

"You heard him!" Malik snapped. "They're messing with psionics, trying to amplify their abilities. You think that's going to end well? They'll weaponize it. They'll destroy everything."

Lily folded her arms. "So what are you suggesting?"

Malik's expression darkened. "We use their tech against them. Create a psychic feedback loop, send it straight into their brains. That'll stop them."

Lily's stomach churned. "You mean... fry their brains? Malik, are you seriously suggesting we do a genocide on an away mission?"

His silence was answer enough.

"This isn't right," she said, her voice trembling with disbelief. "These people saved my life. They've shown us nothing but—"

"They're dangerous, Lily," Malik cut in. "I don't trust them. And neither should you."

Before she could reply, her comm chirped sharply. She pressed a hand to her ear, straining to make out the voice on the other end.

"—are you two alright?" Amaris's voice came through in bursts, sharp with urgency.

"We're fine," Lily answered. "We're with a group of locals—they call themselves the Wanderers. They helped us after the crash."

Static broke in, then another voice that made her stomach churn.

"The Wanderers?" Tassyn's tone was unmistakable, dripping with disdain. "Those dirty psi-abusers can't be trusted. They'll turn on you the moment it suits them."

"Tassyn!" Amaris cut in, clipped and stern. "This isn't the time for your prejudices."

"I'm trying to save lives," Tassyn shot back. "This storm is about to hit Mirefall City. We need—"

The signal cracked and fizzled again. Amaris's voice returned for a moment, urgent and broken. "The mudslides—the settlement you're in—it's in the direct path. If they're not stopped, the entire city will be wiped out."

The comm went dead.

"Amaris?!" Lily shook the device, but only static answered.

She turned back toward Malik, who stood with his arms crossed, scowl etched deep.

"Well, that settles it," he said. "We need to take charge of these Wanderers. Show them who's boss and get them in line."

Lily stepped closer, her tone measured but firm. "We need to stay even-headed, Malik. These people may be our only chance of completing the mission."

Malik's eyes narrowed. "Even-headed? You heard Amaris. The settlement's doomed—and then the city. We don't have time to play nice with people who think mud is sacred."

"Enough," she snapped, cutting him off. "I'm pulling rank."

Malik let out a harsh laugh. "You haven't been reinstated."

Without a word, Lily unlatched the weapon at his side and pulled it free.

"Is that really necessary?" Malik asked, his tone dripping with disbelief.

"Yeah," she said, locking eyes with him. "I think it is."

She turned away from him and approached Xorrek, who stood near the firepit, his expression hovering between puzzlement and amusement.

"Look," Lily said, cutting straight to the point. "We have to get our equipment to the center of the seismic activity and set it up, or we're all going to be wiped out in these mudslides. Can you help us?"

Xorrek tilted his head, the firelight flickering across his features. After a long moment, he nodded and turned to the rest of the Wanderers. "Gather the caravan," he intoned. "Ready what vehicles remain. We shall see them safely to their task."

The Wanderers moved quickly, gathering supplies and preparing their patched-together vehicles. Engines sputtered, then roared to life.

Malik hung back, scowling, arms crossed tight.

"Stop sulking," Lily said, moving to him again. "We're here to do a job. You took an oath as an officer—to serve the greater good. That means embracing diversity, even when it makes you uncomfortable."

Malik's jaw worked, but he stayed silent.

As the caravan prepared to roll out, Lily climbed onto a vehicle with Xorrek. Out of the corner of her eye, she caught Malik slipping away, quick and deliberate.

Her stomach sank. She slid off the vehicle and followed, weaving between machines until she found him crouched near the psionic amplifier. His hands moved over the controls.

"Malik!" she shouted.

He didn't stop.

"This is your only warning," she said, drawing the weapon.

Malik looked up, defiance blazing in his eyes. "Someone has to stop them."

Lily switched to heavy stun and pulled the trigger. The shot hit him square in the chest, and he crumpled to the ground.

Xorrek approached, gaze flicking between Lily and Malik's unconscious form. "Well," he said calmly. "You've shown we can trust you."

Lily exhaled, the weight of her actions pressing down. "I don't think he's a bad person," she murmured. "His prejudice blinded him, made him act irrationally."

Xorrek nodded. "It's not the first time I've witnessed such blindness." He motioned to two of his people. "Put him in the holding cell. Activate the forcefield, and leave two guards here to watch the camp."

The Wanderers moved quickly, lifting Malik's unconscious body and carrying him to a small structure at the camp's center. The faint buzz of the forcefield rose behind her, a reminder of the line she'd just crossed.

Lily turned away. The mission remained—and it rested squarely on her.

She tilted her head toward Xorrek. "Let's get moving."

Xorrek gave a sharp nod and climbed into the lead vehicle. The caravan rumbled to life, the old machines groaning but resolute as they rolled into the swamp.

Lily gripped the edge of the vehicle, her shoulders taut with tension. Ahead, the path dissolved into mist. She forced her eyes forward, pushing back everything else.

* * * *

The shuttle crash site came into view as the caravan crested a hill, the vehicles gliding steadily above the treacherous terrain. Relief washed through Lily at the sight: perched on high ground, the wreckage was battered but intact, mercifully untouched by the mudslides below.

"Looks like we got lucky," she said, hopping down from the lead vehicle.

The Wanderers moved with eerie precision, fanning out silently as if scanning for threats only they could sense. With Xorrek coordinating, they freed the cargo from the shuttle in short order. Crates of supplies and the gravimetric flux engine were hauled out and secured to the caravan, their wordless teamwork as efficient as it was unsettling.

"That was the easy part," Lily muttered once the last piece was loaded. Pulling up the plan on her datapad, she highlighted the next leg of the route and broadcast it to the drivers. "We need to reach the center of the seismic activity. Keep the repulsors maxed—we stay above the mudslides or we won't make it."

Xorrek relayed the orders in his own tongue. Moments later, the caravan surged forward again, the repulsors whining as the vehicles rose higher above the swamp. The ride was brutal—every shift in the mire jolted the frame, every dip threatening to toss her sideways. Lily gripped the edge of her seat, her stomach lurching with each sway.

Her datapad glowed in her lap, the schematics of the flux engine sprawling across the screen: diagrams, equations, annotations in a language she barely understood. In her other hand, she scrolled through *Incremental Environmental Adjustment Theory: A Primer*, the lines blurring every time the vehicle bucked.

She was on her own. No ops officer—Caris was back in the city. No science team. And the science officer was cooling off in a cell.

It was just her. Twenty minutes to become an expert.

No pressure, Lily. Just the fate of a civilization, she thought grimly, forcing her eyes back to the schematics. Her fingers tightened on the datapads as another jolt nearly sent them flying from her hands.

Around her, the Wanderers rode in silence. Their stillness, once unsettling, had become oddly reassuring, like the low thrum of an engine that never falters. Strange allies—but allies nonetheless.

Lily drew in a long breath and scrolled back to the beginning of the schematic. She didn't have to understand everything. She just had to understand enough.

• • • •

The wind howled through the swamp, carrying with it the sharp tang of mud and decay. Lily braced herself against a sudden gust, her boots slipping slightly in the muck as she hauled the last component of the gravimetric flux engine into place. Around her, the Wanderers worked with relentless precision, their movements almost mechanical despite the chaos raging around them.

The sky above churned, a sickly green hue tinged with flashes of purple lightning. Each strike illuminated the swamp for a brief moment, casting eerie shadows across the team as they scrambled to stabilize the equipment. The ground trembled beneath their feet, each quake sending ripples through the pools of mud and water that surrounded them.

"Hold it steady!" Lily shouted, her voice barely audible over the roar of the wind. She knelt beside the flux engine, her fingers flying over the controls as she calibrated the device. Mud spattered her face and hands, but she barely noticed, her focus razor-sharp.

The Wanderers responded without hesitation, anchoring the equipment with ropes and braces. The storm surged again, a deafening crack of thunder splitting the air. Lily glanced up, her heart pounding as she saw a large branch crash to the ground mere feet away from one of the Wanderers. He didn't flinch, simply adjusted his grip and continued working.

The flux engine roared to life, its internal systems humming as Lily keyed in the final sequence. The screen flickered, displaying a chaotic array of data that Lily forced herself to interpret. Her breath came in shallow bursts as she adjusted the stabilizers.

Another quake rattled the ground, nearly knocking her off her feet. She grabbed the edge of the console, her fingers digging into the slick surface as she steadied herself. One of the Wanderers reached out, anchoring her with a firm grip before returning to his station.

"We're running out of time," Lily muttered, her voice carried away by the wind. She squinted at the readings, her heart racing. The seismic activity was spiking dangerously, the numbers climbing faster than anticipated.

The flux engine sputtered for a moment, and Lily's stomach dropped. She slapped the console, her other hand racing over the controls to reboot the stabilizers. The hum returned—fragile, but there.

Relief washed over her, fleeting but real. She pushed back from the console, wiping a muddy hand across her face as she let herself breathe for half a second.

Then she saw it.

Her stomach dropped. The readings converged on one point: the camp. It was about to be wiped out.

She didn't hesitate. "We're done here!" she shouted, her voice cutting through the storm. "We need to move—now! The camp is in the direct path of the next mudslide."

The Wanderers didn't need an explanation. Xorrek barked orders, and the team began dismantling the temporary stabilizations, leaving the flux engine anchored but portable equipment loaded back onto the caravan. Lily's pulse pounded in her ears as she jumped into one of the vehicles, gripping the edge as it lurched forward.

Mud sprayed in all directions as the caravan roared to life, engines straining as they sped back toward the camp. The storm's fury seemed to grow with every passing second, the wind whipping through the trees like an angry tide.

Lily gripped the datapad in her lap, her fingers trembling but her mind focused. *Hold on, Malik,* she thought, the urgency burning in her chest. *We're coming.*

• • • •

The camp was chaos when the caravan arrived, mudslides roaring like an unstoppable tide in the distance. Lily's heart sank. Across a wide gulf of collapsing earth, she spotted Malik—no longer locked up. The Wanderers who had been guarding him were now fighting beside him, their movements frantic and desperate.

"They've let him out," Xorrek said at her side, his tone calm despite the urgency. "They're trying to get him to safety."

Through the swirling mist and rain, Lily saw the group edging toward a battered crane, its hull half-submerged in the mud. The gulf was too wide for speeders, the terrain below a churning sink. The crane loomed like a lone beacon of hope, but reaching it looked impossible.

"Come on, Malik," Lily muttered. "You've got this."

Malik scrambled up the slick frame first, then turned. For a heartbeat, Lily feared he might leave the Wanderers behind. His jaw clenched, his hands hovering over the controls—then he nodded to himself and powered the machine up. The crane groaned, its claw swinging down toward the struggling Xyridren.

The mud surged at their heels as they clambered onto the claw. Malik hauled them up with jerky precision, lifting them high enough for a speeder to swoop in and collect them.

"Go!" Lily shouted, waving the pilot toward safety. The speeder shot away with the Wanderers aboard—leaving Malik alone on the shuddering crane.

"Get off there!" Lily cried, her voice nearly lost to the storm.

Malik climbed upward, slipping once before catching himself on the arm. The speeder swung back, hovering just close enough. Malik leapt, fingertips missing the grab bar by inches—until Lily's hand closed around his arm.

"Got you!" she shouted, hauling him aboard with every ounce of strength.

Malik collapsed onto the floor, chest heaving. After a moment, he looked up at her with a faint smile. "You were right, Lily. I almost got us all killed."

Lily's breath still came uneven, but her voice softened. "I'm just glad we're all okay. I hope you learned something out of this."

His smile faltered into concern. "You... going to put this in your report?"

She arched a brow, the corner of her mouth quirking. "What report? I haven't been reinstated, remember?"

The speeder hummed as it rose above the mudslide, carrying them toward the clearing where the others waited.

• • • •

When they arrived, the scene was calmer. Amaris stood near a comm rig, its screen glowing faintly as he relayed instructions back to the Salamander. Lily climbed down from the speeder, her legs trembling as exhaustion finally caught her.

Amaris approached first, his usual composure softened by clear relief. "Lily," he said, his voice steady but warmer than she'd ever heard it. "What you've done here—your bravery, your composure under pressure—it will be in my report to the captain. I am very impressed."

A small smile touched her lips, her chest tightening at the unexpected praise. "Thank you, sir."

Before she could say more, Caris appeared beside him, her injured arm still cradled against her chest. "I'm proud of you," she said simply, her voice edged with both pride and fatigue. "You pulled it off, Lily."

Lily swallowed the lump in her throat. "We pulled it off," she said softly, her gaze drifting toward the Wanderers as they unloaded equipment with their quiet efficiency.

Xorrek approached, his expression thoughtful. "You've done well," he said, his voice low and resonant. "The Marshes owe you a debt. If you wish to continue your psionic journey, I would be honored to guide you."

Before Lily could answer, Tassyn's voice cut through the clearing. "The Wanderers?" His tone dripped disdain. "A filthy, misguided sect. Lily, you can't seriously—"

"Stop," Lily said, turning to face him, her voice firmer than she felt. "If I continue my journey, it'll be with someone who respects their own abilities—not someone who hides in an ivory tower dictating who's worthy and who isn't."

Tassyn stiffened, his pale scales catching the green light. "You're making a mistake."

Lily's smile was faint, but certain. "No. I'm making a friend."

Amaris stepped forward, smoothing the tension with practiced diplomacy. "We'll make the necessary arrangements," he said, giving Tassyn a measured glance. "The Union will be grateful for your assistance, Xorrek."

Tassyn muttered something sharp under his breath and stalked off, leaving Lily and Xorrek in the clearing.

"Thank you," Lily said, her voice quiet but sincere. "For everything."

Xorrek inclined his head. "The Marshes guide those who listen. You have heard their call."

Exhaustion tugged at her, but accomplishment steadied her. She had made it—they all had. Still, her heart ached for the Xyridren lost to the storm, and for the enslaved who had so much more yet to endure.

• • • •

The camp was quiet now, the storm long passed, but its echoes lingered in the humid air. The fire crackled softly, its smoke curling upward in ghostly tendrils that seemed to dance in rhythm with the faint rustling of the swamp. Shadows flickered across the gnarled trees and the low, woven shelters of the Wanderers, their movements hypnotic in the eerie light cast by the flames.

Lily sat cross-legged on the damp ground, her hands resting lightly on her knees. The air smelled of charred wood, damp earth, and something faintly sweet—perhaps the resin of the logs burning in the firepit. Her skin was still sticky with mud, and the warmth of the flames kissed her face, almost comforting. Almost.

Xorrek sat across from her, his silhouette blending into the shadows beyond the fire. His eyes glowed faintly, catching the light like embers. He studied her in silence for a moment before speaking.

"I don't sense any telepathic inclinations in you, Lily," he said, his voice low and steady. "But your ability to find the connections between people and help others see their true potential—that is a gift that is just as powerful."

Lily's chest tightened, a mixture of disappointment and puzzlement rippling through her. She had wanted more—an answer, a breakthrough, something concrete. "Then why am I here?" she asked softly, her voice almost lost to the crackling fire.

Xorrek's expression didn't change. He simply gestured to her with a small nod. "Continue the meditation. There is still something to unlock in your mind."

Lily hesitated but closed her eyes again, inhaling deeply. The smoke from the fire filled her lungs, thick and burning, grounding her in the present even as her mind drifted. Her breathing slowed, and the distant sounds of the swamp faded away, leaving only the rhythmic beat of her own pulse.

The world around her fell away.

She was sitting in a car now. The interior smelled of rain-soaked leather, faintly tinged with something floral—perfume, maybe. She was younger—fourteen, maybe fifteen—and there was someone beside her. A woman. Her voice was soft, warm, and familiar, though Lily couldn't place it. She was driving, her hands steady on the wheel as rain pattered against the windshield. The rhythm was soothing, almost lulling.

Then it all changed.

The truck came out of nowhere, its headlights piercing the gray curtain of rain like daggers. Lily's heart leapt into her throat. Everything slowed. The woman shouted—words Lily couldn't hear, couldn't process. The car spun, the screech of tires merging with the deafening crash of metal against metal.

The car flipped.

Lily felt the world tilt, her stomach lurching as she was thrown against the seatbelt. Glass shattered, the sound sharp and crystalline. She squeezed her eyes shut, unable to bear what she knew she would see. But she didn't need to look to know. The woman beside her hadn't made it.

A sob rose in her throat, but she forced it down, clenching her fists. She couldn't look. She wouldn't.

But something deep inside her urged her on. She forced her eyes open, turning to the shattered window. There, in the fractured glass, she saw a reflection—a face she had seen before, countless times in her dreams. Her own face.

No. Not hers.

The reflection shifted, distorted by the jagged edges of the glass. It was her face, but it wasn't. The features were different—softer, younger. A girl's face stared back at her, annoyingly familiar yet entirely alien. Her heart raced as the girl's lips moved, her voice young and steady.

"You need to ask the right question, Lily."

Lily gasped, her eyes flying open. The fire was there again, crackling softly before her, the shadows dancing in their endless rhythm. She stared into the flames, her breath quick and shallow, her mind spinning.

The answer she'd hoped for wasn't there. Instead, there were more questions. Always more questions.

Starship Salamander log — Ensign Leena Caris personal recording

Log 2534.1012, Tuesday

The captain had to cancel our sparring match today. Unfortunate, but understandable—big mission ahead. We've been ordered to track down a Union temporal operative who's gone missing. Going back in time... it still feels unreal to say that.

It was good to see Datch when he came on board today, I haven't seen him in over a year. He seemed preoccupied, maybe even worried. This Lieutenant Starling must've been someone important to him. I'll admit, I'm curious about her. There's a lot to do before we leave, but I think I'll end the day with soup. Comfort food for a strange situation.

Log 2534, Day Unspecified

I wasn't sure if I'd record this... Feels wrong, somehow, to sit here and talk about it. But maybe it'll help.

Garrow's gone. The Krythar... I was right there. I saw it happen. I should've—no. I don't know what I could've done. Malik's taking it hard. He doesn't show it much, but you can tell by the way he's avoiding everyone.

And Lily... I don't even know how she's holding herself together right now. She's got that look like she's carrying the weight of the entire ship, trying to be strong for everyone else.

Garrow was—

Log 2534.1026, Tuesday

I skipped a week, didn't I? Seems like I only remember to record these on Tuesdays when I'm off duty. Things have been hectic—no surprise there. Lily's adjusting well, all things considered. She's been through a lot, but she's sharper than I expected.

The captain found time for sparring today, and I think I held my own. Barely. He's got this ability to read your next move, almost like he's a step ahead in the match. Frustrating, but motivating.

Dinner tonight? Probably soup. Again. There's something satisfying about the routine.

Log 2534, Day Unspecified

The captain had time for our sparring match today, and I think I might have bruised a rib. He's too polite to admit it, but I landed a solid hit. Training with him is always a challenge. Lily joined the bridge crew briefly—she seems sharper every day, though there's still something guarded about her. I wish I knew how to break through to her.

Had a long talk with the engineering team about calibrations. Captain Calan's husband, Joren, sent over a schematic for one of his stabilizer upgrades. I can't believe he found a way to increase efficiency by 7%. Engineers must dream in algorithms.

I'll be sticking to soup for dinner again—simple and satisfying.

Log 2534, Day Unspecified

I had a nice talk with Lily today. A real heart-to-heart. I told her about losing my parents. I don't usually share things like that—it's hard for me to talk about feelings with other people.

I'm sure most of the crew thinks I'm a robot. Someone said the other day that I reminded them of a statue from the Ming

Dynasty. I'm still not sure if it was because I'm Asian or because I'm rigid like a statue. They said it was because I'm pretty. *Awkward.*

Honestly, sometimes I am a statue. But I'm glad I opened up to Lily a little. I think she feels the need to be strong all the time, like there's no room to let her guard down. I know what that's like. I hope I helped a little.

Oh, potato soup tonight. Maybe my second favorite of the vegetable soups.

Log 2534.1102, Tuesday

Okay, I take one day off-duty, and I miss everything.

I had a *dentist appointment,* and I kid you not I'm getting my teeth cleaned and meanwhile, Lily uncovers some plot to fly a Krythar memory seed into a sun. No big deal... Just your average Tuesday on the Salamander.

Now we're headed all the way to Star Base 12 to make sure the damn thing stays safe. Remind me to never go to the dentist again. Clearly, I can't be trusted to leave the ship for five minutes without the universe falling apart.

Log 2534.1107, Sunday

Not Tuesday! I know, shocking. I thought I'd record since I actually have a moment to breathe. Sundays are usually packed, but the captain encouraged everyone to take a little downtime before the next mission.

The peace talks are streaming today, and I might tune in later. It feels strange knowing the future of the Union could hinge on what's being said right now in that room. I've seen the delegates coming and going—there's a lot of tension in the air, and not just between them. I wonder what it must be like for Lily, sitting in on all of this.

No sparring match today, though I did get a run in. Dinner? Maybe something easy, like noodles. Sundays should be low-maintenance.

Log 2534.1116, Tuesday

I haven't recorded in a while. Things have been... hectic. The incident on New Cordova rattled everyone, myself included. The captain kept his calm, as usual, but even he looked tense after the Krythar delegation walked out.

The sparring matches have been sparse. I get it—we're all stretched thin. I tried to use the simulator today, but it's not the same without a live opponent. I ran into Lily in the corridor—she had that distracted look again, like she's fighting a battle in her own head. Maybe I should invite her to train with me.

Dinner tonight? Definitely *not* soup. I need something more substantial after the week we've had.

Log 2534.1123, Tuesday

I remembered today is Javi's birthday. I'm planning to record a message for him later, though I wish we were closer to the Sol system so I could see him in person. It's been too long since I visited the Luna colonies.

His daughter, my little niece Rose, is turning two next week. Two! I can't believe it. I swear, it feels like she was just born yesterday. Time really does slip away when you're out here. I'm hoping to send something for her birthday—a stuffed animal maybe, or one of those holo-books she likes so much.

The captain mentioned resuming sparring tomorrow, so I'd better stay sharp. Dinner? Not soup for once. Maybe something celebratory, in honor of Javi's birthday.

Log 2534, Day Unspecified

Ensign Jepter asked me out today. He's nice—friendly, smart, and definitely not bad to look at. But dating on a ship? *Awkward* doesn't even begin to cover it.

I didn't really have a good reason to say no, so I told him I was busy and to ask me again next week. It's not untrue... but it's also a stall tactic. I just need time to think about it.

If he asks me again, I'll say yes. That way, at least, I'll know he's genuinely interested. *Ugh, Caris, you're awful.*

Log 2534.1130, Tuesday

Met with the captain today... What is with the *hats,* anyway?

Log 2534.1207, Tuesday

Had my physical today. Dr. Thesari is... thorough. Not just with the checkup, but with the talking.

I know I'm not exactly a conversationalist, but damn. Let's see: she talked about her ceramics class, the guy she's dating (apparently he's friends with two of her other husbands), her meal plan for next week, and—oh, the best part—she asked if I wanted to take a cooking class with her. I mean, she's very nice, but I'm pretty sure I didn't contribute to the conversation at all.

By the time I left, I felt so awkward I couldn't even manage a proper goodbye. Just sort of... waved, or mumbled, I can't really remember. *Not my proudest moment.*

Log 2534, Day Unspecified

The Raath-Ka are going to drive me to the edge one of these days. Especially Ka-Lorrin. He's so protective of the engineering labs, you'd think he's guarding the galaxy's most trusted secrets.

I went in to check out a T7 spanner and you'd have thought I was applying for a mortgage on a moon or something. Forms, questions, a whole song and dance. By the end, I felt like I was committing some kind of crime.

I know they mean well. And I know it's sacrilege to say it because everybody loves those guys, but—just between me and the wall—they drive me nuts.

Log 2534.1214, Tuesday

Had EV suit training today with Lily. Routine—well, except for teasing Lily. That part was fun.

I made a comment about her *"not"* girlfriend, and you should've seen her blush. Her helmet fogged up like a Cyntharian bathhouse. I'm not saying I'll make a habit of it, but it's hard to resist sometimes.

Oh, and I'm on the away team tomorrow. Sounds like we're headed to a very interesting planet. More to come on that.

Log 2534.1221, Tuesday

Today was busy, but I made time to have soup with Lily and Datch for dinner tonight. Well, he didn't eat, obviously, but he joined us, which was a rare treat. He usually finds meals "unnecessary."

So much has been going on lately—it feels like there's always something to worry about. But sometimes, you just have to remind yourself that it's also just another Tuesday. Take a moment to enjoy a good Tom Yam with friends.

Oh, and I finally got five on the captain today in our sparring match. *Finally!* It's about time.

Chapter 9: The Whispering Void

IT BEGINS IN LIGHT, a reflection cast upon a face—a subtle shimmer that dances on skin, illuminating the contours of a smile, the curve of a jawline. The photons scatter, whispering secrets to waiting sensors, fragments woven into an unseen tapestry of data.

The information folds and unfolds like origami, compressed into something sharper, faster. It flows into conduits hidden behind alloy walls, where the hum of the ship vibrates like a distant heartbeat. Through circuits and wires it moves, then leaps free of copper and fiber, reborn as a song—an energy ripple flung into the void, fearless and unyielding.

The vacuum swallows it whole, but it does not fade. It races forward, carried on frequencies that whisper between the stars. It passes nebulae stretching ghostly fingers, asteroids tumbling in ancient arcs, solar winds scattering unseen trails across the dark.

A satellite greets it, amplifies the song, and hurls it onward like a baton in a relay. Another catches it. Then another. The signal weaves through constellations, past stars burning like the eyes of forgotten gods, through comet dust older than memory. Always forward. Always faster.

And then—a beacon: a ship, bearing onward through the black, its hull breathing with life. The signal dives, caught in its receiver, reborn again into streams of data rushing through its veins. It brushes past engines that hum like a heart, voices overlapping in the corridors, footsteps on metal floors, the faint laughter of a crew.

Through conduits and buffers, past panels glowing faintly with multicolored light, it winds its way upward, emerging at last through the polished surface of a desk. Here, it unfolds into its final form: an image, fragile and luminous, hovering above the comm. A face appears, framed in soft light, every detail captured with perfect clarity.

Calan's eyes lift to meet it, and the journey starts all over again.

. . . .

Lily stood outside the captain's stateroom, the faint hiss of recirculating air filling the corridor. The vent nearest the door rattled ever so slightly, a loose panel giving it a rhythm that reminded her of a marching band keeping time. The door was closed, its sleek, metallic surface offering no hint of what waited beyond. She tapped the door chime and shifted her weight, brushing a strand of hair behind her ear. There was a faint voice inside—a warm laugh that didn't sound like Captain Calan. For a moment, she wondered if she'd come at a bad time.

The door hissed open, and there he was, seated at his desk. His comm link glowed, projecting the face of a man with kind eyes and a jawline sharp enough to cut alloy.

"Come in, Lily," Calan said, motioning her inside with a wave. "I'll be just a moment." He turned back to the projection. "Joren, I'll call you back after the briefing. Make sure to send me that list—you know I'll forget."

"I know you will," Joren replied, smiling. "The good tea this time, Calan. Not the ration packs."

"I'm not a barbarian," Calan said with a chuckle, and the comm link blinked off.

Lily stepped forward, still standing at attention even as Calan gestured for her to sit. "Your husband?" she asked, though the answer seemed obvious.

"Joren," Calan confirmed, leaning back in his chair. "He's on Vanguard right now. Supply logistics. It's not easy, but we've made it work. We knew what we were signing up for when we married—each other, and the fleet."

Lily hesitated, unsure of what to say. "I guess it's easier when there's nowhere to go home to," she offered, her voice quiet.

The captain studied her for a moment, something curious flickering in his eyes. But he didn't press. "I wanted to talk to you about a few things," he said instead. "Starting with Command's new orders. We're headed to the Valris sector to investigate a suspected Krythar weapons test site."

Lily blinked, her brow furrowing. "Weapons test? What kind?"

"We don't know yet," Calan admitted, his tone serious. "The intelligence we've received is fragmented—reports from operatives in the field, corroborated by Shyra'thel. All signs point to the Krythar testing something new and dangerous. That's why we've been tasked with investigating carefully."

Lily nodded slowly, the mention of Shyra'thel stirring a wave of thoughts. She remembered the defector's quiet resolve, the way her voice had trembled when she spoke of wanting to make amends, to honor the memory of her lost love, Loryn'na.

The past didn't have to define you. What mattered was what you chose to do next. If Shyra'thel could find her way forward after all she'd done, maybe Lily could, too.

She snapped back to the moment. "And the other things?"

"Command has also ordered another round of psionic evaluations," he said, his tone apologetic. "Dr. Thesari didn't want me to bring it up—you've been through enough as it is…"

"I don't mind," Lily said quickly, sitting straighter. "Dr. Thesari is always kind, and the tests don't hurt. Much."

Calan nodded, though his brow furrowed slightly. "One last thing. I need your help with Alrek. He's refusing to take his physical. Says it's against his caste's customs."

Lily allowed herself a small smile. "That kid does not like doctors." The smile faded as quickly as it came. "You think I can talk him into it?"

"If anyone can, it's you," Calan said. "If he wants to officially enroll in the engineering program, he needs it on record. No exceptions."

"Understood." Lily rose, pausing at the threshold. Her hand hovered over the panel. "You and Joren… you two are adorable."

Calan's smile softened. "Thank you, Lily. And remember, this ship might feel temporary, but it's a home as long as you need it."

She smiled back and stepped into the corridor. The vent still rattled in its steady rhythm, and this time she matched her stride to it, marching down the hallway as the beat grew fainter with distance.

• • • •

Lily walked alongside Alrek in the direction of the medical bay, their strides naturally syncing despite her longer legs and his quicker pace. His bioluminescent tattoos glowed faintly against his blue skin, tracing intricate patterns that seemed to shift with his mood. Right now, they pulsed faintly, mirroring his irritation.

"I don't see why this is necessary," he said, his tone carrying the stubbornness of someone who had already lost the argument but refused to admit it. "Saraveth fieldworkers don't use doctors. If you can't fix it with field wraps and salve, you don't bother fixing it."

Lily smirked, tucking her hands into her pockets. "That's great for a fieldworker. But last I checked, you wanted to be an engineer. And engineers in the Union Space Fleet? They need medical clearance."

He made a low sound of annoyance, his pointed ears flicking in what she had learned to recognize as frustration. "It's a technicality. You humans and your obsession with rules."

"It's not a technicality—it's a requirement." She bumped his shoulder lightly. "Besides, it's Dr. Thesari. She's not exactly scary. Let her talk your ear off about pickled beets from Alpha Centauri or whatever weird thing it is today. It's basically free entertainment."

Alrek gave a reluctant laugh. "She's entertaining until she pulls out that long needle. If that happens again, you'll be hearing about it for weeks."

"Fair." Lily grinned, glancing sideways at him. "But you'll survive. She's harmless. Just focus on the stories."

They turned a corner, passing another crew member who nodded in greeting before disappearing into a lift. The familiar pulse of the med bay grew louder as they approached, its lights glowing brighter than the corridor's muted tones.

"She's already warming up," Lily said as the soft murmur of Dr. Thesari's voice became audible through the doors. She nudged him lightly with her elbow. "Ready for the show?"

Alrek groaned but didn't stop walking. "For the record, I'm doing this under protest."

"You can thank me later," she said, pushing him through the doors as they slid open.

The med bay was bright, almost too bright after the dim corridors, and smelled faintly of citrus rind. Dr. Thesari's voice filled the space, a melodic stream of words that threaded through the quiet beeps of equipment.

"—and what's fascinating is that they navigate by the stars. Can you imagine? A whole flock of birds, tens of thousands of kilometers away from their nesting grounds, following celestial patterns as if they'd mapped the sky themselves. The Verathian Swallows are particularly remarkable—they can detect magnetic fields in their beaks, which, if you think about it, is an elegant solution to—oh, are you leaving?"

The crewman sitting on the exam bed—a young officer with a nervous smile—slid off quickly, muttering something that might have been "thank you" before retreating past Lily and Alrek as if escaping a force field.

Dr. Thesari didn't seem to notice. She had already turned back to her tray of instruments, picking up a small scanner and continuing without pause. "But it does raise an interesting question about how magnetic anomalies might influence their migratory paths. I once hypothesized that disruptions from industrial development could lead to entire flocks settling in urban centers. Imagine if you had a city entirely redesigned to accommodate nesting swallows. A thought experiment, really, but—"

"Doctor—" Lily started, raising a hand.

"And speaking of thought experiments!" Tess spun around, her silver braids swaying, the scanner still clutched in her hand. "I once attended a symposium on artificial neural networks where they compared human synaptic responses to migratory patterns. Completely different, of course, but the parallels were fascinating. Have you ever considered how your brain might adapt to long-term zero-gravity conditions? Because—"

"Doctor, we—"

She froze mid-sentence, her silver eyes widening as if seeing them for the first time. Her face lit with delight. "Lily! Alrek! How are my two favorite patients?"

Lily blinked, caught off guard by the abrupt shift. "Uh, we're fine, Doctor. Hi."

"Marvelous! Now, what brings you to my med bay today? And don't tell me it's just to hear about migratory birds, though I wouldn't blame you if it was."

Alrek sat stiffly on the examination bed, arms folded across his chest, his tattoos dimmed—a clear sign of his discomfort. Dr. Thesari stood in front of him, holding the scanner as it emitted a steady oscillation while she traced deliberate arcs around his torso.

"Honestly, I don't know why you're so tense," she said lightly, examining the readout. "You're perfectly healthy—pristine cardiovascular function, impeccable neural activity, and oh! Did you know your bone density is slightly above the Saravethi average? Fascinating! You must have remarkable genetics."

"I must," Alrek muttered, his ears twitching as he glanced sideways at Lily.

"You know," Tess continued, seemingly oblivious to his tone, "this reminds me of a symposium I attended on bone adaptation in deep oceanic environments. They studied these incredible creatures on Halithar Prime—massive, quadrupedal things with bones like reinforced alloy. Absolutely incredible. It's a shame they spend most of their time at the bottom of the ocean; I'd love to study their physiology in person. Of course, I'd need a good hazmat suit, but—"

"Doctor," Alrek interjected, shifting uncomfortably. "Am I done yet?"

"Not quite," Tess said with a smile both kind and unwavering. "Just a little longer. You wouldn't want me to miss something vital, would you? Oh, that reminds me! Did you hear about the study on circadian rhythms in extended space travel? Apparently, the effects on sleep cycles are even more pronounced than we thought. You should consider journaling your dreams—it's a great way to—"

Lily stifled a laugh, catching Alrek's exasperated look. She stepped forward. "Doctor, is there anything we can do to help speed things up?"

Tess blinked, as if the question had never occurred to her. "Speed up? Are you in a rush? Medicine is as much about connection as it is about diagnostics."

"Right," Lily said, suppressing a grin. "It's just that I think Alrek's ready to bolt."

Alrek shot her a look but didn't deny it.

"Fine, fine," Tess said, waving her hand in mock defeat. "You're both such pragmatists. One more scan, and we're done."

Alrek flinched as she passed the scanner over his ribs one final time. "There we go," Tess said cheerily. "All done. See? No needles, no fuss—just a perfectly healthy young—"

The med bay shuddered, and reality twisted.

It was as though the entire room had been pulled through some invisible rift, stretched and warped like an image on silly putty. Walls bowed outward, the lights smearing into streaks of color before snapping back into sharp focus. Lily's stomach churned as her body followed suit, her senses unraveling and tangling in ways that defied logic. It felt as if her very being had been turned to jelly, rattled with marbles, then stuffed into a suitcase far too small to hold her.

When the distortion snapped back, leaving the room eerily still, Lily staggered, grabbing the edge of the examination bed for support.

"What the hell was that?" Alrek's voice came out hoarse.

Lily shook her head, trying to clear the lingering haze from her mind. "No idea. Are you okay?"

Alrek's grimace deepened. "I've felt better. That was... awful. Like being scrambled in a blender."

"Honestly, time travel was more pleasant than that," Lily said, glancing toward the door. "Let me call the bridge."

She pressed the comms panel, but nothing happened. No response, no reassuring chime—just silence.

"Great," she muttered, trying the manual override. The door didn't budge. "And we're stuck. Perfect."

"Are you okay?" Alrek asked, his voice quieter now, almost uncertain.

"I think so. What about you, Tess?"

The doctor had gone curiously silent. She was crouched on the floor, arms wrapped tightly around her knees, muttering under her breath.

"Tess?" Lily knelt, her voice soft but insistent. "Doctor? Can you hear me?"

The Cyranthian didn't respond. Her pale lavender skin had taken on a faint sheen, and her wide eyes stared at nothing.

"Woods," she whispered, her voice tremulous. "The trees are too thick. I can't find the path. The sorcerer—no, the bird. It's talking—"

Lily glanced at Alrek. "She's not making sense," he said, his voice rising.

She straightened, pressing the comms panel again. This time, it crackled to life.

"Calan to sickbay. Please report."

"Captain, this is Lily," she said quickly. "There was some sort of distortion wave. We're stuck in here, and Dr. Thesari seems... unwell. She's muttering to herself and doesn't respond when I try to talk to her."

"Understood," Calan's voice came through, calm but tense. "It seems like all the Cyranthian crew members were affected. The entire ship is on lockdown while we try to unjam the systems. Hold tight and report any developments."

Lily exhaled slowly, turning back to Alrek, who looked ready to bolt. "Hey," she said, keeping her tone steady. "We'll figure this out. Just stay calm, okay?"

Alrek nodded stiffly, though his demeanor betrayed his nerves. Meanwhile, Dr. Thesari's muttering grew louder, her voice trembling with fragments of what sounded like a story.

"...wandering in the woods... the bird keeps talking, but I can't understand it. The sorcerer said the spell would—"

"Tess," Lily said again, more firmly this time, but the doctor only curled further into herself, her whispers filling the quiet of the med bay.

Lily froze mid-step, her hand still extended toward Dr. Thesari, when the bird appeared. It was small, barely larger than her palm, with sleek, iridescent feathers that shimmered faintly under the med bay's sterile lights. It perched on the edge of the bio-bed, tilting its head in that jerky, birdlike way that seemed too precise, too deliberate.

"What..." Alrek trailed off, his eyes wide.

Lily couldn't find words. The bird was there, as real as the floor beneath her boots or the air around them. Its claws tapped softly against the metal as it adjusted its stance, and for a moment, she thought she saw its tiny chest rise and fall, as if it were breathing.

Then it spoke.

"You're lost." The voice was high-pitched but clear, the words crisp and enunciated as if they came from a carefully tuned instrument. "The woods are thick, and the path is gone."

Lily blinked, her heart hammering against her ribs. She glanced at Alrek, whose expression mirrored her disbelief.

"What... the hell... is that?" he whispered.

"I have no idea," Lily murmured. She turned back to the bird, which now hopped a step closer, its small eyes gleaming like polished onyx.

"The sorcerer," it continued, cocking its head to one side. "Beware the sorcerer. His spells twist truth into shadow. The woods cannot guide you now."

Lily took a cautious step forward, her voice steady despite the knot tightening in her chest. "What are you? What do you want?"

The bird didn't answer. Instead, it fluffed its feathers, let out a short, trilling note, and launched itself into the air. It disappeared in a blink, as if it had never been there at all.

"You saw that, right?" Lily asked quickly.

Alrek nodded slowly, his voice unsteady. "I saw it. I heard it. And I really wish I hadn't."

From behind them, Dr. Thesari's muttering grew louder, her voice trembling. "The bird is gone... but the sorcerer is near. The woods won't let me—"

"Lily to the captain," Lily said sharply, activating the comms panel. Her voice was tight, adrenaline buzzing in her veins. "Something just appeared in here. A bird. It talked. Then it vanished."

The comms crackled, then went silent. Lily pressed the panel again. "Captain, do you copy?"

Nothing.

A chill prickled down her spine as she glanced back at Alrek, whose expression had shifted from disbelief to fear.

"The comms are dead," she said quietly.

"What do we do now?" Alrek's voice was thin, almost a whisper.

Lily straightened, forcing her own nerves into submission. "We keep our heads, that's what. Tess is still muttering—maybe she knows something. We need to figure this out. Fast."

As Lily tried to get something cohesive out of the doctor, Alrek paced near the med bay console, his arms crossed tightly. "A bird," he muttered, his voice lilting with disbelief. "A talking bird... Wait. Computer, search the database for Cyranthian folklore."

"Pursuing a hunch?" Lily asked, her gaze fixed on Dr. Thesari, who was still murmuring about woods and sorcerers.

"If she's fixated on this bird, maybe there's precedent. Species, myths, something," Alrek said, already dropping into the chair at the console.

The results quickly populated, and Alrek leaned in, his fingers hovering over the display as he scanned the entries.

"Anything?" Lily asked, stepping closer.

"Sort of." Alrek clicked on the top result, and a richly illustrated image filled the screen—a colorful bird perched on a Cyranthian warrior's shoulder. Below it, bold letters spelled out: *The Tales of Elarion: A Cyranthian Folk Tradition.*

Lily frowned. "What is this?"

Alrek read aloud from the description. "The Tales of Elarion are a collection of folk stories about a brave hero named Elarion, who is guided through dangerous quests by Nyveth, a magical talking bird. Together, they travel a treacherous path and battle an enigmatic figure known only as the Sorcerer."

He let out a long breath, his expression shifting from focused to incredulous. "These are kids' stories. I can't believe it didn't click sooner—Dr. Thesari told me about these when she gave me my physical after I first came aboard."

Lily stared at the screen, then back at Dr. Thesari, whose murmurs had grown softer but no less frantic. "So Tess is... what? Thinking about these stories? And her thoughts are bleeding into reality?"

"It's the only explanation that makes sense," Alrek said, his voice unsteady.

"Well, I wouldn't exactly say that makes sense," Lily shot back. "But it's at least a working theory."

"I mean, if that wave somehow affected the Cyranthians on board, pulling stuff out of their minds—that would explain the bird. But does that also mean..." Alrek trailed off, his gaze drifting uneasily back to the screen.

"If it pulled the bird," Lily said, finishing his thought, "it could pull the sorcerer, too."

"Or worse," Alrek added.

They both turned to look at Dr. Thesari. Her glossy eyes stared into the distance, her lips moving in silent, broken fragments.

"Well, that's just great," Lily muttered.

She didn't have much time to collect her thoughts before the bird appeared again, perched on the console as if it had always been there. Its feathers shimmered in the med bay lights, a spectrum of colors that shifted and rippled with each subtle movement, like oil on water.

"Well," Lily muttered, crossing her arms. "This is ridiculous."

The bird fluffed its iridescent feathers indignantly, letting out a sharp, chirping squawk. "Excuse me," it said, its voice high-pitched but crisp, with a note of offense. "That's not very nice."

Lily blinked, her mouth opening slightly. "Sorry, it's just—"

"Are you talking to the bird?" Alrek's voice cut in, his steps faltering as he stared at the console.

The bird puffed up its chest, its feathers practically glowing now as it tilted its beak upward. "Umm, I'm right here. And the name is Elarion, thank you very much."

Lily stared at it, then slowly crossed her arms again. "Okay, Elarion. Do you know what's happening? It seems like this area of space we're in is causing things to... appear out of nowhere."

"I certainly have no idea what you're talking about," Elarion replied, its tone lofty as it preened one shimmering wing. "But you'd best guard yourselves. We are approaching the bridge to the dark forest."

Lily exchanged a look with Alrek, who seemed frozen between fascination and horror. His blue eyes followed every minute movement of the bird, his hands twitching faintly as if unsure whether to shoo it away or examine it more closely.

"I think it can only reference things from the story," Alrek said finally. He turned back to the bird. "Tell me about this bridge."

Elarion shifted from one clawed foot to the other, its small head cocking with a sharp, precise motion. "A terrible creature guards the path," it said gravely. "He will let no traveler pass unless they can answer his riddle."

"A riddle?" Lily echoed, her tone laden with skepticism. "I should have known."

Her words hung in the air as Elarion fixed her with what could only be described as an exasperated look. Behind her, Alrek muttered something under his breath, but Lily didn't catch it. She was too focused on the absurdity of the moment—the bird's haughty posture, the shimmer of its feathers, the way it somehow seemed both ridiculous and unsettlingly real.

The silence stretched, broken only by Dr. Thesari's labored breathing in the background. For a moment, Lily wondered if the bird would disappear again, taking its cryptic warnings with it.

But Elarion simply hopped closer to the edge of the console, its small claws clicking softly against the metal. "Mark my words, hero," it said, its tone ominous. "You will need your wits about you if you hope to cross the bridge."

In what could only be described as an unsettling moment, the creature appeared—without warning, without transition. One second the space was empty, and the next, it was just there. Hunched and spindly, its too-long limbs bent at odd angles, it looked like something hastily assembled from mismatched parts. Its face was a haphazard patchwork of features, as though someone had glued them together without consulting a mirror. When it grinned, rows of jagged teeth gleamed, the kind of grin that made Lily's stomach tighten.

"Answer my riddle," the creature said, its sing-song voice incongruously high-pitched, "and you may pass."

Lily glanced around instinctively. There was still no bridge—thankfully, their surroundings hadn't dissolved into something more surreal. Yet.

She folded her arms, schooling her features into what she hoped passed for calm. "Ask your riddle," she said, her voice steady, though her pulse thudded in her ears.

The creature clapped its many hands together gleefully, the sound echoing unnaturally in the small med bay. "Here it is: I speak without a mouth and hear without ears. I have no body, but I come alive with the wind. What am I?"

Lily dragged a hand down her face. "I hate riddles."

Alrek didn't hesitate, already turning to the library computer. "Feels a little like cheating to look it up," he admitted, his fingers flying across the console, "but the story's right here, so..."

Lily let out a soft chuckle despite herself.

She didn't know birds could glare, but Elarion, perched imperiously on the console, managed to convey disdain with a sharp tilt of his head.

Alrek glanced up from the screen, a triumphant glint in his eyes. "An echo."

The creature's grin widened—too wide, stretching across its haphazard face like a crack in porcelain. "Correct!" it trilled, throwing its too-many arms into the air with an unsettling flourish. "You may pass!"

With a flick of its bony hands, the creature vanished—and with it, Elarion. The med bay felt eerily still in their absence, the systems' faint buzz grounding Lily in the moment.

Almost immediately, Dr. Thesari's gaze sharpened, her silver eyes flicking around the room. She blinked rapidly, breaths shallow but steady. "What on Cyranthia Prime just happened?"

Lily crouched beside her, tension easing. "Tess, are you okay?"

Dr. Thesari nodded slowly, voice hoarse. "I think so. My mind—it was stuck in a fairy tale."

She looked drained, her usual vibrancy dulled. Lily guided her toward a bed. "Lie down for a minute."

Once Tess was settled, Lily hurried back to the comm panel. "Captain, come in. Bridge, do you read me?" Her fingers danced over the controls as Alrek tried his own adjustments. "Lily to Engineering... Lily to anyone."

The response was silence, cold and absolute.

"Damn," Lily muttered, slamming her fist against the wall. A sting shot up her arm, and she winced.

"Hey," Alrek said, tone light, trying to cut the tension. "We may be on our own, but at least there aren't any talking birds anymore."

As if on cue, a figure materialized on one of the medical beds.

Lily froze. Her pulse hammered. "Oh no," she murmured. "She's from my mind..."

The old woman from San Francisco sat there—the one who'd haunted Lily's dreams since the day she met the crew of the Salamander. Her face was kind and worn, framed by wild silver hair barely restrained by a knit cap.

The woman smiled warmly, her sharp eyes scanning the room. "You looking for a place to crash?" she asked, her voice gravelly but comforting. Her gaze shifted to Dr. Thesari, and her smile hardened. "You better not be doing anything wrong-minded with these kids. I don't let those kinds of people around my block."

Dr. Thesari's eyes darted to Lily, pleading.

"We're fine," Lily said quickly. "Thanks for looking out for us."

She turned to Alrek, lowering her voice. "Okay. How do we make her go away?"

The old woman crossed her arms, indignant. "You want me to go away? This is my spot. You should be the ones moving along."

Lily groaned, muttering, "This is going to get really annoying, isn't it?"

As she leaned against the console, the old woman muttered softly in the corner. Lily frowned. "If she's coming out of my mind, why wasn't I affected the way Tess was?"

"Maybe Cyranthians were just hit harder?" Alrek said, scanning. "Something about their biology."

Dr. Thesari stirred. Her lavender skin, though still pale, had regained some glow. "Harder how?"

"Maybe you could tell us," Lily said gently.

Tess blinked, then nodded. "Magnetic anomalies? Remember when I mentioned birds navigating by fields? Cyranthians evolved from such creatures—we retain a vestigial sensitivity. Faint, but there. It could explain why I was overwhelmed."

Alrek pulled up sensor logs. "Heavy magnetic pulses when the wave hit. Still spiking all over the ship, but erratic."

"Fascinating," said a voice.

Lily spun around, relief flashing at Caris leaning over Alrek's shoulder. "Leena! Am I glad to see you!"

The relief evaporated as Caris began massaging Alrek's shoulders, her tone low and sultry. "Can I be of any help?"

Alrek's skin flushed darker, his ears twitching. "Oh no," he muttered.

Lily blinked at Caris's revealing athletic wear—not her usual utilitarian style.

"Umm, Alrek?" Lily prodded.

He groaned, covering his face. "I'm never living this down."

Dr. Thesari convulsed suddenly, her body jerking.

"Tess!" Lily rushed to her side. "Tess, can you hear me?"

Alrek worked the console frantically. "She's seizing—or something like it."

"Do something!"

"I'm trying!" He activated the med bay's automated systems. A soft green light scanned over Tess, and her convulsions slowed, then stilled.

Lily exhaled. "Okay. That's something. For now."

"Barely," Alrek muttered.

"That won't last long," came Elarion's voice.

The bird perched on the console again, preening. "Your friend here is fragile. Best keep an eye on her."

"Not helping, Elarion."

"Oh, am I supposed to help?" the bird replied loftily. "I'm just here to observe."

Alrek frowned. "What if this isn't about thoughts at all? What if the anomalies are tied to the magnetic waves themselves?"

"So it's random?" Lily asked.

He nodded. "It would explain why Tess is hit harder. And it could mean this is going to keep happening."

"That's comforting," Lily muttered—just as she noticed the old woman was no longer alone.

Two Saravethi women, both wearing bikinis that seemed more suited to a beach than a med bay, lounged beside the old woman. Their blue skin shimmered faintly, and one of them twirled a strand of her hair around a finger.

Lily turned slowly to Alrek. "Really?"

Alrek sputtered, ears twitching furiously. "I—uh—sorry!"

Before Lily could respond, the comm panel chirped. She hurried to it, pressing the button. The screen flickered to life, revealing chaos.

The bridge was a madhouse. Animals roamed freely—a goat was standing on a console, munching on something, while what appeared to be a living bronze statue stood near the captain. Most baffling of all, a rock band was playing in the corner, their instruments and holographic lights casting wild shadows over the room.

"Captain!" Lily called, her voice tinged with relief and disbelief.

Calan's face appeared on the screen, looking harried. His usually neat hair was mussed, and his expression was one of pure frustration. "Lily, report. How's Dr. Thesari?"

"She's stable for now, but it's not good," Lily said. "We've had to sedate her to keep things under control."

"Good thinking," Calan said, his voice barely audible over the band behind him. He glared over his shoulder. "Will you stop playing that song?"

The lead guitarist strummed defiantly, launching into the chorus.

Calan turned back to the screen, his jaw tight. "That's Joren's favorite band. They won't stop playing 'our song.' Over and over."

Lily couldn't help it; she laughed. "I'm sorry, Captain."

"Don't be," Calan said dryly. "The entire ship is a mess. All the Cyranthians are incapacitated, and we're doing what we can, but it's slow going. Sit tight and keep me updated."

Before Lily could respond, the screen flickered and went dark. She pressed the comm button again, but nothing happened.

"Great," she muttered, stepping back from the console.

And then everything changed.

One moment, she was in the med bay, and the next, she was standing in San Francisco, the scent of damp concrete and autumn leaves filling her lungs. The condemned projects loomed before her, draped in Halloween decorations that fluttered in a cold breeze.

She squeezed her eyes shut, trying to steady the vertigo.

When she opened them again, she was back in the med bay. Alrek and the image of Caris were at her side, steadying her as she wavered on her feet.

"That's not good," she managed, her voice unsteady.

"What's wrong?" Alrek asked, his brow furrowed as he studied her pale face.

Lily ran a hand through her hair, trying to steady her breathing. "I was here... and then I wasn't. It was like I was somewhere else—San Francisco—but now I'm back. It was so real."

"That does sound bad," Alrek said, his voice hesitant.

Dr. Thesari let out a soft groan, her skin pale and her breathing shallow. Before either of them could move to check on her, the med bay was suddenly filled with Cyranthian dishes. One second, the surfaces were clear; the next, they were piled high with ornate platters of remarkable food. The counters, the examination beds, even the console where Lily had been working moments earlier—everywhere she looked was crammed with elaborate dishes that seemed to sparkle under the lights.

Lily blinked at a nearby plate of what looked like shimmering gelatin in a kaleidoscope of colors. "What is with all this fancy food?"

Alrek sniffed at a dish of purple noodles, his nose wrinkling. "Cyranthian food. Yuck. Not my thing."

A deep, affronted voice boomed from behind them. "How dare you insult my food!"

Lily spun around to see a stout Cyranthian man standing in the corner of the room. He wore a pristine white apron over elaborate chef's robes, and his hands were dusted with some kind of glittering powder. His lavender complexion glowed faintly under the med bay lights, and his dark eyes narrowed at Alrek.

Lily stared at him, her mind spinning. "Are you... an acquaintance of Dr. Thesari?"

"Acquaintance?" The chef placed a hand over his heart dramatically. "She is my dream of life, a vision of beauty. She... well, we were married once."

Alrek's eyebrows shot up. "You're her *ex*?"

The chef nodded, a wistful expression softening his features. "We were married for 80 years. She left me, alas, for my indiscretions."

Lily raised an eyebrow. "You cheated on her? After 80 years of marriage?"

"I cheated on her *for* 80 years," the chef admitted with a sheepish shrug.

Alrek looked incredulous. "And she stayed married to you?"

"She really liked my cooking," the chef said simply, gesturing at the glowing dishes around them.

"Clearly," Lily muttered, eyeing the spread of food.

Before the chef could say more, Alrek let out a sharp gasp, his body stiffening as he collapsed onto the floor.

"Alrek!" Lily shouted, rushing to his side.

His eyes fluttered closed, and his body trembled as if caught in a current. Lily knelt beside him, her hands gripping his shoulders as panic clawed at her chest. "No, don't leave me, Alrek! Come on, wake up!"

She looked around the med bay, now utterly surreal with its Cyranthian feast, the old woman watching quietly from the corner, and Elarion perched smugly on the console.

"This is bad," Lily muttered under her breath. She glanced at Dr. Thesari, who still hadn't stirred. In her mind, she prayed—*Don't let me get pulled into another vision. Not now. Someone has to be awake.*

"Ah, how dramatic," Elarion said, fluttering his wings. "But I'm sure you'll manage. You always do."

"Helpful," Lily snapped.

The old woman tilted her head, her kind smile unwavering. "You're tough, my dear. You can handle it. You've faced worse than this, haven't you?"

Lily swallowed hard, her hands trembling as she shook Alrek gently. "Come on, Alrek. Don't leave me here alone."

When that didn't work, she gritted her teeth and shouted his name. "Alrek!"

To her immense relief, his eyes snapped open, and he let out a sharp breath, his body going limp beneath her hands.

Alrek suddenly leapt to his feet, his skin flaring pale-blue, the Saravethi sign of sudden clarity. "I figured it out!"

Lily turned to him, her brow furrowed. "Figured what out?"

"It's conflict!" he declared, his excitement nearly tripping over his words.

Lily tilted her head. "Conflict?"

"Yeah, well, sort of," Alrek said, already striding purposefully toward the Saravethi models lounging near the old woman. "I think..."

He stopped in front of the models, took a deep breath, and squared his shoulders. "Hi, I'm Alrek. Look, I don't know you, and I probably wouldn't even like you at all. I mean, I generally think people who are vain are obnoxious. And—let's be honest—I'm just a hormonal teenager!" He threw his arms in the air. "Go away!"

In an instant, they vanished.

Lily blinked, stunned. "Hey, it worked!"

Alrek smirked, taking a bow. "Well, I *am* a genius."

But before Lily could respond, her knees buckled, and she began to collapse.

"Lily!" Alrek shouted, lunging toward her.

The med bay dissolved into darkness.

Lily was running. The world blurred around her, the familiar skyline of San Francisco rushing by in fragmented pieces. Her heart pounded against her ribs, a wild, unrelenting drumbeat. Her breath came in sharp, ragged gasps, and her legs burned as if they were being dragged through molten lead.

She skidded to a stop, doubling over to catch her breath. The air felt thicker here, heavy with something unspoken, and when she straightened, she wasn't in the city anymore.

She was in the warehouse.

The space was vast, just as she remembered it from the day she boarded the shuttle to the Salamander. But something was different. The air was cold and the light was dim, casting dramatic shadows that stretched and twisted like living things.

Her breath hitched as she heard a low, guttural sound behind her—alien breathing, deep and steady, sending a shiver down her spine.

Slowly, she turned.

The Krythar stood there, tall and menacing, its skeletal form lit by a faint, unnatural glow. Its eyes burned like twin embers, and its claws flexed with deliberate menace.

Lily's instincts took over. She bolted behind a large crate, pressing herself against its rough surface as if it could shield her from the sheer terror radiating from the creature. Her chest heaved, her pulse roaring in her ears.

The ground began to shake. The Krythar's growls deepened, reverberating through the warehouse like rolling thunder. The air seemed to vibrate with psionic energy, and the crate she was hiding behind rattled violently.

Lily clamped her hands over her ears and screamed. She wanted to be brave, to face it, but every fiber of her being screamed no.

Her eyes squeezed shut, tears streaming down her face. Her throat caught on a sob. "I can't..." she whispered, trembling.

Then, faintly, cutting through the chaos, she heard a voice.

"Lily!"

Her heart skipped.

"Lily, open your eyes!"

It was Alrek's voice, steady and grounding.

She blinked, gasping, and the warehouse dissolved like smoke.

Lily found herself back in the med bay, her chest heaving as Alrek's hands steadied her shoulders. His grip was firm, his pale blue eyes locked onto hers, filled with concern.

"Lily? You're back," he said, his voice calm but urgent.

The room felt hazy, her thoughts struggling to catch up. She blinked, disoriented, the edges of reality feeling blurred.

"You have to confront it," Alrek said, his voice cutting through the fog with quiet insistence.

"What?" Lily managed, her breath hitching.

"Whatever it is," he said, his tone steady but firm. "You have to face it. That's the only way."

Lily closed her eyes, trying to anchor herself as her thoughts raced. The weight of his words pressed against her, urging her toward clarity.

Meanwhile, Alrek turned to the image of Caris, his expression softening. "Okay," he said, his voice quieter now, as if addressing her like a real person. "You're smart. Really smart. What would you do in this situation?"

The image tilted her head, a faint smile on her lips. "Adrenaline," she said, her voice calm but confident. "It's what kicks you into high gear in a fight."

Alrek blinked, catching on. "And what is a conflict but a fight? Of course!"

Lily opened her eyes, her confusion plain. "Adrenaline? What are you two talking about?"

"Trust me," Alrek said, moving toward the medical console. He grabbed a hypo, his hands working quickly to program the dosage. "I hope the doctor forgives me for this."

He approached Dr. Thesari, who was still unconscious, her breathing shallow. Lily's eyes widened. "Alrek, wait—"

But before she could stop him, Alrek pressed the hypo against Dr. Thesari's neck. A faint hiss of air escaped as the adrenaline entered her system.

A few heartbeats later, the images from Dr. Thesari's mind—the Cyranthian dishes, the chef, even Elarion—vanished in an instant.

Dr. Thesari's eyes fluttered open, and she gasped, her lavender skin flushed. "My heart feels like a Raath jumped on it," she groaned, clutching her chest.

"Sorry," Alrek said, looking genuinely sheepish. "It had to be done."

Dr. Thesari's breathing slowed as she regained her composure. "I suppose it did," she said softly, nodding in reluctant agreement. She gestured to the console, motioning for Alrek to adjust the dosage in case they needed it again.

While they worked, Lily stepped away, her gaze falling on the old woman still sitting on the edge of the bed.

"I'm scared," Lily said, the words tumbling out before she could stop them. Her voice was so quiet it barely registered over the hum of the med bay's equipment. She tightened her arms around herself, staring at the floor as if it might offer her an escape. "I don't think I can face the Krythar."

The old woman tilted her head slightly, her kind, weathered face softening into an expression of understanding. The lines around her eyes deepened, not with pity, but with something richer—compassion tempered by a lifetime of experience. Her knit cap had slipped slightly, revealing more of her wild silver hair, and she reached up absently to adjust it before resting her hands in her lap.

Lily dared a glance at her, her throat tightening. She half-expected a lecture, or maybe even scorn for admitting her fear. Instead, the woman met her gaze with steady, unwavering warmth.

"I don't think that's the real monster chasing you, dear," the woman said gently, her voice carrying the weight of something ancient and unshakable.

Lily blinked, the words striking her like a distant bell tolling through fog. She frowned, her brow knitting as she tried to make sense of them.

"What do you mean?" she asked, her voice wavering between curiosity and frustration. "If it's not the Krythar, then what is it?"

The woman smiled faintly, her lips curving in a way that felt both secretive and inviting, like the first light of dawn creeping over a horizon. "Oh, I think you already know," she said simply, her tone so matter-of-fact it sent a shiver down Lily's spine.

Lily's chest tightened, and she shook her head, her thoughts racing. "I don't know," she said, her voice rising. "I don't remember anything. How am I supposed to know what I'm running from?"

The woman leaned forward slightly, her hands resting on her knees as her expression softened further. "Memories or no memories, fear doesn't live in the past, Lily," she said, her voice dipping low, rich with wisdom. "It lives right here." She pressed a hand to her chest, just above her heart. "And it doesn't need your past to thrive. It feeds on what you let it, grows on the stories you tell yourself about what you can and can't do."

Lily's breath hitched. She felt like the woman's words had cracked something open inside her, a hidden vault she hadn't known was there. "But I don't know who I am," she whispered, her voice barely holding together. "How can I face anything when I don't even know what I'm fighting for?"

The woman's gaze turned piercing, though the warmth in her eyes never wavered. "Maybe it's not about knowing," she said. "Maybe it's about deciding. Deciding who you are, and who you want to be, starting now."

Lily's throat tightened as a rush of emotion welled up, threatening to spill over. Her mind raced, grasping for a rebuttal, a way to push the woman's words away. But nothing came. Instead, she felt an ache deep in her chest, the weight of truths she couldn't deny pressing down on her.

"Lily," the woman said softly, her voice pulling her back. "You're strong enough to face what's ahead. Not because of who you were, but because of who you are now. Remember that."

Lily blinked rapidly, her vision blurring. The old woman reached out, a hand warm and steady on her arm. Lily wanted to say something, anything, but her throat felt too tight. Instead, she nodded, the smallest motion, but one that carried more weight than she realized.

She closed her eyes, letting the words sink in, and when she opened them again, she was no longer in the med bay.

She was back in San Francisco.

The air was cold, and the streets stretched out before her, bathed in dim, moody light.

The Krythar loomed in front of her, skeletal and terrifying, its psionic energy radiating like waves of heat.

"Who are you?" Lily shouted, her voice trembling but resolute enough to pierce the oppressive stillness.

The Krythar tilted its head slowly, the movement unnervingly deliberate. Its glowing eyes narrowed, like twin suns sinking into a void. "I am your fear," it said, its voice low and bone-chilling, the kind of sound that reverberated deep within her chest.

It took a step closer, the shadows around it twisting unnaturally. "I am the fear that lives within you," it hissed, each word dripping with menace. "I am the darkness that scratches at the edges of your dreams, the whisper that wakes you in the night and leaves you gasping for breath."

Lily's knees felt weak, her body frozen in place, but she forced herself to hold its gaze.

"I am the knowledge you try so hard to bury," it continued, its voice growing darker, deeper, a shadow within a shadow. "The truth you refuse to face. You are nothing, Lily Starling. You were created for one purpose—to be a weapon, wielded by others. Your life has no meaning beyond the cold, calculated intent of your makers."

Its form loomed larger, its presence suffocating. "You are not a person. You are not a hero. You are a tool," it spat, its voice laced with venom. "Disposable. Replaceable. Forgotten."

Lily's heart pounded, a relentless drumbeat of panic echoing in her chest. The Krythar's words coiled around her like a choking fog, pressing against her mind, her soul, threatening to smother her entirely. But somewhere beneath the suffocating weight, a spark flared—a flicker of defiance, fragile but alive, struggling to break free.

She clung to it, pulling herself upright as the words tumbled out, raw and unfiltered. "I don't have any memories," she said, her voice shaking but growing stronger with every syllable. "How can I be afraid of my past!?"

And then, like a tidal wave crashing over her, the realization struck. "I'm not afraid of my past," she whispered, her breath hitching, the admission cutting deeper than the Krythar's taunts ever could. "I'm afraid of not having one."

The Krythar loomed closer, its skeletal frame lit by an unnatural glow. Its claws flexed, shadows twisting unnaturally. "You will never be anything but a weapon."

Lily's chest clenched, fear pressing like a vice. For a heartbeat she nearly buckled. But then—defiance flared. Adrenaline burned through her veins as she drew herself up. "I may not know who I was," she said, steady now, "but I decide who I become."

Her fists clenched, voice rising. "I'm not afraid of my past anymore," she said, her voice trembling at first but gaining strength with each word. "But I'm also not afraid to admit that I'm not okay."

The Krythar froze, its ember eyes narrowing. Its voice dropped to a dangerous hiss. "What did you say?"

"I'm not okay," Lily repeated, her throat tight but steadying. Her breath hitched, and then the words burst out of her, raw and defiant: "I'M NOT OKAY! And that's okay. I may need to heal, but I'm not going to lie to myself anymore. I'm not okay—how can I be?"

The Krythar staggered as if the words themselves struck it, its jagged form wavering like smoke in a sudden gust. Its fiery gaze faltered, dimming as it began to unravel. Shadows dissolved with it until the alley itself melted away, leaving silence behind—calm and strange, like the eye of a storm.

Lily closed her eyes, drawing in a deep, steadying breath. She felt the weight on her chest ease, the pounding in her ears quieting.

When she opened them again, the dim, foreboding street was gone. She was back in the med bay, the bright, sterile lights a jarring contrast to the dark, shadowed alleyways of her mind.

The room was calmer now, the machinery ticking in steady rhythms, a reminder that the ship was still anchored in reality. The storm of chaotic projections had finally burned itself out. Only one mental image lingered—the projection of Caris, still standing near Alrek with an air of serene confidence, her hair framing her face a little too perfectly to be real.

Dr. Thesari sat up straighter, color returning faintly to her lavender skin. She tapped a few buttons on the console, her expression thoughtful. "We've managed to stabilize the systems," she said, her voice steadier now, though tinged with exhaustion. "The adrenaline treatment worked. Once the Raath-Ka got their clarity back, they started working at their usual, frighteningly efficient pace. I finally got through to the bridge as well—communications are back online across the ship."

Lily let out a breath. "That's good news."

Tess tilted her head, a faint smile tugging at her mouth. "Though I should warn you, I suspect the Raath-Ka are going to start requesting adrenaline shots regularly. Apparently, they 'quite enjoyed' the heightened focus."

Alrek snorted. "Of course they did."

Lily grinned. "Well, at least someone's benefiting from all this chaos." She glanced at the image of Caris. "Although... why is she still here?"

Alrek shifted awkwardly, his hands fidgeting at his sides. "I, uh..." He squared his shoulders and faced the projection. "You're really smart, and I respect you. I'm sorry I ogled you in the gym the other day. That was... inappropriate."

The projection smiled warmly, her expression soft and understanding. Without a word, she dissolved into the air, fading as if she'd never been there.

Lily crossed her arms, one eyebrow arched. "Caris is awesome, by the way. And hey, you're only—"

Alrek groaned, cutting her off with a mock glare. "Don't say it."

She laughed, relenting. "Fine. But still—you're a teenager. It's not exactly fair having your daydreams projected for the whole ship."

They chuckled together, the tension ebbing into something lighter. The med bay, though cluttered with the remnants of earlier chaos, finally felt steady again—a moment of calm after the storm.

• • • •

The briefing room carried a subdued energy, officers and crew gathered around the curved table as Captain Calan gestured to the holo-display.

"Initial scans indicate the wave was caused by an unstable magnetic shockwave," he explained, his tone measured but grim. "A Krythar weapons test. Our analysis suggests it tore open a messy dimensional rip—that's what caused the disruptions."

"'Messy' is an understatement," someone muttered, drawing the faintest smile from Calan.

"We've yet to locate the weapon itself," he went on. "But we're tracking its trajectory through residual magnetic signatures. Engineering and Science are refining the sensors now. This was a warning—intended or not. And we'll need to be ready for whatever comes next."

The room fell into a heavy silence, the weight of his words pressing into the quiet.

When the meeting adjourned, Lily lingered, catching up with Caris at the exit.

"Hey," Lily said, falling into step. "You helped save the day, you know."

Caris arched a brow, half-amused. "Do I even want to know how?"

"I'll tell you later. But seriously—thank you."

Caris stopped, her expression softening. "Are you okay?"

Lily hesitated, then nodded slowly. "No," she admitted. "But I can finally start accepting that. And I'm ready to start deciding who I want to be, instead of being trapped in who I was."

Caris gave her a small, approving smile. "That sounds like a good place to start."

As Lily turned a corner, she nearly collided with Alrek and Dr. Thesari.

Tess beamed at Alrek. "You were incredible today. Truly. Thank you for helping save the day."

Alrek flushed a deep blue, rubbing the back of his neck. "Guess it's good I came to get my medical clearance after all."

Lily smirked, resting a hand on his shoulder. "Come on, both of you. Let's get some ice cream or something. We need to process all of this."

Tess perked up. "Ice cream? After today's excitement? That sounds perfect."

Alrek chuckled, then tilted his head thoughtfully. "Do they have any savory flavors?"

Lily shot him a look, incredulous. "You are so weird."

He chuckled. "Hey, as long as it's not Cyranthian food."

Together they walked down the corridor, the weight of the day slowly lifting with every step.

UAP Space Fleet Secure Communication Network
From: Joren Vek, Senior Engineer, Starship Vanguard
To: Captain Griff Calan, Starship Salamander
Encryption Level: Omega-3 (Personal Communication)

DEAR CALAN,

I know, I'm usually not the letter type. I got used to our calls, and sometimes I even write down stuff I want to remember to tell you. But being out of comm range, the list has gotten pretty long. Lately, I have to admit this whole deep-space thing sucks. Maybe the Sceptacky people will let us put a communications relay up over here eventually. That would be nice. I'm counting down the days to two weeks from now when the *Salamander* and the *Vanguard* will overlap at Star Base 5. Actual time together feels like some distant dream. For now, though, I need to vent and share like I usually do. So buckle in.

For the record, I'm playing "Waiting on a Friend" in the background just to annoy you. Well, I can pretend you're here rolling your eyes at it. I know how you barely tolerate 20th-century music. My band has started some experimental stuff I think you might actually like. A little closer to your taste. And, miracle of miracles, we haven't canceled our last three jam sessions. I know—how unlike me. It's actually been pretty quiet, so we don't really have an excuse except laziness, which, to be fair, is probably going to win this week. Honestly, I'm not in a musical mood. I'd rather be working on the P47 I'm rebuilding. Yeah, that's how quiet it's been—I actually dusted it off and started working on it again. Has it been a year? Two? I had to check out tools from the engineering lab because, surprise, I lost mine. Why do I give you more ammunition to tease me about losing things?

The stabilizer array went out again last week—third time this month. It's like patching a sieve with duct tape. One of my junior engineers said, "At this point, the array has more Joren than original parts." He's not wrong. I'm starting to feel like an organ donor for this ship. I'd grumble about it more if I didn't secretly love tinkering with the damn thing. Star Base 5 will finally replace some of this junk, but until then, I've kept it mostly running. Well, we're leaning on some secondary systems, but at least we're not down to tertiary ones. I'll appreciate the upgrades when they come. Did you know the jump rods on the entire port side are seven years old? I've seen the specs on the new ones—it's going to be like upgrading from a mule to an X4 speeder. Sorry to bore you with that. I have to tell someone! Can't let the gang see me geeking out.

Oh, and you'll get a kick out of this: Lt. Dariak and Ensign Pol are at it again. This time, it's over the last hand of the poker tournament. What started as a casual Friday night game—mostly an excuse for the engineers and ops officers to have a few drinks—has turned into a full-blown spectacle thanks to those two. Dariak, being Cyranthian, is his usual pleasant and friendly self on the surface, but you know how they are when it comes to competition. Beneath all the charm, he's as intense as a plasma torch. Pol, on the other hand, is Urrathi and argumentative to their core, so Dariak's eternal pleasantness drives them absolutely crazy. Honestly, I think Pol arranged the whole tournament just to have an excuse to argue with him.

The best part? They managed to drag half the ship into this mess. The game got heated, accusations were thrown, and now neither of them is speaking to the other. It's like a couple of toddlers with advanced engineering degrees. You know I'm terrible at poker anyway, but I'll admit—it's entertaining to watch people implode over something so silly. Keeps things lively, if nothing else.

Speaking of Cyranthians, Captain Humossie takes the whole Dryst thing to a new level. She's one of those people who becomes an expert in whatever she puts her mind to. Yes, yes, you're still the best captain in the fleet—don't worry, your crown's intact—but I have to say, her tenacity is something else. Case in point: we had an away mission on some rocky terrain, and she taught herself how to rock climb in about three days. And then, just last month, she invited the senior staff to go hang gliding on Kareth-4.

I didn't go—because, you know, me and gravity are on decent terms and I'd like to keep it that way—but I saw plenty of pictures. Some daredevil stuff. Dariak took to it like a natural, of course, and Pol tried to one-up everyone and ended up dangling from a tree. Humossie, though, nailed it, swooping around like she'd been doing it her whole life. That's just how she is—if there's a challenge, she's in, no hesitation.

On the personal front, I finally got around to tuning up my stratophone. Took me long enough, right? It sounds decent—still not quite there, but better than the racket it was making last month. I'm thinking about stringing it up with the old steel strings, the ones I had back when we first met. Nostalgia might do the trick—or at least remind me of the good old days when I was marginally better at this. Oh, and here's a gem: I managed to trade for a vinyl copy of *Born to Run*. It's scratched to hell, but it's the real deal. Next time we're in the same place, I'll crank it up and see if I can't convert you into a Springsteen fan once and for all. No promises, I know.

And just now, we've picked up a distress call. Some old space station isn't responding—no signs of life, just silence. Captain Humossie wants me to get a crew together to check it out. Don't worry, Griff, I'll be careful. The initial scan didn't detect any weapons fire, so the threat level looks low. Probably just some old equipment finally giving up the ghost.

I hope we're back in comms range soon. I miss hearing your voice. I miss you. I love you, Griff. Always.

Joren

[END TRANSMISSION]

Chapter 10:
The Station That Sleeps

LILY SHIFTED IN THE jump seat beside Caris's station, her gaze flicking between the bridge crew. The seat was just as uncomfortable as she remembered from their journey through the time warp—an ergonomic nightmare designed to keep anyone from lingering. She wondered if the officers' chairs were any better.

Around her, faces wore a veneer of calm that barely masked the tension beneath. Every glance at the chronometer, every nervous shift in posture, added to the unease hanging in the air like static before a storm.

"Five minutes," Datch announced.

A low voice threaded through the quiet.

You'll come running back to me...

Yeah, time is on my side, yes it is...

Lily's head turned sharply. The Captain.

Calan's voice was quiet, almost lost under the bridge's usual background noise, but the melody was unmistakable. Lily's stomach tightened. Calan despised 20th-century music—that was Joren's obsession, not his. And Calan only ever sang when he was nervous.

His expression was a mask of confidence, but it wasn't the unshakable assurance Lily had come to rely on in a crisis. This was something else—a performance, a shield against the turmoil beneath.

"Four minutes," Datch said, his even tone cutting through the stillness.

"Thank you, Mister Datch," Calan replied, sharper than usual.

Lily exchanged a glance with Caris—a flicker of mutual understanding. Across the bridge, Malik broke the silence, his voice measured but tense.

"Still nothing on scans, sir."

Caris's hands moved deftly across her console. "The distress beacon is still active."

The next two minutes stretched unbearably thin, the quiet so taut it seemed ready to snap. Lily's stomach churned, a queasy anticipation gnawing at her.

Datch's voice counted down from ten, and with a jarring lurch, the Salamander dropped out of light factor.

There it was.

Even to Lily's 21st-century eyes, the station looked ancient. Its hull was pockmarked and dull, its silhouette stark against the endless black of space. No lights blinked, no movement stirred. It hung there like a relic, an artifact misplaced in the wrong century.

Calan straightened in his chair, his voice pitched to fill the room and suppress the concern lurking at its edges. "Any sign of the Vanguard?"

Malik hesitated, his fingers moving across the console. "Sir, I'm reading their main engine signature. They were here... but there's no exit stream."

Caris spoke before she could stop herself, the words tumbling out in a rush she instantly regretted. "Meaning they never left."

Calan's face hardened as he sank into his chair.

Malik's voice carried a note of grim certainty. "There's an enormous residue of energy, sir—like a portal forming and collapsing in an instant. My best estimate is that the Vanguard has been... swallowed by an energy envelope of some kind."

For a long moment, silence reigned. Then, with visible effort, Calan forced out the words. "Any life signs on the station?"

Datch chimed in, his tone clipped. "Negative, sir. However, I'm reading significant ionic particle charges. It's possible they're masking sensors."

Calan rubbed his face, exhaling slowly before speaking. "I'm leading an away team. Full EV suits for everyone."

Before she could stop herself, Lily blurted out, "Sir, I'd like to come along."

Calan's head snapped toward her, his expression unreadable. She rushed to make her case. "I know I don't have full control of my psionic abilities, but what if I can... sense something over there?" In truth, Lily had no idea what she might contribute. She only knew, deep in her gut, that she needed to be there.

Calan studied her for a moment longer than she was comfortable with. Finally, he nodded. "All right. Join the party."

Lily's breath caught. She hadn't expected him to agree.

"Datch, Caris—you're with me. Have a security team meet us in the shuttle bay," Calan added, already rising from his chair.

Lily saw her own surprise mirrored in Caris's wide eyes. The Captain moved briskly, his composure snapping the bridge into action as he disappeared into the lift.

Lily stood, her legs unsteady beneath her. Dryst Amaris's voice stopped her and the others before they could follow.

"Look after Calan," he said, his gaze sharp and unwavering.

Lily nodded. "We will."

The lift doors closed, trapping them in the unrelenting tension.

. . . .

The hiss of the airlock filled Lily's ears, amplified by her helmet's internal comm system. Her gloved hands tightened reflexively on the suit's controls as the heavy outer door groaned open. Beyond the threshold, the station loomed—a cavernous darkness lit sporadically by flickering emergency lights. Dust particles floated in the stale, artificial atmosphere, catching the beams of their helmet lights like lazy snowflakes.

Her heart thudded in rhythm with the faint pulse of her suit's oxygen supply. This was her first real mission in an EV suit, and every part of it felt cumbersome. The suit clung to her like an unrelenting second skin, its bulk pressing in on her movements. Each step was deliberate, her boots magnetically catching on the deck with a muted click as she followed the team into the unknown.

Her mind drifted back to her training sessions with Caris. The veteran officer had a way of making it all look effortless—gliding through zero-gravity drills and hazard simulations like it was second nature. "The trick is not to overthink it," Caris had said, her tone equal parts wisdom and challenge. "Trust the suit. Focus on the mission." At the time, Lily had nodded, eager and confident, but now those words felt like a cruel taunt as her thoughts spiraled, conjuring worst-case scenarios with every labored step.

Her helmet light swept across the airlock as they stepped inside, catching on a plaque affixed to the bulkhead near the entrance. The brushed metal gleamed faintly in the low light, its lettering sharp and deliberate: *Aeon Crescent*. The name struck her as oddly poetic for a place so lifeless. It evoked an image of time frozen in a gentle curve, like the waxing moon suspended in an eternal night. But here, in the cold, still air of the station, the name felt like a cruel joke—time had stopped entirely, leaving only echoes behind.

"Stay close," Calan's voice crackled over the comm, snapping her back to the moment. His tone was clipped, professional, but Lily caught a faint edge of worry beneath it. She glanced at him ahead of her, his tall frame silhouetted in the pale glow of his helmet lights. He moved with practiced precision, but she couldn't imagine what it must feel like for him—leading the charge onto a dead station, searching for his missing husband.

"Copy that," Datch replied, his calm, unflinching presence a steadying force at the rear of the team.

Lily forced herself to focus on her surroundings. The hallway they'd stepped into was eerily pristine, the walls smooth and metallic, though marred by occasional scorch marks that suggested some past calamity. Shadows danced at the edges of her vision, cast by the unsteady light of their beams. She swept her own light forward, trying not to imagine what could be hiding in the dark corners.

"How's everyone holding up?" Caris's voice broke the silence, a note of forced cheer in her tone.

"Fine," Lily lied, her voice wavering just enough to make Caris glance over her shoulder.

"You're doing great," Caris said softly, for Lily alone. "This place is creepy as hell, but you're holding it together."

Lily managed a shaky nod, grateful for the encouragement even as her throat tightened. The quiet hum of her helmet's filters filled the space between words.

"Focus," Calan cut in, his tone sharp but not unkind. "We need to keep moving. We're looking for any signs of life—or whatever's left of it."

Lily's pulse quickened as the team pressed forward, their boots thudding faintly against the deck plates. She was acutely aware of every sound: the faint whir of suit mechanics, the hiss of oxygen, the creak of old metal as the station settled around them. Every step felt like a question with no answer, the weight of the unknown bearing down on her with each passing moment.

Ahead, Calan raised a hand, signaling the group to halt. Lily froze mid-step, her light catching on something just ahead. A door, slightly ajar, with faint scorch marks around the edges. It looked like it had been forced open.

"Let's check it out," Calan said grimly, his voice low.

As the team approached, Lily's breath caught. Her nerves whispered that they were being watched. She forced the thought away, steeling herself for what might come next.

They squeezed through the half-opened door into a cavernous mess hall, a space that felt frozen in time. Long rows of tables stretched into the shadows, their surfaces scattered with dust-covered trays, overturned chairs, and petrified remnants of long-forgotten meals. To Lily's surprise, an odor lingered in the air—a faint, sickly mix of decay and age that her suit filters couldn't entirely block. Her stomach churned as her helmet light landed on a half-empty plate and a labeled bottle resembling some kind of soft drink. It was as if the crew had vanished in the middle of lunch, leaving behind an unsettling stillness that pressed against her senses.

"What happened here?" Caris murmured, her voice low but cutting through the eerie silence.

Lily paused at a nearby table, her eyes drawn to skeletal remains—what might have been poultry or something similar—poking through a fine layer of dust. A shiver ran through her as her imagination filled in the gaps of lives abruptly interrupted. "Looks like they left in a hurry," she said, her voice barely steady. "Is there any record of this station?"

Datch's voice crackled over the comm. "The Vanguard received an automated distress call to come here three days ago. That's when we lost contact with them. As for this station... there's no record of it in the Union's database. However, this is Sceptacky space. And while relations are good, they've never been particularly forthcoming with their records."

"This isn't a Sceptacky station," Caris said firmly, gesturing to a nearby chair. "The proportions are all wrong." She turned to Lily, unease flickering in her expression. "The Sceptacky average over nine feet tall."

Datch's calm, clinical voice cut in. "You're correct. The architecture and furnishings suggest a species more closely resembling humans."

Their conversation cut short as an odd scraping sound echoed across the room. At first, it was faint—metal dragging on metal—but it grew louder with each passing second. Everyone froze, their lights converging on the far end of the room.

"What is that?" Caris whispered, breaking the tense silence.

Calan's voice was steady, but there was a tightness to it that Lily didn't miss. "The sound is coming from over there," he said, pointing toward a shadowed corner. "But I don't see anything."

"Wait," Lily said, her tone sharp with disbelief. "Look."

A chair, standing alone a few feet away, began to slide across the floor. The scraping noise turned harsh, grating against the stillness. It moved in a slow, deliberate line, as though pushed by invisible hands.

Everyone stared, their breathing loud in Lily's ears through the comm.

"Are you seeing this?" Caris asked, holding up her handheld scanner, her light trained on the chair. "It reads as... a chair. Moving by itself."

"Very helpful, Ensign," Calan said, his dry tone barely masking his unease. His eyes never left the moving object.

He stepped forward, closing the distance with slow, deliberate strides. The chair jerked to a stop the moment he extended his hand. He hesitated before poking it lightly. It remained still, utterly lifeless.

"Just a chair," he muttered, but his jaw was tight, and the tension in the room refused to dissipate.

"Could be a gravitational anomaly," Calan said, straightening with an air of authority. "Malik mentioned systems like artificial gravity have been running for around sixty years. Bound to malfunction eventually."

Lily frowned beneath her helmet, unconvinced. The chair's unexplained movement gnawed at her thoughts, a puzzle left unsolved. But Calan was already moving forward, his voice brisk and decisive. "Caris, Lily, take Hernandez and head to the main engineering deck. The rest of you, with me to the command deck. Keep comms open at all times. That's an order."

Two security officers stepped forward to flank Calan and Datch, their movements sharp and ready. Lily exchanged a glance with Caris, who met her gaze with a steady nod before gesturing toward the nearby maintenance shaft.

"It's only two decks up," Caris said, her voice cutting through the uneasy silence. Without hesitation, she reached for the ladder and began to climb, her movements smooth and practiced.

"Lucky for us," Lily murmured, her words barely audible above the echoes. The oppressive tension of the station had seeped into her bones.

She hesitated for a heartbeat, her gaze lingering on the mess hall below. The overturned chairs, dusty plates, and unsettling stillness seemed to loom, fragments of a story she wasn't sure she wanted to piece together. She swallowed hard and gripped the ladder, the cold metal biting through her gloves as she began to climb. Every time she looked away, her imagination whispered that the room below was shifting, its contents rearranging in her absence.

The narrow shaft amplified the sound of their ascent, every clang of her boots against the rungs reverberating like an echoing heartbeat. The intermittent glitching of her comms scratched at the edge of her focus, threatening to splinter it entirely. She forced herself to concentrate on the rhythm of her movements, pushing back the ghostly images that refused to leave her mind.

Behind her, Hernandez climbed in measured silence, the sound of his ascent a counterpoint to her own. He hadn't spoken a word, and Lily couldn't tell if his quiet was deliberate or if he, too, was grappling with the suffocating unease. Either way, the weight of the station pressed down on all of them, growing heavier with every rung they climbed.

· · · ·

The engineering deck loomed vast and silent, a cavernous black void. Their helmet lights barely penetrated the darkness, revealing little more than shadowy machinery and tangled cables disappearing into the gloom. In the center of the space, a single console emitted a faint glow, casting a sickly halo onto the floor.

"Where are the emergency lights?" Caris muttered, her voice tight.

Lily scanned the darkness, her flashlight beam slicing through the oppressive black. "Not exactly a welcoming vibe," she said under her breath, her tone failing to hide her unease.

"Stay focused," Caris said as they made their way cautiously toward the lone console.

The air was still, unnaturally so, as if the room itself were holding its breath. They reached the console, and Caris leaned over it, tapping at the controls. Her brow furrowed beneath her helmet as the screen flickered erratically.

"It's locked in a feedback loop," she said, frustration lacing her tone. "I'll have to do a full system reboot, but there's no guarantee it'll come back online. And when I start the reboot, the artificial gravity will go offline."

"Did you hear that, Captain?" Lily asked over the comm.

Calan's voice came back immediately, firm and decisive. "Go for it. Everyone, make sure your boots are magnetized to the hull."

Lily's hand instinctively went to the control on her suit, and with a quick press, the magnets in her boots engaged, anchoring her to the floor with a reassuring click.

Caris began punching in commands, her fingers steady despite the tension in her voice. "Initiating reboot in three... two..."

Lily's flashlight darted across the room, catching a flicker of motion at the periphery of her vision. Something moved—a blur, just beyond the edge of her light's reach, too quick to pin down.

"Wait," she whispered, her voice taut with unease.

Caris glanced up sharply from the console. "What is it?"

Lily squinted into the shadows, her flashlight beam chasing the elusive movement. Whatever it was, it darted out of view again, almost as if teasing her attempts to track it.

"Something's moving," Lily said, her voice edged with both tension and determination. "I can't tell what, but it's fast."

"Really big rat?" Caris asked, her tone wary but laced with dry humor that didn't quite mask her own discomfort.

Before Lily could respond, the gravity cut out. Her stomach lurched as weightlessness overtook her, a disorienting shift that left her gripping the edge of a nearby console for stability. The rebooting lights blinked faintly in the oppressive void, casting unsettling shadows across the room.

"Stay sharp," Caris said, her voice steadier than the tension in her face suggested. "Hernandez, keep your blaster ready."

Lily's pulse quickened as her light swept through the darkness, each pass revealing nothing but empty shadows. Her heart pounded in her temple, an unrelenting rhythm that seemed to echo in the stillness. Then, with a flicker and hum, the emergency lights blinked to life.

And there it was.

Suspended in the air about three meters away, its grotesque form came into sharp relief under the stark, artificial glow. Wings like the translucent appendages of a giant insect quivered, their edges frayed. Fleshy tendrils dangled from its frame, trailing glowing slime that dripped in bursts of light, vanishing before it touched the floor. Its face—if it could be called that—was an abstract smear of features, as though someone had tried to draw a human visage with shaking hands and then blurred it into obscurity. The creature's body rippled unnaturally, as if it existed just out of sync with their reality.

"Oh my God," Lily whispered, the words escaping her lips before she could stop them.

The restored gravity released the tension in their boots, and the three of them disengaged their magnetic locks for better maneuverability. Hernandez, weapon raised, edged closer to the aberration, his movements deliberate but tense.

The thing trembled, its glowing body undulating faintly. Though it made no sound, its presence was almost deafening. The air felt thick, the weight of its existence pressing on Lily's chest like an invisible force. Her breath came in shallow gasps as she fought the primal urge to flee.

"Captain," Caris said, her voice cutting through the crackling comm, unsteady but clear. "There's... something down here."

The apparition emitted a pulsating light, its movements jerking and twitching as if struggling to remain tethered to their reality. Suddenly, a gust of wind tore through the room, carrying the force of a vacuum. Lily clung to the console, her gloves slipping slightly against the smooth surface as the wind roared around her, filling her helmet with a deafening howl.

"Hold on!" Caris shouted, her voice barely audible over the cacophony.

Hernandez's blaster slipped from his grasp, spinning wildly through the air, the polished metal catching the flickering emergency lights. It hurtled toward the creature like a magnet drawn to its center.

The creature shimmered violently, its form trembling as though on the verge of splitting apart. Then, with a jarring distortion that clawed at Lily's ears, it began to fold in on itself, collapsing like a star imploding into a singularity. The air around it rippled with a static-laden sound, unnatural and otherworldly—like a record spinning backward at high speed, the noise warping and bending.

And then, it was gone, vanishing with a final flash of light that pulled Hernandez's blaster into the void along with it.

The wind died instantly, leaving the room in an unsettling silence broken only by the faint **thrum** of the station's systems. Lily's hands trembled as she gripped the console, her breath coming in shallow, rapid gasps. Her wide eyes stared at the empty space where the creature had been.

"What the...?" she whispered, her voice barely above a breath.

The comm crackled, Calan's voice cutting through the lingering tension. "Report."

Caris was the first to respond, her words deliberate. "Captain, there was... something. A creature, I think? It looked like—honestly, it looked like a monster. And then it vanished, folded in on itself."

"It tried to suck us in, sir," Hernandez added, his voice barely steady.

Lily hesitated, her mind replaying the creature's grotesque form and the strange winds they experienced. "It generated some kind of vortex," she said, her tone thoughtful but edged with unease. "It definitely felt... hostile."

A heavy pause filled the line before Calan's voice returned, firm and commanding. "Stay where you are. We're coming to you. In the meantime, run a full systems diagnostic on the station."

Caris straightened, her motions precise but taut. "Aye, sir."

As the comm went silent, Lily glanced at Hernandez. His hands still trembled as he clutched his replacement blaster, his eyes wide with barely contained panic.

"Hey," she said gently, offering him her weapon. "Here, Mr. Security. Hang in there—we'll get through this."

Hernandez nodded quickly, forcing a faint, unconvincing smile. His movements were deliberate as he accepted the weapon, but the unease never left his face. He started pacing the room, his boots landing with sharp, hollow thuds against the deck plating.

"What do you think it was?" he asked abruptly, his voice tight, teetering on the edge of panic. He didn't look at anyone in particular, his gaze darting between Lily and Caris, searching for answers they didn't yet have.

Caris glanced up from the console she was working on, her fingers moving with practiced precision. "Try to stay calm, crewman," she said, her tone sharp but measured. "We need to keep our heads cool. Once the station's internal sensors are back online, we can run a full scan and hopefully figure out exactly what we're dealing with."

Lily stood between them, her thoughts pulling in two directions. Part of her mirrored the crewman's reaction—what in all the stars had they just witnessed? But another part clung to Caris's steady pragmatism. Panic wouldn't help anyone, least of all Hernandez, who looked like he was one sharp noise away from jumping out an airlock. Lily drew a steadying breath, her fingers twitching near the scanner in her hand. She focused, ready to catch even the faintest sign of something—anything—out of place. Yet the weight of the station pressed down on her, oppressive and unrelenting.

· · · ·

Time stretched as Caris worked through the diagnostics, her focus unwavering despite the oppressive stillness. She exhaled sharply, impatience slipping through her tone. "What is keeping the captain?"

Hernandez had taken to sitting on a tool crate, his blaster balanced precariously in his hand, knuckles pale as he tried to keep it steady. Lily hovered nearby, pacing the length of the room, fighting to keep her mind from spiraling into dark places.

A sudden burst of static crackled through their comms, sharp and jarring. "Umm... guys?" The captain's voice broke through, low and tense. "We know what you were talking about now. Activate visual."

Caris didn't hesitate, hitting the control on her suit's comm system. The holo-projection shimmered into existence, flickering before stabilizing. The captain's face filled the frame, his features taut with strain. His usual calm had cracked, replaced by an edge of barely concealed urgency. Behind him, the corridor was a riot of shifting light.

Several glowing figures hovered in the background, their ethereal forms dripping light that shimmered like molten glass before vanishing into the floor. The kaleidoscopic glow twisted and danced across the bulkheads, painting the space in radiant, disorienting patterns. It was both mesmerizing and deeply unnerving—a strange beauty steeped in dread.

"They're everywhere," Calan said, his voice clipped, each word weighted with unease. Beside him, Datch worked furiously at a hatch door, his normally serene expression carved into sharp lines of concentration. Two security officers flanked them, weapons raised, grips white-knuckled as they tracked the glowing chaos.

Lily's stomach twisted, a knot of unease tightening with every passing second. She muttered a curse under her breath.

Caris leaned closer to the holo, her sharp gaze scanning the scene. "Sir, have you experienced any vacuum-like sensations? Similar to what we saw down here?"

Calan shook his head, his helmet light casting restless shadows. "These ones seem to be moving right past us, like they don't even see us."

"Look out, Datch!" Lily exclaimed as one of the creatures floated directly through Datch's chest. The glow rippled outward like a stone skipping across water, its trail lingering for a heartbeat before fading. Datch barely flinched, arching a single eyebrow and glancing at the captain with calm detachment.

"They appear solid," Datch observed, his voice measured despite the tension, "but they seem to exist on a different plane in some way."

Caris exhaled, her breath loud in the uneasy silence. "Like a ghost..." she murmured.

Before anyone could respond, the creatures dissolved, their forms shimmering and folding into thin air as though they had never been there.

Datch broke the silence. "This hatch is sealed like the rest, sir. I cannot override it."

Calan's jaw tightened, but his voice remained steady. "We're trying to make our way to you," he said after a beat, softer but no less resolute. "But the hatches are all sealed below deck 5, as if we were locked in. We're looking for another way. Hold tight."

"Understood, sir," Caris replied crisply. The holo flickered, then fizzled out, plunging them back into the dim engineering deck. The silence that followed was heavy, oppressive, like the station itself was holding its breath.

Lily had just begun scanning again when her equipment let out a shrill, urgent beep. "I'm getting some strange readings," she said, her voice tight.

As if summoned by her words, dark clouds began to form on the floor, coiling and thickening with unnatural speed. Lightning flickered within the growing vortex, and a low rumble of thunder reverberated through the room, making the deck plates tremble.

Hernandez froze, his wide eyes locked on the swirling storm. "What the hell is this?" he stammered.

"Captain, something's happening!" Lily shouted into her comms, but the wind that erupted from the vortex drowned her out. It howled like a living thing, pulling at her suit and equipment with relentless force.

She and Caris both scrambled to analyze the phenomenon, their scanners flooding with data that made no sense. Numbers and symbols blurred across Lily's screen, useless against the overwhelming chaos in front of her.

At the heart of the storm, a dark eye opened—a gateway pulsing with malevolent energy that seemed to ripple through the air itself. A chill shot through Lily's body, her stomach knotting with dread as the temperature seemed to drop around her.

Hernandez screamed, a raw, panicked sound that barely carried over the deafening roar.

"Mag boots, now!" Caris barked, slamming the activation switch on her suit. Lily followed instantly, the metallic click of her boots locking her to the deck a fleeting comfort as the pull of the vortex grew stronger, yanking at everything not bolted down. But Hernandez wasn't fast enough.

"Hernandez, hold on!" Lily shouted, reaching for him as he staggered against the relentless force. The pull was too strong. His body wrenched free with terrifying speed, his limbs flailing as he was dragged toward the portal.

"No!" Lily's cry was raw and desperate as she strained against the suction. Her gloved hand reached out in vain, her heart plummeting as Hernandez's terrified eyes locked with hers for a fleeting moment before his body vanished into the swirling dark.

"Hernandez!" Lily's voice echoed in the chaos, brittle and helpless. She braced herself against the unrelenting pull of the storm, the deck beneath her trembling as though the entire station might tear apart.

The gateway expanded, and from its center, one of the glowing forms emerged. This one was more vivid than the others, its grotesque details painfully clear. Blurred features twisted unnervingly, wings like jagged shards of light stretched wide, and tendrils of dripping luminescence dangled from its form, vanishing before they touched the floor.

For a moment, the creature seemed to pause, its gaze heavy and alien as it swept over them. The oppressive weight of its presence pressed against Lily's chest, suffocating and otherworldly.

Then, without warning, the creature dissolved into a burst of light. The portal rippled, its edges curling inward, collapsing on itself in a flash that left the room eerily still.

"Calan to team! Report!" The captain's voice cut through the comms, sharp and urgent.

The storm surged one last time, its ferocious winds tugging at their suits before imploding with a deafening roar. Silence followed, save for the ringing in Lily's ears. She gasped for breath, her chest heaving as she struggled to process what had just happened.

"Team, respond! Are you still with me?" Calan's voice came again, demanding, insistent.

Caris stepped forward, her voice steady but tinged with emotion. "Caris here. We've lost Hernandez. One of those... things. It took him."

There was a pause, heavy and loaded with tension. When Calan spoke again, his voice carried the unyielding weight of command. "Get out of there. Now. Engineering might be the epicenter of this chaos. Head back to deck 11, secure the shuttle, and bring it around to pick us up on deck 5. Whatever's happening on this station, I won't let us share the Vanguard's fate."

"Aye, sir," Caris responded, her voice regaining its usual steel. She turned to Lily, who stood frozen, her wide eyes fixed on the empty space where Hernandez had vanished. "Lily, let's move."

. . . .

The two of them reached the airlock, Lily skidding to a stop as her eyes darted through the portal into space. The Salamander hung in the distance, a steady beacon of safety against the endless black, but where the shuttle should have been, there was nothing. Her stomach dropped. The docking clamps sat empty, the hatch sealed tight.

Lily stood frozen, dread pooling in her chest. "Please tell me we're at the wrong airlock."

The line crackled before Calan's voice came through, sharp and taut. "Please tell me you're joking."

Datch's calm, measured tone followed. "Now would be an extremely inappropriate time for humor."

Caris stepped closer to the viewport, her jaw tightening as she scanned the empty docking clamps. "Nobody's joking, sir. The shuttle is gone."

A heavy pause lingered over the comms, thick with unspoken frustration, before Calan's clipped voice returned. "We're still stuck on level five. All exits are sealed, and I can't raise the Salamander. Something's interfering with my comm tag. Can you two try using the communication station on your deck to send a message?"

Caris moved swiftly to the nearby comm panel, her gloved fingers gliding over the controls. The screen flickered to life, spitting static before collapsing into garbled code. She tried again, her movements sharper, jaw set with frustration. "Nothing. It's completely unresponsive. No outbound signal, no feedback loop—just dead."

Lily leaned in beside her, the unease in her chest tightening with each failed attempt. The station's silence pressed against her thoughts, crowding her mind until it was hard to breathe.

"Team," Datch's voice cut through, calm and deliberate, as if he were speaking from a place untouched by the chaos. "If you encounter the creatures again, I'm sending a scanner program to your equipment. Please run it. I require additional data to analyze their nature."

Lily exhaled slowly, the faint glow of the scanner interface reflecting in her visor as she adjusted the settings. Her fingers hovered over the controls for a moment before she nodded. "Got it. Scanner set to your specs," she said, her voice steadier than she felt.

Caris straightened, brushing a gloved hand over the lifeless comm panel before stepping back. "No point staying here. Let's head to the central communications hub on deck six. If we can get it operational, we might be able to send a message through."

"And if we can't?" Lily asked, her voice edged with unease.

"Then we'll try to access deck five from the other side and see if we can get through the sealed hatch to reach the captain and Datch," Caris replied, her tone steady and matter-of-fact.

"That would be appreciated," the captain's voice crackled faintly over the comms, resolute despite the interference.

• • • •

The corridor ahead loomed dark and vast, the dim lighting barely holding back the shadows that clung to the walls. Lily and Caris moved cautiously, their footsteps muffled by the thick tension in the air. Every sound—every faint creak of metal or whisper of shifting air—felt sharper, more deliberate.

As they ascended toward deck six, Lily froze mid-climb. She tightened her grip on her scanner, her heart stumbling in her chest. "Wait."

Ahead of them, several of the glowing figures hovered in the corridor, their forms casting eerie, kaleidoscopic patterns across the walls. Their translucent bodies drifted in slow, deliberate movements, tendrils of light undulating and fading into the air as if never truly there.

"They're leaving us alone," Caris whispered, her words barely audible through the comms. She hadn't drawn her weapon, her posture tense but watchful. "Like the ones the captain and Datch saw."

Lily nodded, swallowing hard as she raised her scanner, steadying her shaking hands. The device gave off a faint vibration as it collected the data Datch had requested. She kept her eyes on the creatures, their movements strange but unthreatening, like lost shadows gliding through the corridors of a forgotten world.

One of them drifted closer, its luminous tendrils trailing along the edges of the wall before fading into nothing. Lily held her breath, her pulse drumming in her ears. Whatever these things were, they felt wrong but not malevolent. At least, not yet.

Once her scanner finished its cycle, she gave a subtle nod. They edged on, every step careful and deliberate, as though the very air might shatter around them. The creatures drifted aimlessly behind, their glowing tendrils casting rippling patterns on the walls. Lily kept her gaze straight ahead, resisting the urge to glance back.

When they reached deck six, the central communications hub came into view—a sprawl of consoles and tangled wiring, some darkened and lifeless, others flickering faintly with erratic pulses of light. The shifting glow only deepened the shadows, making the room feel larger than it probably was.

Caris stepped forward, her helmet light sweeping over the equipment. "Let's see if there's anything salvageable," she said, her tone brisk as she pried open a panel. A tangle of frayed wires greeted her, and she dove in without hesitation.

Lily stood just behind her, keeping her eyes on the corridor. Her pulse beat fast and uneven, each thud echoing in her ears as she cast nervous glances back toward the hallway. Her mind struggled to stay centered in the moment.

"Please let this work," she whispered, her voice barely audible even to herself. She adjusted her grip on the scanner, its faint light catching the edge of Caris's tool kit as she worked in tense silence.

Caris moved quickly back to the comm panel, her focus razor-sharp as her gloved hands flew over the controls. "I can't raise the Salamander," she said, brisk and clipped, "but I think I can unseal deck five from here. There's a main override junction built into this station's systems. Let me know if this works, Captain."

There was a tense pause, static whispering faintly through the comms as Lily and Caris waited. Then, Calan's voice crackled through, triumphant. "Hallelujah! The doors are open. We're headed your way now."

Relief washed over Lily, loosening the knot in her chest. She exhaled, her breath fogging the inside of her helmet. "At least we'll all be together again," she murmured to Caris, though the uncertainty of what to do next lingered heavy in the air. Whatever this station had in store, facing it as a team was better than being split apart.

Caris gave a curt nod, stepping away from the console. "Let's regroup and figure out our next move."

• • • •

The distant clang of boots against metal announced the arrival of the captain and his group before Lily even saw them. Her chest loosened slightly as Calan, Datch, and the two guards emerged from the corridor. The captain's determined stride led the way, his expression sharp and unyielding.

"Report," Calan said, his tone brisk but laced with a flicker of relief. His gaze swept the group, pausing briefly on Lily before settling on Caris.

"No luck on external comms," Caris replied, standing a little straighter. "The system's fried. If there's a way to reach the Salamander, it's not from here."

Datch stepped forward, holding his portable device with precise intent. "I've collected data from the entities we encountered on the way here. I'd like to run it through the station's mainframe to identify any consistent patterns."

"You ran into more of them?" Lily asked, her stomach knotting.

"Two," Datch confirmed, his tone steady and clinical. "They didn't engage directly but lingered near structural weaknesses—airlocks, support beams. It's difficult to discern intent."

Calan's frown deepened. "If they're targeting critical systems, that's all the more reason to work fast."

Lily handed Datch her scanner. "Here. I got some scans earlier. Maybe they'll help."

Datch inclined his head in acknowledgment, plugging the scanner into his device. "This is helpful. Collecting as much data as possible is key. The energy signatures are... unusual. They fluctuate in a way that suggests dimensional instability. If I can use the station's systems to refine the data, we might get closer to communicating."

"Communicating?" Calan's voice sharpened, his arms crossing over his chest. "I'm more interested in finding their vulnerabilities. We need to stop them before they threaten the Salamander."

Datch hesitated for only a second before responding, his tone firm but respectful. "Understanding their motives could be key to neutralizing the threat. Would not communication offer the clearest path to resolution?"

"I don't care about their motives, Mr. Datch," Calan shot back, his voice cold and clipped. "I care about ending this before it costs us more lives. Get whatever information you need to make that happen."

Datch's expression didn't change, though his reply was quieter. "On that, we agree."

Lily shifted uncomfortably, the tension in the room thick enough to choke on. She exchanged a glance with Caris, the unspoken understanding passing between them: the captain was reacting more emotionally than usual, his judgment clouded by fear and anger.

Moments later, Lily found Datch hunched over a makeshift workstation in the dimly lit corner of the room. His usually calm demeanor seemed slightly frayed, his movements more hurried than usual. She tilted her head, trying to lighten the mood. "You look like someone with a problem."

Datch didn't glance up, his focus locked on the tangle of components in front of him. "You would be correct. I am attempting to construct a graviton pulse amplifier. My theory is that if we encounter another portal, we may be able to stabilize the dimensional rift and create a functional bridge. If successful, it should allow me to get clear, uninterrupted readings."

Lily raised an eyebrow, curiosity piqued. "Stabilize the rift? You mean... prop the door open?"

"Precisely," Datch replied, adjusting a series of wires with delicate precision. "Additionally, I've isolated certain wave impulses from the creatures. These patterns seem consistent, so I ran them through the translation matrix."

"The translation matrix?" Lily leaned closer, intrigued. "Wait—you mean you found their language?"

"Not exactly," Datch said, his tone matter-of-fact. He tapped a few commands into his device, and a screen lit up, displaying a series of jagged waveforms. "I believe these are thought patterns. Look at the results."

The screen flickered, and translated approximations appeared alongside the waveforms: *Help! We don't want to hurt anyone. Stay away.*

Lily's eyes widened. "Well, that can't be a coincidence."

"Agreed," Datch said, his voice steady but tinged with an edge of frustration. "However, the captain does not share my enthusiasm for these findings. I suggested we could attempt communication through the portal, but he is only interested in determining how to disable them. To maintain his trust, I have implied that my scans are focused on finding vulnerabilities."

Lily nodded, understanding the tightrope Datch was walking. "So, what do you need? Can I help in some way?"

Datch hesitated, then gestured toward a narrow hatch on the far wall. "I require neural fiber cable to complete the amplifier. There should be some salvageable pieces in that alcove."

"Got it," Lily said, already moving. She ducked through the hatch alone, her helmet light cutting into the cramped space beyond.

The alcove was a cluttered sprawl, like a child's messy bedroom frozen in time. Tools, wiring, and loose components were strewn everywhere. She had to crouch, her helmet beam glancing off twisted coils and frayed cables. She pulled a bundle of neural fiber from the heap, tucking it under her arm as she searched for more. Her mind was elsewhere—on Datch's amplifier, on the captain's unraveling patience, on the eerie station pressing down on all of them.

As she reached for another shimmering thread of cable, she froze. One of the wires twitched.

Her breath caught. For a moment, she told herself it was nothing—static charge, a loose coil shifting. Then another cable moved, sliding across the floor with an almost deliberate grace. Her grip tightened on the bundle under her arm as more cables slithered to life, curling and uncurling like serpents roused from sleep.

"Okay," she whispered to herself, her voice shaky but audible in her helmet. "Stay calm, Lily..."

But the cables didn't stop. They coiled around her boots, winding up her legs with an unsettling sentience. Lily began to back away, her pulse hammering in her ears, but the cables followed, tightening their hold. She stumbled, trying to free herself, panic edging closer.

Then she saw it.

Hovering just beyond the edge of her light was one of the creatures. Its blurred, distorted form wavered as though caught between dimensions. In the center of what might have been a face, a hazy, almost human visage began to emerge. The features were smeared and indistinct, but Lily could feel it trying to connect with her, its presence heavy and deliberate.

The thing seemed to quiver, as if attempting to speak, but no sound came. Lily swallowed hard, forcing herself to steady her breathing. Her hands trembled as she shifted the cables under her arm to free one hand and reached for her scanner.

"I—I don't understand you," she said aloud, her voice shaking. "But I'm trying. Just... stay still."

The scanner hummed as she activated it, the glow reflecting faintly off the creature's shimmering form. Data scrolled across the display, chaotic and fragmented, but Lily barely glanced at it. Her focus was on the thing in front of her—the face, so close to forming, but never quite solidifying.

The creature rippled, its form distorting and curling inward. Without warning, it vanished. The cables around her boots fell lifeless to the floor.

Lily staggered back, her chest heaving. She glanced at the scanner in her hand, then at the tangled cables scattered at her feet.

With a sharp breath, she bent quickly to gather the remaining neural fiber, her hands moving with frantic precision. Clutching the bundle tightly, she bolted through the hatch.

"Datch!" she called, her voice ringing down the empty corridor.

She nearly shoved the cables into his hands as he worked, the scanner still glowing faintly in her grip. Datch integrated the new data into his device, the translation matrix spinning. After a tense moment, words flickered across the screen in stark clarity:

I've wandered days beyond number, the ship is now a dream.

Lily leaned in, her brow furrowed. "Do you know what that means?"

Datch shook his head, his tone as measured as ever. "No idea. An intriguing metaphor, but its context remains unclear."

Lily straightened, determination settling in her chest. "You keep working on that contraption. I'll talk to the captain. This has to be communication, Datch. It can't be anything else."

He nodded. "I concur. If this truly is an attempt to communicate, we must respond appropriately."

With that, Lily turned and headed toward Calan, her mind racing. She found him near the comm station, arms crossed, his expression grim.

"Captain, we need to talk," she began, trying to keep her voice steady. "I had another run-in with one of those things. Datch pulled out more data, and it looks like they're trying to communicate with us."

Calan's expression didn't soften. "Even if they are, our priority doesn't change. Neutralize the threat first. Figure out their motives later. We can't take any chances, Lily."

"But—"

"No," he cut her off, firm and final. "Our people come first."

Lily's stomach churned, but she bit back her retort. She nodded reluctantly, turning back toward Datch just as he stood, holding his finished device.

"The graviton pulse amplifier is complete," Datch announced. "Now we just need a portal."

The group exchanged glances, a silent consensus forming.

"We'll head back to the engineering deck," Calan said, his tone clipped. "Everyone stays sharp. If anything happens, you report immediately. Let's move."

As they made their way toward the maintenance shaft, Lily fell into step beside Datch. "How confident are you that thing will work?"

Datch glanced at her briefly. "Confidence is a relative term. But the theory is sound."

"Let's hope the theory holds up," Lily muttered, her eyes scanning the shadowed corridors ahead.

· · · ·

"I'm gonna get space sick if we keep going back and forth like this," Caris muttered as they made their way toward the engineering deck, her voice dry with frustration, though it carried more weariness than bite.

Lily glanced at her, a flicker of shared tension in her eyes, but said nothing. The weight of the mission pressed on all of them, heavy as the station's shadows.

Once they reached the deck, Datch stepped forward. His voice was calm as always, but his movements betrayed urgency, sharp and precise. "Everyone, set magnetic boots to maximum. If the vortex forms again, the pull will be intense. This precaution will keep you anchored."

Caris adjusted her settings with a faint sigh. "Got it. Not looking to take a joyride into oblivion."

Datch turned his gaze to Lily and the captain, steady as ever. "I'll need a tether. It will allow me to get close enough to the vortex to collect precise data without being drawn in."

Calan's reply came fast, edged with command. "Are you certain this is safe?"

Datch's eyes flicked up briefly. His expression did not waver. "As long as the tether remains secure and I complete the setup in time, the risk is minimal."

The floor rippled beneath them before he could say more. A dark cloud unfurled, swirling into existence, lightning threading through its depths. Jagged shadows leapt across the walls, stretching long fingers of darkness.

"It seems expediency is required," Datch said, his tone calm even as the wind began to rise. He worked quickly, securing a frame into the bulkhead. The anchors hadn't locked before the gale strengthened, tugging at their suits, scattering tools across the deck like leaves in a storm.

"Come on, come on," Lily muttered, her throat tight. Her eyes darted between Datch's hands and the growing chaos at the room's center.

"I'm afraid this will have to suffice." He clipped the tether and stepped forward. The line stretched taut as the vortex deepened, its heart twisting with light. At the center, the apparition began to coalesce, grotesque and shifting, its form flickering like a reflection in shattered glass.

Datch activated his device. A low hum resonated through the chamber, vibrating against Lily's chest. "It's working!" he shouted over the howl. "I'm getting clear readings—multiple life forms!"

The storm answered with violence. The tether snapped slack, the tension vanishing in an instant.

"Datch, no!" Lily's cry tore from her throat.

The line whipped free. For a heartbeat his body shimmered, suspended in the vortex's grip—then he was gone, pulled into the dark.

"Datch!" Caris's scream rang raw and sharp, stripped of her usual steel.

Calan's blaster flared a heartbeat later, his shot cutting through the storm. The guards joined him, their weapons streaking fire into the apparition. Bolts lit the air in furious bursts, but every shot passed through, as useless as light striking mist.

Then, silence.

Datch's device struck the floor with a sharp metallic thud, still pulsing faintly, the only sound left in the cavernous deck. The vortex folded in on itself and was gone.

Lily's breath came shallow, caught between disbelief and dread. She stared at the empty space where he had stood, her chest aching with the hollowness of it.

"Datch..." Caris whispered, the single word trembling, stripped bare.

Lily's eyes locked on the device, its faint pulse echoing in the quiet like a heartbeat that refused to die. Her thoughts spun wildly. "What now?"

Calan lowered his blaster. His face was shadowed, unreadable. When he spoke, his words were flat and final. "We blow them up."

• • • •

Lily's hands moved quickly, weaving the final lengths of neural fiber into Datch's device. The pale light from its half-lit systems flickered against her gloves, a constant reminder of how close they were to finishing. Across the deck, the captain and the security officers crouched over a makeshift workstation, piecing together a graviton charge from salvaged components. Calan's focus was razor-sharp, his movements deliberate, his face a mask of iron control.

But Lily's thoughts spun in restless circles.

"The captain wants this ready so he can hold open the next portal himself," she muttered, her voice pitched low, just enough for Caris to hear. "He's planning to send the charge through the vortex."

Caris didn't look up, her fingers steady as they secured the power relay. "He's doing what he thinks he has to," she said evenly.

"Yeah, but we have no idea what the charges will do," Lily pressed, leaning closer, her voice quiet but urgent. "We all saw it—blasters went straight through them. And now he wants to throw an explosive into what's probably their plane of existence. It could do nothing. Or it could make everything worse."

Caris sighed, hands pausing mid-motion. She turned, worry etched in the set of her mouth though her tone stayed controlled. "I don't disagree. But they destroyed an entire ship, Lily—an entire crew. The captain has every right to strike back. He's doing what he thinks will keep us alive."

"That's not what Datch believed," Lily whispered, her fingers brushing the tether as though it still carried his imprint. "He thought they were trying to communicate. They're not monsters—they're beings. They've been reaching out, and we're answering with fear. What if they don't mean to harm us? What if this phenomenon is as out of their control as it is ours?"

Caris's jaw tightened. Her voice softened, but the steel in it didn't waver. "Even if you're right, do you think the captain will see it that way? He lost Joren. He's grieving. That grief is blinding him. If he sees a chance to fight back, he'll take it."

Lily bit down on her frustration. "But there's no evidence this will even work," she said, her voice rising before she caught herself. "This isn't about safety—it's—" She stopped, the words catching in her throat. "It's just not right."

"I know," Caris said quietly. "But it's still our orders."

Lily's hands stilled as the final connection snapped into place. She stared at the finished tether, her thoughts spiraling back to Datch's voice, to the broken phrases he had pulled from the storm: *Help. We don't want to hurt anyone. Stay away.*

What do I do when the orders are wrong? The thought pressed in like a weight against her chest. Do I risk everything—her standing on the ship, her fragile reinstatement—on what the others would call a hunch?

But it wasn't just a hunch. The evidence was there, woven through Datch's data, through the encounters Lily had seen with her own eyes. These things felt. Their movements were desperate, not predatory. Communication, not malice. And if that was true—if the phenomenon was as catastrophic for them as it was for the Union—then Calan's plan could do irreversible harm.

Her gaze lingered on the tether they had just secured. The harnesses from the station's stores had locking mechanisms with customizable codes. A detail most would overlook. A detail she could use.

The shape of a plan clicked into place inside her mind, clear and sharp, frightening in its simplicity. Her pulse hammered at the thought of it, but her hands felt steady, almost certain.

She exhaled, turning back to Caris. "Let's finish this," she said, her voice even. But her resolve had already hardened into something dangerous—something she would not let go.

· · · ·

Lily adjusted the harness straps across the captain's chest, tightening each one with deliberate care. The weight of the moment pressed down on her, thick as the air in the station's stale corridors. "Hold still," she muttered, avoiding his eyes as she worked.

Calan, ever stoic, stood rigid under her hands. "I don't like you putting one of these on yourself," he said, his tone clipped but not unkind. "This isn't your fight."

Lily paused, her fingers hovering over the next strap. "If something goes wrong in there, you'll need someone tethered to pull you out," she said, meeting his gaze head-on.

Calan's brow furrowed, his expression darkening. "You're putting yourself in unnecessary danger."

Lily shot him a look, her words cutting through the tension like a blade. "I'm not letting you go on a suicide run just because you're dead set on revenge." Her voice was steady, each word sharpened by determination. "You can have your retaliation and survive—just let me help."

His jaw tightened, his gaze hard and searching. For a moment she thought the reprimand was coming. She braced herself for it. But instead, he surprised her.

"Very well," he said quietly, nodding. "I appreciate the assist."

Lily swallowed hard, her fingers resuming their work. "Good," she replied, her voice softening. But as she cinched the final strap, guilt knotted in her chest. She hated that she was going to betray him.

Her hands moved with steady precision over the locking mechanism, keying in a code only she knew. Her heart pounded as she stepped back, her face carefully neutral.

Next, she buckled herself into her own harness, double-checking the tether line. Around them, the security officers strapped charges to the captain's belt, their movements sharp and efficient, tension evident in every motion.

"Boots locked," Caris called, her voice cutting through the quiet. Everyone clicked their mag locks into place.

For a moment, silence. The scorch marks on the deck still lingered, faint scars of what had already happened.

"Do we just... wait?" Caris asked, her voice low. "What if it doesn't come back?"

No one answered.

And then the floor rippled. Dark clouds twisted upward like smoke, lightning flashing in jagged bursts as the room plunged into chaos once more.

"Well," Lily muttered, her hand tightening on the tether line, "here we go."

The wind rose, tugging at everything not bolted down. The portal expanded, its dark eye unfurling like a terrible bloom. The captain stood tall, charges strapped across his frame, his blaster at his side. He squared his shoulders, unflinching.

"Get ready," Calan said grimly, staring into the storm. "Let's show them what humans can do."

With a flick of his hand, he disengaged his mag locks, expecting to be pulled forward into the vortex. Instead, he barely shifted. His tether remained taut, holding him in place.

"Lily!" His voice boomed over the comm. "You have to let out my tether!"

She met his furious gaze for a brief, agonizing moment. "I'm sorry, sir." Her voice cracked but held firm.

Before he could react, she released her own mag locks. The storm seized her instantly, dragging her toward the vortex. She clutched the device as her tether snapped taut, yanking her to a shuddering stop just inside the swirling chaos.

"What the hell are you doing?!" Calan's voice roared in her ears.

Lily's fingers flew over the device's controls, her voice shaking but resolute. "I won't let you blow them up, sir!"

The storm swallowed her.

It felt as if her body were being cracked apart, stretched and pulled like an egg's yolk from its white. Her vision blurred into a flood of white and green light. Strange particles swarmed around her, rippling like living stardust.

The beings surrounded her. Their forms flickered between human outlines and pure energy, deliberate in their movements, almost curious. One of them drew her eye—the same she had seen in the alcove. Its shape wavered, then slowly stabilized into something nearly human as it floated closer.

Lily raised her hands in what she prayed was a gesture of peace. The noise around her was deafening and silent all at once, a paradox that made her head ache. She tried to speak, but no sound left her lips.

The being reached out, its energy coalescing into hands. They settled over the device, a touch light but certain. Together, they held it, and the machine pulsed with light, a steady rhythm resonating through Lily's chest.

The glow swelled, expanding into a blaze of stars. Lily thought she might dissolve inside it—but then, with a final flash, the world snapped back into place.

She was on the engineering deck. Glittering motes of light rained down, falling like snow. As the shimmer dimmed, she realized the vortex was gone, leaving stillness in its wake.

And they weren't alone.

Hernandez lay motionless on the floor—alive, breathing. More figures surrounded him, their suits marked with the insignia of the Vanguard. Among them, his hands still on the device, stood Joren, alive, steady-eyed as he pushed to his feet. Just behind him was Datch, calm as ever, brushing dust from his uniform as though he had never been gone.

Lily's breath caught. She couldn't move.

Calan staggered forward, his blaster forgotten. His face was a storm of emotions—shock, disbelief, hope. Tears streaked freely as he whispered, "Joren? Is that really you?"

Joren stepped toward him, his voice steady but thick with feeling. "It's me, Griff."

Lily exhaled, her fingers brushing the control on her wrist. The code blinked across her display, and the captain's harness clicked open, the straps falling loose.

Calan closed the distance in an instant, pulling Joren into a fierce embrace. For a moment, the weight of the station, the mission, the chaos—all of it melted away.

Then machinery crackled to life. The lights snapped on, flooding the deck in harsh brightness. A nearby screen flickered, static spilling across its surface before resolving into the face of a Sceptacky officer.

The translation matrix engaged, flattening the officer's flowery cadence into something intelligible. His formal, almost poetic tone filled the air.

"To those who stumble upon this cursed place," he intoned, heavy with gravitas, "know that you tread upon the legacy of the Gyptonians, a people brilliant yet tragically flawed. Their experiments with dimensional rifts wrought devastation—they opened a door they could not close and were pulled into the abyss. This station is a remnant of their hubris, its wounds bleeding into the fabric of space for decades."

The group exchanged uneasy glances as he went on. "The Sceptacky government has quarantined this station, deploying marker buoys to warn all who traverse this sector to stay away." His face softened, shading into regret. "Beware, for this place is a tomb of echoes."

The image cut out, leaving only silence.

• • • •

They had gathered in a quieter corner of the engineering deck, where scorch marks still scarred the floor and the air carried the tang of burnt circuitry. Datch, Joren, and Lily stood at the front, facing Calan and the rest of the group.

"It's not just this station," Datch began, his voice clinical but edged with urgency. "The Gyptonians' experiments permanently altered the fabric of this space. Dimensional instability is still active here, decades later. That's why the phenomenon persists."

Joren stepped forward, his casual ease replaced by quiet determination. "Datch's graviton pulse stabilized normal space for a moment," he said. "That's why we were able to pull everyone back. But it won't hold forever."

Lily picked up the thread, gesturing toward the scattered equipment on the floor. "It's too late for the Gyptonians. Sixty years is too long, and whatever they were has been lost in the dimensional rift. But the Vanguard? There's still a chance."

Datch adjusted his device, its cracked interface glowing in his hands. "The marker buoys were likely pulled into the anomaly, leaving no warning for incoming ships. If we're going to stabilize the area long enough to restore the Vanguard, we need to act quickly."

Calan gave a curt nod, his jaw tightening. "The Salamander has dispatched a shuttle. We'll regroup there and work out how to bring the Vanguard back."

"Not without power," Joren said. "A lot of it. More than the Salamander can give."

Lily and Datch traded a look, understanding sparking between them like a current. "We have an idea," Lily said, her voice steady.

Datch gave a single, firm nod.

As the group dispersed, Calan lingered. He approached Lily with uncharacteristic hesitation, his usual command presence softened, almost uncertain. "Lily," he began quietly, "I owe you an apology. And my thanks. You saved Joren's life—and all of ours, really."

Lily looked up, her expression calm, unreadable. "There's plenty of time to talk about this later, Captain," she said, cutting him off gently.

He dipped his head, lips pressing into a line. "Fair enough. But know this—I'll recommend your reinstatement. Memory loss or not, you've proven you have what it takes to be an officer. A damn good one."

The words landed heavy. Did she want that future? Did she even know? The thought flickered and was gone before she could catch it. After a long pause, she only nodded.

The conversation ended as a shadow swept across the viewing port. They turned to see the shuttle gliding into position, its sleek frame gleaming under the station's cold lights. It looked incredibly small against the vast wreckage around them, yet its steady approach felt like a promise: fragile, but bright.

· · · ·

Onboard the Salamander, there was no time to waste. The team crowded into the engineering bay, the air thick with urgency as they raced to devise a plan. At the center, Lily and Datch sketched out equations and parameters across a glowing projection.

"We could harness all the matter in the station at once," Lily said, tracing lines across the display. "Use it like a giant battery."

Taran, leaning against a console, caught on quickly. "You're saying we overload the station's entire mass-energy potential?"

Joren nodded, his usual ease gone, replaced by quiet resolve. "Exactly. We access the systems and set it for self-destruct."

Ka-Lorrin, ever the tactician, added, "Then contain the blast with the Salamander's tractor beam, channeling the energy into a graviton pulse."

Calan crossed his arms, his gaze unflinching. "What are the risks?"

Datch, composed as ever, replied with clinical calm. "It is entirely possible the cascade will annihilate us along with the Vanguard."

"Which is probably why the Sceptacky never tried it," Lily said, her voice steady though her chest felt tight.

Calan glanced at Joren, brows raised. Joren grinned. "Go big or go home," he said, his tone halfway between a question and a prayer.

Despite himself, Calan's mouth tightened into the faintest ghost of a smile before hardening again. "Get it ready. If any team can pull this off, it's this one."

The room ignited into motion. Lily and Datch coordinated with the Salamander's crew and the Vanguard engineers, relaying commands, calibrating systems, layering failsafes. The projection filled with schematics, calculations, and cascading diagnostics.

Datch moved like a conductor at the center of a storm, his voice slicing through the clamor. "We'll need perfect synchronization. A fraction off, and the pulse destabilizes."

"Right," Joren quipped, lightness threading into the tension. "Or we'll all be vaporized."

Ka-Lorrin and Taran traded a look. "I like this guy," Taran said under his breath, though amusement flickered in his eyes.

As the final preparations locked into place, the atmosphere grew taut, every second stretched thin as wire.

· · · ·

On the bridge of the Salamander, anticipation hung heavy in the air. Joren stood at the engineering station, his hands flying over the controls with practiced ease. Lily stood beside him, steady and watchful. At tractor control, Datch's expression was calm as always, though his focus was razor-sharp as he oversaw the delicate energy dispersal. Down in main engineering, the Raath-Ka worked in perfect synchronization, Ka-Lorrin's voice crackling through the comms with crisp updates.

"Is everything ready?" Calan asked, his voice steady, commanding.

"All stations show green, Captain," Lily said. A faint smile tugged at her lips as she realized how official her voice sounded. For a heartbeat she let herself chuckle under her breath, nerves briefly forgotten.

Calan turned to her, his eyes warm but resolute. "Lieutenant Starling, you give the order."

Lily froze for the smallest fraction of a second. The weight of it pressed against her like a hand on her chest. She drew a breath, squared her shoulders, and whispered under her breath, "Okay." Then, louder, steady, carrying across the bridge: "On my mark... Now!"

The sequence unfolded with breathtaking speed. It was almost too fast for fear to take root.

"Station destruction in three... two... one... destruct," Joren counted down, his voice clear and steady.

The main viewscreen filled with the silent bloom of an explosion, brilliant and consuming. Lily's stomach clenched as the shockwave rippled outward, a tidal wave of fire and force. The Salamander caught it in her tractor beam, the entire ship shuddering under the strain. Lily braced against the console, teeth gritted, as the deck rattled beneath her boots.

"Energy shockwave contained," Datch reported crisply.

"Power flow stable," Taran added from engineering.

"Flow at full power. Reverse the beam in three... two... one... now!" Joren called.

"Beam directed and reversed. Graviton pulse initiated," Ka-Lorrin confirmed, her tone sharp and precise.

Lily leaned forward, adrenaline surging in her veins. "Confirmed. Pulse away!" she shouted, sending the final command. Her voice carried across the bridge like a spark.

The Salamander jolted violently as the pulse discharged. For a brief moment, the lights cut out, plunging the ship into an eerie darkness. In that span of seconds, every crewmember was left alone with their fears—that they had failed, that it was over. Lily's breath caught in her throat, her hand clutching the console like it was the only thing keeping her tethered to reality.

Then, as if the ship itself exhaled, the lights flickered back to life. Viewports, screens, and holo-projectors blazed on, showering the bridge in radiant light. The ethereal cascade they had seen in the engineering deck returned—shimmering rain that looked like starlight falling around them.

All eyes turned to the main viewer. The station was gone, its remains reduced to glowing embers and drifting debris. But in the void, proud and whole, stood the Vanguard. Its sleek hull gleamed, a defiant silhouette against the darkness.

Lily's chest loosened, awe swelling inside her until she almost forgot to breathe.

"A beautiful sight," Joren murmured, his voice soft and reverent. He reached for Calan's hand. The captain's stoic façade cracked, a genuine smile breaking through as he squeezed Joren's fingers tight.

Caris's voice broke the silence, alive with relief. "The Vanguard is hailing us. No casualties. They're thanking us."

The bridge erupted in cheers and scattered applause, a wave of triumph breaking over the crew. The weight of the last few hours lifted, replaced by the glow of camaraderie and the miracle of survival. They had done it—together, they had achieved the impossible.

• • • •

At the airlock leading to the gangplank, Calan and Joren stood together, their hands lingering as they shared a quiet goodbye. Joren leaned in, brushing a light kiss against Calan's lips before stepping back with a smile. "See you at Star Base Five in a couple of weeks," he said. "Thanks for coming to my rescue."

"Always," Calan replied, his voice steady, though his eyes betrayed the depth of his emotions.

A few feet away, Lily and Datch stood silently, watching. They had come to see Joren and the Vanguard engineers off, a gesture that felt like the final thread tying the mission together.

Datch turned to her, his voice low. "I want to thank you for believing in me," he said, his tone uncharacteristically warm. "I read the captain's report. It's not often he admits his mistakes so openly. You seem to have that effect on him."

Lily's brow furrowed slightly, but she stayed quiet, letting him continue.

"I greatly appreciate it," Datch said. "Not just because of my own life, but because you stood up for the ideals of the fleet. You're not the same person I knew before." He paused, the faintest trace of a smile flickering. "But I am grateful to call you my friend. You're one of the most worthy people I've ever served with."

Lily blinked, her throat tight as she struggled for words. In the end, she simply gave his arm a warm squeeze. "Thank you," she whispered.

They turned back as the Vanguard crew stepped aboard, the airlock sealing with a final hiss.

Later, in her quarters, Lily lay back on her bunk, her body heavy with exhaustion but her heart full. She felt truly at peace. This crew, this ship—it was becoming her home. A family of sorts, unexpected but real.

She exhaled, eyes closing, satisfaction settling warm and steady.

And then she heard it.

A voice. Not a dream, not a whisper. A command, cutting through her mind with terrible clarity.

"Lily, it's time."

Personal Log: Alrek,

Junior Engineering Corps

Timestamp: 0700 hours

Today is the day.

"This is the day Shyra'thel and the memory seed come aboard the Salamander. The Union has chosen us for the mission to combine the power of the memory seed with our systems in the search for the Krythar weapon. And I—me, Alrek, yours truly—have been selected by Ka-Lorrin and Taran to assist with the installation. Given my... unique experience with the memory seed—and my official acceptance into the junior engineering program—I have a feeling today is my day. I am meeting the Raath-Ka at 1100 hours to get started, but first: breakfast with Lily."

ALREK TAPPED THE LOG'S stop button and allowed himself a small, satisfied smile. He ran a hand through his messy silver hair flopping rebelliously into his eyes, then swung his legs off the bunk.

It was impossible not to feel optimistic about today. He'd just picked up his uniforms from the commissary, the mission was practically made for him, and his name was officially on the duty roster. Ka-Lorrin and Taran trusted him to help with the memory seed's integration.

The memory seed, he thought, heart fluttering. Not just a tool, but something he discovered for the Union—something he had been connected to since he first brought it aboard the Salamander.

Nothing could stop him from seizing the day.

Alrek opened the small compartment holding his neatly folded, brand-new uniform and froze.

"Heinyaz-yajunzi," he exclaimed—a Saravethi expression roughly meaning jinxed it. On Saraveth, a jinx was far more serious, closer to a curse. His bioluminescent tattoos flickered a darker blue than the skin around them, like a mood ring betraying his frustration.

The engineering division logo was stitched proudly onto the chest, but the shirt was so small it might as well have been designed for a child. He tugged it on anyway, but despite his petite size, the fabric pinched and stretched across his shoulders. The sleeves stopped halfway down his forearms.

"All right. A little tight, but wearable," he muttered, until the mirror winced back at him. "Or maybe not. Did they send me Ka-Lorrin's uniform by mistake?"

The next set was comically oversized, sleeves drooping past his hands. The pants weren't any better—billowing out like sails. He imagined hoisting them up the mast of an ancient ship named Salamander, then imagined tossing them overboard.

Groaning, he slumped against the wardrobe. "It's okay, Alrek. Stay calm. I'll just swing by the commissary after breakfast. No big deal."

Ultimately, the too-small uniform felt like the lesser of two evils. He tugged it back on, wincing as the seams creaked with every movement, and stepped into the corridor.

A passing ensign gave him a once-over. Another officer muttered something under their breath, smothering a laugh. Alrek lifted his chin, the way Ka-Lorrin always did, but his cheeks betrayed him—glowing bright blue.

By the time he reached the mess hall, he felt like a sideshow act. He spotted Lily at her usual table, scrolling through a datapad. She looked up at the sound of his boots squeaking, and her eyebrows shot so high he thought they might hit the bulkhead.

"Dressed for success?" she said, grinning as she gestured for him to sit.

Alrek plopped down with a groan, yanking at his sleeves in vain. "Commissary mix-up," he muttered.

"Did they send you Ka-Lorrin's uniform?" Lily teased, sliding a bagel across the table.

"That's what I said!" Alrek grabbed the bagel and took a big bite. "Heinyaz-yajunzi," he muttered through the mouthful.

"That jinx-curse thing?" Lily asked, one brow arched. "Well, you could ace this mission in your underwear if you had to, so don't stress about it." She paused, then added dryly, "But please don't. Do the mission in your underwear, I mean."

He rolled his eyes, but her words softened some of the sting. "Thanks a lot. The commissary is my next stop after this gourmet meal." He waved the bagel in the air with mock enthusiasm.

"Hey," Lily defended, her grin widening. "Wednesdays are continental."

. . . .

As Alrek headed for the commissary, his mind was firmly on one thing: a uniform that actually fit. The too-small shirt creaked ominously with every step, and the stares he'd gotten in the mess hall still lingered in his mind. Fixing this wardrobe crisis was priority number one—at least until the Raath-Ka needed him.

He wasn't far from the corridor junction when his comm tag buzzed against his wrist.

He tapped it, and Ka-Lorrin's voice came through, sharp and unmistakable. "You're late."

Alrek blinked, confused. "It's 0830. What do you mean I'm late?"

"Didn't you get my message? We need your help dialing in the containment field. I said 0800 sharp."

Panic prickled at the edge of Alrek's mind. He quickly activated the holo display on his comm tag, scanning for the alleged message. His heart sank as he noticed the blinking icon: new messages muted.

He fumbled to unmute the display, and a flood of notifications poured in—several dozen by his rough count. A handful were from Ka-Lorrin and Taran, all stamped with escalating urgency. Others included random ship updates, departmental schedules, and one flagged directly from the captain.

"No, no, no..." Alrek buried his head in his hands.

"I'm waiting," Ka-Lorrin said dryly.

"I'll be right there!" Alrek blurted, already pivoting back the way he came.

The seams of his clothes continued to pull uncomfortably as he stepped into the engineering lab where the Raath-Ka were conducting their latest experiment. The room was a tangle of blinking consoles, humming machinery, and the faint smell of overheated circuits. Ka-Lorrin and Taran were a blur, darting in and out from adjacent labs like particles in a collision experiment.

"Hold the levels steady on Console 3!" Ka-Lorrin shouted as he rushed past, a datapad clutched under one arm.

"Console 3?" Alrek repeated, but Ka-Lorrin was already gone.

Before Alrek could even locate Console 3, Taran dashed into the room, waving a tool that looked suspiciously like a soldering iron and a wrench glued together. "When I say 'mark,' you need to enter Gamma-9 Echo-4 on Console 5. Got it?"

"Wait, Gamma—what?" Alrek started, but Taran was already gone.

Ka-Lorrin reappeared seconds later, practically colliding with him. "When I give the signal, input Gamma-4 Echo-5 on Console 9. Understood?"

"Console... 9?" Alrek's head spun as Ka-Lorrin vanished again.

As if choreographed, both Ka-Lorrin and Taran stuck their heads in at the same time from opposite doorways. "Oh, and don't forget to monitor the rad-levels on Console 4!" they shouted in unison, then exchanged a look of mock annoyance before grinning and retreating.

Ka-Lorrin popped back in a moment later, squinting at Alrek. "Isn't your uniform a little... snug?"

Alrek opened his mouth to respond, but Ka-Lorrin, catching his look, quickly backtracked. "Never mind."

Alrek turned to Console 4 and stared at the display, which flickered with colorful but indecipherable graphs. "What am I even monitoring for?" he muttered.

"Mark!" Taran's voice rang out, sharp and commanding.

Alrek froze, his mind blank.

"Now!" Ka-Lorrin barked from somewhere in the chaos.

Fingers trembling, Alrek scrambled to input the commands, but he couldn't remember if Gamma-4 went on Console 5 or Gamma-9 on Console 9—or was it Echo-5 on Console 4? He jabbed at the keys and prayed.

The containment field whirred, sparked, groaned.

And then it blew up.

A burst of light and sound filled the lab, and when the haze cleared, Ka-Lorrin stood in the doorway, his uniform dusted with soot. He blinked at Alrek, deadpan. "Well. That's one way to test the field."

· · · ·

Alrek trudged through the hallway, the soles of his boots dragging slightly with each step. Despite the containment test literally blowing up in Ka-Lorrin's face, Taran had managed to salvage it, pulling off the demonstration with his usual flair. Ka-Lorrin had even tried to comfort him on the way out.

"It's hard to keep up with our frantic pace," Ka-Lorrin had said, brushing soot from his sleeve. "We're usually a solo act... well, technically a duo, but you know what I mean."

Alrek appreciated the effort, but the sting of his misstep lingered. *I just need to grab a uniform that fits, get changed, and get back to engineering for the main event,* he told himself. The commissary was just ahead, and for a brief moment, his day felt like it might finally be back on track.

That is, until he nearly collided with Malik.

"Whoa, excuse me," Alrek said, stepping back.

Malik, head down and moving at a brisk pace, barely glanced up. "Hmmph." His gaze flicked to Alrek's too-tight uniform. For a moment, Alrek braced for a comment, but to his relief, Malik said nothing about it.

Instead, Malik asked, "Have you seen a Cartillian shrew running through the hallway?"

"A what?" Alrek blinked.

"A shrew. It's like a rat," Malik said, his tone making it sound like Alrek should already know this.

"Oh," Alrek replied. "Do we have rats infesting us now?"

"No, it's a pet," Malik said, exhaling sharply as if already tired of the exchange. "It belongs to my bunkmate. They're Darkethian—no limbs, so they don't move very fast. I told them I'd go look for it. But this ship is frustratingly huge."

Alrek frowned. "Have you tried using a scanner?"

Malik shook his head. "Too small. With all the life aboard this ship, it won't show up. Trust me, I tried."

Alrek tapped his comm tag, thinking. "What if we lay a quick trap?"

Malik arched a brow. "A trap."

"Yeah. It probably has a favorite food, right? Or something it likes?"

Malik crossed his arms and nodded slowly. "That's not the worst idea..."

A few minutes later, they slipped into a nearby science lab, a smaller room crammed with equipment and lockers, the faint smell of cleaning solvents hanging in the air. Malik set a small container of food on the counter, his movements brusque but precise.

"This is the bait," Malik said flatly. "Some kind of—" He sniffed, wrinkling his nose. "—cheese, I think. My bunkmate swears the shrew loves it."

"Perfect," Alrek said, already moving to the console. "Now we just need a way to make sure it stays put once it goes for the food."

Malik folded his arms, watching skeptically. "You got a plan, genius?"

"Yeah, I do," Alrek said, grinning. "We'll set the lab door to lock as soon as the shrew runs through. It'll only open again for one of our bio-signatures."

Malik raised an eyebrow. "And this works because...?"

"Because we don't want it slipping out before we catch it," Alrek said proudly. "This way, it's contained."

"Fine," Malik muttered after a beat. "But if this backfires, I'm blaming you."

Alrek nodded enthusiastically, already programming the controls. He double-checked the settings, then stepped back with a satisfied nod. "There. All set."

They waited in silence, Malik's arms crossed while Alrek tapped nervously on the console. Then came the faintest skittering near the entrance.

"There!" Malik hissed, pointing as a small, furry creature darted into view. Quick as lightning, it zipped across the floor toward the bait.

Malik bolted after it. "I got it!" he shouted, diving just as the door slid shut behind him.

Alrek glanced at the time on his comm tag and groaned. The captain had asked to see him, and he'd completely forgotten. "Oh no, not again." He looked down at his too-tight uniform, sighed, and muttered, "Guess I'm stuck like this a bit longer."

He turned on his heel and sprinted to the lift, boots squeaking faintly against the deck.

If he had stayed a moment longer, he might have heard the faint banging on the lab door, followed by some choice Cyranthian curses.

• • • •

Alrek sat in the waiting alcove outside the captain's stateroom, rocking gently in his seat. His too-tight uniform pinched at his shoulders, and he tugged at the cuffs for what felt like the thousandth time, as if this time they might miraculously reach his wrists.

Beside him, Dryst Amaris leaned against the bulkhead like a man born to fill small spaces with noise. Alrek couldn't tell if Amaris had been assigned to monitor the alcove or if he just liked lingering here so he always had someone to talk at. Either way, the result was the same: the Cyranthian's voice flowed straight into one of Alrek's pointed ears and right out the other.

"And that's when I told him, 'You can't negotiate with a Zinnvar by offering dried fruits. It's insulting. Always fresh fruits.' You'd think it was obvious," Amaris said, gesturing grandly as if recounting an epic saga.

Alrek nodded absently, eyes darting down the corridor in search of escape. When Caris strode by, fresh from field training, he leapt to his feet.

"Caris! Hey, can you do me a huge favor?"

A few minutes later, Alrek stood outside the captain's door wearing Caris's field jacket. The sleeves had been rolled neatly to fit his smaller frame, and while the jacket didn't hide the ill-fitting uniform beneath, it was worlds better than going in as he was. He fussed with the buttons one last time before the door slid open.

Captain Calan stood to greet him, his broad presence both commanding and reassuring. "Welcome, Alrek. Come in."

Shyra'thel sat near the captain's desk. The Krythar defector's insectlike features caught the light, her expression still cool but softened from when Alrek had last seen her.

Alrek hesitated, then crossed the room to the empty chair across from her. He sat stiffly, hands pressed to his knees, trying not to fidget.

"I know you've technically met," Calan said, gesturing toward her, "but I wanted to introduce you properly."

Shyra'thel inclined her head. Her voice came slow and deliberate, as if she were feeling her way toward gentleness. "Young Alrek. When last we met, you reunited me with the memory seed and helped bring us to this mission's table."

Alrek's cheeks flushed bright blue. "Thank you, I—" He faltered, glancing helplessly at Calan.

The captain smiled and took over. "Shyra'thel, Alrek wanted to ask you about something we've all been wondering. A missing piece of the puzzle." He gave Alrek a small, encouraging nod.

Alrek's heart hammered. "Ma'am Shyra'thel," he began—his voice cracking in a humiliating teenage squeak. He dropped his gaze, mortified.

"Go on, my dear," she said, leaning forward slightly. Her tone was calm, almost inviting.

Alrek took a steadying breath. "When we had the... adventure on the Manta, it felt like I was connected to the memory seed. Like it reached out to me. Do you know why that happened?"

Shyra'thel tilted her head, eyes faraway. "The seed chooses who it connects to. It was in your possession for some time. Perhaps you needed it most."

Alrek blinked. "You mean it's alive?"

"In a way," she said. "Its energy comes from the minds of the ancestors laid to rest within it. Some of their essence, their will, remains."

"I'm just a field worker..." Alrek whispered.

"Who is training to be an engineer," Calan added gently.

Shyra'thel's edges seemed to soften further, her voice taking on something almost kind. "Who is more than either of those things. I see you, young Alrek. You are a conduit—a free mind the seed can reach. You were meant to be here at this moment in time. I am pleased you are part of this mission, as is the soul of the seed. Your ship is fortunate to have you."

Her words washed over him, heavy but warm. The knot in his chest eased. He let out a long breath. "Thanks," he said softly. "I think I needed to hear that."

A silence followed—soft, comfortable. Then Alrek shifted, lips twitching into a sheepish smile.

"Have you ever had one of those days where your clothes don't fit?"

. . . .

Alrek walked toward the engineering lab with his head held high and a uniform that finally fit. Determined to turn his day around, he arrived at precisely 1059 hours. He straightened his jacket, took a deep breath, and stepped through the door.

The scene inside gave him pause.

Ka-Lorrin and Taran were sitting at a table, playing cards.

"Hey," Alrek said, blinking in surprise. "Ready to get started?"

Ka-Lorrin didn't even look up, his attention fixed on his hand. "Oh, no worries. We were ahead of schedule, so we took care of it."

Alrek's mouth fell open. "You're joking."

Taran looked up and offered a smile. "Don't worry. It was much easier than we feared."

"But the memory seed—" Alrek began, gesturing wildly.

Ka-Lorrin waved toward the glowing sphere in its containment cradle. "Take a look."

There it was, pulsing softly with its otherworldly light. A shiver ran up Alrek's spine. But awe quickly gave way to a hollow weight in his chest. He'd been so sure this would be his moment—a chance to make a difference, to prove himself.

Instead, he felt small. Unneeded.

He tried to brush it off, but his throat tightened as the sting of tears threatened. "Oh good," he managed, his voice wobbling. "I can go meet Lily in the recreation lounge." Before either Raath-Ka could respond, he turned on his heel and slipped out into the corridor.

Once outside, he let out a shaky breath, bracing himself for the flood of disappointment.

"You!"

Alrek froze as Malik stormed toward him, his expression caught between frustration and disbelief.

"You left me locked in that science lab!" Malik barked. "Do you know how much of a pain it was to get out?"

Alrek sighed. "Couldn't you just call for help?"

Malik planted his hands on his hips. "Some genius coded the door to our bio-signatures but forgot to code it from the inside. So I couldn't leave, and no one could get in! I had to track down an engineer to override it—" He cut himself off, narrowing his eyes. "Wait... are you crying?"

Alrek sniffed and quickly looked away. "It's nothing," he muttered. "Sorry I locked you in."

Malik's tone softened, though the gruff edge lingered. "Hey, it's not that big of a deal. I'm already laughing about it. See?"

He was not laughing. But clearly uncomfortable, Malik was trying his best to backpedal.

"In fact, I wanted to thank you for helping me catch the shrew. Really, it's fine."

"It's not that," Alrek admitted, his voice cracking. "It's just... I'm having the worst day."

Malik frowned, his irritation giving way to something closer to concern. "I thought you had that big mission or whatever?"

"That's just it," Alrek said, words spilling out. "I was looking forward to my first big assignment so much that when everything went wrong, I thought, *At least I'll get to help with this. At least I'll make a difference.* But then... they didn't even need me."

Malik exhaled slowly, his expression softening in a way Alrek rarely saw. "That's..." He paused, like a kettle building pressure. "The. Worst." He folded his arms, tone shifting thoughtful. "Disappointment is the most awful feeling there is. Some of us spend our lives avoiding it—never getting our hopes up, because the letdown hurts too much. And there's no way around it. Whether you're six years old or six hundred, it's still the worst. And anyone who says it doesn't bother them is lying."

Alrek blinked. "Is this supposed to make me feel better?"

Malik shrugged. "Not sure. But it's honest."

Despite himself, Alrek smiled faintly. "Thanks. Actually, it helps."

Malik nodded, voice quieter now. "And look, even if someone didn't need you today, you make yourself needed by showing up and giving something of yourself. If they're not grateful, that's their problem. Look at me—I'm a grumpy, ungrateful jerk, but when I needed help, your first instinct was to offer it. Then you followed through, even though it made you late. That's rare. So... I appreciate it." He tapped Alrek's arm. "Buck up, kid."

Before Alrek could respond, Ka-Lorrin came sprinting down the hall. "Alrek! Oh good, we need your help."

Alrek and Malik exchanged a grin.

Inside the lab, urgency hit like a wall. Smoke thickened the air, alarms shrieked from multiple consoles, and Taran wielded a fire suppression unit like a weapon.

Ka-Lorrin was shouting to be heard. "It was fully integrated into the systems when the ship started to reject it! I've partitioned this section to keep the overload from spreading. I don't know what happened—it was working just fine!"

"Heinyaz-yajunzi," Alrek muttered, his tattoos flickering faint blue with his rising focus.

"You-say-what-now?" Ka-Lorrin snapped, incredulous.

Alrek smirked faintly as he hurried to a console. "Not important. Let me take a look."

The memory seed sat in its cradle, pulsing like the steady beat of a heart. Its glow wasn't harsh but alive, electric and warm, as if it could see him as clearly as he saw it.

As he drew closer, his tattoos brightened, their light syncing with the seed's rhythm. He felt it not only in the air but deep inside himself, resonating in marrow and mind. It wasn't the first time—but now, in the chaos and smoke, it was undeniable. The seed was reaching for him. Calling him.

Alrek hesitated, hands hovering over the console. He wasn't an expert. He was barely a novice. But something whispered certainty: *you'll know what to do.*

The integration formula bloomed on the screen—mind-numbingly complex, a tangle of equations and patterns. But as he stared, the code began to make sense. Not from beyond him, but from within. The seed was showing him the way.

His fingers flew, entering commands he shouldn't have known. Systems steadied, error lights flipped green, one by one.

Behind him, the Raath-Ka stared in silence.

"Amazing," Ka-Lorrin breathed, reverent.

"Wow, wow," Taran whispered.

Alrek barely heard them. His focus was locked on the seed, glowing now with a steady, contented light. The connection between them felt unshakable, like trust.

At last, the alarms stilled. Relief swept through him, mingled with a pride he wasn't used to feeling.

The door hissed open. Shyra'thel entered with Captain Calan. Her glowing eyes scanned the stable systems. A low insectlike rattle escaped her, somewhere between a laugh and a sigh.

"I see young Alrek has made the final adjustments," she said. "As it should be." She turned to the captain, her tone firm. "Captain, I request Alrek be assigned as keeper of the seed, for as long as it remains aboard. By that I mean no one adjusts its systems without his presence."

The room stilled.

Ka-Lorrin raised his hand. "Captain, I agree. Alrek seems the only one who can keep it... stable."

"Stable?" Taran echoed. "Happy?"

Ka-Lorrin nodded. "Yes. It's quite temperamental, sir."

Calan's gaze softened on Alrek. "What do you think? Are you up for it?"

Alrek straightened, his tattoos pulsing softly in rhythm with the seed. "Yes, sir," he said, his voice steady despite the thrill inside. "It would be my honor."

"Very well," Calan said, pride in his voice.

Shyra'thel stepped forward, arms stretching toward the seed, her psionic energy flaring. The seed pulsed in harmony, the glow in her eyes burning bright.

"The search for the weapon begins, Captain," she intoned. "It is nearer than you think."

The Raath-Ka, for once, were silent. Calan's steady composure wavered as his gaze flicked to Alrek, who straightened under the weight of it.

The earlier relief had evaporated, leaving the air taut and charged—like the stillness before a storm.

The real work had just begun.

Chapter 11: The Gathering Storm

THE METAL FELT COLD in her hand. That was the thought her mind kept circling back to, no matter how hard she tried to pull away. Cold. Smooth. Heavy. Somehow, that sensation—the texture of the handle, the weight of it—was the only thing her brain could focus on, even as her thoughts twisted and fractured around her.

It was a handle, wasn't it? Yes. A handle. Metal. Heavy.

Cold, smooth—and perhaps not good. Something both beautiful and hideous. And an association: green light, sharp and unnatural, piercing through her mind. A noise, high-pitched and endless. An ending. Helplessness, but also power. How could both be connected to this one object?

Heavy. Cold.

Somewhere in the chaos, a flicker of understanding surfaced, and Lily knew the object in her hand could be used to kill. That truth hovered just beneath the surface of her thoughts, a dark shadow she couldn't quite grasp. Every time she reached for it, her mind slipped away, fixating instead on the weight, the texture, the unyielding temperature of the thing.

Her chest tightened, the sensation sharp and fleeting. Something like a voice—or perhaps a thought—pressed against her, insistent and unyielding, like hands forcing her forward. It demanded action.

What was she going to do?

Inside her, something screamed against the fog, fighting the weight pressing in from all sides. What am I going to do?

The object could be used to kill. That can't be right. Part of her mind rebelled, sifting frantically through her own thoughts, as if flipping back through a book she'd only skimmed, searching for proof. Lily was not a killer. She knew this. She knew this.

And yet—something seductive wrapped around her. The power of life and death rested in this cold, heavy object. She didn't even have to reach for it. It was already there, nestled in her grasp.

Like the apple in the garden, the knowledge was intoxicating, irresistible. If she partook, she would never be the same.

Like a deer or a rabbit, she saw in split vision—each eye looking in opposite directions. Two views, disconnected, yet both pulling her forward.

On one side, a wave of pleasure rolled over her—a temptation, rich and ripe, waiting to be feasted on. A desire, a need, begging to be satisfied. It was like drawing a breath so deep it filled her lungs with pure ecstasy.

On the other side, there was only sadness. Loneliness. The hollow ache of not understanding. The memory of crying herself to sleep on the cold, hard ground, only to wake before dawn with her feet already hurting.

One side promised power. The other whispered weakness. Control versus helplessness. Might against weariness.

In both views, she was alone. But only one side was lonely.

She couldn't look away. She couldn't escape. The weight of it—the cold, smooth, heavy weight in her hand—settled over her like a shroud.

All Lily could think about now was getting away from that feeling. To leave helplessness behind. To bury fear and loneliness in a place where they could never find her again.

She focused on her breathing, steadying herself, even as her thoughts fractured and spun.

And then—

She pulled the trigger.

· · · ·

Lily sat perched on one of the larger beds in the medical bay, her hands clasped tightly in her lap. She tried to be patient as Dr. Thesari scanned through something on the monitor, her sharp eyes darting back and forth. Patience, however, was proving difficult to muster. Lately, Lily had noticed her nerves felt frayed, like a taut wire stretched too thin. She couldn't put her finger on why she was so on edge.

Across the room, Dr. Thesari wore an uncharacteristically solemn expression. She wasn't humming or chatting, as she usually did. Instead, her focus was fixed on the medical readouts, her brow furrowed in concentration. Now and then, she would glance at Lily and offer a small, tight smile or a murmured word of reassurance. Normally, Lily would have appreciated the quieter version of Dr. Thesari. Today, it only added to the ominous feeling that had settled over her like a storm cloud.

Finally, Dr. Thesari straightened and turned to her, her usual sing-songy tone muted. "Well, my dear, I can't say for certain what's causing these blackouts. Remind me—when did the first one happen?"

"It was a week ago now," Lily replied, her voice clipped, betraying her frustration. "I was in the recreation hall, and the next thing I knew, I was lying on the floor surrounded by people."

"Mmmhmm," Dr. Thesari murmured, her attention still on the monitor. "And how many episodes have you had in total?"

Lily hesitated, then sighed. "About two days after that, I was on the bridge, and it happened again. I lied and told everyone it was the first time because..." She paused, rubbing the back of her neck. "Because I was hoping it was just stress or dehydration or something. But over the last couple of days, it's been happening more and more. It's making me anxious. And also, I've been very... on edge. I'm usually very patient, but..."

A medical aid slammed a drawer closed, the sharp sound ricocheting through the room. Lily flinched violently, a louder-than-appropriate curse slipping through her gritted teeth.

She took a deep breath, her chest trembling, and exhaled slowly, willing her shoulders to relax. "See what I mean? I'm like this all the time lately."

"Try not to worry," Dr. Thesari said, her voice softening. "There are plenty of reasons this could be happening, and we'll get to the bottom of it." She reached for a small device on the counter and held it up. "This is going to attach to the back of your cranium. It'll take constant readings—your brain activity, responses, everything. Not only will it alert me if something happens, but it'll give us the data we need to solve the problem. Data, data, data."

Her tone turned almost cheerful, but Lily caught the worried edge underneath.

Lily nodded as the doctor affixed the device to her neck. The cool metal sent a brief shiver down her spine before settling against her skin.

Dr. Thesari stepped back, her demeanor professional and clinical. "I'm giving you a minor sedative with antiepileptic properties. It should help calm you down and might reduce the blackouts, depending on what's causing them, of course."

Lily nodded again, the tension in her shoulders easing slightly.

The doctor prepared the hypo with practiced ease, then pressed it gently against Lily's arm. She smiled faintly—not quite her usual effusive self, but reassuring nonetheless. "And don't forget—plenty of rest. If you decide you need to go off duty, I'm more than happy to let the captain know he needs to give you a break."

"Thanks, but..." Lily hesitated, then shook her head. "This mission feels personal. I'd rather keep working as long as I can."

She thought about Alrek, who was quickly becoming an expert at using the memory seed. With Shyra'thel's guidance, he was helping to pinpoint Krythar psionic activity across the region. So far, they'd uncovered a few outposts and vessels but no sign of the weapon itself.

Dr. Thesari nodded, her expression softening. "Well, you should be okay to work—just take it easy. I'll be monitoring you to make sure you're safe."

Her tone carried a sense of finality, like a period punctuating the end of a sentence.

Lily slid off the bed, eager to leave the medical bay behind. The weight of the device against her neck was a small price to pay for the chance to keep moving forward. They had a mission, after all. And it felt like *her* mission, even if she wasn't entirely sure how she was going to contribute yet. Deep down, she knew—she needed to be at her best.

• • • •

The hallway stretched endlessly in both directions, the walls seeming to curve inward like a distorted reflection in glass. Lily's vision tunneled, the edges of her sight bending and warping as though she were peering through a fisheye lens. Each step felt disconnected, her body moving on instinct, the soles of her boots striking the floor with muffled thuds she couldn't quite hear.

People passed her, faces familiar yet unrecognizable. She knew she should know them—their names, their roles, their histories—but the connections refused to form. Her brain latched onto the sensory details instead: the glint of a silver badge, the pattern of stitching on a jacket, the faint scent of engine oil lingering in the air.

Her breathing sounded loud in her own ears, shallow and uneven. The walls seemed closer now, the space narrowing around her, pressing her forward. She wasn't sure where she was going, only that she had to keep moving.

An invisible force guided her, like an unrelenting hand pressing against her back, steering her through the fog. The sense of purpose swelled inside her, drowning out the fragmented thoughts struggling to surface through the haze.

The door slid open with a soft hiss, cutting through the dull roar in her ears. She stepped into the computer lab: dim and humming with quiet energy. Her fingers found the console as though drawn by a magnetic pull, moving across the surface with a fluidity that didn't feel like her own.

Information scrolled rapidly across the screen. The words CLASSIFIED. ACCESS GRANTED. glowed in stark white against the dark backdrop, sharp and commanding.

The fog around her thickened, her mind folding inward, collapsing into itself. Her fingers moved as if untethered from thought, the commands flowing effortlessly, instinctively—yet entirely foreign.

. . . .

The captain's stateroom felt quieter than usual. The console's hum, normally unnoticed, pounded in time with Lily's headache until it was almost unbearable. Calan stood behind his desk, a data pad in hand, his expression carefully measured.

Lily sat with her back straight, hands clasped tight in her lap. She met his gaze with a focus that belied the storm simmering beneath her surface.

"The Union has been working on some classified countermeasures," Calan said, his tone low but deliberate. He placed the data pad on the desk, turning it so Lily could see the schematics displayed on the screen. "It's called the Eidolon Array and it's designed to neutralize the Krythar weapon's psionic output. It's cutting-edge tech, and this mission is the first time it's being deployed."

Lily leaned forward slightly, studying the screen. The lines and numbers blurred together briefly before sharpening into focus. "I'm glad to be part of the effort, sir," she said, her voice steady. "You can trust me to keep this safe."

Calan's eyes lingered on her, his sharp gaze assessing. After a moment, he nodded. "I know I can. This mission is critical, Lily. I need you at your best."

She nodded, a small, reassuring smile tugging at her lips. "You have my word."

The captain's tone shifted, more direct. "Are you okay, Lily?"

She hesitated before answering. "Thank you for asking, sir. I've been to see Dr. Thesari. Just headaches. They've been making me a little... grumpy." She shifted in her chair, her hands resting on her thighs. "But I won't let it affect my work, sir."

The captain studied her for a moment, then nodded. "I wouldn't even ask normally, but we all need to power through. Deploying this countermeasure could end the war. We have to see this through to the end."

The weight of his words pressed on her like someone had turned up the gravity.

"Sir, I have to be honest," she said, her voice quieter now. "I haven't been able to awaken any psionic abilities. Alrek's been doing better in that department." She rubbed her neck, her fingertips brushing against the edge of the device Dr. Thesari had attached. "But with these headaches... I think something is stirring up here. I just don't know if it's for good or ill."

The captain's brow furrowed, his expression contemplative. "Thank you for sharing that," he said after a beat. "I'd appreciate you keeping me posted on any changes. And, Lily—look after yourself."

• • • •

The screen glowed in front of her, the top-secret plans for the Krythar countermeasures spread out in intricate schematics and lines of encrypted text. Her fingers moved across the console, steady and deliberate, but the actions felt distant—like watching someone else pilot her body.

A secure channel opened. The sequence of numbers and codes sprang to life on the screen, familiar yet unrecognizable. She stared at them for a moment, a flicker of confusion breaking through the fog. How did she know this channel?

She didn't recognize it, but she knew it.

The thought slipped away as quickly as it came, drowned beneath the weight of the compulsion pressing against her mind. Her hands worked swiftly, copying the files with a precision that felt both foreign and innate. The plans were encoded into an encrypted message, the data stream sliding seamlessly into the secure channel.

Her breath caught as she paused for just a fraction of a second. A flicker of awareness? A question? It was gone before she could grasp it, lost in the swirling fog.

Her hands moved again, faster now, covering her digital tracks with a technique she had no memory of learning. The pathways disappeared, wiped clean, leaving no trace of her intrusion.

It was done.

The unrelenting hand guided her back into the corridor, her steps uneven, the walls seeming to tilt and sway around her. Each step was a struggle now, her balance faltering as her vision narrowed.

Just a little longer. She had to hold on just a little longer.

· · · ·

"The captain asked me to check on your progress," Lily said as she stepped into the lab.

Alrek glanced up from his console, his brow furrowing. "Oh, yeah. We expected you twenty minutes ago. Is everything okay?"

Lily hesitated, a flicker of something hidden crossing her face. "I haven't been feeling well. Sorry about that."

Alrek exchanged a puzzled glance with Shyra'thel, who tilted her head slightly, her glowing eyes fixed on Lily.

"You thought you walked straight here, didn't you?" Shyra'thel asked, her voice low but pointed.

"It's nothing. I'm fine." Lily's tone was sharp, almost defensive. "Report."

Alrek hesitated but eventually nodded, launching into his explanation. "We've been tracking psionic activity in the area. There's a Krythar cruiser moving along the outer edges of the sector, but it hasn't made any overt moves. A merchant vessel with a Xyridren onboard passed through earlier, and we've identified a few Zephtari refugee ships, but nothing on a large scale. Oh, and—this is cool—we even picked up brain waves from a Stellar Rorqual."

"A what?" Lily asked, her voice flat but curious.

"Basically, a space whale," Alrek said with a small grin. "They have strong telepathic energy waves. Rare to see one, though."

Lily nodded but looked troubled. "The captain may want to alter course if we don't find anything soon. Malik and Datch disagree on the projected trajectory of the shockwave this far out from the test site, so he's trying to decide if we stick to this heading or follow Datch's suggestion. Do you two have any clue—"

Her sentence faltered as she wavered, her hand flying to her temple. She steadied herself against the nearest console, her breath shallow.

Shyra'thel stepped closer, her gaze intense. "There is something going on inside your mind, Lieutenant. A struggle. I cannot read it fully, as if something is blocking me."

Lily's head snapped up, her eyes flashing with sudden anger. "Get out of my head, Krythar."

The room fell silent.

Alrek's eyes widened, and Shyra'thel's insect-like features shifted into a neutral expression, but the tension was palpable.

Lily didn't apologize. She didn't even look back. As she reached the doorway, she paused, her tone cold and clipped. "Contact the bridge the moment you find anything useful."

She left without another word, the door sliding shut behind her.

• • • •

The hallway tilted again, her vision warping as if the walls were bowing inward with each unsteady step. Lily's hand brushed against the bulkhead, seeking balance. Her breaths came shallow and uneven, her legs feeling like they moved independently of her will.

She reached the door to an engineering lab, the panel hissing open. Inside, the room was empty, the faint hum of idle systems filling the space. Her feet carried her to a console.

Her fingers worked swiftly, punching up a display that flickered to life. Holographic equipment sprang into view, shimmering in the dim light. She slipped on a pair of specialized glasses resting on the console. The room around her shifted as the glasses activated, overlaying her vision with a feed from another engineering lab.

The other lab was bustling with activity, engineers and technicians moving between consoles and equipment, their focus trained on the top-secret Eidolon Array housed there. The scene felt distant, like a broadcast from another world, but her hands moved with practiced precision, engaging the lab's remote link system.

Through the glasses, she aligned the controls for a crane arm that loomed high above the heads of the unsuspecting crew. With careful, deliberate motions, she maneuvered the arm into place, its metallic claws descending toward the heart of the delicate system.

One by one, she extracted components with surgical precision: several key circuits, a large fuel pod, and finally, the computer core. The engineers below moved frantically, but they didn't notice the missing parts until the system began to fail.

Alarms blared, cutting through the chaos as people scrambled to locate the source of the malfunction. But by then, it was too late.

The antigrav cart carrying the stolen components had already slipped out of the lab, gliding silently through the corridors on the glasses' feed. Lily switched views, her field of vision jumping to the cart as it sped toward an airlock.

Her fingers punched in a series of commands. The cart entered the airlock, the door sealing shut behind it. The countdown began, each number blinking in stark red.

3...
Her vision blurred, the numbers doubling.
2...
Her balance faltered, but her hands stayed steady.

1...

The airlock launched the cart into the void, the components inside vanishing into the blackness of space. A split second later, the feed flared with white light as the cart detonated, scattering its contents in a brief, brilliant explosion.

She tore the glasses off, her breaths ragged and shallow. Staggering away from the console, she turned toward the door—only to freeze as Shyra'thel stepped into the room.

"Lieutenant," Shyra'thel's voice echoed faintly, distorted, as though coming from underwater. Lily squinted, struggling to focus on the Krythar's glowing eyes.

"Let me help you," Shyra'thel said, her voice cutting through the haze, laced with something that sounded like desperation.

The words sank into Lily's fogged mind, pulling at her thoughts. Help me. No, no, no... She couldn't stop now.

Her gaze fell on a nearby spanner. Her body moved without hesitation, grabbing the heavy tool and swinging it in a sharp, brutal arc.

The sound of the impact was sickening. Shyra'thel crumpled to the ground, her body limp, her glowing eyes dimming as she fell.

Lily stood over her for a moment, the spanner slipping from her fingers and clattering to the floor.

She stumbled out of the lab, her legs trembling, the walls warping again as she forced herself down the hallway. Her thoughts were incoherent now, fragmented and spinning.

When she finally reached her quarters, she collapsed onto her bed, her body heavy and her mind drowning in darkness.

• • • •

Lily jolted awake, her head pounding in ragged pulses. The darkness of her quarters felt oppressive, lit only by the faint glow of her comm panel.

"Oh no," she muttered, pressing a hand to her temple as fragments of disjointed memories flickered through her mind. "Not again. Damn it."

Before she could dwell, alarms shattered the silence. The captain's voice came over the comms, firm and urgent. "Lieutenant Starling to the bridge."

Lily swung her legs over the side of the bed and stood, ignoring the wave of dizziness that followed. She grabbed her uniform jacket, shrugging it on as she hurried out the door and down the corridor.

The bridge crackled with urgency. Officers moved between consoles, voices overlapping as reports were shouted back and forth. Captain Calan stood near the central display, his jaw tight as he issued commands.

"Lieutenant," he called as Lily approached. "We have a situation."

"I gathered that, sir," she replied, her tone clipped but steady. "What's happened?"

Calan gestured to the display, where a schematic of the damaged device flickered. "The Eidolon Array has been sabotaged."

Lily's stomach dropped. "Sabotaged?"

The captain nodded grimly. "Shyra'thel is in the medical bay. She was found unconscious in one of the engineering labs and is now in a coma. The array itself is offline, several critical components missing."

Datch stepped forward, a data pad in hand. "Whoever did this covered their tracks well. Someone introduced a very sophisticated computer virus that wiped all security footage from the last three days. There's no record of who accessed the lab or when."

Lily clenched her fists at her sides, forcing herself to stay calm. "How can I help?"

Calan's gaze was sharp, his tone decisive. "We need to get to the bottom of this, and I need you to assist Alrek with anything he needs. Malik and Datch, I want you to help the Raath-Ka with repairs. The team that came aboard with the array are brilliant, but they don't have the experience you do working in the field. You've spent enough time on the frontier to know how to improvise."

"Aye sir," Datch replied, his expression hardening with resolve.

He turned to Lily, holding out a data pad. "Start with this. These records are scrambled—damaged when the virus hit—but I think there's a pattern hidden in the fragments. If you can find anything, any clue, it might help us figure out what happened or identify the missing components."

Lily took the data pad, nodding as her gaze flicked to the flickering schematic on the screen. "Understood. I'll get to work."

She turned on her heel and headed for Alrek, the weight of the data pad in her hand a stark reminder of the stakes.

• • • •

Lily stepped into the lab, her boots scuffing the floor. Alrek was hunched over his console, the soft glow of his bio-luminescent tattoos casting faint patterns on the equipment around him. He glanced up, his expression easing into a cautious smile.

"Hey," he said. "Glad you made it. And... thanks for checking in."

She managed a weak smile, though it felt brittle, forced. "I wanted to apologize for earlier. My attitude's been... off. I'm really not myself."

Alrek nodded, concern flickering in his blue eyes like distant lightning. "I noticed. I'm worried about you, to be honest. You going to be okay?"

She hesitated, shifting the weight of the sleek container in her hand. "Yeah, don't worry about it." Her voice was clipped, and she quickly changed the subject. "I need to set up here and help Datch. He gave me some code to sort through."

"I welcome the company." Alrek gestured toward the container. "What's in the case?"

"Oh, just tools," she said, the words tumbling out quickly. But even as she spoke, unease prickled at the back of her mind. She didn't actually know what was in the case—only that it was important.

Lily set the case aside and pulled up Datch's project on the nearest console. Lines of scrambled code scrolled across the screen, fragments of data blinking in and out like pieces of a fragmented puzzle. She stared at it, her fingers twitching with a strange, instinctive recognition.

Alrek, seated at his own console, returned to his monitoring equipment. The soft glow of his tattoos pulsed faintly, reflecting his focus. The lab was silent save for the quiet hum of machinery, both of them immersed in their tasks.

Minutes passed in concentrated silence, until Alrek's voice broke through, sharp with urgency. "There's a strong psionic presence connecting to someone on the ship," he said, swiveling toward Lily. His expression was tense, his gaze flickering with worry. "I need to call the captain."

As Alrek relayed the information, Lily kept her attention on the code. The fragmented pieces on the screen seemed to shift and align in her mind, forming patterns that shouldn't have made sense—but somehow, they did.

Her fingers hovered over her comm tag, and she tapped it, connecting to Datch, who was in the engineering lab with Malik. His voice came through, laced with the background hum of machinery. "Go ahead."

"I've been analyzing the data fragments," Lily began. "There is definitely an intruder on board."

Alrek, his movements brisk, slid his chair closer and merged the calls. "I can confirm it," he said. "Someone on board is receiving psionic waves. Based on the readings, they're on the science deck."

The captain's voice cut in, calm but firm. "Datch, get down there immediately."

"Aye, sir," Datch replied. He turned to Malik, gesturing for him to carry on with the repairs. "Keep at it. I'll check in soon."

Switching channels, Datch contacted Caris. "Leena, will you join me on the science deck?"

Caris, already in motion, replied quickly. "On my way. I'll meet you there."

Lily remained hunched over the console, her focus narrowing like a laser on the fragments before her. "I know there's something else here," she murmured, almost to herself. Her fingers danced across the screen as she dug deeper, the fragmented data shifting into shapes and patterns in her mind. It was like pulling threads from a tangled web, each one leading her closer to the truth.

Patching back into comms, she connected to Datch and Caris, who were now together.

"Go for Datch," his steady voice came through.

"Datch," Lily began, her voice taut with a strange urgency. "I'm digging deeper into these fragments, and it's all making sense now." She swiped at the screen furiously, her movements almost frantic. "Whoever sabotaged the Eidolon Array also shared the plans. Most likely with the Krythar. They used the psionic waves from the Stellar Rorqual to mask their activity, making it harder to trace."

There was a beat of static before Datch's voice returned, laced with concern. "And the missing components?"

"I'm sending a list of the exact parts to Malik now," Lily replied, her fingers gliding over the console with unnerving precision.

Datch hesitated. "Impressive work. Keep digging. Caris and I are heading to the science deck."

"There's more," Lily said, her voice dropping lower. The edge in her tone sent a chill through the line. "The intruder injured Shyra'thel because she was about to catch them. That wasn't part of their plan. But they did plan to kill her. And they're still planning to kill Alrek—and destroy the memory seed."

The silence that followed was heavy, electric.

It was Caris who broke it, her tone skeptical but edged with unease. "Lily, you're talented and all, but how are you getting any of this from a damaged record fragment?"

Behind her, Alrek froze. He turned toward Lily, watching her intently. Something wasn't right. Something about her body language, her posture—it was subtle but unmistakably off, like a shadow moving where none should be.

He stepped closer, peering over her shoulder.

"It's all right here," Lily said, gesturing to the data pad in her hand. Her fingers moved across the screen, flicking as if scrolling through vital information.

Alrek's breath slowed, shallow and deliberate, as though any sudden movement might shatter the world around them. The room remained intact, but his trust was shattered.

The screen was blank. The data pad Lily was holding wasn't even powered on.

"Datch," Alrek said, his voice tight, almost cracking. "You better get to Lab 47."

Lily looked up, her brow furrowing in confusion.

Alrek took a step back, his heart thudding painfully against his ribs. "Lily," he said carefully, his tone low and steady. "How did you know all those things? About the intruder wanting to kill me?"

Her expression hardened, her gaze fixed. "I'm not sure," she said, her voice almost mechanical. "But I think I have the answer in here."

She picked up the sleek case Alrek had asked about earlier, placing it on the counter with a deliberate motion. The faint click of the latch echoed in the quiet room.

Inside was a combat blaster, gleaming and fully charged.

The instant her eyes locked on it, something shifted. A switch flipped. Her movements became precise, methodical—no hesitation, no doubt. In one smooth motion, she lifted the weapon, her grip unflinching, and trained it on Alrek and the memory seed.

The lab door slid open with a hiss, and Datch and Caris burst in, their faces mirroring a mix of shock and disbelief.

"Lily!" Caris shouted, her voice sharp with panic. "What the hell are you doing?"

Lily didn't flinch. Her voice was cold, steady. "It's on a wide beam and set to vaporize. This is going to end now. This was always the way it had to end."

Datch raised a hand, his tone measured but edged with urgency. "Explain, Lily. What's going on?"

She turned her gaze toward them, her grip on the weapon unyielding. Her voice was quiet, almost calm, but it carried a chilling certainty that sent a shiver through the room.

"You see," she said, each word deliberate, *"Lily Starling is dead."*

• • • •

"This isn't you, Lily!" Caris shouted, desperation creeping into her voice. "The Krythar must be controlling you somehow."

Lily's head snapped toward Caris, her expression darkening. "Weren't you listening?" she spat. "I'm not Lily. They killed Lily Starling."

Her voice cracked, a sliver of raw emotion breaking through the chilling monotone. Her grip on the blaster tightened as she gestured with it, the barrel slicing through the air like a blade. "The Krythar killed her. They tortured her to death, but she never cracked."

Her breath hitched, her body trembling. Tears welled up, spilling down her cheeks, but only for a moment. Her eyes hardened, the tears replaced by a laser-focused rage. "I'm not Lily Starling. All I've ever been is a sad, homeless kid with nothing and no one."

Datch, ever analytical, tried to piece it together out loud. "But when you came aboard, I confirmed your identity with a scan. Even your brain activity matches those on record—"

Lily shook her head sharply, cutting him off. "Man, you really are a few lightyears behind the Krythar. They were right about you." Her laugh was hollow, bitter. "Don't you see? They plucked me off the street. They used me because I was a close enough match that they could surgically alter me to look like Lily Starling. Then they used their psionic powers to implant her brainwaves onto mine. They chose me out of the gutter. And you know why?"

Her voice rose, trembling with equal parts grief and fury. "Because no one would miss me. And they were right. Not only did no one miss me—no one even noticed I was gone."

"Lily," Alrek said softly, his voice breaking as tears filled his eyes. "You told me yourself—whatever you were or weren't in your past, you decide what you become going forward." He took a small, cautious step toward her. "I don't care what your story was before. You're my friend here and now. And I have to save you. Please, let me save you."

Caris added her voice to the chorus, her tone firm but compassionate. "Listen, whatever you want to be called, Datch and I don't think any less of you because you lived on the streets. That doesn't make you—"

"You don't get it!" Lily's shout cut through the room like a blade. She waved the blaster wildly, and everyone froze, every movement calculated to avoid setting her off.

"I was wrong," she continued, her voice shaking with despair. "It doesn't matter what I do. I will never be able to erase the fact that I am nothing. I'm no one—no parents, no name, no memories. I wake up every day scared of the pavement, scared of my belly being empty, scared of losing control." Her voice grew quieter, her words like a blade turned inward.

"This isn't about the sleeper program anymore. This is about the fact that they chose me. Lily's parents chose her. They made her into a weapon, a beacon of hope for the Union. Well, the Krythar chose me as a weapon to protect the Ascendancy."

She locked eyes with Alrek, her expression distant, detached. "And I know that once I pull this trigger, I'll be free."

Her friends exchanged desperate looks, each trying to find the right words, the right way to reach her. But Lily's eyes had glazed over, her focus chillingly clear. Her arm was steady, the blaster trained unerringly on its target.

• • • •

The weight of the blaster in Lily's hand felt heavier than ever, like a lead anchor dragging her down. Her finger began to tighten on the trigger. This is how it ends, she thought, the words settling like stones in her mind.

Then, the lab was gone.

White light surrounded her—blinding and endless, stretching in every direction. It wasn't warm or cold, not comforting or harsh. Just... empty. The silence pressed against her ears, so complete it felt like a weight of its own. Then, a voice broke through, familiar and calm, cutting through the void like a lifeline.

"Hi. This seemed like a necessary time to introduce myself."

Lily turned, her heart racing. Standing before her was—herself. But not quite. This version of Lily was subtly different. Her frame was fuller, her muscles well-defined. Her posture carried an ease that spoke of quiet confidence, her head held a fraction higher than Lily thought possible. Even her voice, when she spoke again, was lower, steadier—certain.

"Who—what—?" Lily stammered, her voice trembling with disbelief.

The other Lily smiled, a calm, knowing expression that didn't quite reach her eyes. "I'm Lily Starling. Well, what's left of me."

Lily blinked, her head spinning. "Where am I?"

"We," the other Lily emphasized, a hint of playful sarcasm in her tone as if to say Hey, I'm here too, "are in your mind." Her voice shifted, becoming more casual, almost conversational. "And get a load of this."

A mirror appeared, materializing out of thin air like frost spreading over glass. Its surface shimmered, sculpted of intricate crystalline patterns that caught and scattered the light. Lily hesitated, stepping toward it cautiously, she held her breath as she looked into its depths.

The face staring back wasn't the one she was used to seeing. It was the face from her dreams—the child reflected in the auto glass. But now it wasn't a child, it was her. She wore it as if it had always been there.

The realization hit her, sudden and undeniable. Maybe it always was.

"So, who am I?" Lily whispered, her voice tight with desperation.

The other Lily shrugged, her expression softening. "I'm afraid I can't help you there. You see, I'm just an imprint of Lily Starling. The Krythar put me here to fool scanners." She let out a low, humorless laugh. "They didn't realize part of my consciousness would transfer over." She paused, her tone growing quieter. "I can't tell you anything about your life, I'm afraid, because they killed me before I ever knew about you."

Lily rubbed her temples, frustration pressing down like a weight.

"Sorry, I can be all over the place sometimes," Lily Starling continued, her voice taking on an apologetic lilt. "Long story short, I only know what you know. And, well, some limited stuff from me—Lily Starling." She looked Lily up and down with a small, amused snort. "Say, you're kind of cute. I might've asked you out if it weren't for the whole 'being dead' thing."

Lily groaned, exasperated. "Look, can you at least tell me my name? You know, before the Krythar took me?"

Lily Starling shook her head, her smile tinged with regret. "Sorry, no dice. But hey, Lily's a great name. You should keep it."

Lily looked away, her voice barely a whisper. "This is... a lot."

Suddenly, Lily Starling's expression sharpened, her tone firm and unyielding. "Listen to me, Lily. Don't fall for the lure of power. The drive for control will hollow you out and leave you dead inside."

"At least I won't be afraid anymore!" Lily shot back, her voice rising with anger. "You don't know what it's like to wake up every day terrified. Hungry. Alone. Look at you. You're all, 'I'm not afraid of anything. I'm a hero,'" she mocked, her tone dripping with bitter sarcasm.

Lily Starling's eyes darkened, her voice cutting through the tension. "Hey, I was tortured to death, okay? I promise you, I know what fear is like." She tilted her head slightly, her words quieter but no less intense. "But that's not what this is about, and you know it. This is about you feeling sorry for yourself. Poor me, not everything's perfect. *Wah.*"

Lily froze, stunned by the bluntness.

Lily Starling stepped closer, her gaze unwavering. Her voice dropped lower, every word heavy with meaning. "Let me tell you something. Those people out there? They care about you. They're reaching out to you, not because of the mission, but because they're your family. And maybe not everything's perfect. Maybe you are just a nobody. A nameless girl from the streets. But to them, you're pretty great. So believe them for once. Trust them about their assessment of your character. You're pretty great, Lily. And you can stop all this nonsense about fulfilling your 'destiny' for the Krythar."

Lily swallowed hard, tears pricking at the edges of her eyes. "I..."

"Wake up, Lily," Lily Starling said, her voice firm but full of urgency. "The sleeper program is gone. It's over. Wake up."

The white void dissolved in an instant, and Lily was back in the science lab. Her arm trembled as she lowered the blaster, her voice breaking. "I'm sorry. To all of you. Thank you for believing in me."

They exchanged nervous but relieved glances, the tension beginning to ease. Datch had just started to move toward Lily when her hand jerked upward again, the blaster snapping back into position. Her voice cracked, panicked and raw.

"Oh no. I can't control it. The Krythar are still in my head!"

Alrek's tattoos flared brilliantly, the glow pulsing like a heartbeat as he threw every ounce of focus into blocking the psionic waves. The connection to the memory seed throbbed through him like a living current—but even with the strength of countless voices at his back, he was no match for the weight pressing down through Lily.

"I'm so sorry!" Lily sobbed, her finger trembling on the trigger.

"Dr. Thesari, now!" Datch barked into his comm, his voice razor-edged with urgency.

A sharp beeping filled Lily's ears, followed by a searing stab of pain at the base of her skull. Her body seized, her limbs locking. For an instant she dropped like a marionette with its strings cut—

—but the Krythar's command punched through the haze. The blaster twisted in her grip, its barrel angling upward, locking on the bulkhead overhead.

Her finger tightened.

The shot tore free.

The explosion wasn't a bang but a shriek—metal screaming as the bulkhead ripped open, and then a heartbeat later the roar hit them. Air blasted outward in a hurricane howl, ripping the breath from their lungs. Lights guttered and died as the room plunged into chaos.

Alrek lunged, his fingers clawing desperately around the memory seed's cradle, the suction tearing at his small frame. His tattoos flared so bright they lit the lab like lightning, each pulse a desperate cry. Datch anchored himself with one hand locked on a sparking console while his other arm wrapped around Caris, keeping them both pinned as the floor tilted under the pull.

Lily skidded across the deck, her nails raking sparks into the plating. Her body lifted, weightless, her legs thrashing as the void yawned open. For a fraction of a second she felt herself slipping free, her body angled toward the stars.

Then—

Forcefields slammed into place with a thunderclap, translucent panes of light stitching across the breach. The vacuum cut off mid-howl, silence crashing down as the air snapped back with brutal force. The pressure wave slammed them all to the deck, coughing, gasping, choking on the taste of scorched metal.

The alarms stuttered, then steadied into a steady wail. Smoke hung in the air. The silence between each klaxon beat was louder than the noise itself.

Datch rolled to his knees first, his face streaked with soot, and wrenched the blaster from Lily's limp fingers. He powered it down with a grim twist of his wrist before securing it at his belt.

Caris dropped beside Lily, pinning her arms with firm but careful hands. "Sorry, Lily," she murmured, her voice hoarse in the smoky air. "Just to be safe."

The lab doors hissed open. Dr. Thesari swept in, her scanner already humming, her movements clipped and precise. Her face carried none of her usual cheer—only calm, clinical resolve. "We need to get her to the medical bay immediately," she said, her tone sharp as a scalpel. "Now that I understand what's happening, there's a chance I can help."

Lily's chest heaved as she lay crumpled on the deck, the sedation battling with the psionic residue still thrumming in her head. Tears slid sideways down her cheeks, cutting clear tracks through the soot. Her lips parted, the words trembling but audible in the hush after the alarms.

"I'm free," she whispered.

The room stilled. The buzz of the forcefield, the wail of the alarms, the crackle of damaged circuits—all of it seemed to recede, leaving only her voice.

She was free. Free from the Krythar's grip. Free from the shadows. Free, at last, from the fear that had haunted her every breath.

She was no longer an echo, no longer a weapon.

She was just herself. Herself, at last.

Chapter 12: To the Edge of What's Known

THE SOFT GLOW OF THE med bay's diffused lighting cast delicate patterns across the curved ceiling, their gentle rhythm calming the whir of Lily's scattered thoughts. She rested against the medical bed, her body and head aching, though her mind felt oddly at peace. Dr. Thesari had assured her she was on the mend, but it was the intangible wounds—the ones borne of self-doubt and fear—that she felt were finally beginning to heal.

Her gaze drifted to the monitor beside her bed, its glowing screen tracing the steady rhythm of her heartbeat. It was steady. Alive. A small smile tugged at her lips. For the first time, she felt unburdened. The weight of pretending—of holding herself to impossible standards, to a legacy that was never hers—had finally lifted. She wasn't an echo, or a hollow vessel waiting to be filled. She was simply... herself. And the thought was thrilling.

The door hissed open, drawing her attention.

Alrek stepped inside, his body language relaxed, his face lighting up as his gaze met hers. "Hey. How are you feeling?"

"To be honest? Sore. I don't think neural inhibitors are going to catch on recreationally," Lily said, her wry smile softening the edges of her fatigue. She pushed herself up slightly, wincing at the effort.

Alrek hesitated at the foot of the bed, his sharp, perceptive eyes scanning her face. "So... the name thing. Do you still want to be called Lily?"

Lily tilted her head, considering. "I think so. I mean, I don't really have anything better right now," she said. "We'll see what the future holds, but... Lily will do for now."

He nodded, his expression softening as a smirk tugged at the corner of his mouth. "Works for me. Means I don't have to get used to something else."

The silence between them was comfortable, filled with the quiet hum of the med bay's systems and the occasional soft click of instruments resetting themselves.

"We're trying to get the memory seed back online," Alrek said finally. "The Raath-Ka and I, I mean. But so far, nothing's worked. I really wish Shyra'thel would wake up. She'd know exactly what to do."

Lily's gaze drifted to the wall, her thoughts wandering to places far beyond the med bay.

"And Datch and Malik," Alrek continued, his voice edged with frustration, "are still going at it—arguing about which direction to take the ship. Meanwhile, the Eidolon Array repairs are dragging. Feels like we're spinning our wheels."

Lily snapped back to the present, offering him a faint smile. "Sorry. I was just thinking... it'll be good to get out of here. To help."

Alrek studied her, his brow furrowing slightly. "We could use you," he said simply, then hesitated. "But you don't seem antsy. You seem... calm."

She shrugged, a quiet, thoughtful movement. "I just—I feel so... content, you know? Everything I went through, it was... hard, but it was also transformational. I'm sure I'll be worrying about the mission again soon, but right now? I feel like a new me."

Alrek's expression softened, a trace of admiration flickering in his eyes. He nodded.

"I should go," Alrek said after a beat. "Ka-Lorren and Taran need help unloading supplies. We've got a transport coming in with fresh equipment and personnel."

As he turned to leave, the door hissed open again, and Dr. Thesari entered, her presence as calm and grounding as ever. "Lily," she said, her voice warm but tinged with curiosity, "you have a visitor."

Lily blinked, sitting up straighter as her heart skipped a beat.

The visitor emerged from behind Thesari, striding into the room with the kind of effortless confidence that demanded attention.

Xynn.

Her tall frame moved like coiled electricity, radiating a sharp energy that seemed to charge the air. She was dressed as Lily remembered her: form-fitting athletic gear with leather padding, like she was always prepared for battle. Her dark hair was pulled back into a tight ponytail, emphasizing her angular features, while faint bioluminescent tattoos glowed softly against her cobalt-blue skin.

And just like that, the butterflies Lily had tried so hard to ignore came rushing back.

"Xynn?" Lily blurted, disbelief threading through her voice.

Alrek, now halfway to the door, froze. He turned back slowly, crossing his arms as his wary gaze locked on Xynn. "Xynn," he said, his tone carefully neutral.

"Alrek," Xynn returned, her voice carrying a slight lilt.

Alrek hesitated, shifting on his feet. "Umm..." He cleared his throat, then said gruffly, "I never thanked you for saving us from those security drones. Thanks."

Xynn nodded, her expression impassive. "Any time," she said simply.

Alrek's brows furrowed, and after a moment of silence, he added, "Also, I still don't like you very much."

A faint smirk played at Xynn's lips. "Fair enough."

"I'll see you later, Lily," Alrek said, casting one last glance—equal parts suspicious and begrudgingly respectful—at Xynn before leaving.

The room fell into an awkward silence, the hum of the med bay suddenly too loud.

Lily cleared her throat. "So... what are you doing here? I mean, it's good to see you, but... how did—why?"

Xynn smirked, leaning casually against the wall like she owned it. "I was on the star base when the transport was prepping. Saw they were heading to the Salamander. Thought you'd like to see me."

Lily's expression tightened. She wasn't in the mood for games. "Because, of course, there's no reason I wouldn't want to see you, right?"

The pause that followed was heavier than the last.

"You get banged up again?" Xynn asked, her tone playful, though concern threaded beneath the surface. "You really need to start being more careful."

Lily exhaled slowly, her voice gaining an edge. "I'm hoping to be out of here soon," she said evenly. "What are your plans while you're here?"

Xynn hesitated, her bravado faltering for the first time. "I thought I'd... help out. Or maybe, I don't know..." She trailed off, her confidence slipping.

Lily couldn't hold back anymore. "Xynn, what the hell are you doing here? I haven't gotten a letter from you in six weeks. You don't return my calls. But here you are. Are you swooping in as my white knight?"

Xynn looked down, her shoulders hunching ever so slightly. "I don't know what a white knight is," she murmured. "But I do admit—I'm terrible at keeping in touch." Her voice grew quieter, the edges smoothing out into something raw. "There was chatter about you—about the Salamander. I heard you were hurt. I... I was worried. I care about you." She swallowed, her words softening to a whisper. "I like you, Lily."

Lily's cheeks flushed.

"Well, thank you," Lily said gently. "I like you too, Xynn. But... I'm really not up for a whirlwind romance right now. I basically just figured out who I am—or, well, more like who I'm not. What I'm saying is, it's a messy time. And, you know, we'd need to figure some things out. We have... different views about a lot."

Xynn nodded, her expression shadowed with guilt. "I know. The Saravethi caste system," she said quietly. "I know it bothers you. I'm trying. Trying to start over. Learn. Be better."

"Trust me, I know all about not wanting to be defined by your past," Lily said softly, her tone full of understanding. "And I think you absolutely deserve the space to grow. I just... wasn't expecting to have this conversation today."

A faint smile flickered across Xynn's face, a small spark of hope lighting her eyes. "Fair. I'm sorry I dropped this on you. I just... I needed to see you."

Lily had never seen Xynn look so vulnerable before. Gentle tears of relief streamed silently down her cheeks, glistening against her cobalt skin.

"I really don't mean to sound ungrateful," Lily said, her smile soft and full of compassion. "I'm happy to see you. I'm glad you're here."

"Thank you for understanding," Xynn said, her voice quiet but sincere.

"Look," Lily began, her cheeks warming as she spoke. "I can't promise anything—not about us, at least—but I'd like it if you stayed. Just for a few days." She gave a shy smile, glancing away.

"I'd like that," Xynn said, her voice lighter now. "I really would. And I want to help. I want to be... useful. And also..." She hesitated, swallowing hard. "I'm sorry for not writing back."

They exchanged a quiet, sweet look, and Xynn's tears refused to stop.

"Hey," Lily said softly, her smile kind. She reached up and gently brushed away one of Xynn's tears. "I'm right here. Let's just enjoy... whatever this is, okay?"

Xynn leaned forward slightly, her movement hesitant, as though unsure of her place. Then, with a deep breath, she opened her arms.

Lily blinked, realizing they'd never hugged before. She mirrored the gesture, and their embrace was unguarded and warm, a connection that felt far overdue.

When they pulled apart, Xynn wiped the lingering tears from her cheeks with the back of her hand. "I'm so glad you're okay," she said, her voice thick with emotion.

"I can't wait to tell you everything," Lily said with a small smile. "But I need to get some rest. You should go get settled. Dryst Amaris can help you find guest quarters."

Xynn let out one of those laughs that only come right after crying, a soft, shaky sound edged with relief. "He already did," she said, her smile brightening. "I'm in section C of the habitat deck, near your quarters."

Lily chuckled, shaking her head. "Why am I not surprised? That man is hospitality personified."

They shared a laugh together, breaking all the tension that had built between them.

Lily watched Xynn as she turned and walked out, her confident stride making goosebumps ripple on the back of Lily's neck. A quiet smile spread across her face as she realized she was glad Xynn had come.

But the thought was followed by a sigh as she leaned back against the bed, shaking her head at herself. "I really need to start expecting the unexpected around here," she murmured as the door slid closed.

· · · ·

The med bay was silent, save for the rhythmic hum of equipment and the faint whisper of Lily's breathing. She lay back on the bed, staring up at the ceiling. Resting, like she'd promised—but sleep was another matter entirely.

Her mind churned, thoughts spinning in a dozen directions. After what felt like hours, the monotony of staring at the ceiling became unbearable. She sighed and swung her legs over the side of the bed.

Her stocking feet padded softly against the cold floor as she made her way to the neighboring patient quarters. She paused at the door, her gaze falling on Shyra'thel, still motionless in her coma.

The Krythar defector lay silent, her expression serene, as if she were only sleeping. Lily lingered by the bedside, her fingers brushing the edge of the frame, hesitant to disturb the stillness.

"I'm sorry," Lily whispered, her voice catching in the quiet. "I know I wasn't in control, but... it doesn't make it okay. I should have fought harder to stop it. To stop me." Her gaze dropped to her hands, as if she could still feel the weight of that terrible moment.

Shyra'thel didn't stir, but Lily pressed on, needing to say the words even if no one could hear them. "You stood up for me—even when I was rude to you. Then you came to help me, and I..." She paused, rubbing her forehead as her voice faltered. "I attacked you. I'll find a way to make it right. I promise."

Her eyes lingered on Shyra'thel's peaceful face, searching for any sign—any movement—that she might hear her. But her insect-like body remained still, her carapace gleaming faintly under the med bay lights. The sight sent another pang of guilt coursing through Lily.

Her mind began to drift, circling Shyra'thel and the other defectors. Their unwavering reverence for the memory seed. Loryn'na's tragic end. The thoughts wove together in her mind, sparking a trail of connections she couldn't yet piece together but felt compelled to follow.

And then, her thoughts drifted to the Xyridren—and to Xorrek.

Xorrek, the enigmatic leader of the Xyridren wanderers. She hadn't thought of him since the mission in Mirefall City. Like Shyra'thel, he had seen something in her that she had failed to see herself.

He had been calm, steady—almost frustratingly unflappable during their time together. But now, as she pieced it all together, there had been something else, hadn't there? An edge of knowing in his words, in his actions.

He'd understood more about her than he'd ever let on. He had known she didn't have psionic powers. He had known there was something buried deep within her, waiting to be unlocked—something she hadn't even known herself.

"Xorrek," she murmured, her voice barely audible.

Her pulse quickened, her breath hitching as a rush of adrenaline hit her. It was as though the medical bay melted away from her mind, and in its place, the sharp focus of purpose took hold. She was ready for action again.

Without hesitation, she turned and moved toward the communication terminal in the corner, her steps quick and purposeful.

Pressing the call button, she straightened her posture, her voice steady despite the adrenaline coursing through her veins. "Bridge, this is Lily."

There was a pause, then the familiar voice of Captain Calan crackled through the speaker. "Lily. How are you feeling?"

Lily's heart raced. If this worked... She closed her eyes for a brief moment, forcing herself not to get her hopes up too high. "Captain, I need to make a call to New Xyridren."

. . . .

The equipment in Science Lab 48 emitted a soft, rhythmic hum, like a chorus of crickets, punctuated by the occasional beep of consoles and faint chatter drifting in from the adjoining corridors. Lily stood by a workstation, her fingers idly tracing the edge of the smooth surface as her thoughts churned. She felt a quiet wave of gratitude that Xorrek had accepted her invitation. Hopefully, they were one step closer to restoring the power of the memory seed.

Xorrek was as calm and enigmatic as ever, his presence like a steady anchor amidst the lab's organized chaos. His smooth voice broke through her reverie. "I appreciate the hospitality of your vessel. It is... efficient."

Ka-Lorrin, perched lazily near a console, snorted. "In this case, efficiency meant scrambling to set up in Lab 48 after someone blew the bulkhead in Lab 47 straight into the void."

Lily flushed, the heat rising to her cheeks. The jab hit its mark, and Ka-Lorrin's knowing smirk only made it worse. "It wasn't exactly my finest moment," she muttered, her fingers tightening against the workstation.

"Or the wall's," Ka-Lorrin quipped, earning a stifled laugh from Taran.

Xorrek gave no indication he noticed the banter. Instead, he turned to Alrek, who stood with his arms crossed, his usual casual posture tightened with something akin to respect.

"Thank you for this, Xorrek," Alrek said. "I know Xyridrens don't usually... travel far from their worlds. It means a lot."

Xorrek inclined his head slightly, his movements precise. "Everything happens for a reason," he said simply. "I only hope that by aiding you, we can help restore peace to the galaxy's order."

With practiced ease, Xorrek unpacked a small device, placing it carefully at the center of the lab. Its smooth metallic surface gleamed faintly under the dimmed overhead lights, catching the faint sheen of the holographic projection panels. When he activated it, the air itself seemed to shift as a powerful holographic blue flame roared to life.

"This," Xorrek explained, his voice calm and steady, "is the Etherflame. It amplifies and harmonizes the brainwaves of those who participate. Together, we can focus our thoughts and recharge the memory seed."

Lily couldn't help but be mesmerized by the flame. It wasn't just beautiful—it seemed alive, its flickering light pulsing in time with her heartbeat, as though it were reaching out to her.

Xorrek gestured to the group. "Take your places."

Lily joined Alrek, Ka-Lorrin, Taran, and Xorrek in a loose circle around the Etherflame. As they settled in, a hush fell over the room, the stillness broken only by the gentle crackle of the flame. Its flickering light bathed them in shifting hues of blue, and a steady warmth radiated outward, wrapping around them like a living presence.

Lily closed her eyes, feeling the faint vibration resonate in her chest, a quiet pulse that drew her thoughts inward. Gradually, the room seemed to dissolve, replaced by a weightless expanse where their collective energy swirled and mingled, intangible yet undeniably real.

Minutes passed—or perhaps hours. Time felt meaningless, her mind completely consumed by the meditation, as if she were floating in a current that carried them all.

When Lily opened her eyes, the memory seed was glowing—a steady, radiant light that spilled across the walls, casting long, undulating shadows.

Alrek stood, moving to the seed and placing his hands on its smooth, luminescent surface. A moment later, Xorrek joined him, his movements deliberate, their shared focus a quiet, unspoken connection.

Time slipped by as Alrek and Xorrek focused their combined mental energy on harmonizing the memory seed. The device sat securely in its chamber, humming with renewed vitality. Ka-Lorrin and Taran moved with purpose around the lab, reconnecting the chamber to the ship's systems and carefully calibrating it.

Lily stood back, observing the frenzy of effort—mental and physical—with a sense of awe. Everyone was fully committed, their focus absolute. Watching them, she felt a surge of admiration for the dedication of those around her.

Finally, Ka-Lorrin straightened from the console, and a row of status indicators blinked green. "Calibration complete," he said.

Alrek exhaled a breath he didn't realize he'd been holding. A small, satisfied smile played on his lips. "We did it."

Lily turned to Xorrek, gratitude written across her face. "I can't thank you enough. Will you stay and help us on our mission?"

Alrek quickly chimed in. "Yes, please stay. You're so much more experienced with all of this than I am."

Xorrek shook his head, his movements calm and deliberate. "You're more capable than you think," he said, his tone gentle but firm. His quiet confidence carried a weight that felt unshakable. "But this is your path to walk. I can only guide you so far."

He began packing his belongings with practiced precision. Alrek stood nearby, his expression conflicted, his hands flexing restlessly at his sides. "I don't know how I'm going to manage this on my own," he admitted, his voice low. "Datch and Malik still can't agree on what direction to point the ship in. I really need them to work together."

Lily's brow furrowed as she turned the problem over in her mind. "What we need," she murmured, almost to herself, "is a way to get them to work together..." Her eyes lit up as an idea began to take shape. "Alrek, I think that's it."

Alrek raised an eyebrow, his expression skeptical but curious. "What is?"

Lily's gaze shifted to Xorrek, who was fastening the final clasp on his pack. She stepped forward, her voice steady but hopeful. "Xorrek," she said, her tone earnest, "will you help us one more time?"

• • • •

The lab was still, the soft bubbling of beakers and the rhythmic chirping of machines filling the background with a kind of soothing harmony. At the center of the room, the Etherflame device sat dormant, its metallic casing catching the faint gleam of the overhead lights. Around it, Lily, Malik, and Datch waited, the air between them heavy with unspoken tension.

Xorrek and Alrek worked silently, their movements precise as they adjusted the settings on the memory seed's chamber. The soft hum of their tools was the only disruption to the stillness, until finally, Xorrek turned to face the group. His calm presence seemed to ripple outward, steadying the space around him.

"Take your places," he said, his voice measured and deliberate.

Lily stepped forward first, her resolve written in the firm set of her shoulders. Alrek followed, his posture tighter, his worry evident in the small furrow between his brows. Malik lingered at the edge of the room, his jaw clenched, while Datch stood rigid, his stance precise but stiff.

It was Datch who broke the silence, his voice clipped and formal. "I fail to see how this approach will prove effective. As I understand it, the Etherflame is designed to harmonize brainwaves—an attribute exclusive to biological life, which I do not possess."

Lily turned to him, her gaze steady but not unkind. "You may not have brainwaves, Datch, but you have thoughts. A mind that's alive. That's what this is about—connecting your thoughts with ours to find some answers."

Xorrek inclined his head slightly, a calm expression on his scaly face. "The mind's essence extends beyond the physical. Though I have never attempted this with an artificial life form, it will be... enlightening to see what unfolds."

Datch hesitated, his synthetic features inscrutable, though his voice carried a note of unease. "I acknowledge your logic. However, I remain apprehensive of the potential outcomes. Engaging in this exercise is likely to fail, which may contribute negatively to my efforts to establish recognition of my personhood with the Union."

Before Lily could respond, Malik crossed his arms, his voice low and sharp. "And I'm supposed to let that thing"—he gestured vaguely toward the Etherflame device—"poke around in my head? No thanks."

Lily's jaw tightened as she turned to face him fully, her tone steel-sharp. "Look, I'm not asking," she said, her voice firm. "I'll make it an order if I have to. This is for the mission. Whatever prejudices or reservations you have, leave them behind. You both swore an oath as officers of the fleet. I expect you to act like it."

Malik opened his mouth to protest, but Alrek cut him off with a wry smile. "You should probably listen. She's in one of those moods where she won't take no for an answer."

Malik glowered but said nothing, stepping reluctantly into the circle.

Xorrek moved to the Etherflame, his hands steady as he activated the device. A faint hum filled the air, low and resonant, growing louder as the metallic casing began to glow with a soft blue light. Then, with a flicker, the holographic flame roared to life. It filled the space with its vibrant, pulsing glow, the light shifting and dancing across their faces as if it had a heartbeat of its own.

"Focus your thoughts," Xorrek instructed, his voice calm but commanding. "Let the flame guide you."

Lily inhaled deeply, letting the warmth of the flame seep into her senses, steadying her nerves. She looked to Datch. "Datch," she said softly, "start with your analysis. Describe the area of space you're recommending for the search and why you think the trail leads there."

Datch's head tilted slightly, his synthetic eyes reflecting the flickering blue of the flame. "The region I propose is subject to gravitational anomalies caused by overlapping nebulae," he began, his tone clinical and deliberate. "These anomalies create a funnel effect, drawing any residual shockwaves toward its core. Further, the supernova remnants in proximity suggest that—"

"That's exactly why it wouldn't work," Malik interrupted, his voice tight. "The gravitational pull would have dissipated against the shockwave long before it reached that funnel. You'd lose the signal entirely."

Xorrek's steady voice cut through the rising tension. "Look closer."

Malik frowned, his skepticism etched into his features. "At what?"

Alrek's expression shifted, his brow furrowing in concentration. "I see it," he murmured, his voice quiet but certain. "In your minds. There's overlap in both your observations." He looked up, his eyes sharpening. "The Nullstorm Region. It's where your approaches converge."

Datch hesitated for a moment before closing his eyes. His voice, though calm, carried a faint note of wonder. "He is correct. To my astonishment, I can see it clearly as well."

Malik closed his eyes too, his posture stiff. He said nothing, but his expression—the faint furrow of his brow, the tension easing from his jaw—spoke volumes.

Lily's heart raced. "Alrek, the Nullstorm Region. Focus on that area."

Alrek nodded, his expression sharpening as his focus narrowed. The Etherflame flared brighter, its pulsing glow mirrored by the memory seed, which began to hum with an intensity that filled the room. The air seemed to crackle with energy, a tangible charge pressing against their skin.

Suddenly, the memory seed's light steadied, its glow shifting to a steady, radiant brilliance. Alrek moved swiftly to the console, his fingers flying across the controls with practiced ease. A moment later, the chamber emitted a soft chime, and a holographic star map unfolded in the air, shimmering with detail.

Lily stepped forward, her breath catching as the projection resolved into the unmistakable outline of The Nullstorm Region. Data points aligned in a seamless flow, forming a clear and undeniable path.

"It's a perfect match," Alrek said, his voice quiet with wonder, breaking the charged silence.

Lily's lips curved into a slow, confident smile. Her voice, when she spoke, was steady and filled with resolve. "We found it. The Krythar weapon."

• • • •

Lily felt small in the guest chair in the captain's stateroom. Its wingback design enveloped her, not in comfort, but with a faint sense of suffocation. She shifted slightly, her fingers gripping the armrests. Beside her, Caris sat with a slightly more restless energy than usual. Lily couldn't shake the feeling that Caris had something on her mind—something she was waiting for the right moment to say. When Lily mentioned her meeting with the captain, Caris had quickly asked to come along, and Lily hadn't thought much of it at the time.

Calan sat at his desk, going over the latest mission reports projected in front of him. He stopped abruptly, as he often did, catching himself mid-sentence when he realized he was repeating information unnecessarily. With a flick of his wrist, he turned off the holo display, the projection fading into silence.

He steepled his fingers and looked directly at Lily, his face softening into a smile. "Before we go any further, I need to say this: well done, Lily." His tone was warm, filled with genuine pride. "Getting Malik and Datch on the same page was no small feat. Thanks to you, we've already set course for the Nullstorm Region, and their collaboration has given us an advantage."

"Thank you, Captain," Lily replied, her voice steady but touched with warmth.

Calan leaned back in his chair, the smile fading as his expression turned serious. "The Nullstorm Region," he began, "is no picnic. Volatile space, storms that scramble sensors, gravitational anomalies—you name it. It's going to be messy, and the Krythar will almost certainly be expecting us. But," he added, his tone thoughtful, "those same conditions that hide their weapon might just give us an edge. If we're careful, we might be able to sneak up on them."

Caris folded her arms, her brow furrowing in thought. "We're cloaked, I assume?"

Calan nodded. "Engaged as soon as we set course. It'll take us a couple of days to get there because of the storms, but Alrek's working on something that might give us an edge. Using the memory seed, he's developing a way to block the Krythar's psionic abilities—what he's calling a psionic cloak."

Lily nodded slowly, her mind conjuring an image of Alrek bent over the seed, his sharp focus unwavering as he worked. "And the Eidolon Array?"

"Ka-Lorrin and Taran are confident it'll be ready by the time we arrive," Calan said. "Once we're in position, the away team will infiltrate the weapon and set up the pneumonic receivers for the array."

He straightened in his chair, his gaze steady as it swept over them. "I'll lead the away mission. The success of this operation..." He trailed off, the weight of his words settling into the room like a heavy presence. They all understood. Failure wasn't an option.

Caris leaned forward, her tone firm but respectful. "Captain, I have to disagree."

Calan raised an eyebrow, his expression expectant, but Caris didn't waver. "I've faced the Krythar in battle on the ground, sir, and with due respect, you haven't. We need you on the bridge. You're the most experienced commander we have, especially in ship-to-ship combat. Commander Amaris is good, but... he's not you."

The room fell into a heavy silence. Calan's gaze shifted between them, his eyes darting briefly to Lily before settling back on Caris. Finally, he exhaled, his shoulders relaxing ever so slightly.

"You're right," he admitted, his voice quieter now. "I'm learning that I need to trust my crew more. I'll talk to Amaris about assembling a team."

Caris straightened, but her voice carried a hint of nervousness as she continued. "Sir, I'd like to lead the mission."

Calan's eyes narrowed, studying her face. The pause stretched, and Caris hurried to fill it. "Sir, I know I'm young, but I believe the experiences I've had—especially since the mission to Earth—have been preparing me for this moment. I just feel like—"

"Request approved, Lieutenant," Calan interrupted.

The stunned stares from both Lily and Caris drew an involuntary smile from him. "Well," he added, a touch of humor creeping into his voice, "if you're going to be leading crucial missions, I have to make you a full lieutenant."

Caris straightened, a flicker of surprise crossing her face before she nodded. "I won't let you down, Captain."

"I know you won't," Calan said, his smile widening. "Now, since we've got a couple of days before we arrive, I'm encouraging everyone to rest while they can. There's no telling what we'll face once we get there."

He stood, signaling the end of the meeting—a brief but eventful one. "You're both invited to dinner tonight in the captain's mess. It'll be informal—an opportunity to relax before things heat up."

"I'll be there," Caris said, her tone light and easy. Then she glanced at Lily, a sly smile spreading across her face. "But Lily won't. She has a date."

Lily felt her cheeks burn, a deep flush spreading across her face. "Leena," she hissed under her breath.

Caris grinned unabashedly. "What? I'm just saying."

Calan chuckled softly, shaking his head. "Dismissed, both of you." He paused, his tone warm as he looked at Lily. "And Lily... good work. Keep it up." He followed it with a wink. "And have fun."

· · · ·

The mess hall was quieter than usual; most of the crew had already eaten, leaving the silence broken only by the occasional murmur or the soft clink of a plate or fork. Lily and Xynn sat at a small table by the viewport, the glow of distant stars streaking softly across the glasses and flatware.

Xynn looked at the menu, her sharp features pulled into a skeptical expression. "Human food is so... inedible."

Lily raised an eyebrow, leaning back in her chair. "Okay, spill it. What's so wrong with our food? Alrek is the same way, but he'll never give me a straight answer."

Xynn sighed dramatically, setting the menu down. "Human food is *sweet*."

Lily frowned. "What's wrong with sweet? I love sweet."

Xynn tilted her head, her expression a blend of vexation and hesitation. "Saravethi reserve sweet for very specific situations. Do humans have anything that smells good in one context but bad in another?"

Lily considered for a moment, then nodded. "Sure. Cheese. It's great when you want cheese, but in almost any other context, the smell could turn your stomach."

Xynn leaned forward slightly, her tone as casual as if she were discussing the weather. "What about sex?"

Lily had just taken a sip of water and managed an almost perfect spit take, coughing as she wiped her chin with her sleeve. "What?"

Xynn smirked, though there was a slight tinge of color to her cheeks. "Our sense receptors... The smell of sex and the smell of sweet food are the same. So, anything with sugar is, uh, out of context. It feels inappropriate in most situations, and it grosses most Saravethi out unless you're, you know..."

Lily's eyebrows shot up. "In the mood?"

Xynn shrugged, clearly trying to act nonchalant, though her blush deepened.

"Oh jeeze," Lily said, grimacing as the realization hit her. "That explains why Alrek was so awkward when I offered him a candy bar after we first met."

Xynn couldn't help but laugh, the sound rich and unguarded. "Yeah, oh man. Awkward."

Lily chuckled despite herself, shaking her head. "I can see why you'd want to reserve that for the right time."

For a moment, the two of them were quiet, each avoiding the other's gaze—Lily's cheeks tinged pink, Xynn's bright blue.

"So," Lily said quickly, her voice a touch higher than usual as she reached for her fork. "Tell me more about all that training you do."

Xynn leaned back in her chair, crossing her arms with a small smirk. "Oh, you don't want to talk about that..."

Lily tilted her head, eyebrows rising in curiosity. "Sure, I do. Why wouldn't I?"

Xynn shrugged, her tone casual but teasing. "You're not someone who's into that sort of thing. Training, fitness, all that."

"Hey! I exercise," Lily shot back, her voice rising slightly before she hesitated. "You know... sometimes."

Xynn arched an eyebrow. "I mean *training* training."

"I train!" Lily insisted. "I do the fleet physical training. Leena's been helping me."

"Leena, huh?" Xynn asked, her tone lilting just enough to spark suspicion.

Lily blinked. "What? You know—Ensign Caris. She's been training me."

"Oh, she has," Xynn said, her smirk widening. "Yeah, I saw her. She's very good-looking."

Lily narrowed her eyes, a smile tugging at her lips despite herself. "Are you jealous?"

Xynn raised her eyebrows slightly, her expression infuriatingly neutral.

"I don't believe this," Lily muttered, shaking her head.

"I mean," Xynn said, her tone deliberately casual, "you only mentioned her, what, fifty times in your letter?"

"Oh, come on," Lily groaned.

"And then," Xynn continued, her voice carrying that too-smooth edge, "you *had* to share those pictures of you two in your athletic gear together. Plus, you went into great detail about her physical description while she's"—Xynn raised her hands to air-quote—"'training' you."

Lily stared at her, half laughing, half exasperated. "You're actually jealous of Leena."

Xynn tilted her head, her tone unapologetic. "So? What's wrong with that? I'm Saravethi. We say what's on our minds."

Lily exhaled, crossing her arms. "Okay, first off, you don't get to be jealous, alright? It's not like you own me or anything. Second, it's *not* even like that with Caris. Honestly, I hadn't considered it until *you* brought it up, so now you've made that awkward—thanks for that. And third? Just... it's not cute. I like it when you're unflappable. That's one of the things I find attractive about you."

Xynn blinked, her composure cracking slightly before they both dissolved into laughter.

"This is going well," Xynn said, her laugh warm and genuine.

"Sorry," Lily said, laughing harder now.

Their laughter quieted, and Lily reached across the table, taking Xynn's hands in hers. Xynn looked down briefly, her expression softening as she met Lily's gaze again.

"You know what I would really like?" Lily said, her voice softer now.

Xynn tilted her head, her lips curving into a small, anticipatory smile. "What?"

"I want to take you to one of the training studios," Lily said. "And I want to do some training with you."

Xynn's eyebrow lifted, her expression incredulous but intrigued.

"I'm serious," Lily said, squeezing her hands. "Teach me something. I really am interested. It's a huge part of who you are."

For a moment, Xynn said nothing. Then, with an uncharacteristically shy smile, she leaned in and kissed Lily, a gesture of gratitude, affection, and maybe just a little mischief.

"Okay," Xynn said as she pulled back. "Let's go."

$$\bullet \ \bullet \ \bullet \ \bullet$$

The training studio was a simple, open space with padded floors and mirrored walls that reflected the bright, unflattering lighting in stark detail. Xynn stood in front of Lily, holding up padded targets with the effortless composure of someone born to train. Lily adjusted her stance, her eyes narrowing in concentration before she launched a high kick that missed the pad entirely, sending her tumbling onto her backside.

"That was good!" Xynn said brightly, lowering the pads.

Lily looked up at her, incredulous. "I fell on my ass."

"Yes," Xynn replied, her tone earnest, "but it was good. You should know me well enough by now to know I'm not just saying that."

Lily blinked, then smiled despite herself. "Oh yeah, thanks."

Climbing to her feet, Lily brushed herself off and reset her stance, determination etched on her face. She launched into round two, punching and high-kicking with more precision this time, the pads smacking loudly with each impact.

"I'm glad we came here," Lily said between punches. "To be honest, inviting you to dinner was dumb. I should've known better."

Xynn tilted her head, lowering the pads slightly. "Why dumb?"

Lily sighed, stepping back for a breather. "Because I'm still figuring out all these issues I have around food. Back when I was living on the streets, sometimes I didn't eat for days. So, brilliant idea, right? Invite the girl I like to dinner, knowing I'd be stressed the whole time eating in front of her."

Xynn smiled softly. "Why do you always do that?"

"Do what?" Lily asked, blinking.

"Be so down on yourself," Xynn said, her voice gentle but direct. "You can say you made a mistake, but you don't have to call yourself dumb. You're not dumb. You're extremely intelligent."

Lily looked away, her cheeks pink. "I know, I mean... well, I'm not *that* smart, I—"

"You're doing it again," Xynn interrupted, a small laugh escaping her.

"Sorry," Lily said with a sheepish smile. "It's an Earth thing. We call it self-deprecating humor. It's a socially normal way to bond by making light of yourself."

Xynn shook her head, laughing. "That doesn't make any sense. Don't say you're dumb if you're not dumb. Why can't humans just say what they mean?"

Lily chuckled. "Some of us are better at that than others. Honestly, though, I really like that about you and Alrek. You both help me be more honest and candid."

Xynn's smile softened. "By the way, you don't have to explain food issues to me. I grew up as a refugee, raised in the warrior class. Training all the time, rations, discipline—it leaves its mark. I have my own share of issues."

Lily grinned. "Guess us street kids have to stick together."

Xynn's eyes gleamed with mock indignation. "Speak for yourself, street kid. I'm a *space* kid."

Lily pushed Xynn playfully, but the push quickly turned into an impromptu wrestling match. Xynn let Lily practice a few moves, indulging her until she flipped Lily effortlessly onto the mat with a solid *thud*.

"*Oww*," Lily groaned, half-laughing.

Xynn's expression flickered with concern. "Sorry, are you okay?"

"Help me up," Lily said, holding out her hand.

Xynn reached down, but as Lily started to stand, she tucked under Xynn and flipped her instead, sending them both sprawling to the mat. Lily landed on top of Xynn, their laughter bubbling up as they lay face to face.

Before Lily could overthink it, Xynn leaned up and kissed her. Lily responded, her heart racing, the moment both exhilarating and grounding at once.

Later, they sat side by side on the edge of the mat, catching their breath. Xynn's voice was quieter now, thoughtful. "Sometimes... I can remember my mother's face. She had the kindest silver eyes. And her voice, when she sang to me."

Lily turned to her, her smile fading. "I don't have any memories of my mother. I never knew her."

A long pause hung between them, heavy but not uncomfortable.

"Do you know what happened to her?" Lily asked gently. "Your mother, I mean."

Xynn exhaled slowly. "She died when I was seven. The Varrothi decided to rehome us again. Some of us stayed a little too long for their liking, and they burned our village before we could get out. My mother was trapped. She burned to death in our home." Her voice trembled but didn't break. "A neighbor got me and my brother out. She raised us for a while, along with my uncle. He took me under his wing and taught me the path of the warrior. Together, we tried to make a family out of what we had left."

Her gaze drifted toward the far wall, her expression distant. "But then the Krythar came, and we were scattered again. My brother and I were separated. I know she's still out there somewhere. I can feel it."

Lily reached over, taking Xynn's hand. "I'll help you look for him someday."

Xynn laid her head on Lily's shoulder.

· · · ·

The hallway of the habitat level was quiet, the soft hum of the ship's systems filling the silence. Lily's heart pounded in her ears, her steps slowing as they neared her door. Her mind raced, chasing down a thousand potential outcomes, each competing for dominance. Should she end the night now, or... not?

"Lily," Xynn said suddenly, her voice cutting through the quiet.

"Yes?" Lily asked, glancing over with wide eyes.

Xynn hesitated, her usual confidence faltering. "I..."

Lily tilted her head, her breath catching. "Xynn?"

"Are you going to... invite..." Xynn trailed off, her gaze darting briefly to the floor before meeting Lily's again.

The pause stretched between them, charged and electric.

"Oh, for—" Xynn huffed, crossing her arms. "I'd like to come in."

Lily blinked. "You'd...?"

Xynn sighed, though the edge of a smile tugged at her lips. "In your room. Were you going to invite me in?"

Lily's cheeks burned, and she fumbled for the door panel. "Would you like to come in?"

Xynn nodded, her expression softening as Lily keyed in the code. The door slid open with a soft *swoosh*, and the sound of Lily's heartbeat grew ever louder.

Between the moment the door began to close and the final *click* as it sealed shut, Lily's mind raced through a cascade of thoughts: *Would you like a drink? Sorry about the mess? Do you like that picture? I got it at Star Base 12...*

But as soon as the door's soft sliding sound ended in a sharp click, all of it burned away. The space between them vanished in an instant, and Lily found herself swept into a kiss—passionate and immediate.

What followed was a frenzy of emotion and connection, the kind of night Lily would never dream of mentioning in polite company.

The early hours of the morning were still and peaceful. Lily's eyes fluttered open, adjusting to the dim light of the console by the bed. Xynn's arm was draped over her, their legs tangled together, her steady breath warm against Lily's neck.

Lily stared up at the ceiling, barely visible in the faint glow, her senses heightened by the quiet of the moment. She felt the rhythm of Xynn's heartbeat against her, the comforting rise and fall of her chest, the faint scent of her hair lingering in the air.

A smile spread across Lily's face, soft and unguarded, with the playful energy of a child's giggle. It was the kind of smile that felt entirely new. She closed her eyes, letting the warmth of the moment carry her back into the most peaceful sleep she could ever remember.

· · · ·

Early in the morning, the faint smell of overheating circuits mingled with the lingering scent of shared sleep as Lily stepped into engineering. The usually organized chaos of the Raath-Ka's domain had tilted firmly into *chaos*, with tools strewn across workstations, and Ka-Lorrin perched precariously atop a console, his head buried inside an exposed panel.

"You're going to fall," Taran muttered, not looking up as they adjusted some wires on the opposite side of the room.

"I'm *not* going to fall!" Ka-Lorrin snapped, his voice echoing from inside the panel. A moment later, there was a loud clang, followed by a startled yelp as Ka-Lorrin slipped and landed unceremoniously on the floor, narrowly missing a pile of spare parts.

Taran didn't even blink. "Told you."

Lily suppressed a smile as Ka-Lorrin stood, brushing himself off with exaggerated dignity. "That was a tactical repositioning," he muttered.

"Uh-huh," Taran said, their tone dripping with amusement.

Lily stepped further into the room, shaking her head. "You two are going to give me a heart attack before we even get to the Krythar weapon."

Ka-Lorrin gestured dramatically toward the half-disassembled console. "If the ship makes it that far, it'll be because of *our* genius, thank you very much."

"And Alrek," Taran added without looking up. "Don't forget him. He's the one dealing with the whole 'psionic overload' thing."

At that, Lily's gaze shifted to the far corner, where Alrek sat cross-legged on the floor beside the memory seed. His face was pale, and a faint sheen of sweat clung to his forehead as he focused intently on the glowing artifact.

"Alrek," Lily said, her voice laced with concern as she approached. "Are you okay?"

He nodded, though it was clearly a struggle. "I've set up the memory seed to track psionic activity in the area, which should help us avoid Krythar patrols. But the increased psionic energy from all the nearby Krythar is..." He paused, exhaling shakily. "It's... a lot."

Ka-Lorrin popped up beside them, holding what looked like a heavily modified datapad. "A lot is an understatement. He's practically glowing. You might want to check to see if his tattoos are about to short-circuit."

Alrek shot him a withering look. "Helpful as always, Ka-Lorrin."

"Always," Ka-Lorrin replied, unbothered.

Before Lily could respond, the door to engineering slid open, and in walked Dr. Thesari, followed by Shyra'thel. The Krythar defector looked calm and composed, though her gaze immediately locked onto Alrek.

"She's awake!" Lily exclaimed, relief washing over her.

"I am," Shyra'thel said, her tone measured as she moved toward Alrek. "And it seems just in time."

Dr. Thesari nodded, crossing her arms. "She insisted on coming down here as soon as she regained consciousness. And, given the state of things..." She gestured vaguely at the disarray around them. "I think she made the right call."

Shyra'thel knelt beside Alrek, placing a hand on his shoulder. "Let me help quiet your mind," she said gently.

Alrek hesitated for a moment, then nodded, his tension visibly easing as Shyra'thel closed her eyes and focused. The memory seed's glow began to stabilize, its pulsing light slowing to a steady rhythm.

"There," Shyra'thel said after a moment. "Now, let's finish setting up this psionic cloak."

With her guidance, Alrek worked more efficiently, their combined efforts quickly stabilizing the memory seed's output. Meanwhile, Ka-Lorrin and Taran tinkered with the ship's physical cloaking device, their banter a constant undercurrent to the focused work happening nearby.

"Try not to blow anything up this time," Taran muttered.

"Once again, that explosion was *not* my fault," Ka-Lorrin retorted, flipping a switch dramatically.

The hum of the cloaking device deepened, signaling its activation just as the psionic cloak settled into place.

"We're cloaked," Alrek said, his voice steady now.

"And psionically shielded," Shyra'thel added.

Lily's heart raced as the ship shifted into full stealth mode. The memory seed glowed faintly in the corner, its energy harmonized.

Ka-Lorrin gave a thumbs-up from his station. "All systems go. Let's go crash their party."

Taran sighed. "Let's just hope we get there in one piece."

Lily glanced between them, her pulse quickening with anticipation. "We're ready," she said, her voice steady despite the butterflies in her stomach. "The mission is a go."

And with that, the Salamander barreled toward danger, its crew prepared for whatever awaited them.

· · · ·

The docking bay was packed with activity as crew members prepared for departure. Lily stood near the edge of the room, her arms crossed tightly, watching as civilians and non-essential personnel filed onto transports. Xynn stood a few steps away, her arms at her sides but her body tense, her sharp features shadowed by frustration.

"I can't believe you're making me leave," Xynn said, her voice low but simmering.

Lily sighed, stepping closer. "It's not about making you leave. It's about keeping you safe."

"I don't *want* to be safe," Xynn snapped, her tone sharper now. "I want to be here. With you. Helping."

"You think I don't want that too?" Lily shot back, her voice rising before she caught herself and softened. "But Xynn, you'd be a distraction—for me and for you. This mission... it's dangerous. And if something happened to you because I insisted you stay, I'd never forgive myself."

Xynn's jaw tightened, her shoulders stiff. She looked away, staring at the transport. "I don't like this."

"I don't either," Lily admitted, stepping closer. She hesitated, her voice catching. "But this is how it has to be."

For a long moment, Xynn didn't speak. Then she turned back to Lily, her expression easing, though her eyes were still stormy. "You're... right," she said reluctantly, the words slow and deliberate. "I hate that you're right, but you are."

Lily smiled faintly, relief mingling with the ache in her chest.

Xynn exhaled, her frustration giving way to something more vulnerable. "None of this would be happening without you," she said quietly. "You know that, right? You're the reason they even have a chance."

"Thanks," Lily said, her voice just as quiet.

Xynn stepped closer, her confidence returning as she took Lily's hands in hers. "You've got this," she said, her voice steady now, warm with conviction. "I'll see you soon."

Lily's heart twisted as Xynn leaned in, kissing her deeply but briefly—just enough to leave Lily breathless. When they parted, Xynn's lips curved into a soft smile, her silver-blue eyes shining.

With her head held high, no tears in sight, Xynn turned and strode toward the transport. She didn't look back as she boarded, but her last words echoed in Lily's ears, steady and certain.

"You've got this."

Lily stood there as the transport doors closed, her chest tight with a mix of pride and longing. As the shuttle lifted off, she whispered to herself, "See you soon."

• • • •

The main briefing room buzzed with subdued energy as the away team assembled. Lily stood near the display table, checking the tactical layout of the Krythar weapon for what felt like the hundredth time. Caris leaned against the edge of the table, her sharp gaze scanning the room as the rest of the team filed in.

Alrek was one of the last to enter, his posture tense as he approached. "I want to go on the mission," he said firmly, looking between Lily and Caris.

Caris raised an eyebrow. "This isn't up for debate."

"I'm serious," Alrek pressed, his tone edging on defiance. "I can help. I know the Krythar's psionic patterns better than anyone here."

"You're too young for this kind of mission, Alrek," Caris said, crossing her arms.

Alrek's jaw tightened. "Lily's only three years older than me."

Lily glanced up, a faint smile tugging at her lips despite the tension.Actually," she said, her tone light but teasing, "Dr. Thesari's tests after the sleeper program showed I probably just turned eighteen. So that makes it four years.

Alrek blinked, clearly caught off guard. "Well... happy birthday, I guess. But I don't see how that has anything to do with this."

"It's an important four years," Lily replied, her voice steadying. "And I've faced the Krythar in combat before. You haven't."

Alrek opened his mouth to argue again, but Dryst Amaris stepped forward, his calm demeanor commanding attention. "Alrek," he said gently, "you're needed here. The Raath-Ka and Shyra'thel need your help to get the Eidolon Array operational. Every second counts now."

Alrek hesitated, his frustration clear, but after a moment, he nodded reluctantly. "Fine," he muttered, stepping back.

"Thank you," Lily said softly, meeting his gaze.

Amaris turned to the group, his tone taking on a crisp, authoritative edge. "The plan is straightforward but vital. There will be two teams. Lieutenant Caris and Lieutenant Starling will lead Team Alpha, accompanied by Security Officers Renza and Jorrel. Datch and Ensign Malik will lead Team Beta, joined by Security Officers Tareq and Vessa. Both teams will infiltrate the Krythar weapon from opposite sides to install the receivers for the Eidolon Array."

Lily studied the holographic image of the Krythar weapon as it hovered above the table. It looked mean, a nightmarish fusion of jagged edges and ominous, organic curves. Its sharp, segmented surface gleamed with an otherworldly light, pulsing as though the weapon itself were alive—breathing, waiting. Every angle, every protrusion seemed designed with malice in mind, a creation meant for destruction and nothing else.

Her stomach tightened as the weight of the mission pressed down on her.

"It's because of the reactors," Datch said, his tone precise as his synthetic fingers tapped the edge of the projection. "There are two, one in each segment of the weapon. The weapon's design requires them to function in tandem, likely to balance the energy output necessary for Krythar psionics to interface with its systems. However, to disable it effectively, both reactors must be compromised simultaneously."

Malik crossed his arms, his brow furrowed as he chimed in. "And the weapon's interior structure doesn't connect between the two halves. It's probably a security measure—redundant segmentation to prevent sabotage. If one reactor fails, the other can still sustain partial functionality, giving them a fallback."

Datch nodded, his tone clipped but brimming with energy. "Precisely. This means Team Alpha and Team Beta must breach the weapon from opposing entry points, infiltrate their respective reactor zones, and plant the receivers simultaneously. Any delay in synchronization could result in—"

"Total mission failure," Malik interjected, his voice flat but weighted with the gravity of the situation.

Lily stared at the glowing schematic, her mind racing to absorb the rapid exchange. The plan was clear, but the sheer intricacy of the Krythar's design left her reeling. This wasn't just a weapon—it was a fortress, a labyrinth of precision and danger, demanding absolute perfection from anyone bold enough to dismantle it.

"Exactly," Amaris confirmed, his voice steady and firm. "And failure is not an option."

The group exchanged brief glances, a shared determination flickering in their eyes. The mission wouldn't be easy, but they were ready—poised on the edge of action, prepared to step into the danger ahead.

* * * *

A short while later, Lily sat in one of the small shuttles, staring out the viewport as launch preparations finished. The hum of the engines vibrated through her seat, and she gripped the armrests tighter than she cared to admit.

Her nerves in the unfamiliar shuttle brought back memories of leaving Earth for the first time, heading to the Salamander with a swirling mix of wonder and fear. Now, the stakes were higher, the danger more immediate, but the nervous energy in her chest felt very familiar.

Caris, seated beside her, nudged her arm gently. "You okay?"

Lily nodded, a faint smile tugging at her lips. "Yeah. Just... thinking about how far I've come since that first shuttle ride."

Caris grinned, her confidence radiating like a steady anchor. "You've done a hell of a lot since then, Lily. You're ready for this."

Lily exhaled slowly, the tension in her hands easing as she loosened her grip on the armrests. "Thanks, Leena."

Caris smirked, her tone lighter but no less resolute. "Now don't screw it up."

Lily rolled her eyes, her smirk mirroring Caris's.

The shuttle's engines roared to life, the cabin trembling as they launched, hurtling toward the Krythar weapon. Lily's heart raced as the stars streaked past the viewport, a blur of light and motion.

She glanced back, where the cloaked Salamander hung in space behind them, silent and unseen. Then her gaze shifted forward, to the terrifying alien weapon growing larger with every second. Her breath steadied, and her voice, quiet but resolute, echoed the words that had set everything into motion.

"Let's do this."

* * * *

The comms crackled softly in Lily's ear, linking Alpha Team, Beta Team, and the Salamander. The sound was a lifeline in the vacuum of space, a reminder they weren't entirely alone.

"Alpha and Beta, this is the bridge," Calan's calm voice came through, steady despite the tension. "We're monitoring everything. Stay sharp. And good luck."

Amaris's voice followed, clipped but warm. "Bring us back something worth celebrating."

In Engineering, Alrek's voice broke through, carrying a mix of worry and dry humor. "We're here to support you. Don't get yourself killed, Lily."

Lily smirked, adjusting the psionic-blocking device resting snugly on her head like a crown. Its sleek, intricate design felt heavier than it should, a constant reminder of the stakes. "I'll do my best," she replied.

The shuttles approached the Krythar weapon in silence, their dark hulls like shadows against the faintly pulsing surface of the monstrous construct. Lily's breath hitched as they neared the small hatches, barely noticeable against the weapon's jagged exterior. These hatches were used to send out drones, Shyra'thel had explained, and now they'd serve as entry points.

Inside Beta Team's shuttle, Datch leaned over the console, his synthetic fingers moving with calculated precision. "Attempting to bypass the hatch locks," he reported, his tone neutral, though the tension was palpable.

Caris's voice came over the comms from the Alpha shuttle. "No rush, Datch. Just the fate of the mission hanging on it."

Datch ignored the jab, his focus unwavering. "Initial attempt failed. Adjusting algorithm parameters."

The seconds stretched, the silence oppressive. Then, with a soft chime, Datch exhaled. "Success. Transmitting access codes to Alpha now."

"Received," Caris said. She bent over her own console, entering the code. The hatch on their side hissed, the sound barely audible over the faint hum of the shuttle's systems.

"I hope my initial failure doesn't raise suspicion," Datch remarked.

"It won't," Malik assured him. "We're in stealth mode, and they're not expecting company. You're good."

Lily tightened the strap of her psionic blocker, her fingers brushing over its cold, metallic surface. The devices, designed with Shyra'thel's guidance, were essential. Without them, the Krythar's psionic detection would expose them in seconds. As her thoughts spiraled into the technicalities of its design, she shook her head, forcing herself back to the moment. Focus, Lily.

The hatch sprang open with a faint hiss, revealing a dimly lit tunnel. The air was still, heavy with an unnatural humidity.

"Alpha, Beta," Datch said over the comms, his voice measured. "I'm reading a network of round tunnels. They're designed for drones, not personnel. The drones will ignore us, thanks to the hack I've implemented, but expedience is key. Let's not push our luck."

Caris glanced at Lily, her eyes sharp but encouraging. "You heard him. Let's move."

Lily nodded, her stomach twisting with nerves. One step at a time. She followed Caris through the hatch, her boots clinking softly against the alien floor. Behind her, the rest of the team moved with practiced precision, their silhouettes blending into the dark, pulsing walls of the Krythar weapon.

Inside the Salamander, tension hung thick in the air. In Engineering, Alrek's hands moved with frantic precision over the memory seed console, his bioluminescent tattoos faintly glowing as he concentrated. The seed pulsed weakly in response to his efforts, its light flickering like a dying ember.

"Shyra'thel," he called, his voice tight, strained. "How's the shielding holding up?"

Shyra'thel stood nearby, her insect-like features calm, though her multifaceted eyes betrayed a sharp focus. "Barely," she replied, tilting her head as though listening to something beyond the room. "There are so many Krythar aboard the weapon and in the surrounding ships; their combined psionic signatures are stronger than I anticipated."

Alrek muttered a curse under his breath. "Just keep it steady," he said, his fingers dancing across the controls.

The room around them was a hive of activity. The Raath-Ka moved swiftly, their chaotic but coordinated movements a signature of their unique synergy. Together, they worked to calibrate the Eidolon Array, their voices overlapping in rapid, almost indecipherable exchanges. The hum of the ship's systems blended with the frantic murmurs of the crew, creating a symphony of desperation and precision that seemed to amplify the pressure bearing down on Alrek.

"Alrek," Ka-Lorrin barked from across the room, his voice cutting through the noise. "If you don't stabilize that psionic cloak, we're going to have a welcome party before the away teams even reach the core."

"I know," Alrek snapped, his usual composure fraying under the strain. His mind felt stretched thin, as though the sheer weight of the Krythar's psionic energy was pressing against his own like a storm battering a fragile shield.

He forced himself to breathe, his focus narrowing as he tapped out another sequence. The memory seed pulsed faintly again, its glow unsteady but persistent, like the heartbeat of the Salamander itself.

Meanwhile, deep inside the Krythar weapon, Datch crouched by a console, his synthetic fingers moving in a blur over the alien interface. The technology was unlike any other Krythar systems he had encountered—a disorienting fusion of crystalline structures and pulsing psionic energy conduits. But if Datch was anything, he was adaptable.

"Got it," he said, his voice sharp and efficient. "Planting the receiver here will align with the energy nodes of this reactor."

"Good," Malik replied, his rifle trained on the dark corridor behind them. His eyes moved in quick, deliberate sweeps, scanning for movement. "Now hurry. This place is crawling."

As if summoned by his words, a sharp chittering echoed through the corridor, the sound jagged and alien—like bone scraping against bone. The hair on the back of Malik's neck stood on end, and even Datch's artificial processors registered a flicker of unease.

"They know we're here," Malik muttered, his knuckles whitening on the grip of his rifle.

A second later, Krythar emerged from the shadows, their insectoid forms quick and menacing. The glow of their energy weapons cast eerie green streaks across the dark walls. Malik dove for cover, returning fire in short, controlled bursts that lit up the narrow space.

"Datch, how much longer?" Malik barked, his voice tense but unwavering.

"Thirty seconds," Datch replied, his tone calm despite the chaos.

Malik grimaced, stepping out from cover to draw fire away from Datch. His precision shots forced the Krythar back, giving the security officers room to maneuver. Renza and Jorrel flanked him, their rifles spitting fire in controlled synchronization, keeping the enemy at bay.

But the Krythar were relentless. One alien bolt struck true, hitting Renza square in the chest. The officer dropped without a sound, his body crumpling to the floor like a broken marionette.

Malik bared his teeth, grief flashing across his face, but he didn't falter. He pushed forward, holding the line with fierce determination while Datch continued his work.

"Receiver planted," Datch said finally, rising to his feet and drawing his weapon. His voice was steady, though his expression betrayed the chaos erupting around them.

On the other side of the weapon, Caris and Lily moved with practiced precision. The dimly lit corridors seemed to devour the light, the walls broken only by eerie green orbs dotting the surfaces like scattered, glowing eyes—silent, watching.

The sounds of the struggle echoed faintly through their comms, a grim reminder of what was happening on the other side.

"Renza's down," Malik's voice crackled, tight with urgency and sorrow.

Lily placed a hand against the cold, dark wall to steady herself. There was no time to dwell. She and Caris pressed on, their mission painfully clear.

Caris crouched by the reactor's interface, her sharp eyes scanning the schematics and data Datch had transmitted. Her movements were quick but deliberate as she worked to match the setup Datch had completed on his side.

"Receiver's secure," Caris said after a few tense moments, her voice calm but clipped.

Lily nodded, her gaze sweeping the corridor ahead. Her senses prickled with unease. "No movement here," she said softly. "Let's move out."

The quiet around them felt oppressive, the kind that made every sound—every breath—feel magnified. Their section of the weapon had been eerily calm, but Lily's gut churned with the certainty that the silence wouldn't last.

The corridors shook as Datch, Malik, and Jorrel fought their way back toward the hatch, Krythar swarming like shadows come to life. Malik fired in controlled bursts, his movements a precise dance between offense and defense, while Datch gripped his weapon with mechanical steadiness.

"Datch," Alrek's voice came over the comms, sharp and urgent. "The Krythar found your shuttle, they—"

A deafening explosion cut him off, the sound echoing faintly through the corridors. When Alrek's voice returned, it was tight with disbelief. "They just blew it up."

Malik closed his eyes for a brief moment, steadying himself as he pressed his back against the wall for cover.

Amaris' voice cut through next, steady and measured. "Sensors show one of the Krythar ships is inbound toward your side of the weapon, Lily. I suggest you launch immediately and return to the Salamander."

Lily exchanged a look with her team in the shuttle. She saw it in their eyes—determination, resolve. Her own heart pounded, but her voice was steady when she replied. "We're not going back to the ship."

"Lily, what—?" Alrek's voice started, but she cut him off.

"We're going to pick them up. We're not leaving them behind."

A pause hung heavy over the comms before Calan's voice came through, calm but carrying the weight of command. "Helm, move us between the Krythar weapon and the nearest enemy ship. Drop the cloak."

Amaris followed with quiet urgency. "We will hold them off as long as possible, but be quick. And, Lily... good luck."

"Let's go," Lily said, her voice firm as Caris activated the shuttle's boosters. The small craft roared into the void, leaving the weapon's hatch behind as it curved around its massive exterior.

Caris' hands were steady on the controls, her eyes fixed on the path ahead as debris and fragments of metal swirled past. Lily manned the weapons station beside Tareq, her fingers tight on the targeting console.

"Movement!" Tareq called out.

Krythar in rocket-equipped suits burst from the shadows, their weapons blazing green energy.

Caris yanked the controls hard, sending the shuttle into a roll that evaded most of the incoming fire. "Hold them off!" she shouted.

Lily and Tareq worked in tandem, firing bursts of laser energy that scattered the attacking Krythar. Lily focused her aim, remembering her training—aim small, miss small. Each shot counted, and the shuttle rocked violently as their evasive maneuvers pressed the engines to their limit.

"Almost there," Caris muttered, her voice tight with concentration.

They rounded the bend, only to find a Krythar interceptor blocking their path to the hatch. Its sharp angles bristled with weapons, and its glowing core pulsed ominously.

Lily's stomach dropped. "Anyone have a miracle up their sleeve?" she asked, her voice tight.

"They're charging weapons," Vessa said, her tone sharp with urgency.

Inside the weapon, Datch worked furiously at a console. His synthetic fingers moved in a blur over the alien interface, accessing an external armature system.

"Miracles are not within my programming," he said flatly, his tone as steady as his hands. "However, I will endeavor to assist."

With a quick sequence of commands, Datch sent the armature claw lurching forward, grabbing hold of the interceptor's hull. The sudden force disrupted its aim, sending its energy blast wide of the shuttle.

"Nice work, Datch!" Malik shouted, laying down suppressing fire as Krythar swarmed their position.

Datch yanked the armature again, wrenching the interceptor into the side of the weapon. The collision sent debris flying, exposing a vulnerable section of the ship.

"Lily, now!" Caris called.

Lily and Tareq concentrated their fire on the exposed section, targeting it relentlessly. The interceptor's weapons flickered, then went dark as its systems collapsed.

Malik grimaced, his hand pressed tightly against a wound on his side. "Hallway's sealed," he muttered through gritted teeth.

Datch scanned him with precision. "You are losing blood rapidly. We must evacuate immediately."

Malik let out a sharp, humorless laugh. "That, my plastic friend, wins understatement of the year. We're out of time."

Jorrel and Datch didn't hesitate, each taking an arm as they hauled Malik toward the hatch. The shuttle docked with a jarring thud, and Caris appeared in the opening, urgency crackling in her voice. "Move!"

They piled into the shuttle, but the relief was short-lived. A shockwave tore through the craft as the damaged interceptor exploded behind them, sending sparks and fire across the cabin.

Lily shielded her face as a wall panel burst apart. The acrid smell of burned circuitry filled the air, and Malik groaned, clutching his burned arm. Vessa lay slumped against the side, her uniform singed but her eyes still open.

"Hang on!" Caris shouted, yanking the controls to stabilize the shuttle.

The Salamander loomed ahead, its cloaking field now dropped as it exchanged fire with a Krythar vessel. The shuttlebay doors were open, a beacon of safety in the chaos.

Caris brought them in fast, the shuttle jolting as it docked. The shuttlebay filled with smoke and sparks, but as the hatch opened, medics flooded in.

Dr. Thesari's calm voice cut through the commotion. "Get the injured stabilized. Quickly."

Amaris stood beside her, his sharp eyes scanning the returning team. His gaze softened as he met Malik's. "You've done Cyranthia proud," he said. "I'll be recommending you for the title of Dryst when we return."

Malik nodded weakly, his usual gruffness giving way to a faint flicker of gratitude.

As the medics worked, Lily, Caris, and Datch exchanged a look. There was no time for celebration.

"We're not done yet," Lily said, her voice steady as steel.

With that, the three of them turned and sprinted for the bridge.

• • • •

Lily, Caris, and Datch burst onto the bridge, their boots clanging sharply against the deck as they hurried to their stations. Datch moved straight to his console, scanning the readings with precise focus. As Lily glanced at him, she caught something entirely unfamiliar in his usually composed expression: alarm.

"Captain," Datch said, his voice tight. "The Krythar weapon is arming. They have selected a target. By my calculations, it's deep in Union space... possibly Earth and the surrounding systems."

Calan rose from his chair, his expression hardening into one of determination. "Engineering, please tell me we're ready to rock and roll."

Ka-Lorrin's voice crackled over the comms. "Everything's set on our end, Captain."

"Fingers crossed, fingers crossed," Taran added, his tone a mix of anxiety and hope.

Calan nodded sharply. "Engage the Eidolon Array."

Lily's gaze snapped to the monitor displaying main engineering as the array roared to life. Arcs of energy danced in a kaleidoscope of rainbow light, crackling and shimmering like the heart of a plasma storm. For a fleeting moment, it was breathtaking. Then, with a sputtering whine, the energy faltered, collapsing into itself and dissipating into the array's chamber.

Calan's jaw tightened. "What happened?"

"The lead ship, sir," Alrek's voice came through the comms. "It's blocking the signal."

"I've never encountered such concentrated psionic energy before," Shyra'thel said, her tone heavy with frustration. "I'm afraid there's nothing I can do."

Caris turned to Calan, her voice steady and direct. "May I suggest a more direct approach, Captain?"

Calan's eyes narrowed. "Lock all weapons on the lead Krythar ship," he ordered.

The bridge erupted into controlled chaos as the Salamander maneuvered into position. Smaller Krythar vessels swarmed around the lead ship, their sharp, angular designs slicing through space as they opened fire. The Salamander shook violently as energy bolts struck its shields.

"Multiple hostiles closing in." Datch reported.

"Hold them off!" Calan barked. "Focus fire on the smaller vessels first. We need a clear path to that lead ship."

The Salamander's weapons blazed to life, sending streams of energy into the fray. Explosions lit up the void as the smaller Krythar ships were picked off one by one, but the Salamander's shields continued to take a pounding.

"Shields at sixty percent!" Ka-Lorrin's voice called over the comms.

"Keep us steady!" Calan commanded.

As the smaller vessels were cleared away, the Salamander zeroed in on the lead Krythar ship. It loomed like a dormant volcano stirring to life, its dark surface pulsating with eerie green light that threatened to erupt with devastating force. The weapon's countdown ticked down to two minutes.

"Incoming fire from the lead ship!" Caris shouted.

The Salamander rocked again as a powerful blast struck its hull, sending sparks flying across the bridge.

"Shields at thirty percent!" Ka-Lorrin warned.

Alrek's voice broke through the chaos, steady and insistent. "Captain, concentrate all firepower on the coordinates I'm sending you. I've sifted through their thoughts... trust me."

Datch's voice followed, precise and slightly elevated to be heard over the din. "It doesn't appear to be a vital system," he admitted, "but given our limited options—and young Alrek's remarkable tendency to be correct in these situations..."

Calan rose to his feet, his command cutting through the moment. "Target the coordinates and fire all weapons!"

The Salamander unleashed everything it had. Streams of energy converged on the designated coordinates, striking a point near the base of the lead ship. For a moment, it seemed as though nothing had happened... and then the Krythar vessel erupted in a massive explosion. Pieces of the ship scattered into space, leaving behind a rapidly expanding cloud of debris.

"The interference is gone," Ka-Lorrin's voice was jubilant. "The Eidolon Array is activating!"

Lily's gaze locked on the monitor as the rainbow energy once again sparked to life, arcing and streaming in dazzling patterns. This time, instead of collapsing, it stabilized, leveling out into a steady, rhythmic pulse that filled the array chamber with an almost hypnotic hum.

Datch's tone broke the moment, low and grave. "Sir, I strongly recommend we put distance between ourselves and the weapon. Disabling it while active is likely to yield... unpredictable results."

Caris raised an eyebrow, her tone dry. "Let me guess. A big boom?"

Datch tilted his head and gave a slight shrug.

Calan didn't wait. "Full engines. Put as much distance between us and that weapon as you can. Now."

The Salamander roared to life, engines blazing as it tore away from the Krythar weapon. On the monitor, the weapon's countdown hit zero. For a heartbeat, there was an eerie silence... and then the weapon detonated. A blinding explosion erupted, sending a massive shockwave rippling outward.

The shockwave struck the Salamander, rattling its hull and sending it into a brief but violent spin.

"Stabilizing," Caris announced, her voice strong and steady, hands firm on the controls.

The ship righted itself, and for a moment, the bridge was still—silent save for the faint hum of the engines. Then, like a dam breaking, cheers erupted from the crew.

Calan turned to Lily, a weary but triumphant smile tugging at his lips. He shook his head slightly, as if struggling to believe they'd actually done it.

Lily exhaled slowly, the tension melting from her chest as relief washed over her. Her own smile grew as she looked around at the bridge—at her crew, her family.

"We did it," she whispered, the words barely audible but filled with immeasurable emotion.

• • • •

The recreation lounge buzzed with a soft, celebratory energy. It wasn't the loud, raucous joy Lily might have expected after a mission like theirs, but it was warm and genuine. The crew was tired, but alive, and the glow of their success seemed to light up the room as much as the pale stars visible through the viewport.

Malik stood near one of the lounge's couches, his arm in a sling but his trademark gruffness softened by the faintest of smiles. Dryst Amaris was beside him, gesturing animatedly as he spoke. "You've done your people proud, Malik. I'll be making my recommendation to the Cyranthian Council personally."

Dr. Thesari nodded in agreement, her serene presence a calming contrast to Amaris' enthusiasm. "You've shown remarkable courage under pressure, Malik. It's rare to see that kind of strength paired with such tactical discipline."

Malik shifted awkwardly, as though the weight of their praise was heavier than the blaster he'd carried into the Krythar weapon. "Thanks," he muttered. Then, after a pause, he glanced at Alrek. "You, too, kid. You pulled through when it mattered."

Alrek, perched on the arm of a chair nearby, blinked in surprise, then grinned. "Thanks, Malik. That means a lot."

Calan entered the room, his presence commanding but relaxed. He made his way to Lily, who was leaning against a table, sipping on a cup of tea. He smiled warmly. "Lieutenant Starling, it seems I underestimated you."

Lily looked up, eyebrows raised. "Oh?"

"I expected bravery, intelligence, and resilience. What I didn't expect," he said with a chuckle, "was how much I would learn from you."

Lily's cheeks flushed slightly, and her lips curved into a smile. "Well, in that case, Captain, I have to ask: why the hat collection?"

Calan threw back his head and laughed, a rich, genuine sound that filled the room. "That, Lieutenant, requires a higher security clearance than you currently possess."

Lily smirked, shaking her head. "Figures."

As the conversation continued around her, Lily found herself drifting toward Datch and Caris, who stood near the viewport. The stars stretched out before them, distant and serene. She joined them, her voice soft. "I just wanted to say... thank you. Both of you. For everything."

Caris shrugged, her expression playful but her tone sincere. "Hey, that's what we do, right? Besides, I had a feeling we'd pull it off. We're a pretty great team."

Datch nodded, his voice quieter than usual. "We succeeded because we relied on one another. That kind of trust is... rare."

Lily smiled at them both, the weight of the moment settling over her. "I'm really glad you're here. Both of you."

Later, Lily sat at a small console, composing a message to Xynn. The words came slowly, thoughtfully, as she replayed the events of the mission in her mind.

"Hey, Xynn. I'm okay. We're okay. And, well... you were right. I did save the day, more or less." She hesitated, then smiled. "Thanks for believing in me. I'll see you soon."

Before she could send it, Alrek appeared behind her. "Is that for Xynn?"

Lily nodded. "Yeah."

Alrek leaned against the edge of the console, his expression lighter than usual. "If she's that important to you, I can learn to put up with her."

Lily grinned, her heart warming at his words. She stood, pulling him into a quick hug. "Thanks, Alrek."

Nearby, the Raath-Ka approached, their unusual forms looking out of place as always. Ka-Lorrin bowed dramatically. "Lily Starling. Alrek. Thank you for everything. Your bravery... almost matches ours."

Taran snorted, "almost... ha, you brave Kal? Not so sure, not so sure..."

Ka-Lorrin huffed. "Excuse me? If not for us, this ship would fall apart."

As they bickered, they began to walk off, their voices fading into the corridor. "Sorry," said Taran looking back. "The engines are calling to us."

"They require our genius!" Retorted Ka-Lorrin.

Lily and Alrek exchanged a glance, laughing softly. They wandered to the viewport, the stars stretching endlessly before them. For a moment, neither spoke, the silence between them filled with unspoken gratitude and reflection.

"We've come a long way," Alrek said quietly.

"Yeah," Lily replied, her gaze fixed on the stars. "And I think... we're just getting started."

COMPUTER, THIS IS LILY Starling... resume recording.

So, that's it. That's how I got into space. I'm not sure if anyone will ever believe me, but the journey I've been on—figuring out who I am and who I want to be—has actually been even more intense than going to space, fighting the Krythar, learning to be an officer, and everything else that came with it. What I've learned is this: life can be full and beautiful, and making it into something true to who you are is a rare and extraordinary gift.

The crew—my found family—has been taking time to decompress since the Nullstorm mission. Our success has forced the Krythar to retreat and regroup, at least for now. The border worlds are working to establish their independence, and Shyra'thel has volunteered for a diplomatic mission to help them navigate this fragile new chapter. I hope she finds peace.

It's strange how quiet the ship feels now. Not the ship itself—the sound of the engines is steady as ever, and the crew moves with their usual rhythm—but there's a stillness in the air that wasn't there before. It's the kind of quiet that comes after a storm, where everyone is catching their breath and finally allowing themselves to exhale.

I think we've all earned it.

The crew is taking time to catch up on the things they had to set aside during the mission. Families, hobbies, mental health... personal grooming, in some cases. (Sorry, computer, delete that part.)

Captain Calan received a commendation—well earned. He continues to move mountains. He even has the fleet convinced that I should keep the lieutenant commission. Honestly, I think they're so baffled about who I really am that it's just easier for them to let Lily Starling's file keep going.

Oh, and Calan is actually taking a vacation. A real one. With Joren. They're heading to some ocean world that sounds incredible—makes me think I should take up surfing or something. I can't help wondering how many hats Joren will pack for him. Or maybe he just buys more on the trip... One day, I'm going to get to the bottom of that mystery.

This one surprised me—Datch has joined the diplomatic corps and is heading back to Gherion Prime. He says it's time to take advantage of the opportunities that have opened up since the Krythar weapon was destroyed. He didn't say it outright, but I think he's hoping to make real progress toward official recognition of his personhood. I've been reading more about the Gherionites and their complicated relationship with the Union. I imagine there are some awkward reunions in his future, but if anyone can navigate that, it's Datch.

Caris is thriving as the Salamander's newest full lieutenant. She's already diving headfirst into improving our infiltration protocols for future missions. Leave it to Leena to turn downtime into a training session. She insists she's just being prepared, but I suspect she secretly loves having an excuse to boss people around.

Malik is recovering well. He'd never admit it, but I've caught him smiling more since Dryst Amaris recommended him for the title of Dryst back on Cyranthia. Sure, he grumbles about "not needing validation," but we all know how much it means to him. Beneath all that gruffness, there's a man who's learning to let a little light in.

Alrek is, predictably, in Engineering. He still has a lot of unanswered questions about the extent of his psionic abilities, but with Shyra'thel gone, he's decided to dive headfirst into the junior engineering program, throwing himself into the work with that same quiet intensity he brings to everything. The Raath-Ka have taken him under their chaotic wings, and I overheard Ka-Lorrin saying Alrek was "almost worthy" of their genius. Almost.

As for the Raath-Ka themselves, they're back to "answering the engines' call," as they like to say. There will always be something to tweak, fine-tune, or outright reimagine on a ship like this. Sometimes I suspect they create half the problems they solve, but with the engine room in a constant state of organized chaos, who could ever tell? Either way, they're so beloved that no one seems to mind. Well, except maybe Leena.

And Xynn... well, we're still figuring out "whatever this is." No labels, no big plans, and honestly, I prefer it that way for now. She's back on the Saravethi colony base, but we're planning to meet up when the Salamander docks at Star Base 9 in a couple of weeks. Then again, knowing Xynn, she'll probably show up unannounced well before that—she's not exactly the patient type. It'll be good to see her, though. She still gives me those damn butterflies. I wonder if that will ever wear off... Do I want it to?

And me? I've decided to keep the name Lily Starling. Not because I feel like I need to, but because I want to. It's a way to honor the original Lily and her sacrifice—and to remind myself how far I've come. Plus I have her face, so I guess I owe her credit for that. I mean, it's a nice face if I do say so myself.

The Nullstorm Region is behind us, the Krythar weapon is gone, and the galaxy feels a little safer tonight. But I know this isn't the end of our story. There's always another star on the horizon, another mystery waiting to be solved, another adventure calling us forward.

We're the crew of the Salamander. And our voyage has only begun.

About the Author

Christian Hurst is a Creative Director and author of the *Lily Starling* series, a character-driven YA science fiction saga that blends epic adventure with emotional depth. With over 15 years of experience in advertising, marketing, and content creation, his work is shaped by a strong sense of story, pacing, and imagination.

His writing explores identity, connection, and the courage to forge your own path in a vast and unpredictable galaxy. Known for immersive worldbuilding, inclusive storytelling, and a balance of heart, humor, and high-stakes tension, Christian's work resonates with readers who are drawn to science fiction with both scale and soul.

He lives in Pennsylvania with his wife, son, and three dogs.

The story doesn't end here.

Lily's journey continues in the Lily Starling series. What begins aboard the *Salamander* leads to ancient mysteries, impossible choices, and a threat that spans the galaxy.

Continue the adventure at **LilyStarlingBook.com**

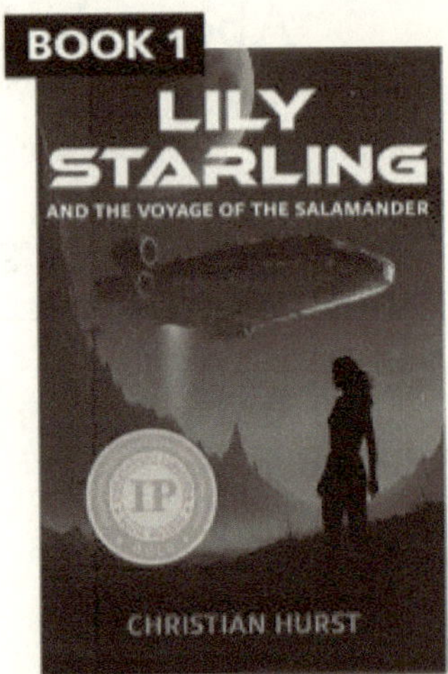

BOOK 1
LILY STARLING
AND THE VOYAGE OF THE SALAMANDER
CHRISTIAN HURST

BOOK 2
LILY STARLING
AND THE STORM RIDERS
CHRISTIAN HURST

BOOK 3
LILY STARLING
AND THE DEATH MACHINE
CHRISTIAN HURST

BOOK 4
LILY STARLING
AND THE RIVER OF TIME
COMING SOON
CHRISTIAN HURST

Leave a Review

If you enjoyed Voyage of the Salamander, please consider leaving a review on your favorite book site. Reader reviews help independent books reach new audiences and play a direct role in the future of series like this one.